My Forgotten Demons

Book Two

Elm Jed

To Deadwood,
My Marine Brother & confidant
Thank you for being the ground I needed
when I felt like I was falling

<u>Semper Fi</u>

Contents

Content Warnings

This Book Contains ON PAGE:
Self-harm with sharp objects, attempted self-harm, unlawful arrest, stalking, minor starvation, interrogation, torture, gun violence, minor blood/gore, medical malpractice,
Panic/anxiety attacks, and PTSD flashbacks.
Cliffhanger.

-Discussed-
Sexual assault, thoughts of suicide, forced hospitalization/surgeries, death/loss, homelessness, alcohol & drug abuse, and domestic violence.
Components of BDSM are used such as honorifics, titles, and the stoplight method.

Prologue

Before the Americano

I should've taken the damn socks.

The gloves on my hands have practically frozen over my fingers from the melted snow. Grumbling about poor decisions from what I took at the soup kitchen, I head down the busy street. Constantly, I check over my shoulder, hyperaware of the people moving past. The small envelope also feels frozen in my hands, even as I clutch it to my chest.

A few feet more. Almost there.

I check my surroundings again. No one. Not anyone who cares about a girl with ratty hair and a tattered, stained coat. The scarf wrapped around me is barely a scrap of cloth. I could pass as an orphan in *Annie*, any version, or just any other homeless person. Then again, I *am* one.

One more time I check, body bristling, hating this part. My anxiety spikes, fearful of being followed even though I know in my gut I'm not. Approaching the drop point, I veer around some couples and make it to the abandoned mailbox. The envelope falls into the slot as I keep walking toward the park, stomach dropping as I come upon the once green area. Winter hasn't been kind the past few weeks. Once I cross the street, I glimpse to the mailbox and turn away, knowing I can't linger. A stiff breeze blows past. I wrap my arms tighter and pause before my usual exit, turning down toward downtown instead. I need to avoid certain parts of the park, best to avoid all together.

My feet feel fucking frozen; toes beginning to go numb. They'll thaw when I get to the soup kitchen. Hopefully. Just have to get there first. It'll take longer walking through Lower Manhattan, but it'll be safer and I know I won't cross any territories. Could stop at one of the closer shelters, but they weren't approved by Roger. Further south I go.

People bump me as I pass, and I ignore their ignoring of me. I chance gazing up at the skyscrapers above, noticing more snow beginning to fall. Here's hoping it doesn't turn into hail or freezing rain. Freezing rain means down powerlines, making it harder to hack into computer networks. Unless I bypass—

I shake my head, knowing I don't have time to figure that out. It's been easier sneaking into the back of the clubs, but harder to skim past those who may recognize my face. Last thing I need is one of Steve's buddies calling him up of where I am. He may have found a place, but like fuck am I staying in another drug, rat-infested, hell-hole. Steve thinks I'm staying at some brothel, reality, I've been homeless for weeks. It keeps me moving, staying on target to finally get the fuck out of this situation.

And it's kept Leanne and Nan safe; the only two in my life who truly matter.

Shivering violently, I come down a block where fancy buildings glisten. They practically glitter from the gold lining their doors, lights illuminating from the overhangs, and silvery windows. I chance a look inside one, noticing marble and pristine cleanliness as those with gowns and tuxedos walk about.

They're gorgeous.

I'm so entranced by the shimmering sight, my foot catches a patch of ice and I go tumbling down. I bite back a yelp as my hip hits the pavement, wincing at the sharp pain. People pass, ignoring me still as I groan and rub at my backside when someone stops in front of me.

A man dressed in fancy black shoes stops before me, holding his hand down for me. "Are you alright?"

"Fine," I mutter, ignoring the hand and get up on my own. I keep my face lowered, trying not to let him see it and wipe at my running nose with the holey glove I'm wearing.

"Why don't you come inside?" His voice is smooth, too fucking smooth and kind.

"I'm fine. Sorry." I start to pass him, pulling my scarf up more around my face. I do *not* need pity from some guy wearing shoes worth more than my college courses. My entire back throbs and the cold is beginning to give me a headache.

"You're apologizing for falling?"

"I need to go."

He goes to grab my arm. "Wait—"

"Sorry," I say again, dodging the hand. I practically run away from him. The wind picks up and I quicken my pace, fearful he may be trying to follow me. This fear makes me flash a look behind me, noticing he hasn't seemed to move, but staring in my direction.

Swallowing hard, I turn away and concentrate on finding a cot for tonight. I hasten my steps, flexing my hands to regain some feeling. As I'm about to turn the corner, I look one last time. He's gone.

I think…he had hazel eyes.

Chapter 1

Beginning of the End

It smells of fabric softener and cheap carpet, muted by the lingering staleness of cigarettes. Roger "used" to smoke. Seems like his house didn't quit.

My head throbs as I lay on the bed I've been "sleeping" in for the past four days. How the fuck am I supposed to sleep when all I see is his face? Hear Jameson calling after me? Running through the hotel, and then it all conjoins with memories I've long wanted to forget. It feels like there's a thousand pounds sitting on my chest. Swallowing hard, I get up and groan at the lingering pain along my shoulders and down my thighs. Yanking on the same clothes I've worn since I left New York City, I pull the shabby sweater over my head. The house is quiet as I go down the creaky, wooden stairs and shiver at every noise. In the kitchen, coffee has already been brewed.

He must be up.

I grab a mug, pouring the coffee and sit down at the small table. My head throbs more as I lean into my hands, rubbing my temples. The coffee is burnt. It leaves a dry taste in my mouth as I grimace at the crappy stuff. Roger can't even buy good fucking beans. The brown liquid stares back at me, and my chest tightens along with my throat as a memory flashes.

Leo's stunned expression, while latte foam and coffee drip down my front. Hazel eyes staring at me in surprise as I lick the foam from my finger. Those furrowed brows. The coffee weighs heavy in my stomach, twisting as the pain of the past few days comes back and obliterates the memory.

I put the mug down, clutching the table and try to breathe through the piercing pain. It's felt like I've been drowning the past four days. Confusion, loneliness, and fear keep swirling in circles. I've not left Detective Roger Caltz's house, barely slept or ate. Haven't showered. I've just stayed in his guest bedroom, phone still turned off, wondering what to do or where to go next. I can't contact anyone. It'd be too dangerous. Doesn't help that Roger keeps telling me to hand over my phone, but I just can't.

It's my only lifeline. All I have left.

I continue wishing this wasn't real, staring at the mug of coffee, when Roger walks in and drops a notepad in front of me. A pen follows it, thumping against the paper. He doesn't look at me, heading to the coffee pot.

"What is this?" I rasp.

"Write down everything." He grabs a thermos. "What you saw. Heard. Smelled and tasted for all I care. Everything gets written down. Your memory was always the fucking best." He pours the coffee, adding a crap ton of sugar.

Yeah, that ain't gonna save it.

"You mentioned getting into his country house, note anything about that, too. We know about it, but that's it. Include any vehicles he drove, places he went, phone numbers…actually that part, just hand over your phone with all of it, and I'll get everything else."

My mouth slackens. "You're kidding right now."

He snorts. "Fuck no. It's been four days. We need this info."

"The fuck you do." He turns, frowning at me and I frown back.

I'm not sure why I'm arguing, knowing I'm the one who came to him worried of falling back into the mafia, but the empty notepad before me feels wrong. I'm not his insider anymore. I'm not working for him anymore. Sinking emotions roar at me to toss the paper on the floor and run. And then I remember why I'm feeling this way. Similar feelings under bright, fluorescent lights and a cold, grey room.

"We need everything. Make your time worthwhile. Tell us everything."

And then I lost everything.

I've given him enough already. Scared or not, mob or not, I'm not giving over shit that feels like a violation of my own life. *Again.*

"I didn't see or hear anything that was mob related, that's *why* I came to you. For you to do your job. Figure it out. Find the evidence."

He scoffs, "Fucking god damn it, not again, Sarah—"

My old name claws at my ears. "What I *did* see, I told you already. If I'd known I'd have left sooner, so you know everything—"

"Except *I* need the info on how he lives, layouts of his buildings and hotel, who works for him, where he goes—"

"Put a fucking tail on him!" Roger's eyes darken, narrowing them. "You don't even need a hacker to figure out the building layouts. He's a fucking public figure, not that hard. Go to the municipal building or whatever for floor plans. Do *your* job."

"It'll be easier if you just gave it all over. What you know."

I sneer at him, "I'm not your informant anymore. Remember?"

"You still have a duty—"

"He goes to restaurants, shops, businesses like everyone else. *Nothing* he did was out of the ordinary or hidden. He's just a businessman like more than half of Lower Manhattan. It's not like you don't know where his hotel locations already are—"

"But not the layouts of his offices, his home—"

"Fuck no." I shove the notepad away.

No. No fucking way was I being that invasive. I'm terrified of what could happen next, who Leo is, what he does for his brothers, and being near the mob again, but no way. He could be the guy who kills for Matteo. Finishes deals. I don't care. Roger was asking for an invasion of privacy, part of Leo's life and *mine* that had nothing to do with this shit. I won't cross that line again. It wasn't the same as Steve or Gabriel, right? Deep down I worried because what if I was wrong?

What if I subjected Leo to all of this, make him go through what I had? Having your entire life scourged to be yanked apart, but to be wrong?

"I came here for help. Not to be your little toy...*again*."

"Do you want to help stop them or not? Do the right thing?"

"Don't pull that on me." My voice shakes, wanting to crumble under the harshness of his.

Roger slams his thermos down, and I flinch as I stare at where it made contact with the counter. "We need this information to catch them. Take them down. Put a stop to the Marchetti Family and count-less others, once and for all. This could be the breakthrough we need to—"

"You said that last time! Still, none of what you're asking has to do with mafia shit. It's his personal life, his privacy, and businesses. He walked away, at least... he tried."

"And you believe that?"

"Yes! It's his life and I'm not handing over—"

"Privacy doesn't fucking matter when it comes to people's safety. No such fucking thing, especially when it could be the key to getting inside." He points his callused finger at me, and my heart pounds in my chest. The same words. He's using the same words from years ago. Stomach clenching, my hands start to shake. "You know what it takes. How much we have to sacrifice to get inside."

"I saw paperwork that may connect him, that's it. Apart from him being related to the Marchettis, that's all I know, which *you* already knew. Figure out the rest. It's your job. Find out if I'm right in being worried I've been found out or not."

"And my job includes getting info from witnesses."

"I gave you that when I got here."

"Not enough." He grabs his thermos, muttering, "You should've swiped the folders. Losing your fucking touch...*Sarah*."

He talks like I never left. Like I hadn't tried for three years to have a normal life. And the idea that he still considers me his informant, boils me from the inside out. I stand, sneering at him as my body trembles. "I had to get out. I left on instinct."

"You panicked. *Again.*" I stumble back at the tone of his voice. "If you'd just been calm, did your job—"

"I'm not police! It wasn't my job!"

"You still knew better. We trained you enough."

"What training?" I scoff. The walls are closing in, pressing tightly as I struggle to breathe. "Even if I had, you'd still just send me back into that mess? Years out?" I point at him next, but my hands are shaking, and he gives me a look of disapproval. "It's your damn job. Not mine. I didn't get trained by *you*. What I did get was PTSD, pain, injuries, a stripped future, paranoia…"

"Calm down."

"Don't tell me to calm down!" I scream, slamming a fist into the table. It reverberates through my arm. I stare at the wood under my fist and then the empty notepad. Anger twists in my gut.

Not enough. Never enough.

Roger steps closer and speaks in a low tone. "Give me what you know. If you want to help, if you want to be safe again…with everyone you love, you'll write it all down. No matter how small. It could keep you safe."

"It won't help you," I say exasperated. My sleepless nights are catching up with me, along with empty stomach and pounding head. I feel weak and empty. Tired. "I told you what I saw, what may be connected. You'll get far enough on your own. I don't want part of this anymore. I came here to get out."

He's quiet. His expression stern, eyes flashing down over me and then back up. "Why are you protecting him?"

"I'm not—"

"Yes, you are. Whatever feelings you have for him, let it go. Probably all a lie to get what he wants, which is you in his fucking bed. Man might be private, but everyone fucking knows he sleeps around. He'll do whatever is needed to get what he wants. His type…his *family* does that…using people, if you even remember."

"More than you do." Those nights flash in my mind. The yelling. The broken skin and blood. Those nights before the end came. No calm before the storm, it was all a fucking hurricane for the final days of Sarah Marie.

"Then you know the moment he realizes who *you* are, you'll wish he'll only kill you."

"You don't—"

"Think I'm wrong? You want to chance it? Like you did with Steve? Like you did with the rest of them? As you said, he tried to leave, but came back…who's the one who put his brother behind bars? Why his younger brother is in Italy?" Fury builds within me, mixed with terror as I glare at him. A few tears fall from my eyes, and he smirks. "That's what I thought. This is your only way out." Roger points at the notepad. "I'm gonna keep reminding you of the reality here. *I'm* your only way out, it's why you came to me. Do you want a repeat learning the hard way?"

"Fuck you!" I spit out at him.

I shove against his chest, making him almost drop his coffee. He glowers at me, shaking off the drops of coffee on his hand. "It wasn't your life that was stolen!" I yell at him. "You weren't abused and picked apart for over a year. You didn't lose jackshit when it all went down, instead you got your fucking promotion, this house, and the life you wanted. The entire NYPD and FBI got what they wanted, with their praise and recognition, while I laid in a hospital bed. Half-dead ripped apart. You won and I lost for that *damn* cause of yours."

I spin on my heel to leave the kitchen, but stop saying, "And *no one* is like the monster Steve was, including the five *you* let loose."

The screen door slams open as I storm out into the early morning. A breeze causes me to shiver. Mindlessly, I go down the sidewalk heading nowhere. Tears stream down my cheeks. My throat tightens, hurting as the ache moves through my body. My feet drag me down one block. Then another. Then another. I aimlessly walk, mind spinning and distraught over what to do. I'm too damn tired to think. I don't even check over my shoulder or survey my surroundings, even with pricks crawling up my neck.

I don't care.

Let them fucking take me.

Nearing an entrance for a park, Washington I think, I stop and look up at the clouds. Dark skies fill the air, and I can smell the rain coming. Can take the girl out of the Midwest but can't take the Midwest out of her. Even if she presumably died.

Deeply breathing in the cool air, I scrub at my head, feeling the oily sensation in my hair as I continue on. Faintly, I memorize each car that passes and the streets of the quiet neighborhood. There's rumbling in the distance, echoing through the skies. I find myself quite a few blocks from Roger's house, and I stop outside a small outlet of stores with a parking lot half filled with cars. An empty bench calls my name, and I sit, looking out at the store fronts. Another breeze passes and I shiver, realizing I don't have shit to survive the winter if I kept running. Sure, I knew how to navigate the homeless shelters, but that was back in New York. Back into the lion's den, back...

My foot taps as I attempt to concentrate. I remember this game that Roger's playing with me. What the FBI will do and every other "good guy" I've helped. The rules had been simple and I followed them to the letter, only to be screwed over. They stripped everything from me, except for the pieces I hid from them. Kept close like precious gems, except even now...I have nothing.

Fuck. Why did I come back to him? I knew what he'd argue for. Demand from me. Now I'm trapped in the damn snare he'd gotten me in last time. Once again, nowhere else to go.

Fool me once, shame on me. Fool me twice...

I pull my phone out. My heart pounds as I stare at the device, turning it on and allowing it to find some Wi-Fi. As soon as it does, it dings with a message.

Neither of my friends or Nan would've called. They'd have waited until I contacted them. The one voicemail I have is from a number I hadn't blocked.

Isaac.

My hands shake as I press the button, curiosity overriding the fear inside. Bringing it to my ear, I hear Isaac talk, *"I don't know how far you've gotten or where, but please...please listen to this. Just listen."*

There's a pause, and I wait as he mumbles something, sounding frustrated. *"Come back. He needs you. Leo fucking needs you. Please. Just come back, we'll talk. I swear to you, whatever happens it can be discussed. Allow us to explain. He will explain everything…just come back."* Another pause and he lets out a long exhale. *"At the very least, I ask you, let him know you're okay. It'll kill him if he thinks you're hurt or dead, please Miss Autumn. Please."*

My hand fumbles to my lap as tears fall. I stare at the concrete, chest feeling heavier and heavier with each breath. I wipe at my face, staring up at the sky and hoping for answers. Hands trembling, I close my eyes and recite a few stanzas from *The Raven*, but barely feel any ease. The emptiness is all consuming, writhing as I feel lost. I swallow hard, steady my breath, and look back at the phone.

Thirty seconds. I can give them that at least. And it's not enough time for them to find me. They deserve something.

I press the call button, checking the time, standing, and begin pacing. It rings once before being picked up. "Don't speak or I hang up," I instruct. "Tell him I'm safe. I'm fine. I won't rat him or any of you out, apart from the damage I may have already done. Whatever is asked of me, the one thing I won't give is personal shit. I'm going to respect the relationship we have…had, 'cause it was real to me. But know that the police will start looking into the hotel, and I tell you this 'cause I don't want innocent people being dragged into a tidal wave. They don't deserve that. Do you understand?"

There's a moment of silence before Isaac responds in that familiar British accent, "Yes, Miss Autumn."

A sob breaks in my throat, hanging up and turning everything off again. Tears land on the block of technology, trying to hold back sobs as I walk again. Rain begins to drizzle, falling harder as I walk until I see a flashing sign of a small diner. The clouds release a crash of thunder through the sky and it downpours. I shove through the glass door, stepping into warmth.

It's like one of those 1950s aesthetic places, but with a hint of Waffle House. There're red-topped seats, including the booths that line the windows of the place. The high-top counter makes up most seats, leading to the few booths near the back. I move past the counter and into the furthest booth, climbing in and stare at the wooden tabletop as my hair drips onto the surface. There are a few people inside for late breakfast, utensils clink through the air with an occasional sizzle of a skillet. Thunder continues outside as the white noise of the diner floods my head. I concentrate on it all, trying to find peace in the very everyday of it all. I'm startled when a mug of coffee is placed down before me and a slice of apple pie.

I look up to see an older, curvy woman with deep gray hair, lighter silver strands amongst them. A dark headband holds back the stray hairs, and she's wearing a short-sleeved button up with an apron. She smiles warmly with umber eyes behind some rounded glasses.

My mouth works a little, trying to get words out, but nothing comes. Instead, all I can do is shake my head.

"No worries about it, honey," she says in a soft tone with a small accent that's not from here. "Might be a bit gray outside, but everything is always better after some pie."

My gaze flicks to her name tag, and I whisper in a scratchy rasp, "Thank you…Cheryl."

"Take your time, I'll be right over here if you need anything else." She pats my hand, her aged tawny skin seemingly more human than my paled, wet skin. I stare at where her warm hand touched me, even after she walks away.

Days. It's been days since I've been given a kind gesture. A kind word.

As the numbing emptiness consumes me, I begin to sob silently.

Chapter 2

Apple Pie

"Oh, sweetie, now." Cheryl comes back around, and there's a lull in the diner noise. There's shuffling, and I try to hide some of my tears from being noticed. I used to hide them a lot better than this.

Cheryl sits next to me, putting her arm around my shoulders while rubbing my leg with her other hand. "It's just a bit of pie. Nothing to cry over," she attempts to soothe. I try to apologize, but she doesn't let me get half the words out. "Now, now it's only morning and already crying, no need to apologize for tears."

"What'd you do now, Cheryl?" A man's voice comes from across the way.

"Nothing. Go back to eating," she responds swiftly.

"Nothing?" A chair scrapes. "Young girl crying all over you, dripping like a cat drug in from a river."

"Leave her alone, you old coot," she chastises him, and some of my sobbing subsides. She reminds me of Nan. The thought is both amusing and saddening. "Don't pay him any attention. Thinks he's a big wig for owning a company and such."

Someone sits across from us, and I glance up through tear-filled eyes. Before me must be said Rob. An older gentleman with round-wire glasses and a bald head. His face is covered in wrinkles, his fair skin now weathered from sun and age. I notice a few freckles as he gives me an easy expression. "Did she poison your pie? Could happen. She gets jealous easy."

"Rob," she chastises him again.

"What? I didn't tell her it was the coffee, that'd be a real damn shame." He winks. A small-choked laugh escapes me, and I reach up to cover my mouth. He leans back. "Ahh, she's got a sense of humor. See? Takes more than pie, Cheryl."

She pats my arm, clicking her tongue at him. "Shush. Don't you have a lunch to finish?"

"Nope." He continues smiling like a mischievous young boy. "But don't you have a diner to wait on?"

"I'm waiting on a customer right here." She gestures toward me. "And Mindy can take care of the other two tables."

I look past Rob, noticing the place has become almost empty. Apart from the cook, another waitress, and two other customers. Was I sitting here long? I couldn't be that out of it with time, could I? Looking at the clock, I realize it's been a while since I've left Roger's house. Fuck. I must've been wandering around for hours.

I rub my head, letting out a long sigh at how fuzzy everything feels. Whatever the two had started bickering about, they stop. My hands shake, perhaps more from the chilly AC, as I reach for the coffee, taking a few sips of the dark blend that doesn't taste like shit.

"Sorry," I rasp with a hoarse throat. "It's been a long week, and I haven't…haven't had a lot of kindness lately."

"Oh, sweetie." She hugs me a bit closer. A small, tentative smile rises on my face, because yeah, she is a lot like Nan. Maybe I accidentally found her long lost sister, especially since I detect a southern accent. Nan lost hers years ago. "Well, you can cry and eat if you'd like. You look like you need something in you besides pie, I can get you something whipped up."

She stands, calling out to the cook about the special for today. Rob remains where he is, and I notice his collared shirt and jacket. He holds his hand out to me over the table. "Name's Robert, but everyone calls me Rob. Frequent regular here and father to four daughters, so cry all you need. Looking like you've been through some trouble there."

I take his hand and shake it. "Name's Autumn."

"Pleasure to meet you." Rob looks over his shoulder at Cheryl, who's clearing some dishes. I grab the fork left behind and stab into the pie, taking a bit of the pastry and almost moan at the delicious taste. I've missed diner food, especially with how sweet the desserts can be and even better after the four days of bad take-out Roger has gotten. Seriously, he found the worst places in town to eat from. Relief fills me as I take another bite, flinching when a clap of thunder echoes outside.

"So," I start between bites, looking up at Rob. "Do you always try to comfort women who come in crying from the rain? Or is this part of the lunch special?"

He chuckles, spreading out his arms behind him as he gets comfortable. "Not of late. But today is just one of those days, I guess. Must be the weather," he smirks, but it drops a smidge. "And as I said, father of four, I can see heartbreak from a mile away." I pause, staring at him. "My girls had their own share too many times, beyond what I could count."

The pie becomes more interesting as I pick at it, staring at the flecks of cinnamon amongst the apple slices. He brings his hands down to the table. "You don't gotta talk about it. Just observing. Old man senses, you know."

A half-hearted snort is my response, glancing up at the man across from me. Well, he's much better company than Roger. He's better company than myself right now.

I swallow hard, pushing at the pie absentmindedly. "How'd your daughters handle it?"

"What I advised them with. You move on, don't waste time—"

Cheryl's laughter cuts him off as she plops down a plate with a BLT, fries, and a few pickle spears. "Don't let him fool you. He's a softie for romance and gushes over happy endings. He'll be the first to tell you to run to the airport. He'll drive you, too."

"Do not."

"Have to."

"One time."

"See?" She gestures at him.

"Special occasions only."

"What about Hannah, then?" She crosses her arms.

"Misunderstanding, and we both know it. She'd have gone herself, but I had a full tank of gas," Rob argues. "Alex said the wrong thing, and she needed reassurance. Sometimes we men fuck up."

"Don't I know it," she comments with a snort. The gesture makes me sputter out a weak laugh. Both turn toward me.

"Sorry." I wipe at my mouth.

"Don't be, sweetie." Cheryl tilts her head as I stare at her a moment. "Wondering why the pie is so good or why I don't sound like a local?"

I clear my throat and shrug. "Well…"

"She's afraid to tell you the pie is lackluster," Rob intervenes.

Cheryl smacks him as he laughs, nabbing a fry from my plate. I narrow my eyes at him, and he winks again. Cheryl sighs, and then answers, "Originally from South Carolina, moved up here cause my husband's business. Empty nest and I needed a hobby. Waitressing felt like a good fit. I like meeting people."

"Don't forget stubborn," Rob mutters.

"Always been a working woman. Always will be." She narrows her eyes at him, while her tone drops. "Long as there's someone who needs pie during a storm, I'll be there."

Flashing my gaze between them, finally with my tired brain, it clicks. I huff out a laugh. "You're married."

"It's our undying love showing, ain't it?" Rob asks with a wide smile filled with mischief.

"Secrets out, darling." She pats his shoulder, walking away. "Over forty-two years, and he's still complaining about my pies."

"Cause you keep giving them away. Barely makes any at home for me anymore." Even though he mutters the last part, Cheryl still pauses to give him a look. He holds up both hands in defense, shrugging like he didn't do anything. He turns back smiling still. "She's a good woman. Keeps me on my toes."

"You moved up here for business?" He nods as I pick at my fries. "What business?" I ask, taking the direct route of distraction and liking this simple human interaction.

The more I eat and listen to him and Cheryl, the more the emptiness feels less heavy. The dark feelings aren't so consuming as Rob tells me about his construction company, moving to New York, and his daughters. It reminds me of the slow days at the coffee shop, learning about customers lives. All four of their daughters are married and close to my age. They have five grandchildren, all girls, too. A small detail Rob keeps bringing up with pride, showing me all their newest pictures. It feels like hours before Rob leaves for work and he kisses Cheryl on the cheek. It's still raining, and he runs out to his truck, disappearing into the downpour.

People come and go. Hours pass. Cheryl keeps my coffee refilled while my clothes dry, but I still shiver from time to time, holding onto the warm drink. It's still drizzling against the windows when someone replaces Cheryl, but she comes over to sit where Rob was with her own mug of tea.

"So, tell me about this heartbreak," she says with a soft smile.

"Sure you want to hear about it? Heartbreak from one to the next can't be that much different or interesting."

"Except people are different," she says, picking up her mug. "Sometimes the best conversations we have are the kinship we find in strangers. We're all human and crave a bit of human companionship when our hearts hurt."

"I guess."

"And no judgement from me, sweetie. Whether it was a man, woman, friend, or whoever. Anyone can cause our hearts to break."

Skimming my finger around the mug's rim, I whisper, "I tried to do that with people as a barista. Conversations were always short. But there were ones I cherished."

"Best stories, huh? Well, not the heartbreak ones, but hearing about others. Another reason I kept waitressing. People intrigue me, no matter who they are." She hums, sipping her tea.

"Yeah…" My voice trails off as my mind does.

Hazel, inquisitive eyes that watched me across the counter. The confusion on his face as I reject his fifty dollars, and the touch of his hand. His eyes always finding mine. Him staying for hours in the shop, not daring to leave me alone that last, long day. I remember the fluttering in my stomach. The ease of conversation and questions. My heart squeezes, replaying him calling me, "Dear Watson" for the first time. That sultry, quiet voice.

My chin quivers, trying to stop the tears from coming back. I inhale sharply as my hands begin to tremble. I clutch the mug, pushing my knees tightly against the table leg to keep from shaking, too.

"Wanna talk about it?" Cheryl reaches across to touch my hand. "Might make you feel better. Getting it all out."

A moment passes as I look down at the hand touching mine, gentle and kind.

Kind eyes find mine and I talk.

The next hour I tell her about Leo, opting out certain information, especially the end part. I do explain the, I guess, fast relationship of him and I of the past few months, telling her about dates, the coffee shop, our conversations, and everything that has weighed on my chest. By the end I feel exhausted, leaning back into the booth. She sits silently, rain fading outside as twilight begins. I gulp, knowing Roger will be back from work soon and I'll need to get back before he launches a fucking search party.

She hums, and the noise brings my attention back to her. "You love him still."

"I don't know anymore," I whisper, shrugging weakly. My story stopped before I found the folders and the pictures, telling her I left because he'd been lying about stuff, like his family. She also thinks I'm staying with my "uncle" at the moment.

"Did you talk to him? About what upset you?"

"I was too scared, after my last relationship…I, uh, didn't want it to end the same way. Or worse. It felt like history was repeating itself…and I…"

"But it's not, honey, you can change it." I stare at her, and she grips my hand tenderly. "Your future is up to you. You won't know his true intentions 'til you talk to him. From what you told me, I think he'd listen."

"Don't think he's fake? That he was using me?"

"I think someone from before made you believe that's all you deserve, cause no one who believes another was using them, I think…would speak so kindly about them."

Cheryl shakes her head, taking her mug and mine to put on the ledge behind her where another waitress can grab them. I start to wring my hands together and whisper, "I'm just not sure anymore. Not sure how to trust my instincts."

"Then perhaps, I can help," she says, settling back into her seat. "No man who's faking will go to the kinds of lengths your man did for a ruse. Maybe the fancy dinners or rides, but not taking his time to listen, to care, and be patient with you. Those are traits of a man who loves you. Adores you."

Except, how much does that change when he finds out you ruined his family? Shaking off those thoughts, I ask, "You know this cause of your own marriage?"

She laughs under her breath. "Oh yes, and he tried the wrong route, too. All couples do. Rob tried to buy me fancy things and dinners like a proud peacock. Thought I wanted all that stuff, but all I wanted was a partner. Someone to be there when the sun is shining and not. Through good or bad."

Small streams of sunlight peak through the clouds. I exhale sharply, staring at the light reflecting off the windows. We both stand, and I pull out a few bills and place them on the table. She tries to stop me, but I shake my head at her. "I'll be back tomorrow. Don't want a bad reputation of eating all that pie and running."

Cheryl laughs gently, nodding. "If you insist, honey. I'll see you tomorrow then, and maybe it'll be a bit drier. Better for both our health, but I'll even bring you extra clothes just in case." She winks just like Rob.

"Thanks."

"And then you can tell me more about this Leo of yours. Help get you where you want to be."

I nod, walking out of the diner with her, and parting ways at the sidewalk. I turn my gaze toward where the city is, knowing where I want to be, but fearful it didn't want me back.

Chapter 3

This House Isn't Home

I'm back at Roger's house before he is. His answering machine beeps, and I hit the button, barely hearing the message he left for me. Something about being late and to lock up. Don't open the door for anyone. The message ends with a click as I try to shrug off the exhaustion. The emptiness that's been gone comes creeping back like a toxic waste.

Slowly, I go up the stairs and into the small bedroom. All I've got are the clothes I escaped here with, which are still dirty and smell musty. Roger left some clothes for me, piled on a chair I've yet to go through. I randomly grab a shirt and sweatpants, heading into the bathroom and strip out of the damp clothes. Then I'm just standing. Frozen in the bathroom.

A shower. I should take a shower.

All I do is stare at the crinkly shower curtain, unable to move. The weight on my shoulders too much and abruptly, the food I ate today comes back up. I stumble to the toilet, puking up everything I had at the diner. It burns my throat. I groan against the scratching feeling, stomach clenching at the aftertaste while I clutch the bowl and heave my guts out. Once the torment ends, my entire body shakes as I flush the toilet and curl up on the tiled floor. I hug myself, naked, staring at the cracks in the floor and the dirt that's been there for years I would venture. The bathroom rug is a dark green, its fibers smashed from being stood on. It smells of mildew.

"I don't want to be alone," I whisper.

I'm answered only with silence. Unending, consuming silence.

The dark emotions wrap around me, and I silently rise, almost a robot as I open the medicine cabinet and find Roger's razors. My stomach churns, but there's nothing left in it to expel. Carefully, I hold the razor as I walk into the shower stall and sit with my back against the wall. My entire body convulses from the cold contact, memories flashing at the back of my mind.

I'm alone. I'm alone…

Those words keep repeating in my head. I don't want to be alone. Not again. I can't do this again. I can't.

The blade presses against my calf, pinching at the skin with a tight pressure. I wince as I push further, watching as the blood seeps out and I gasp at the sharp pain. My hands continue shaking, pulling the blade down with a slight harshness. A hiccup comes out of me, a small sob choking out. The pain overrides the darkness in my head, banishing the memories and loneliness for a moment. A painful moment is all it is. Just the sharpness of the blade. Just the blood trickling down my leg.

I gasp, dropping the blade as I slam my head back against the wall. The shaking continues along my arm, while I concentrate on the throbbing sensation where I cut myself. On the feeling of the blood going down my skin like fucked up water. Throat tightening, I struggle to breathe as I squeeze my eyes shut, but all I see is Leo. All I see is him standing at the shower stall, holding a towel out for me.

"You're not broken."

I want him here. To take away these fears. To help me stop myself. Parts of me still ache for him, for his voice, if only for a moment. Even if it meant my damnation, could it be worse than this? Being back in this dark hole of nothing? Bleeding in a shower stall that's not mine?

No monster is worse than Steve.

I exhale sharply, wincing at the small cut as I move a little. How did I get here again? After all these years, I'm back in this damn chasm. If I stay here with Roger, it'll only get worse.

Blood crawls toward the drain.

Because what's the point of being alive if all there is…was pain?

The nightmares are relentless. Every time I snap my eyes open, it's like I'm being crushed or choked. Knives are against my skin and hands are wrapped around my throat. Drowning. I'm drowning and freezing. My legs tremble as I pull them in closely, touching where the bandages are for the cuts. After five days of crying, I somehow still have plenty left to shed.

When morning breaks, I get out of the bed with a pounding head. Roger is already in the kitchen. His thermos in hand, watching me as I blink harshly at the sunlight. "Did you write anything down?"

I go for the coffee pot and pour some into a mug. He asks the question again as I continue not to answer. My body groans, and my calf hurts as I sit at the kitchen table. Could've cut my thigh, but that's a whole other level of chafing hell. My muscles ache from the constant anxiety attacks, lack of sleep, puking, and now from what I've hidden in his guest bathroom. He never knew about the cutting before. He won't now. Roger was always the easiest to hide that shit from.

"Look, my boss is asking for some evidence, anything worth probable cause. I won't get my own contacts in the FBI to agree on anything unless you give me more." I remain mute, and he lets out an exasperated scoff. "Damn sakes, whatever feelings you have for the guy, let it go. It won't be worth the pain. Trust me. You've come this far…don't stop now."

"I have come this far, and I want to stop. I already gave you everything," I whisper in a hoarse voice. "I want out."

"You chose—"

"Almost five years ago I did, but I walked away. You don't need to know how he hangs up his fucking shirts."

"Fine." He slams his cup onto the table, and my brain goes into high alert. The rest is too tired, readying itself to get hit. To prepare for a beating. "Give us the layout of his home, then. The country estate. His hotel, any security you saw—"

"Put a tail on him."

"They won't let me—"

"Never stopped you before."

"It'll be better if you just wrote it down."

I sip the coffee, holding back the grimace of the rough taste. It's quiet and he sighs, sitting down across from me.

"You ran all this way. You came to *me,* fearful of what you saw and what it could mean. Who knows if they've found out who you are now, you can't go back. Don't shut down on me now."

"I'm tired, Roger."

"I know you are—"

"No, you fucking don't." I glare at him, clutching the mug as my fresh wounds pulse under my bandages. His gaze stays on mine, but I don't back down.

He breaks away first, standing up and pours more coffee into his cup. "I'm going to my captain to hopefully continue this Luciano investigation. Start subpoenaing his records and I'm getting into that damn hotel, with or without your cooperation. But, I'm expecting you to have shit written down in the next day or two. You know how this works, I won't get anywhere I need without it, so do your job."

"It's not my—"

"I know a commissioner who's willing to move forward, and he'll definitely do so when he learns that Luciano is a mafia boss."

His last sentence snaps my attention. What? I stare at him stunned. "I never said—"

"Doesn't matter. He's a Marchetti. Connect the damn dots, Sarah."

"That doesn't mean anything!"

"Unless you give me more, I'll *prove* it easily."

"Roger, what the fuck are you—"

"I'm getting the Marchettis once and for all," he growls, pointing at me. "If Luciano wants to keep hiding behind another name, he won't be for much longer. He'll be the link to get Matteo, too. I always fucking wondered if that bastard was involved in some shape or form. My gut is turning out to be right. Those folders you saw could be the start to finally taking down the Marchettis—"

"Is that all you care about?"

"Wouldn't you, after what they did to you? When Gabriel and Steve found out what you were doing?"

"Shut up." My voice trembles with anger, trying to keep back the memories that try to flood forward.

"Or do you want everything you did to go to waste? Think about that. If you don't finish this out, then you *died* for nothing." Roger slams out of the house.

His words sting as he leaves. The house empty and quiet as a graveyard. My stomach aches, and I quickly move to the sink and puke up the coffee I just had. I rub my head, trying to think and figure some way out.

Come on, Autumn. You always have an escape plan.

Except, if what Roger said was true then there's no escaping anywhere.

Shit. I thought briefly if Leo could've been an underboss, enforcer, or something, but not fully if he'd taken over completely as the…

Shit.

I stare at the drain and my heart sinks.

"I took over the family business."

I hold my stomach close, knowing that the last Marchetti is still in the city.

And he's looking for me.

Chapter 4

Lover Lost

I find myself at the diner again. Rob joins me in the same booth as he had the day before. We talk, well he does, while Cheryl checks on us. He leaves after lunch, and I'm left with Cheryl until she leaves before dinner. I leave the diner soon after, holding myself close as I start back to Roger's house. The only comfort I've found in the past few days is gone and my mind spirals back into an abyss of despair and repulsion. Whatever ease they've given vanishes with each step away from the diner. If I could sleep there, I would.

Roger isn't back when I return. Before I know it, I'm back in the damn shower stall. Bathroom door locked with the same blade pressing against my skin as the thoughts of self-hatred, guilt, and fear strangle me. I don't stop with the second searing, sharp pain when he knocks on the door.

"Go away!" I scream, wincing and concentrating on the pain to eddy out my thoughts.

"We need to talk."

"No, we don't. You know what I want."

"And you'll get it when you behave and do what you should."

My hands stop, dropping to my sides as I clutch the razor. The tears don't fall this time. My eyes are dry as I stare at the ceiling feeling like I'm shackled to the floor.

"I talked to a contact within the FBI, he's gonna check things out on his end. We need that information, Sarah."

"Don't use that name." I glare at the locked door. "Don't you *dare*."

"I will if it gets you to understand what's at stake. Your life, along with your friends and others. Or do you want to be responsible for—"

"Shut up!" I scream, dropping the blade and clutching my head. "Stop!"

"Get it through your head. There's no going back. That life is over." Frozen in place, I stare at the dirty tile. The constriction around my chest worsens. My mind zaps back to reality as I feel my veins pulse, the fresh cuts yanking me back to the present.

Pain. A coldness sweeps over my skin. *Finish it.*

I choke at the thought.

I try to remember the warmth of Cheryl's hand. Rob's grin. The smell of bacon cooking in the diner. The drizzle of rain on the window.

Anything real.

Anything good. *Something.*

A memory unlatches. Carbonara. *"Never will I harm you."*

My hand moves down, pressing against the small wounds as I try to stop the blood trickling down my leg. How much had he meant? How deep was that promise?

"Fucking woman," he mutters through the door. "We'll talk tomorrow."

It becomes quiet. The faucet drips. I'm not sure how long I sit there, contemplating what to do, but conjure up nothing. My mind won't think straight, as if my thoughts are covered in a thick dust and I'm crawling through oil. All that seems to come easily are horrid memories, repulsion of myself, and constant horror.

Late in the night, I get off the floor and bandage my cuts with cheap Band-Aids, then fall into bed where I'm plagued with nightmares again. Twice, I barely make it to the bathroom to puke, remembering being tortured and strapped to the hospital bed as they cut into me. So much blood. Red. I wake up on the bathroom floor, peeling myself off the tile. Quickly as I can, I peel off the bloodied bandages, haphazardly putting on new ones before I get dressed, needing to get out of the stifling house.

I bypass the kitchen, heading straight for the door as Roger calls out, ignoring him. He comes outside after me but stops in the yard as I head down the street. Not wanting him to follow, I wander for almost two hours before I see the diner up ahead. Suddenly, that familiar prick returns, tugging at the back of my neck. The hairs on my skin rise, tingling down my spine as I stop and glance around at my surroundings.

There's no one.

There are a few cars passing, and a couple walking into a nearby store. Anxiety ticks through me as I continue for the diner, keeping my eyes moving as I enter the familiar space.

Cheryl isn't in yet, and I sit down at the regular booth as one of the other waitresses takes my order. It's another hour before Cheryl comes in with a surprised expression, coming over as she ties on her apron. "You're here earlier than usual."

"Couldn't sleep." And my legs fucking hurt from cutting. If I'm going down, might as well fall into the deepest pit of self-loathing.

She smiles, and I try to give her one back. "You want more coffee, sweetie?"

"Please." I search outside again, as I have been for the past hour. The worry hasn't left, and I begin to wonder if I'm finally just losing it. Surprised it took this long.

She comes back, topping off my coffee and places down a slice of pie. "Seems sleep hasn't been your friend lately."

"Not, really," I say, adding more cream before drinking more of the hot liquid. It scratches against my throat. "Thank goodness for coffee."

I lift the mug a little as Cheryl eyes me a moment. She nods, pursing her lips and gestures toward the pie. "Heard you already had some waffles, try some pie to get those sugars up. You looking too thin of late."

I snort, half-heartedly. "Yes, mom."

"Careful giving me sass, cause I'll throw it back. Or worse…give you to my husband to deal with." She pats my hand and walks away as more customers enter.

My skin pricks of warning again. None glance my way, all sitting at tables on the other side or at the far end of the counter. A few seem like regulars from the past two days. My heart still pounds, and I rub at my chest.

"You're overthinking. Roger's getting you worked up. No sleep and not keeping down food is just catching up is all," I murmur to myself, stabbing at the pie. "Don't lose it now. One day at a time. Just like before."

Halfway through the rhubarb pie, Cheryl brings over some oatmeal. She says something about good for the stomach and continues to check on me as I nurse my coffee for the next couple of hours. The feeling of being watched doesn't leave. Every ten minutes I check again and again. Nothing changes.

People come in. People leave. People eat. Cars pass.

Lunchtime hits and Robs walks in, raising his hands up when he sees me and claps them together as he sits across from me.

"You had pie without me?" I nod. "Ah, well, must mean you're getting better."

"Does it?"

"Well, it's what my wife says, huh?" He asks as she approaches, bringing him a water. "It's that or getting more sun. Or just seeing my Cheryl with her cheery smile."

"Quit trying to butter me up for extra fries, Rob." She clicks her tongue at him, walking away. He makes a disgruntled noise. "Never works." He brings his attention back to me. "How we doing today, Autumn?"

"Feels like I've been run over by a truck," I say with a sharp exhale.

"You're uh…" he clears his throat, "…your *uncle* being persistent on what you should do again?"

His brow raises, and there's something in his tone that makes me tense. I swallow harshly, nodding as I try to play along with the ruse of Roger being my uncle. I've tried to be vague as possible in explaining the situation of why I'm here, such as a "protective" uncle against what could be a bad guy. He doesn't like him or approve, yadda yadda. To Rob and Cheryl, I'm a distraught, heartbroken woman who's left her ex-boyfriend, unsure where to go next. Not sure how well they'd have taken the truth: hiding from my potential mafia boss boyfriend, who doesn't know I imprisoned his older brother, made him stay in New York to take over the family business, possibly why his younger brother has to be in Italy, and I've been hiding from the mob for three years.

Soap operas are more believable.

I rub at my neck, feeling the prick come back. "Yeah, my uncle, uh…doesn't like him, and that I should stay out of the city. Think he's just…protective"

"More like a jealous woman with a vendetta," Rob comments. I tilt my head, raising a brow as he shrugs and looks over at his wife. "Just saying. Sounds like jealousy. Green-eyed envy. Odd being your uncle and all."

"Yeah…I guess," I mutter under my breath. Pretty sure the jealousy part was not getting *everyone* in the mob years ago. Guess the promotion, recognition, and plaques weren't enough for him.

"Want to know what I think?"

"I think you will anyway," I smirk.

He chuckles under his breath. A few seconds pass as he watches me, then finally says in a calm tone, "Go back to your man."

The bluntness in his voice makes me rear back, staring at him with wide eyes.

"It's your decision, of course, can't tell you what to do. Couldn't with my own daughters, but…" he hums, placing a lingering gaze on Cheryl, "…there's nothing like finding your person. You do what you can to keep them. It's hard, real hard, but when both people want it, then you can withstand the worst the world can offer. I may not have met him but hearing about him in comparison to others well…you sound like me with my wife. And maybe, just maybe, he'd be willing to fix whatever broke."

I clutch my mug, trying to keep myself from shaking. Rob reaches across, patting my hand gently. "You get to decide what you want fixed. What's worth fighting for, but you won't know what he's willing to fix until you talk."

"You trying to tell me…" I clear my throat, swallowing hard, "…I'm being too harsh? That I'm wrong for leaving?"

He shakes his head, while I wait to be chastised. To be told I'm being irrational and too emotional. To just deal with it, go pull on my bootstraps and shit. My body tenses as Rob sighs, waiting for the raised voice. Except, Rob smiles.

"Fear makes us do all kinds of crazy things. But just cause you left from fear from what others have told you, doesn't mean it's set in stone. Won't know you can't go back, unless you try."

At that moment, Cheryl comes up and puts lunch in front of Rob. She wipes her hands over her apron, flicking her gaze between us. "What he telling you now? To put more cream in your coffee or the time our eldest snuck out for a Garth Brooks concert?"

"No, but now I want to hear about it," I say softly, keeping my gaze on Rob who concentrates on his food. I give Cheryl a soft smile. "I'll have to ask about that next."

"Just be sure to hear the version where *he* stayed at the concert with her. He's always been a fan."

"Ain't my fault the man can croon."

She shakes her head at him, walking off as he begins to eat.

Some minutes pass before I ask, "Have you always come to the diner to see her?"

"Oh, yeah." He stabs at the salad. "She always supported me, and I'm gonna support her. If I ain't staying home, neither is she. Gives me a reason to see her a bit more every day, too. And there's something about seeing your loved one doing something they love. She gets all giddy about the pie. Meeting new people. Listening to regulars. Social butterfly. Always has been."

He waves a little at Cheryl, who pretends she doesn't care, but I notice a small blush blossom across her cheeks. She even giggles as she tries to wave him off. I watch her, warmth filling my chest that hasn't been there in days. She reminds me of working at *Blue Java Café*, spending time with customers and being with coworkers I liked. The laughter with Mabel. Quick conversations with regulars. Being excited to see Leo walk in, a glint in his eye as he hid his smile. The smell of an Americano.

Feeling…seen.

Curiosity tickling at my senses, I come back to the present and feel the fog around my brain lifting a bit. Thoughts are clearer as I look at Rob, who watches me with a concentrated expression. I lean forward. "You've known me for like two days, I'm appreciative of the kindness, but why tell me this? To try helping me or…" my fingers tap the table, and I clear my throat as I rub at my chest again, "…thinking I should take the chance?"

A sad smile comes over his face. Eyes softening. "Because I think I understand Leo a bit."

"How so?"

"I messed up, too." His smile doesn't falter. "Beginning of my marriage, I didn't know what love really was. I was young, didn't understand truly consequences of my actions. What being silent can do. Those first few months in marriage, I slept with another woman. I cheated and I didn't tell Cheryl for oh, about six months after the *horrid* affair."

My eyes widen as I flash them toward his wife.

"She listened to me beg for forgiveness. I was ashamed, young, and dumb. Should've told her something was wrong before ever looking outside of her, and I hated myself for it. I didn't see myself good enough for her, beating myself up this way and that for those six months. I tried to be good enough, what I thought that meant to her, because I loved her. When the time came she learned what I'd done…I thought I'd lost her. For the first time, I truly cried in front of her. I confessed, then waited for the destruction that would follow. Waited to be left. Waited to be punished for my actions."

He pauses to take a bite of his sandwich, and I almost roll my eyes at him for the slight dramatic stop. Rob winks as I make a noise for him to continue. Finishing up his sandwich, he leans back in his seat. "She forgave me. On one condition."

"Don't do it again?"

He chuckles, shaking his head. "Well, apart from that. Her condition was for me to never break her trust like that again. Somehow that woman…" he nods toward Cheryl, who's serving a new couple, "…forgave me. She gave me a chance to be better, and to prove to her how much I loved her. Needed her. Had to spend the next few years doing a lot of work, which was hard at times, but she had the patience of all the saints combined. We loved each other and that's what counts the most on some days to help the work not feel so impossible."

My mouth hangs open a little. I've discussed red flags and working on baggage with Leo, but this was a different level. That's rebuilding an entire foundation. Leo lied to me, hid information, but…I'm not sure how I'd forgive him if he was with someone else. And perhaps from the lack of sleep or other influences, I can't comprehend how Cheryl was able to forgive Rob.

"How? How do you rebuild after something like that?"

"With love, but not the cutesy shit they show you. Nah, the hard love; kind where no one besides you and them will know what you're willing to try. Cause no matter what you tell me, Cheryl…" he pauses, dropping his voice, "…or your uncle, only you and your man will know what you truly have. What *you* are willing to do for each other."

"You're another kind of human, Rob. Cheryl is too."

"Nah," he laughs, shaking his head. "Just two people in love. Like I said, sometimes that's all you need to survive. More fun that way."

"Not what society says."

"What *society says* can go fuck off. Usually, those people don't know nothing about a good partnership, unless it means money or other selfish crap."

"Yeah," I whisper with a shrug. "Maybe."

Rob's glasses catch a stream of light as he tilts his head. "Can you live without him?"

"What?"

"Can you live without him?" He asks again. "If yes, then do what I told you when I first met you. Move on. If not, you find a way to fit the pieces together. And you grow. You try."

I nod, trailing a finger around my mug. "The whole, won't know until you try thing?"

"Sure as hell ain't gonna know sitting in this diner all day. Or at a house that ain't yours."

Rob's story sinks into me, along with every bit of advice. Probably the better option to listen to a man who's been in a good relationship for over thirty years. Especially one that's overcome a few obstacles, and not just a daughter sneaking off for a concert.

The conversation turns over to happier topics. After the lunch hour is up, Rob leaves for work and gives Cheryl a big kiss before disappearing through the door. She giggles like a young girl, bringing over a new glass of water for me as the diner almost empties. Only a couple of construction workers sit near the front windows when that prick at my neck comes back. Hairs standing on end.

The water glass pauses at my lips.

Anxiety rises, crawling over my skin like someone is standing behind me. I look up through the windows. It feels like my heart stops when I see him across the street, hands in his pockets as he stares at the diner.

He found me.

Chapter 5

Lover Found

Slowly, I move the glass down to the table as he walks across the street. A part of me screams to run. Get out. Except, him approaching me in a public space is my best option. Not to mention a southern woman on the other side of the counter who may poison his coffee if I asked. My heart races, pounding in my ears, as I take a steadying breath and watch him walk into the diner.

There's no falter in his step. He strides in with comfortable ease. He's wearing a dark blue suit, shirt un-buttoned at the top. I flick my gaze to what could be potential witnesses and straighten myself as he approaches. He sits across from me, gaze finding mine.

Almost seven days have passed, but it's like years since I've seen Jameson. There are shadows under his eyes and the stubble across his jaw is messy like he forgot to shave. He appears to have just woken up to come here, because I notice the wrinkles in his clothing. Guess I'm not the only one who's not getting their beauty sleep.

"How'd you find me?" I whisper.

Jameson smirks, reminding me of a big brother who just found a dirty magazine under my mattress. Odd thing is I see no malicious intent in his gaze. With others it was like looking into someone who's found their prey. Instead, in a tired quiet tone he half-teasingly says, "Learned to be quicker after the elevator."

I tilt my head. After a few seconds, it clicks.

The phone call. Damn. Guess I wasn't as quick as I thought I was.

"Didn't need much time, huh? If you only needed thirty seconds, then that tells me you've got the good tech to triangulate my location." His brows pinch together, frowning. "Or you found me *after* I hung up."

He shifts in his seat. "Isaac's head of security for a reason. But we have another guy who's better."

"CIA?"

"Ex-FBI."

Oh-fucking-joy. Maybe we can swap notes later.

Cheryl comes around, gaze moving between us as she puts her hand on her hip. "Haven't seen you around. What can I get ya?"

"Water's fine," he answers with an easy smile. "Won't be long. Just saying hi to an old friend. Haven't seen her in a bit."

"Uh-huh." She gives me a look, pausing before I nod. She leaves, but comes back promptly, putting the drink down and gives me her full attention. "You need anything, honey? Perhaps some tea, looks like it's gonna rain again."

"Maybe in a bit, Cheryl." My eyes meet hers and she raises a brow. "Just need to have a talk real quick."

She pats my shoulder. "Just holler if you need me, sweetie."

Cheryl leaves as a few more construction workers enter the diner. Jameson watches her. "Find new friends already?"

"Kind of." My hands move down to my lap as I start pulling at my fingers and rubbing my palms against my thighs. "Better being surrounded by friendly faces at the moment. How'd you know I'd be here specifically?"

"Public space. Figured I'd wait until you'd leave, but then realized you're here for hours at a time. Given past experiences, I think I'd regret trying to meet you in a park."

"Not a great track record for you all, huh?" Or me for that matter. My heart races, hands shaking under the table, I flick my gaze toward the gun peeking from his holster. "Been watching me long then?" Had to have been if he knew I'd be here all day or have before.

"Less than 24 hours," he murmurs. "Got only a five-to-seven-mile radius, so you can wave that in Isaac's face." I snort. "But spent the 24 hours prior to that scouring the neighborhoods for you. Found you here by chance. Right before you left yesterday."

He knows where I'm staying then. Son of a fucking moldy biscuit. Damn it.

Jameson sips his water. "Had a pretty effective plan there, and it would've worked if you hadn't called."

I remain quiet. My jaw hurts as I clench my teeth, head pounding as I do my best to keep my entire body from quivering. Fear and loneliness battle within. I'm terrified of what Jameson is doing here, but I miss talking with him at the same time. There's a calm air about him, the same I remembered for the weeks I've known him.

Yet, it all feels changed.

My mind reels, trying to think of what to say. To ask. Why it's him that's here and not Leo. Why they hadn't knocked on Roger's door. What he or Leo wants with me. What they know.

"He needs you." His voice is quiet, but the words instantly bring tears to my eyes.

My hand clenches as they escape, rolling down my cheeks. Jameson shifts again, leaning in, but doesn't touch me. He pulls out a handkerchief and places it on the table.

"He does need you."

"Stop," I weakly plead.

"No matter what you saw, he still cares about you. And he fucking loves you."

"I don't know what to believe anymore. What's real…"

"It was real. You and him." I shut my eyes, yanking more at my hands as my stomach starts to hurt. My legs rub together, and I hold back a wince as I freeze. The food I had earlier becomes like a rock. "He was going to tell you everything. All of it that night at the estate." I snap my head up, brows furrowing. "You were never supposed to see those folders."

"Doesn't change much does it? What's been done."

"What you saw was to protect you."

"Protect me?"

"Yes."

I wipe the tears with his handkerchief. "Why'd you come?"

"Because he asked." Confusion must be seen on my face because he begins to explain swiftly. "He didn't want to smother you. Make you feel like he was manipulating you, forcing you to come back, or worse cause you to run again. He'll never allow for you to feel shackled to him. To his life. He'd rather fucking drown, the stubborn bastard."

"Then why come at all?"

He scoffs, settling back into his seat. "You were gone for almost a week at a *detective's* house. Yet, there's been no warrants or feds calling. No knocking on our doors." His tone is cold, but he also sounds confused. His brows are furrowed, cocking his head to the side as he eyes me. "A few questions arise in general of why you went where you did, but mostly I want to know *why* haven't they come? Especially after what you saw."

"It wasn't enough."

"Not enough?"

"Proof. They need more to do anything."

"And did you? Give it?"

"I said I didn't—"

"Could've been lying."

I look away, staring over at Cheryl who's whispering with another waitress at the end of the counter. Her gaze meets mine, giving me a look, like asking if she needs to intervene. I force a small smile, shaking my head and bring my attention back to Jameson. "No. I didn't lie to Isaac. I didn't tell…them everything. Or won't, I guess."

"Why?"

"Because I can't. I just…I just can't." My chest feels heavy, weighing more and more as the ache of the past week comes back. It drowns me, making me mourn of what can't be anymore. Not if they find out what I've done.

"Why?" He asks again.

"Because..." My voice rasps.

"Autumn—"

"It was real to me," I snap under my breath. A trickling anger spears its way through the hurt and fear. "It was real. I'm going to respect the relationship I had with him. I'm going to respect our privacy because it doesn't need to be given over to anyone as *evidence*, like what we had was wrong or a crime. Maybe I don't know what to believe in but...but..." my voice chokes, and I swallow hard, "...it was real to me. More than any of you may understand."

"It's still fucking real. Just come back."

My head begins to shake automatically. I want to scream as I feel pulled in different directions. I have to concentrate to not throw up my food again. "Answer me one thing."

"Long as you answer me one," he counters. I nod, knowing I won't learn anything to help me figure out what I need unless I agree. He leans in close, folding his hands under his chin. "Who are you really?"

I remain quiet, but my heart plummets through the floor. The pounding in my head is loud as he watches my reaction. Unable to speak, I go still, not knowing what to do or say. Chills run over my bones of the potential consequences, and I can hear Roger's words that I can't go back. That I'll be repeating a mistake. I'll be used and tortured again. I'd escaped only to be dragged back to something, perhaps worse than the first time.

He'll hate me. Like everyone else.

After a minute of silence, he begins to talk, and the chill gets worse.

"After some digging, we think you were caught up in the mob before. Maybe years ago. All we knew is that things weren't adding up. What we found on Autumn Watson and what you told Leo; shit wasn't aligning. Mentioned you left Ohio around 17, but Autumn Watson was from *Kentucky* and left at *18* from her foster home. Which is odd, since you told him you had parents and sister who were still alive."

Brown eyes stay with mine, but I become a stone. My entire body locks up, shutting down as he connects the pieces. I fucked up. I'd been open with Leo, never thinking that those bits of my past would be brought into light and examined. Fuck, I should've been more careful, but I wanted to be honest with him since so much of me felt like a lie.

"After those little realizations, we dug deeper," he continues. "Your job, current bank accounts, even therapy all started around the same time frame. Makes sense given the brutality of your assault, but everything before was like this mirage. From afar, nothing seemed off, but as you stare at the picture a bit closer you begin to notice something's not right."

He pauses, and I wait for the final blow. For what they found. My body tenses, waiting for him to say the name. Jameson takes a drink of water, continuing in a low tone. "The foster home you were supposedly in was shitty with records, so apparently a lot of your information is lost. Not uncommon but must've been hard to get into college cause of that."

"Yeah," I mutter.

"College had everything though. Every document saved, but uh, odd knowing how smart you are, you barely got your degree in English. Not so great grades. Partying too much?"

"Maybe."

"Then why no social media? Just never wanted it?" I shrug. "Or maybe you deleted everything? Not a trace of you, which is impressive. No current public accounts either."

Oh, social media is still up. Just not Autumn Watson's. No, Autumn Watson is a reclusive, book nerd who spends too much time reading and not studying. Autumn Watson wasn't someone you remembered, but always seemed to be in class with you. She was the barista you never looked twice at. The woman who wore thrifted clothes, kept her eyes down, and you wouldn't remember if you bumped into her on the street. That was the cover, and it had worked for the past few years. Until Leo.

"There's stuff," I say, trying to act nonchalant.

"Oh, sure, on Leanne's and Trix's social accounts of the last three years. Even that's few and far between."

"Preferred books and movies over people," I whisper. "You getting at something?"

He inhales sharply, frowning. "The thing is, foster child, loner, or whatever, there should be more. A life lived, especially after the past three years, being freed from an abusive ex. It's like you're still hiding. From what and who though? So, who are you really... Autumn Watson?"

Realization sinks in, straightening myself knowing they haven't made the last connection. The small details I'd interwoven with my old life, making the obvious still hard to see. I'd done everything that the FBI told me to do, even going beyond what I was instructed to hide in plain sight. Guess it worked given they don't know my old name, but how long can I keep that secret?

"Not a double agent or something cool," I murmur, smirking a bit.

"Whoever you are, you had help to hide."

Yeah, no, mostly me. Autumn Watson was a book nerd, but Sarah Marie was a computer forensics nerd. I'll keep that to myself for now.

"Pretty impressive, either way. Had to dig deep, not to mention if you hadn't told Leo, we'd have never known the discrepancies."

"Thanks," I say deadpan.

"What happened?"

"That's two questions."

"Answer the first."

Keeping myself calm, I lean back in my seat as I tap my fingers on the table. I needed to know first. Knowing the truth determined if I even should say out loud who I am. Being an enemy of the mob *and* police isn't good for your health or so I've been told. And I know I'm slowly making an enemy with Roger right now.

"Answer mine first. Then I will."

He clears his throat but agrees. The question spirals in my head, pushing up my throat to finally ask, "Is he *the* boss?"

There's no indication of surprise. He was ready for me to ask it.

His jaw muscles tighten flashing his gaze at the quiet diner. Finally, he whispers, "Yes."

Fear chokes me.

It was me. I fucked up Leo's life and plans to leave. He told me he left, to get away from his family and he came back, only to be stuck here. Guilt weighs on me, along with worry and uncertainty. Just as I had given him snippets of my real life, he'd given me parts of his. Coded sentences and clues. He didn't want this. And yet, because of what I'd done just over three years ago, he became locked in. Not to mention the money I probably cost him. There's no fucking coming back from being the reason why it all was destroyed. I'm why his brother is in jail. I'm why his family's business shattered and why Matteo left for Italy. I'm why businesses went bankrupt. Why the mafia lost millions.

If he knew what I'd done, he'd hate me. For multiple reasons, and I wouldn't blame him.

"Are you gonna tell me—"

"I can't," I state.

Jameson swears under his breath, flexing his hands on the table and I move further back into my seat. He flicks his gaze over me, then down to his hands before he moves them off the table. He pulls a phone out, pushing it toward me next to the handkerchief. "I was given explicit instructions not to touch you."

"Why?"

"Cause Leo would cut off my hands." My eyes widen and he shrugs. "Best friend or not. I meant it when I said he doesn't want to force your hand. And how much he cares about you."

Would he still if he knew what I'd done? I shouldn't feel guilty for taking down more than half the mob, but right now...the guilt festers. "And if I forced his hand?"

"You haven't. Even if you gave over everything you learned to the police, what you saw or heard, we have precautions for it. Not the first time." He gestures toward the phone. "That's a burner phone. It's encrypted. No one can trace who you call, completely private. There's one number already saved, and he'll pick up when you're ready. He said *if* you call, but I'm saying when. Cause deep down, you'll talk to him before you officially disappear. For good."

"You don't know—"

"Don't act dumb with me now." His gaze darkens. "We know how this goes. If you were caught in shit before, and they let you change your identity to stay in New York, what makes you think they'll do it again? I doubt the feds will let you stay on the east coast. You'll wind up in a witness protection program in some random state. So, you might want to consider the last time you saw Nancy. Leanne. Trix. Even Leo. Cause it'll *be* the last time you ever saw them."

He's wrong.

I'd be lucky if Roger allowed me to go into witness protection. Sure, I'd gotten lucky last time for the FBI to allow me to stay in New York, including allowing a handful of people to know about my identity change, but that was when I had shit to trade with. This time? From how Roger sounds, he'll lock me up before allowing me to go further than Atlantic City.

He may actually do that—lock me up if I don't cooperate.

For all I know in a few weeks, I'll *wish* that he sent me states away.

A piercing feeling runs through my heart though at the thought of never seeing Nan or Leanne again. He'd make sure I wouldn't. My lifelines. The only reasons I stayed alive this long.

"Leo won't do that to you," he says quietly, pulling me from my spiraling thoughts. "I know him. Maybe it's hard for you to believe, but he cares about you immensely. Which means, he'll go all in to help. He did it for me, Isaac, and countless others, you should at least let him try and not run at the first sign of trouble."

"Trying to guilt me to come back?"

"Will it work?" I glare at him. "He's not going to. Someone should try."

"You have no right—"

"Don't care. Not gonna apologize for helping him. No matter how dirty I gotta get."

"Why?"

"Because he's a brother to me. Over a decade with him. I'm gonna make sure he finally gets his happiness, and he found it in you."

"Jameson."

"He's been a wreck since you left. Worried you're dead, hurt, or… worse." My calf suddenly throbs and the band-aids itch, the sudden urge to add to them flickers in my mind. "You have pegged him every time on what he wanted, needed, who he is, or what he'd do… come on. Why stop now? You've kept an open heart so far, with him and the rest of us."

"It's called being nice," I scoff.

"Not for us." Jameson leans back, crossing his arms. "People don't remember details about your life or give nicknames to be *nice*. They don't ask how you are or say thank you. They don't look you straight in the eye, wanting truth and not bullshit like weather patterns. Fuck sakes, you did the same with people at this diner, otherwise why is that waitress seem ready to gut me the moment something goes wrong over here?"

I look at Cheryl quickly, noticing her glance our way again. She flicks a gaze between us, nodding a little as I look away and rub my temple.

Sure, I try to be open with people. To be kind and not cruel. I've seen enough cruelty; I didn't want to add more to the world. Fear pushes at me with the truth that could condemn me, no matter how kind or open I was. And then there's that little voice, telling me this is all fake. A ruse like how Steve had done. What Roger has done. Another just like them where there's no escape. Only pain.

Except, I continue to hear Leo's voice at the back of my head. *"You'll always be safe with me, dear Watson. Always."* Could I trust he'd keep his word?

Our gazes become locked, and I see that flicker of sincerity in him. "It was real, Autumn," he whispers, pleading with me once more. "All of it. With him and us. We care about you, not giving a shit who you were before or that you ran."

"You say that now."

"Come back." He scowls, nodding at the handkerchief. "You can give that back when you do."

"I'm not—"

"He won't tell you what to do, but I fucking will. Come back to us. We'll wait however long you need, but some things will always have a time limit. Besides..." he starts to get out of the booth, "... hotel seems a bit dim without you."

"Wait." I hesitate, not entirely certain of what I'm doing as I flag down Cheryl, who comes over with investigative eyes. "Can you bring me something to write with?"

She leaves, coming back with one of her pads of tickets and a pencil. I thank her, and she walks away with a long look at Jameson. He stands still as I shakingly write down the name.

I stare at my handwriting, wondering if it will kill me or free me? Did it matter which at this point? I'd done everything to bury her, so I could live, but not everything stays buried. Another sharp inhale, I hand over the sheet of paper knowing there's no way back once they read it. Once the connections are made.

Jameson takes it, careful not to touch me and glances at the paper. His brows lift as I say in a quiet tone, "She'll have the answers you need."

Chapter 6

Resolve

Fifteen minutes have passed since Jameson left. I stare at the phone, quiet and thinking. Finally, the handkerchief disappears into my pocket, and I grab the phone. I pull out cash to pay for my meal and hand Cheryl her pad and pencil back.

"You alright, honey?" She asks.

"I don't know. I uh, but I need to go." It's early for me at least. But I needed to move, get out and think.

"Alright but come back in if the rain's too much." She nods towards the darkening sky, then gives me a soft smile. "I'll see you tomorrow, then, yeah?"

A sinking feeling hits my stomach as if I'm heading to the guillotine. Dread presses further as I clutch the phone in my hand. I look over the sweet face that's comforted me the past few days. Guilt mixes with the dread. Still, I force a smile and nod. "I'll see you tomorrow."

Throat tightening, I quickly leave and head for the park. My head is on a swivel as I check my surroundings, waiting for Jameson or Isaac to pop up. There's nothing out of the ordinary from before, but knowing I've been watched the past 12 hours puts me on edge. I'm better than this… trained better—

I stop.

No. No I wasn't trained. It wasn't my job. It wasn't my duty. None of it was. Being good at escaping, not being found, manipulating information weren't fucking talents. They were survival.

Talent was me creating software that can penetrate the hardest firewalls without being tracked. Talent was juggling multiple drinks at a time. *Talent* was knowing every fucking line from *The Room*, and with knowing how crappy of a movie it is. And I could also recite every stanza from *The Raven*, too.

All this other shit was survival. I *had* to learn. Or die.

Warning flicks up my spine, I move to the side as I hear footsteps and someone jogs past. I move off the sidewalk into the small park, feeling the wind pick up as I head toward a small gazebo. Once underneath, I sit on the small bench inside and hold the phone in my lap. With trembling fingers, I turn on the encrypted device, hoping Jameson wasn't lying.

Once the screen turns on, there's a singular note app. I press it to find a number I don't know with the message underneath; *I'll answer no matter when -Leo*. And then beneath it are numbers I know with another message, *so you're not alone*.

It's Nan, Leanne, and Trix's personal numbers.

Quickly, feeling a bit rusty, I go through the phone's settings, looking for anything that would show it's tracking my movement. Nothing. I go through every precaution I know, but it's a military grade encrypted phone. Unattached to anything. Not even Leo would be able to track where I go or where I'm calling from.

Shit. A lifeline. He gave me a lifeline if I actually decided to disappear.

Swallowing hard, I quickly put in a familiar number and wait as it rings. The call is picked up and I almost cry when I hear her voice.

"Hello? Autumn, is that you?" Nan's voice drifts over the line.

"It's me."

"Oh, my dear, I'm so relieved to hear your voice. Are you okay? Can you tell me where you are? What happened—?"

"I can't…I can't tell…" the words won't come out, choking me as I try to talk, "…I'm scared, Nan."

There's some scuffling in the background and then a door closes. "I can come get you. I'm in Georgia, but I can come find you."

"No, you can't…no, I can't let you get involved."

"You don't sound well."

"Probably because I'm not," I scoff with a half-hearted, empty laugh. "I don't know what to do. I don't…" pausing to blink, and glance over my shoulder, "…how'd you know it was me?"

A quiet laugh leaves her, empty like mine. "You used to call from blocked numbers all the time. Remember? Thought perhaps you were again, so Caltz wouldn't track you."

How long have I been on the run? Never feeling safe even with those I was supposed to? My memory flashes to being in Leo's apartment at the hotel, eating breakfast as he cooks and not having the constant worry at my back. That memory feels close to shattering, my heart sinking of what he may do when he realizes who I really am.

"Are you coming back?" Nan's voice pulls me from my thoughts.

"I don't know."

"What's wrong, dear? How can I help you?"

"I don't know." I repeat.

I get up, pacing in the gazebo as the sky darkens with clouds rolling in. It's only afternoon, but the sun is mostly covered from the coming rain. Unsure what else to do, confused and feeling more like a caged animal as I pace under the roof, I tell her, "I'm scared, Nan. Scared I'll trust the wrong people again. This time there's no way out. No escape if I choose wrong. That'll I fuck up again…"

"You didn't before."

"Yes, I did—"

"No," she states in a stern voice, but I can hear it breaking. "They used you. That is *not* your fault. You did what you could to stay alive. What we all must do sometimes to protect who we love and ourselves."

Tears fall down my cheeks as I continue to pace, focusing on her voice. "I'm scared," I repeat. "I don't want to be alone."

"You're not alone, dear." I stop pacing, closing my eyes as I feel the breeze across my face. I inhale deeply, trying to keep my thoughts together.

"I don't know what to do, Nan. I feel trapped. And I don't…I don't know who to believe…who to trust."

"What does your gut say?"

"Nan, I'm pretty sure I'm not well enough—"

"You're smart. And your common sense and know-how has always been good. Not your head or heart, as my Finn would say, what does the bottom of your gut tell ya?"

My grip on the phone tightens as the first of the rain falls. The prick at my neck intensifies, and I look over my shoulder. There's a car there. Maroon with the lights on, but the guy inside is smoking and talking on the phone.

What my gut says.

It says to take precautions first.

With a deep breath, I close my eyes and begin devising in my head the first steps to play it smart. No matter what I do, to have plan B and C in place. Just in case.

"Nan, can you do me a favor? When you come back to New York, make sure no one goes through my stuff. It's all I have."

"Of course, dear."

"If I…if I don't show up in a couple of months, there's a locker near Penn Station. The number and code to open the lock are under the drawer on the left side of my bed. Put my movies and whatever books you can fit inside, throw away the rest."

"Autumn—"

"They took everything from me last time, and I want *something* in case they try taking everything from me again. You know what those movies mean to me."

She hums, "The first items you ever owned after you got out."

"Yeah," I mumble, wiping away at stray tears. "Not much, but all I got to my name. Don't let them near my stuff unless I come back. No one, Nan."

She inhales sharply. "Alright. Everything is already safe. You're always welcome home again, dear."

"I know."

"Autumn—"

"I love you, and I'm sorry." Her voice is cut off as I hang up.

I continue staring at the maroon car as the rain begins to come down hard. It pounds against the gazebo roof as I breathe deeply for the first time in days it seems.

What my gut says.

Pocketing the phone, I head out into the rain and take the long route back to Roger's.

***

The razor is in my hand. The room is barely lit by a singular lamp as I sit on the floor against the bed. It's late as I flick my gaze between the phone on the floor and the razor. Roger still isn't home, making the worry gnaw more that the plan which is slowly brewing won't be able to happen. If he surprises me with agents at the door, I'll have to figure other shit out.

After my long walk in the rain, I stripped out of the soaking wet clothes and pulled on the only other set of clothes that were dry. We'll count the rain as a shower. Pretty sure the last time I've taken a proper shower was in Leo's penthouse. I smell of mildew and musty clothes. It makes my stomach twist, but I haven't puked yet. Instead, I've stared at the razor then my calf, and then the phone. Even as I try to think of my next steps, I'm pulled in different directions.

Logic tells me to go with Roger, whatever he says. He's police. The good guys. Leo's a mafia boss, and given his lineage, most likely the head honcho. Don supreme as some like to call it. A dangerous life awaits that side, filled with atrocities I saw and experienced first-hand. The smart thing was to leave. To put Leo, everyone who works for him behind bars like I had with his brother, captains, and under-bosses. With my ex.

I'm not even fucking sure if the mob knew it was all me. If they really looked, perhaps they'd see the connections. Who I was around and where. Steve figured it out, others could have. Even after all the surgeries I had, I could still be recognized. It was what Leanne was always worried about, why she helped me photoshop myself into old photos with "Sarah" like we'd hung out. Hide in plain sight. And I should continue doing that. Hope they never connect the dots that it was some alcoholic, drugged-up girl that pulverized more than half their operations.

The razor presses against my skin, blood beginning to show as the prick makes me wince.

"You're not broken."

The blade drops from my hand, falling to the carpet with a weak thud.

In my mind's eye, I see those hazel eyes and furrowed brows. The hidden smile beneath his frown. The sound of his laugh and the strictness in his voice. Gentle tones as his hands stroke over my skin, holding me in a strong warmth like a barrier against the world. As if he'd been protecting me.

He *had* been protecting me.

In my heart, soul, and gut I still loved him. No matter how terrified I was, I loved him. I wanted to run to him, knowing he could be holding the weapon next to end me. He's given me so much patience over the past few months, but this wasn't any of those times. Those hadn't been dealbreakers, but what I'd done to his family and him had to be.

I deliberately brought down half the mob. And I ran. To a *cop.* What if I went back and he didn't forgive me? What if he hated me now? He didn't want to shackle me to the life he was in, but what if *I'd* already imprisoned *him?*

My gaze flicks to the razor. Death would be kind. It wouldn't hate me or leave me to rot. It wouldn't leave me in darkness alone with memories of horrific pain. It didn't use you. It didn't torture or manipulate you. Reaching for the razor again, I stop.

"Sure, as hell ain't gonna know sitting in this diner all day. Or in a house that ain't yours."

My gaze drifts toward the phone, I slowly start to reach for it instead.

The door opens downstairs, and Roger calls up as it slams, shaking the house. "Autumn!"

Quickly, I snatch the razor and toss it on the dresser and scoop the phone up. Anxiety tickles up my spine as I hide the phone under the bed along with the handkerchief. Taking a deep breath, and swiping a tissue over the small cut, I walk out of the bedroom. Halfway down the stairs I see him pouring himself a drink, and I stop, hugging myself a little. "What is it?"

"Contact called me back. They'll be here tomorrow." He doesn't look at me, his tone passive. Quickly, he knocks back the drink, pouring another and holds up the bottle.

"No," I answer.

He shrugs, making himself a double and turns towards me. "Should be here by mid-afternoon. We'll go over the procedures on what to do next, but again…we'll be able to help you more if you tell us everything. Think about those close to you. How you can keep them safe."

"Roger."

"The more you tell us, the easier it'll be taking those fuckers down. Once and for all. Think about how many people you'll help." He gestures outside with his drink. "About helping them feel safe. Helping *you* feel safe. You won't unless you do the right thing."

His words clang though me, and something deep down just…clicks.

The anxiety and worry sliding over my skin subsides. Another emotion, that's felt buried since I left the city, comes back. I stare down at him, almost going cold as older memories jerk forward, reminding me how *safe* I was with them.

I bring my arms down, and answer, "Okay."

Roger pauses with glass at his lips. "What?"

"Okay. You're right. I *should* do the right thing."

He huffs, easing back against the cabinet and knocks the entire drink back. "Knew you'd finally understand. I know it's harder when you're emotionally tied, but this is for the best. You'll move on. Just gotta cut them off and realize they ain't good for you."

"Yeah."

"Tonight, write everything down if you haven't already. Get it on paper." He starts going through procedure, lounging back into one of the chairs. "I'll need your phone, too. We'll bag and tag tomorrow. And we'll take you to the station."

"The station?"

"Yeah, can't have you stay here much longer. And come on, you were good undercover. Maybe we can get you back in, better eyes on the ground. Someone who people won't expect. Another nobody. Start fresh."

I pinch my brows, and ask, "Putting me back would be dangerous."

"This entire line of work is dangerous," he holds his hands out, then pours another glass. "But think of it. Do this right, and they're no more. We get the bastards. *Finally*. The Marchetti family will be gone."

I nod robotically, barely hearing his words. They run through me, echoing with similar words from the past. And I ask the same question I did years ago, "How long you think?"

"Just a couple of months, tops. In and out—"

"Before I know it," I murmur, finishing his sentence. Some people never change, we just finally see them for who they are. Like an electric shock through the body, I'm seeing clearly how fucking much I fucked up.

Resolve settles in my bones, done being the victim again and no matter how scared I am, it's better than being here. It was better than repeating history, just not the history Roger thinks.

"Have everything written by the time I get back here tomorrow afternoon," he says.

"What about contacting Nan? Or my friends?"

He shakes his head. "Can't. Too risky. But we'll take care of them."

"Right," I mutter.

"For their own good and yours, don't want them caught up in this, right?" His tone is strict, and I just nod. "Sacrifices have to be made when it comes to justice. You know that."

I turn, beginning to head back up the stairs when Roger adds, "You're doing the right thing…Sarah. You'll get your justice, too."

An empty, cold laugh almost leaves me. Instead, I take a steadying breath and clutch the handrail. "We'll see."

Once in the bedroom, I lock the door and quickly grab the notepad. Sentence after sentence goes down, jotting down words and skipping spaces as I go. I try to make it as believable as I can, writing as the night wears on and I can hear Roger go to bed a few hours later. When I get to the last page, I land the final blow. My hands ache from the writing, flexing them as I put the pen down and stack the papers on the dresser.

Next, I go to my own phone, taking the sim card out just in case. I don't trust Roger, even with the damn door locked. Pulling out the handkerchief Jameson gave me I wrap up the card and the razor, hiding it back within my bag.

It's almost two in the morning when I sit down on the bed, holding Jameson's phone in my lap. I glance at the stack of papers on the dresser. Even though I can't go back with Roger, I'm not sure I can go through with one escape plan or the other. I need to know my gut feeling and heart, fragile as they feel, aren't wrong.

"Never will these hands harm you."

Closing my eyes, I take a deep breath. "Please be telling the truth. Please."

I press the call button and the phone rings twice before I hang up. I swear under my breath, tossing the phone next to me on the bed. My head comes down into my hands, and I grumble, "Fuck, come on…just make the damn call, just—"

The phone lights up and the caller ID shows who I tried to call a moment ago.

He's awake.

Swallowing hard, I pick up the phone and bring it to my ear.

There's ragged breathing on the other end, but the first words I hear Leo say are, "Check in."

A choked sob comes up from my chest. "Yellow."

"Are you safe?" There's rustling in the background, sounding like paperwork, not bedsheets.

"Yeah," I rasp.

"Don't lie…I've been worried…fuck, shit," he mutters and my heart squeezes at the tone of his voice. "Autumn—"

"Did Jameson talk to you?"

He's quiet for only a moment. "Yes."

"You know?"

"Yes," he answers. My stomach clenches at the succinct answers, and I stare over at the papers. My vision starts to blur. "Talk to me. Please."

"I can't." His breath hitches, and he swears under his breath. "I needed to call you. Hear your voice. Maybe…maybe one last time." He makes a strangled grunt filled with frustration. "I needed to let you know that…that if you don't hear from me in the next 24 hours I'm gone. I'll be gone."

I sit in silence and wait for his reply. Minutes pass before he lets out a long breath, and says in a soft tone, "I'll let you go."

"What?"

"I won't make you stay or come to me. As much as I want to, trust me I do…to *beg* you to come back, but I can't." Leo's words sink into me. "It's your decision, not mine. If you can't or won't…of all people who may understand, it may be me."

"Leo."

"My promise remains. I'll never bring harm to you, not by my hands. I promise I'll look after Nan, Leanne and Trix, too. Until you return or never. Don't worry, they'll be safe. I will make sure no harm comes to them, keep them out of the line of fire. But that phone will keep you connected with them if you need."

My jaw slackens, stomach dropping as I listen to the strain in his voice. Don't be this kind to me. I don't deserve it, I don't—

"I will wait for you."

I murmur, "You don't even know if I'll...ever come back."

"I'll still wait, whether it's tomorrow, a week, or years down the line you come back on your own fruition. A hundred years if you want me to." Hot tears stream down my cheeks. "It was very real for me, every single moment with you. I meant it, saying I love you and that hasn't changed. I will *always* love you, my dear Watson. And I'll never forget the kindness you gave me and patience. I'll never forget the smile of the woman with latte foam all over her."

"Leo." It feels like time stills for a moment as I ask next in a shaky breath, "Check in."

"Red." A part of my heart shatters as I almost drop the phone. "Take care of yourself, don't let any of those bastards control you. You're free, dear Watson. I won't hinder you. But know that I'll love you, even if you move on without me...Sarah."

The line clicks and goes dead.

Chapter 7

Escape Plan

I don't sleep. Even when I almost doze off, nightmares chase me disguised as memories. All that I've blocked and tried to forget swarms back. The assault. The hospital. The clubs. The docks. How bottom of the barrel my life had been.

I stare at the ceiling, listening to Roger downstairs as small streams of early light peek through the window. Doing my best to block out every emotion, there's a knock on the door and I remain still.

"Hey." My fingers press into the sheets, keeping my breathing level. He swears under his breath, and I can hear him mutter, "Fucking getting lazy. Better be up when I get back."

His steps echo and the door opens, shutting with a thud. I don't move.

Fifteen minutes pass before I finally get up and get to work. All the clothes I had, plus what Roger gave me, are thrown into a bag. Rummaging through the bathroom cabinet next, I grab toiletries and throw them in next, then fold up the blanket and stuff it into the small duffel bag. My old sim card, handkerchief, and phone given to me by Jameson are stuffed into my pockets. I go back into the bathroom, roughly peeling off my bandages with a hiss. Too much in a hurry, I swipe a wet towel over any dried blood, and then hastily put bandages over the cuts, tossing everything I used into a plastic bag to carry out. I grab the duffel bag from the bedroom, and then the papers I wrote last night and head downstairs, making a mess as I go.

The papers are tossed onto the coffee table in his living room, and the bag onto the sofa. Checking the time, I head out through the front door and briskly walk to the small outlet mall a few blocks away. The tiny cellular store is just opening as I enter, and the employee looks at me confused. Quickly, I find a phone similar to mine and sim card that should work. Paying for both with the cash I still have, I walk out and practically jog back to the house. The screen door slams behind me, and I jump clutching my chest. I lock the main door and head into the kitchen to disassemble the phone I bought and double check the new sim card works in my old phone.

I'll *make* it work.

With mine, I turn everything back on, hoping anyone and everyone is watching at this point. Going through sites, I order a train ticket for the afternoon to head to Denver, Colorado. From there I book a hotel in Denver and then order another ticket from Denver to Seattle, Washington for two days after. Using the last of the money in my account, I book two more hotels in small city outside Seattle and then Portland, Oregon. Double checking confirmations have gone through, I take out the sim card and wrap it into the handkerchief. The new card goes into my phone, and I input random numbers from delivery services, stores, and ex-coworkers.

"Guess you'll finally do something useful, Bailey," I mutter, putting hers in last, but naming it as 'Leo's chauffeur.'

I add in a few apps, trying to buy myself more time for when he finds it. My heart pounds in my chest as I finish the dummy phone, placing it on the paperwork. This is it. No more alliances on this side after this. Then again, doubt I ever had a true alliance in the first place.

I shove the handkerchief in my back pocket but take the razor out that I've been cutting with. The weight of it suddenly feels heavier than it should, and the wounds I've given myself pulse with a small ache. Shaking my head, I put it in my back pocket and go to Roger's office and open his safe. First night here, he showed me how to get in, just in case I'd been followed, and he wasn't here. I pull out one of the unmarked guns...one of his illegal ones.

Have fun explaining what happened to it.

I shove it into my pants, hiding it beneath my jacket as I grab the duffel bag. Lastly, I nab a few things from his cabinets, making it seem like I left in a rush as I stuff it all into the bag and head for the back door. Checking the time briefly, I swallow hard as I leave through his backyard, checking my surroundings.

A few dogs bark as I jump the small privacy fence he has, moving my way through another yard and then another. I come to a back alley and dump the food and half the clothes into it. I go the opposite direction I'm heading, splitting up all the stuff I've grabbed, including the plastic bag of my dirty bandages, and finally toss the duffel bag into someone's trash bin. All I have on my person is what I wear, the two phones, gun, cash, and the handkerchief with my old sim card in it. The razor is tossed into another bin as I turn down an alley way, just as the trash collectors pull into an alley.

Perfect timing.

I spend the next hour walking around, checking over my shoulder from time to time as my nerves skyrocket. Paranoia yanks at me as I see the diner up ahead, anxiety ticking up my neck. Looking again, there's no one around apart from the occasional car driving past. Taking a deep breath, I enter the diner and head to my usual booth. Cheryl comes out, giving me a warm smile, but it falters when she sees my face.

She approaches, putting a coffee in front of me. "You've got the look of determination on you."

"Finally made a decision. Do you still have those extra clothes you brought the other day? In case it rains?" My voice doesn't shake, surprising me almost. Guess I *am* pretty certain about my decision.

Eyeing me a moment, she nods. "In the back, why?"

I swallow hard, and whisper, "When you took Rob back after

what he did..." her arms drop, face falling a little, "...how scared were you to trust him again?"

She sighs and walks away to disappear into the back. In a few minutes, she comes back with a bag and places it on the table. "To the core of my being but knew in my heart I was doing the right thing for me."

"Thank you," I breathe out, rubbing my hands over the jeans. "Um, know a taxi driver willing to go into the city? Or another way that's not the ferry?"

"When you leaving?"

"Soonish. I can't stay here long not without being found." I whisper the last part.

Cheryl purses her lips, and then crosses her arms. "I got someone I can call. Go change, and then we'll get some food into you. No good traveling on an empty stomach."

Nodding, I grab the bag, but stop and grab for Cheryl instead. Guilt gnaws at me, and I can't leave her in the dark too much without feeling responsible if anything happens to her. "You'll be helping me evade the law by the way. I should let you know that. Who I'm running from—"

She chuckles, patting my hand. "Sweetie, the moment you talked about your *uncle* I already knew somethin' ain't right. No woman runs to her uncle then comes to a diner every day for hours. Whoever you're running from, I'll help you. Law or not." Cheryl winks. "Not my first time." My eyes widen and she chuckles again. "Some of us have more colorful pasts than we look. Go change."

I head into the bathroom and pull out the jeans, shirt, and sweater. I switch out my clothing, noticing how big the clothes are on my small frame. Wincing as the jeans rub against my cuts, I rip Roger's old shirt and use it as a belt to help hold up the pants. The rest of the clothes he gave me are stuffed into the bottom of the trash. After I pull the sweater over my head, I shove the gun into the back of my pants and hide the rest into the pockets. Satisfied, I head back out to the diner.

There's a plate of eggs, toast, and bacon next to my coffee. I sit as

Cheryl comes over to place some grits down, too. "I've called someone, who'll get you back into the city."

"Thank you. I still don't know why you're helping me, but—"

"Sweetpea, sometimes we need to depend on the kindness of strangers." She pats my hand. "And not to ask questions."

She walks off to attend other customers, acting like it's just another day. I'm not hungry, but I take a few bites of what she's given me and drink the coffee to help calm my nerves. Probably not helping them, but I need the caffeine after barely sleeping the past week. I sit and wait, glancing at the clock as the time passes and the lunchtime rush begins.

On cue, Rob walks in and sits across from me at the booth. He puts both elbows on the table, folding his hands under his chin. "Heard you need a ride." My eyes bulge, looking over to Cheryl.

Shit, no wait. "Rob, you can't, I mean…"

"Done sketchier shit than driving a young woman safely back home," he says holding up a hand. "And I don't like that *uncle* of yours."

Exhaling sharply, I smile faintly. Cheryl comes around, putting down Rob's usual and winks before she goes off to help others.

"You have lunch, I'll be right back," I tell him, getting up and heading outside. I go behind the building, hiding from the street as I punch in the number on the encrypted phone. It rings a few times before a receptionist picks up, "Italian Lily, how may I assist you today?"

"I need to speak to the manager, Chiari. Is she in?"

There's a pause. "I'm sorry, who's—?"

"Please just get me Chiari, and if she's not there, if you could just give me her office number then." My voice has a bit of pleading to it, and I hope it works as I hear shuffling in the background.

"Please hold." Soft music plays and I tap my fingers against the brick wall. My foot starts to tap next as another minute passes before the line clicks.

"This is Chiari." Relief flickers over me as I hear her voice.

"It's Autumn." There's a sharp inhale on the line, and I swallow hard. "I need help, and you're the only one I think who can." And who has access to certain areas without tipping people off.

There's a brief silence and I'm questioning if I should hang up and try another way. Finally, she murmurs low, "I'm listening."

Thank fuck. With a steadying breath, I tell her what I need.

I'm constantly checking outside, not sure when Roger would be back at his house. I needed to be out of the area soon. Except, I couldn't go where I needed until later, and my "safehouses" were compromised.

Rob finishes his lunch, then asks, "Where we going?"

"Here's the thing," I whisper, leaning in close. "I need to be in the city early evening, but I can't stay here. Perhaps there's another diner or place I can be at until then."

"Hmm, well I still have some work to finish up today."

"You can come pick me up after."

"Better yet, I'll just take you with me. No one's gonna look for you at some old construction company. Anyone asks, you're my daughter's friend visiting from Arizona."

"You sure?"

"My trailer is pretty lonely anyhow, get some conversation in today would be nice."

Slowly, I stand up, staring at him and relieved by how helpful he's being. If Roger comes back before I make it into the city, either he'll go directly back to work or follow the breadcrumbs I left. Either way, I needed to stay out of sight and away from public areas until later when the train leaves.

The decision to follow my gut feels better with each moment, and I nod. "Okay. Thank you."

"Can show you what I do, warning though it's boring compared to Cheryl's work." Almost on cue, she comes over and gives me a hug.

Squeezing me a little, she murmurs in my ear, "If anything goes wrong, come on back. Got an extra room if you need."

"You've been a lifesaver."

"Doing what the good Lord asks of us; helping those in need." She pulls back, smiling warmly. Swiftly, she looks at Rob. "Keep an eye on her. Or else no pie for you the rest of the month."

"You wound me, madam." He kisses her on the cheek, beginning to leave the diner. "I'll be back this evening, honey."

I follow Rob out to the parking lot, where his Ford truck waits. It's a large vehicle, dark green and has dust all over it. I get into the cab, thanking him again as he waves it off and starts the engine. We drive away from the diner, and I glance back at the small safe haven.

We're quiet as he pulls onto the highway, driving toward his work. "Told you I watched my daughters go through tough times. Some required the law to be shifted aside. Their wants aren't always aligned with the right thing, if you know what I mean."

"And if the right thing I'm doing is really bad?" I feel the hidden gun at my back.

He snorts. "Autumn, if a woman has to run to another man to keep her safe from the law, I ain't helping the law. It ain't perfect, like the people inside it."

"Learned that from your daughters, too?"

"From growing up. Where I come from, sometimes it was best to take the law into our own hands." He smiles over at me. "Been awhile since I felt this kind of thrill. Thank you for that."

I laugh under my breath, glad someone's getting a bit of glee out of this. He takes us up north and then stops off at a construction site. I follow him into a trailer, where there's an office set up and he starts to go to work. The sofa he has in there is where I sit while he works, talking as he does. Rob keeps me distracted from my thoughts whirling, tumbling into a nervous wreck. A part of me wants to go and jump on that damn train, disappear, and take another train to another city. My fingers scratch at my skin, but I stop whenever Rob looks my way and I force a smile.

I repeat in my head to trust in what Leo said. What my gut says; I can do this. I don't have to be alone. I don't have to keep running.

I'm tired of running.

Hours tick by, and I keep watching the clock he has on the wall. The end of his day arrives, and he gives me a look and I nod. We head back out to his truck, and I scramble in, clutching my hands as my anxiety begins to tick back up.

I'm rocking a little, and suddenly Rob places his hand on my leg. I stop as he pats it, and he whispers, "We'll get you into the city fine, don't worry."

"Not exactly all that I'm worried about."

He hums as we pull onto the highway, heading toward Lincoln Tunnel. "You felt safe with him though, before? Leo?"

"Yeah, yeah I did."

"Did you ever with that uncle—"

"Detective. He's a detective."

"Hmm, well, did you with him?"

I glance out the window, watching lights pass and the atmosphere change as we approach the city. "No."

"He do anything to you? That detective?"

My stomach clenches, and my hands tremble. One of them reaches for his and he squeezes it back. "Yelled. Left me alone. Didn't lift a hand towards me. But…didn't lift a finger to help either."

"Then I'm glad I followed my gut," he says solemnly. The rest of the ride is quiet as the sun begins to set and he drives through the tunnel. "Where am I headed?"

I give him directions, texting Chiari that I'm almost there and she answers for me to arrive in the executive garage entrance along with a code to enter.

Rob navigates the traffic slowly, the busyness of the city pulsing through me. It feels like forever before we come to the familiar block. Directing him to the parking garage, I give him the code to get in and we wind our way down into the private area. We sit, waiting, until Chiari comes out of the hotel entrance and nods in my direction.

I turn back to Rob, leaning over to kiss him briefly on the cheek. "Don't tell Cheryl."

"Secret safe with me." His smile is tight, eyes looking a bit misty. "If you need to leave, come on back. Better yet…" he pulls out a card, placing it into my hand, "…just call."

"You're a very sweet, wonderful man. And a good father."

"Ah, well, just stubborn and a hopeless romantic. This ain't an airport, but I hope it all works out and you catch him." His brown eyes meet mine, and I nod before jumping out of the truck. The door slams behind me, and I remain in that spot until he drives out of the garage.

I turn toward Chiari, who ushers me into the building with her hand at my back. She speaks low and quickly, "Don't say a word until we're in the elevator."

I follow her down a hall, through another and then we pass through the backside of the lobby. My heart rate picks up, looking at the grandeur that now feels foreign. There's a constriction around my chest, clutching me tight. She leads me to the private elevator, getting on after inputting her code, and my legs tremble as we get on. I gulp harshly, glancing at the space.

"Thank you for helping me," I whisper when the doors close.

"He's been miserable since you disappeared." Her tone is low, but the kindness I've known from her is still there. "Seems you haven't had it much better."

"I didn't have a fancy hotel to hide in," I mutter as she huffs out a laugh. "Are you…are you part of the *other* business?"

Gaze meeting mine she answers, "Yes. I worked for his brother."

My stomach drops, putting my attention to the glowing numbers that change. "Really?"

"He was a menace."

My body locks up, my head screaming to shove the button to go back down. To run.

"It got better when Mr. Luciano took over. He's far more kind than any boss should be. Mafia or not. Or whether anyone believes it or not outside of here."

"And what's your job?"

"Helping him get what he wants." She places her hand gently on my shoulder, but I still flinch lightly. Her hand doesn't budge, but her thumb moves over in a caring manner. A moment passes and the gesture helps ease some of my nerves. "I'm glad you're back. And that you trusted me enough to help you."

"Seemed right for the job. That maybe…you'd understand."

She smiles. "Always fun to keep men on their toes, isn't it? Let them think they have control."

"Don't they?"

"*Do* they?" The door opens, revealing the hallway I ran from. She steps out, but I can't seem to make my feet move as I stare as the closed doors of his office. I feel sick to my stomach, while tremors run over my skin with a coldness. She gently takes my hand, bringing me out of the elevator and into the hall to be closer to the doors. "Stay here. Please."

Chiari turns, opening the door and shutting it behind her. My anxiety runs rampant as I close my eyes, concentrating on breathing. It's fine. It'll be fine. The want to do this feels thin as seconds pass. Suddenly, the doors open, and she steps aside.

"It's just him inside," she says, and I take a step when she grabs my arm. "He doesn't know it's you."

Her eyes meet mine and I nod, quietly thanking her.

Clearing my throat and trying to shake off the nerves, I take one more deep breath and walk into the office. I step into the vast space filled with the grey and black tones. Leo leans over his desk. Papers cover everything, including the coffee table near the sitting area. The shirt he wears is rumpled and mostly unbuttoned at the top, revealing a dark v-neck that allows his tattoos to peek out. Dark stubble covers his jaw, longer than I've ever seen it. Even from across the room, I can see the white over his knuckles as he clutches the desk and stares at the paperwork before him.

He doesn't look up even when the door clicks shut behind me. His voice is dark and menacing, almost sneering, "What do you want? I'm fucking busy."

Look at me, I think. *Look at me so I know this wasn't a mistake.*

Silence grows between us, and Leo growls in frustration, "What do you—?"

My knees almost give out when his hazel eyes snap up, hardened with wrathful danger.

Chapter 8

My Heart of Glass

The anger in his eyes disappears instantly.

I want to sob on the spot. It feels like a lifetime since I've seen him. With the stone-cold expression gone, there's tiredness and pain. It's as if he's been through hell and back. Worry lines his face, brows furrowed more than they always were before. He stands fully, watching me intently as he starts to round his desk to approach.

I put my hand up, and say hoarsely, "Red."

He stops immediately.

Whatever tiredness was there before vanishes and turns into an intense want. His shoulders begin to rise heavily with harsh breaths. He remains at the side of his desk, doing as I asked even as I start to walk towards him.

I pull the gun out.

He doesn't blink. He doesn't flinch or move or say a damn thing as I hold the weapon out, pointing it to the ground. It's silent as we stand there. The gun in my hand. Leo's eyes never leave mine.

My jaw tightens as I pull the clip out, moving to put the gun and the clip of bullets onto his desk. I take out the encrypted phone, setting it down next to it and then the handkerchief opening it to reveal the sim card from my old phone. He doesn't even glance at the items.

I step away from the desk and him. Hands shaking, I start talking, "I don't know how much you found, but I'm gonna tell you anyways. My side of it. The whole truth, because you deserve that, especially when...when I told you honesty was important to me. I owe you that."

He visibly relaxes slightly and nods for me to continue.

Running my hand through my hair, I give myself a tiny pep talk in my head and start.

"I met Steve in college, but it wasn't anything more than friendship. We were both seniors at the time. It wasn't until after graduating we started dating. About six years ago, I noticed things weren't...he was acting different. Next thing I knew, there were drugs in our apartment, and I confronted him, but he said he'd quit. It was only weed, but a lot of it. Six months later, there was more...not just weed, but cocaine, heroin, even meth. He was a supplier." I swallow hard, rubbing at my chest as I scoff. "There was over a fucking pound of heroin in our bathroom. I should've left but said nothing. I should've gone to Leanne's. I should've done a lot of things."

I clench my fist, trying to breathe steadily as I continue.

"I went to the police, and I was informed that Steve was this big dealer they'd been trying to catch. But he had connections they wanted, too so they...*employed* me to spy on him. Said it'd only be a few weeks, but then it became months...and then that turned into 19 months. I was undercover in the mobs as an informant for the NYPD."

Leo's face falls, jaw going slack in shock. Yeah, that was Leanne's face too after realizing how long I'd been under.

"No one knew. Not Leanne or Nan. I had no one else, except Steve. Getting the *bad guys* was all that mattered. I was in so deep; I couldn't just leave. Steve would look for me. Or others presumed I owed them money because of him. And the police weren't gonna help me." Leo grips the side of the desk, white knuckling it. His brows furrow deeper, reigning in the frustration I see lining his face.

"During the last months, I became homeless cause Steve lost the apartment and gave away all the money for drugs. He wasn't… keeping up with his numbers, I guess. I couldn't hold a job while undercover, and the police weren't paying me, so I stayed in shelters, boxes, centers…wherever I could go and not be tracked. I believed the police, too that I was doing the right thing. Had to get through the long nights somehow, that it'd end s-soon…" my voice almost cracks, and he takes a step forward, but quickly stops himself when I step back, "…the detective I worked with told me to stay. For the good of the city, I needed to stay. To…*help*." Leo grunts, almost like a snarl while his lip curls. I close my eyes concentrating to finish the damn story, get it over with.

"I don't know how, but Steve found out I was working with the cops. And he snapped. That's when the men showed up and…you know. The assault. And I don't know who else Steve told, who'd come after me next. So, after I dragged myself to the hospital, that's when Trix came in, trying to advocate for me. Trying to…protect me." My hands run over my stomach, feeling sick as I hold myself and concentrate not puking on his carpet. Throat tightening, I shake off that other tidbit of information, not able to get those words out still. What they took from me. "It was what finally broke me, and I gave them what I collected. I identified, with proof and receipts, over two dozen people involved with the mafia. A list of underbosses, captains, dealers, and politicians, not to mention locations and businesses, and…and your brother Gabriel." Pausing, I watch for his reaction, but he keeps the same stern expression. "The five men who assaulted me were let go, being used for…I guess, whatever the police wanted. And Steve was put in jail for drug possession, assault, and murdering…Sarah Marie Mitchell, who died in the hospital from blunt force trauma and blood loss."

"That was *you*," he breathes out.

"I was given the choice to disappear for good, but I didn't want to while the only three people I had were here. And I don't think the police really wanted me to leave either, I think…" I pause, remembering what Roger told me last night, and bile almost comes up,

"....no, they were waiting for me to come back. I was valuable in what I could do. *I* created Autumn Watson, not them. The background friend who watched her friend...Sarah...die."

I'm not sure if the folders I saw the day I left are the ones on the desk now. My stomach clenches as I see where I panicked, and I wring my hands next. "When I saw the folders, what was inside I thought you were coming for me. That I'd been found and you'd finish what your brother would've started. Everything I'd gone through came back in a blur and I *had* to leave. I couldn't chance it, not after all I'd done to get out. Nineteen months I spent my life in lies and deceit, used, and I couldn't...I couldn't...fuck." Closing my eyes tight, I shake my head and clench my fists. "I thought everything was a lie, and even if it wasn't...that you'd never forgive me."

"Forgive you?" He breathes out. "What are you talking about?"

I stare at him, hands falling limp to my sides. "What I just...just told you. You know my old name. And I *just* told you what I've done."

"Autumn."

"I cost you millions. I sold out the mob." I throw my hand out, beginning to feel a bit unhinged at his lack of anger. For some reason, deep down, I want him to yell at me. Throw something. Be like Roger or Steve. Hit me, abuse me like the guilt that gnaws deeper. "They arrested your brother because of me. I tore apart the mafia and connections and businesses...and it was *me* who brought you back into this. *Me.*"

He takes a tentative step toward me. I take one back. He goes still instantly as confusion flits over his face. What is there to be confused about? I fucked him over. I fucked over—

"You tried to walk away. You were blackmailed. You got out and I brought you back." My voice chokes out. The pain of the guilt and self-hate consume me as I hear Steve scream at me. Roger telling me to do better. My parents blaming me. "You made a life for yourself, a good one...away from...from this!" I wave my hands in the air.

"That wasn't you."

"Yes! It was! What I did shackled you back into this. You'd have never become boss if I hadn't put Gabriel in jail. I bankrupted most of the Marchetti fortune, I saw the numbers. I *saw* the accounts. And Matteo has been in Italy because…fuck, it was me, Leo. I *fucked* you over, I took away…"

My breathing becomes harder, and I press at my chest trying to find oxygen as the panic sets in. He takes another step, hand still gripping the desk.

"Breathe," he says gently. "*Upon a midnight dreary…*"

He tries several times to get me to recite the poem, but all I can do is shake my head, gripping at my hair. Why isn't he mad? The lack of reaction and anger digs at my soul. *Hate me. Hate me like the others*, my head screams. *Despise me and throw me away.* The old part comes roaring back, wanting to be hit, thrown, shot, *anything* to tell that part of myself I deserve it. I shake harder and notice he's moved closer, letting go of the desk.

"Red." He stops, hazel eyes burning into me.

I breathe harder, almost pleading, "Hate me."

"No."

"Then be angry with me!"

"Autumn, listen to me," he says in a calm tone. "I'm not angry. Everything was real. You and I were…*are* still real. I don't hate you."

"Why not?" I almost scream. "You should be! You should tell me how much you hate me! I destroyed what you worked for. I betrayed you—"

"No, you didn't. You couldn't betray me if you didn't know me."

"I ruined everything."

"You ruined nothing. Breathe," he pleads as I take another gulping breath. It feels like I'm being choked. I try to concentrate on the gaze before me, finding it hard to. "Breathe, sweetheart."

The tenderness of his voice tears at me. The softness breaks through my barriers, those I've built after the last week at Roger's. My mind and body don't know how to respond to the calm, when it expects to be beaten.

"Be angry with me," I plead. "Hate me, please. I deserve it. *Hate me just like...like...*"

"I am not your ex." There's an undertone of darkness in his voice, but the care in his eyes hasn't subsided. "I am not the FBI. I am not the police. Those fucking thugs, none of them. I promised that you'd only know kindness from my hands. *That* hasn't changed. I will not hate you, no matter how much you beg. I will not be angry with you for trying to survive this shitty world, because not one fragment of what I swore to you has changed."

Tears build inside, wanting to believe him fully. Something still holds me back, unsure and scared. He then takes another step toward me, coming only within a few feet. His hands stay at his sides, not trying to crowd or touch me as he keeps the last of the distance between us.

"I became boss *five* years ago, not three." I go still, the shaking stops as I stare at him with wide eyes. "I won't go into details now, another time if you want, but I was already in charge by the time you came into the picture. And I knew who you were before Jameson left to find you in Jersey. It wasn't me dragged into this; you were. *You* were abused and used like a fucking toy by the police, doing their damn jobs when they should've been."

"How?" I breathe out, different horror beginning to trickle through my veins. "How long did you know?"

"When you disappeared, I called Nancy. I explained very little, but told her how worried I was about you. Thinking the worst. She mentioned more of your past, more than what you let on and said your ex's name. Isaac and I looked into it, thinking it was connected to why you left, but we found him and then we found Sarah. In an old photo, I knew I'd found you when I saw her...*your* eyes." I stumble back, staring wide-eyed. "From there, bits and pieces connected because of what you've told me about your past. Timelines matched, but I didn't know *how* involved you were until now. When you called, I sent Jameson to find you to give you that phone. I have people who are ex-feds, we know how they operate, and you'd be gone forever or worse. They'd have stripped you of your life again, and you do not deserve that."

My mind spins as I try to piece together bits of information, trying to understand. I shake my head and hold it. "I still went to the police…I still…I left you!"

"You were scared, Autumn. What I saw, what they did to you, I don't blame you. They threw you into the worst of the mafia, the fucking underbelly and said die or survive. Even when you survived you were brutalized, I can't be angry with you for being scared." My legs buckle under me, but I remain standing somehow as I lock my knees. "I was going to tell you everything that night when we went upstate. To talk. Except…things got in the way, and I was distracted—"

"By what?"

His jaw tightens, finally averting his gaze and he inhales sharply before looking back at me again. "Finishing business concerning you."

"Such as?"

"You saw the reports on my desk? All of them?" His eyes darken as I nod. "I have people *everywhere*, including prisons and precincts. Your attacker from your first night at the hotel was taken care of because of me."

"When you say…" I gulp, feeling my chest tighten, "…taken care of, do you mean…killed?"

"He had multiple violations of paroles and assault charges," he states in a sudden monotone voice. "Myself and those who work closely with me don't tolerate such existences. They deserve what they have coming to them from my security…or me."

My chin quivers. So, yes.

Someone was killed because of me…no, for me. He did. The Leo I knew did what he did best: control a situation and get what he wants. I blink, tears falling down my cheeks as I try to make sense of the churning emotions. Fifteen minutes ago, I thought he'd hate me, despise me, but instead he was…he was…

I muster more of my courage, coming this far and wanting answers. "What were you doing when I came in here?"

"Check in," he answers.

"Tell me, Leo."

"Check in."

The worry lines over his face haven't left, but there's a passive strictness there. His gaze betrays his concern, which prompts me to answer, "Yellow. Now tell me. I told you the truth, now you tell me."

His jaw muscles tighten, and a coldness sweeps over him. "The men you saw, those who attacked you years ago were brought here. I was going to make them wait, but seeing the aftermath they wrought upon you, I couldn't. They won't ever harm you or anyone again."

"That didn't answer my question," I whisper. His hands flex at his sides, and now I'm even more determined to have answers. "How?" I choke out. "How did you...how did you take care of them?"

"Do you really want to know?"

"Yes."

"Autumn—"

"*Tell me.*"

"Tortured them with knives, bled them out, burned their knuckles and sides, cut their dicks off, and finally put a bullet into each of their heads."

I wait for the screams to come. I stare at him, waiting for the ripple of horror knowing what Leo is capable of. To run from what he's done. But the only emotion that comes is...relief? Pure relief travels through me and I want to fall at the weight of it. He even made the bastards suffer.

"The others have been tracked down," he continues quietly. "One is in jail and the other works for another crime boss, but I can get a hold of them both. Your ex is in max, so it'll be harder to reach him. But I'll wait until you tell me what you want done with them. I took care of the first for the hurt and agony they put you through, but I'll give you the final decision on what to do with the others."

My body slackens. The trembling completely stops. The anxiety and worry of the past week dissipate. This time, I take a small step toward him. His strict expression falls away and I see the distraught man before me. The one I saw the night who picked me up from the club. The one who took his time to help me through a panic attack. The one who tried to barge into my apartment. The man who was trying to understand me, while trying to help and protect me.

"Nothing with you was a lie," he whispers. "I love you. And I want you…want you safe. It tears me apart knowing how much you've had to survive on your own. How much those fuckers put you through, expecting more." I take another small step forward. "I don't understand how you've been able to smile, find happiness in the small things, laugh when you should be screaming. And I cannot, or would ever hate you because I lied, too. I withheld who I was from you. But everything that I hid or lied about, none of it included how I feel about you. That has always been true."

I come within arm's length of him, noticing as his hands flex and fidget at his sides. His arms want to move, but he keeps them there and I know he's fighting from touching me. Even now, he's doing what I asked. Forcing back the last of the worry and fear, I bring my hand up and place it against his stubbled cheek. The sensation is odd as I move my thumb over the coarse hairs. He leans into the touch, closing his eyes as he frowns.

He whispers, "If you want to leave, I understand. I won't make you stay in a world that killed you. But I promise if you do stay, I will do everything I can to keep you safe. Anything, my dear Watson."

Walls inside shatter. The ache in my heart, needing him comes forward full force. And I know now, I don't want to move on without him. My gut was right.

"Leo," I say softly, and he opens his eyes. Hazel eyes sear into me, breaking apart the last of the uncertainty. Far into his soul I can see the truth in his eyes. The promises he's tried to keep and will keep for me. I'm safe here. "I love you."

"Dear Watson—"

"Green."

Once I say the word, Leo swiftly pulls me into his arms. I wrap my arms around his neck, burying my face into his shoulder as I begin to sob. My body becomes wrecked with shivers as he holds me, cradling my head with tender protection.

"You're safe," he murmurs against my ear. "You're safe." He repeats again and again. I'm not sure if he's saying it for me or him.

I clutch him harder, allowing the comfort of his body to sink into my bones. For the first time in almost seven days, I finally feel safe. Keeping hold, he steps back to lean against his desk and tightens his arms with a gentle force. His lips press against my temple, the short beard scratching against my skin.

"I'm sorry," I whisper once the sobs subside. "I'm sorry I ran."

"Don't be. You're here, that's all that matters." He strokes down my back, shifting to allow me to further burrow myself against him. I want to be wrapped up within him and never leave.

He pulls back gently to move my head away and cups my face, stroking his thumb over my skin. Green eyes flecked with gold search my face, misted with tears. "May I kiss you?"

My heart clenches at the ask.

I nod in response, and he dips his head to press his lips against mine. He's tender with me as I melt further against him. A sigh of relief releases, tasting him and feeling the familiar warmth. Leo places another small kiss at the side of my mouth and then at my jaw. I lay my head back against his chest, inhaling deeply. Leo strokes my back, not letting go as he continues the affectionate gesture. We stand in silence for I don't know how long, just reveling in the moment of being together again.

I break the silence first, speaking against his shirt, "You need to know what I told them. What they know—"

"No." He kisses my head. "Don't worry about it."

"Leo, you need to know." I pull back to look up at him. "I didn't tell them much, but it could be enough for them to target you."

He places a hand against my cheek. "I'll take care of it. You don't need to tell me now. Later." I start to protest, but he kisses me briefly to quiet me. "Precautions have already been taken. Don't worry. I'll take care of it."

"Leo. Let me help fix whatever damage I caused. Please. Just...

listen, a moment, okay? It'll make me feel better, even if I'm a bit fragile at the moment."

"You are far from fragile," he says, and I scoff lightly. "You came back to confront a mafia boss in his own hotel, I doubt that counts as fragile, Autumn."

I smile faintly, moving a hand to point towards the items I placed on his desk. "They have my old phone, but a new sim card is inside it with bogus information and messages. That's my actual sim card. Roger wanted me to write down everything, which I kinda did, but again...red herrings and some runaround things that wouldn't implicate you."

"Such as?"

"Wrong addresses and layouts and may have put the police and FBI on a wild goose chase, including thinking that I fled to Denver and am going to Seattle next." His brows shoot up. "Roger kept asking for everything about our relationship...personal things, and it felt more invasive than before. He was pushing too much." A bit obsessively after three years since the investigation finished. Or maybe it never did for him.

"Who's this Roger?" His eyes darken.

"My handler from years ago. Detective Roger Caltz."

"Shit handler if he allowed you to—" he stops, closing his eyes and his brows scrunch together in thought. He leans back to look at me with inquisitive eyes. "Did you say you evaded the FBI?"

"Presumably." He cocks his head at me. "I needed to create a distraction to get back here." My tone becomes a bit blunter.

"Similar how you made us think you were in Cleveland?" He quirks a brow.

"Knew you'd track me. So will Roger and any agents he'll bring in. Y'all are predictable."

Leo grunts and I give him a guilty smile. Amusement flits over his face before he kisses my forehead, whispering, "Good girl."

A shiver runs down my spine, and I breathe out in relief. Leo turns, pressing a button on his desk and almost immediately his office doors open. Chiari walks in with a small smirk.

"Chiari," Leo speaks in a stern tone. "Assemble everyone and come back for further instructions for yourself."

"Yes, sir."

"And Chiari." She stops and I go still, hearing the warning in his voice. Her demeanor doesn't change or flinch as he frowns at her with a forewarning expression. "Thank you. And *never* do that again."

"Yes, sir," she replies promptly, walking out with the door closing behind her.

Worry flickers through me that I may have given her a death sentence. "Leo, I told her what to do. I told her not to tell you, please don't punish—"

"I won't." He cups my face, his expression becoming gentle, and I believe him. I nod, leaning back into chest. "Do you still trust me?"

The screaming voice from all week tells me to run. To cower and hide. It's been so long since I've heard it, yet it's been the loudest this week. I ignore it, focusing on the steady hold Leo has on me.

"Yes."

"I need to get you out of the city." I stiffen, and he instantly starts to stroke my back again, soothing my fears. "The police and FBI will be looking for you, we both know that. They'll try to grab you, along with others. You need to be somewhere safe for the time being away from here. I won't let anything happen to you, dear Watson. But first I have to settle a few things, set plans in place and it'll be a few hours."

"Um, do I need to go somewhere?"

"I don't want you out of my sight." Leo adjusts, nodding toward the doorway at the back of his office. "That's my bar area. You'll stay there until I'm done. I swear I'll be as quick as I can," he promises, kissing my cheek. I can't help the small smile at the gentle touches and careful reminders he's giving me that I'm safe. "When did you eat last?"

Oh, damn it.

My brain goes fuzzy, trying to remember and the last 48 hours feel like a blur. Body and mind begin to feel heavy, catching up to the fact that I've barely slept in days, rarely ate, and everything hurts from being on pins and needles for a week. "This morning."

Leo looks me over, quirking a brow. "These aren't your clothes either."

"Look, it's been a long fucking week, mister," I mutter.

A half grin comes up on his face, and I respond with my own.

The door opens, and a multitude of footsteps come into the room. I turn to see Jameson, Isaac, Chiari, Rudolph, and others I don't know enter. Some stay near the door, staring at us, while relief flashes over the three men I know.

Jameson crosses his arms over his chest. "Took you long enough. But thank fuck you made it back." Two of the men exchange a look. "You look terrible though."

A slight growl comes from Leo, and he opens his mouth to respond, but I beat him to it with my tired and no fucks given tone, "Blow it up your ass."

Isaac snorts a laugh and Rudolph grunts. Jameson smirks smugly.

"We'll be implementing the *Estate* protocols," Leo speaks directly to them, and a few men leave the room. Jameson pulls out his phone, moving to the cabinets to the far right of the office, where a computer is pulled out. "Chiari, I want fresh clothes for Autumn. Order the # 3 and #21 from *Sole Blu*, and I want it up here ASAP. Afterwards, ready everything downstairs with security. I want everything to be taken care of after my departure." She nods, walking out. "Isaac, assist Chiari."

"Normal checks after?"

"Yes."

Isaac leaves next and Owen comes into the room, joining Jameson with a digital pad in hand.

Leo guides me toward the bar, which is in a long rectangular room set up much like a dive bar. There's a long counter on the right side, lined with high back stools of shiny leather with lights hanging low from the ceiling. There are shelves of liquor against the back of the bar with a mirror and the entire space is a deep brown with amber light. I almost forgot how fancy his shit is.

I'm sat on one of the chairs, and he cages me in with his arms as he leans over. His lips press against mine, the soft touch making me grab at his shirt to remain close. Leo breaks away, worried eyes looking over me. "Isaac will be back here with you. Rudolph at the doorway. At anytime you need me, tell them or yell 'red', do you understand?"

"Yes." He kisses me again, then brings his forehead against mine. I move my hand over his neck, keeping him there as I breathe in his scent. "You won't be far?"

"Stone's throw away."

I nod, feeling myself begin to crash as the last couple of days collide. Someone calls out for Leo, and he grumbles, turning toward the sound. Grunting under his breath, he places another kiss on my cheek before stepping back.

"Eat and change."

"Yes, bossy pants," I murmur. My heart skips a beat when he smiles, but it quickly disappears as he turns and heads back into his office. From where I sit, I can see his desk and the windowed area, which is where he goes.

Not out of my sight.

A few more minutes pass before Isaac walks back with some clothes in hand. He places them on the bar next to me, then gestures toward the end of the bar. "Bathroom there to change in."

I stare at the stubble on his cheeks, and disheveled hair. Bags are under his blue eyes. Did any of us sleep? Knowing it wasn't just me who worried, not the only one who cared, brings up tears. It solidifies that I made the right choice, even though I wished I'd come back sooner. Wished I never ran. I throw my arms around him, and he stiffens a moment before hugging me back. A small moment passes, and I tense, looking past Isaac to the office. Leo's bent over his desk with a phone to his ear, but he passes a glance to us. I pull back, and Isaac smirks at the worried expression on my face.

"He's not *that* possessive, Miss Autumn. He's still the same Leo. It's good to see you."

"You're not, um, not mad?"

He shakes his head. "Can't blame you for what you did. Understand why."

I huff out a loud breath and grab the clothes he brought. "You all are pretty forgiving, you know that?"

"Quite certain it should be the other way around. We're the mob, not you. Besides, you've made some of us quite smitten with you. Not like the boss is, though."

I snort walking to the bathroom, which is decorated with suede and leather, and change out of the clothes Cheryl gave me. I pull on leggings, a shirt, and a cardigan that finally fit me. While I fold up the clothes, I pause when I see my reflection in the mirror.

My hair is greasy and a mess, dark circles are under my eyes, and I appear paler than I should be. Some of the color in my face is gone, and even though it's only been a week, the puking and barely eating has made me look gaunt. Even with Cheryl trying to get me to eat, it obviously wasn't enough. I smooth back my hair, ignoring the tired look in my eyes as I walk out.

There's a tray with a metal lid over it where I was sitting. Putting the old clothes down beside me, I sit as Isaac pulls the metal lid off. There's squash soup, toast, pasta, and a salad. He goes behind the counter, dipping low to pull out a water from a small fridge. "Can I get you some tea or coffee?"

"I…" I stare down at the food and my stomach churns.

"You're safe now, Miss Autumn. Ask for whatever you want."

"I know," I whisper, and give him a weak smile. "Maybe some tea. Thanks."

He nods, walking out for me to eat in the quiet atmosphere.

I continue staring at the food, listening to the muted conversations in the office. Thoughts beginning to fuzz, I carefully pick up the spoon and start on the soup. It's delicious, making my stomach twist and grumble for more. Each bite I take is slow, trying not to overwhelm myself and accidentally cause my body to reject it. Isaac comes back with the tea, keeping to the side to give me space. I only get through the soup and some of the toast, not touching anything else as I sip the tea. He removes the tray and I rest my head on my arms upon the counter.

Exhaustion pulls at me.

I drift into a light slumber, but awake what feels like minutes after with a start. My hands grasp the counter. It feels like a gaping hole is in my chest. A scream tries to bubble up, pressing its way as terror washes over me. Someone grabs at my shoulder, and I flinch reaching for the closest utensil. My head snaps to the side as I clutch the spoon in my hand.

Isaac stares at me with wide eyes, holding his hands up. "You're alright. It's okay."

Breathing heavily, my head throbs which presses a weight down against my skull. Hands shaking, I drop the spoon and let go of the counter. Tremors begin in my body as I stare at the wood, finding it hard to concentrate as I wring my hands. The dark shadows envelop me, and fears of the past week begin to seep back into me.

Isaac speaks, but I can't make out what he says. The words don't register as I grip the counter again, rocking in my seat as despair gnaws. There's noise and talking.

Through the fog I hear *his* voice softly behind me, "Check in."

Words won't come out. I barely let go of the counter as my hands shake, trying to reach for him. "R...r-re—"

His arms become instantly around me, hugging me to his chest as I bury my face against him.

"You're safe." He shifts, lifting my entire body into a bridal carry. "We're leaving."

I wrap my arms around his neck, holding on as he carries me into the office. There are people. I can feel them watching. I can feel them staring. I bury myself further against him, trying to disappear.

We're soon in the elevator with a few others, but we're only there a moment it seems. I smell fresh air and a breeze passes my face. I peek out and see we're on top of his hotel, and he's walking toward his helicopter. My grip tightens around him, and he kisses my head. "Don't worry, I'm not flying the damn thing. *Rudy* is."

A choked laugh comes out of me as he sets me into the same seat from the first time we flew. He goes through procedures, strapping me in and getting my headset on, then gets settled in next to me. The blades begin to rotate, the engines firing up as Leo wraps his arm around my shoulders. My eyes start to close again as the helicopter lifts into the air.

I drift as we leave the city, sealing my decision and fate.

Chapter 9

Come Daylight

A soundless scream rips from my throat.

It feels like bricks have been placed on my chest, burying me into the darkness that threatens to choke me. Pressure forms around my throat and I struggle to breathe. My hand flails, hitting a body next to me and I jerk away in terror.

Steve. He's going to punch me again. He's going to—

"You're safe."

A voice pierces through the darkness that swallows me, and I jolt as hands grab at me. I struggle, flinching at the contact as hands try to hold onto me and someone presses me into the bed. My legs kick, trying to get them off as I fight them and the terrible darkness.

"You're safe, dear Watson…you're safe."

The voice comes again and my eyes open as I finally find breath. Hazel eyes. They look down at me as a gentle hand strokes my hair back, while the other keeps my arms crossed at my front. His body practically engulfs mine, keeping me secure beneath him against a soft bed.

My voice comes out as a rasp, "Leo?"

"I'm here, sweetheart."

"Are you real?" I say my thoughts out loud, wanting to know if this was part of the nightmare. I'll think he's here, but then I'll wake up in Roger's house. On the street. In that damn, rat-infested apartment of Steve's.

He clutches my face, pressing a kiss to my forehead. "Very real. I'm here."

I choke out a sob, relief flooding me as I take in the scruff on his face. The gold in his eyes. The dark strands of his hair, unkempt and still unwashed. Last night. I went back to him last night.

Wiggling my arms, Leo let's go so I can grab him. He shifts to the side but wraps his arms around me tightly. My breath stutters, trying to catch breath and fight off the sobs as I clutch him. In silence, we remain there as I get my bearings. Eyes blinking against a few tears I look at where I am.

It's a bedroom with deep cherry wood walls and beams that cross overhead. There's a fireplace on the far side, near a porch with wide double doors, the windows revealing a countryside being lit by a grey dawn. There's a chandelier sparkling in the first rays of morning, and it smells of pine and cedar. It's inviting and warm.

"Where are we?"

"You don't remember?" I shake my head against his shoulder. "We flew to my country estate; the one I brought you to before. You seemed somewhat awake, trying to take a shower because you didn't want to dirty the bed. Except, you kept falling asleep and I thought it was best to wait til morning. That's why you're still in the clothes I gave you last night."

My legs rub together, feeling the soft leggings and I hide a wince as my calves' brush against each other. Guilt pangs me as I remember what I'd done. Everything I'd done from running, cutting, telling Roger about him. The self-blame builds, and I shake my head trying to rid the thoughts.

"Autumn?" Leo asks, pulling back to cradle my face. "What is—"

"I'm sorry," I say, squeezing my eyes shut. "I'm sorry. I'm sorry—"

"Stop." I quiet, beginning to tremble as I feel myself unravel all over again. Fuck, it's been forever since it was this bad to keep control. Why can't I keep control of myself? "Open your eyes, sweetheart."

Slowly, I do as he says, and he wipes away a tear with his thumb. There's concern in his gaze, filled with concentration as he furrows his brow. I touch where the line always forms on his forehead as his expression softens. He turns his head, kissing the palm of my hand and whispers, "Good girl."

A whimper comes out of me. Leo carefully pulls me up, sitting us both upright as he keeps me in his embrace. I lean my head against his chest, listening to his heartbeat and following the tattooed lines. Leo strokes my back, gently calming me and my breathing becomes more at ease. I inhale deeply and exhale, relaxing against him as the trembling disappears.

"Do you want or need to talk?" I shrug. He kisses my head, inhaling deeply himself. "I won't make you. Not until you're ready, but I'll be here to listen."

I nod, cuddling as close as I can with him and glance at the room. It's like the parts I've already seen. Woodsy. Quaint. And far more inviting than his other two places. Not sure if I can believe it was the same decorator still.

A few more long breaths, and I speak, "I didn't sleep while I was gone, the nightmares were too much. Too real. I could barely keep down the food I tried to eat, but I always seemed to puke it up." Leo's movements still for a second before he continues to stroke my back. "It felt like I was back in the same spot again. Alone. On my own. Everything hurt and…" I stop, feeling the self-given wounds pulse against my skin, and I gulp, "…it felt never ending."

"Did that detective notice at all?" I shake my head. "Not even that you weren't eating or sleeping for a whole week?"

Not the only thing he didn't notice. My mind flits back to me cutting while he was yelling at me through the door. Maybe Leo doesn't need to know about that.

"He had…other priorities."

"Like using you as a mule? Some info dump source?"

"Didn't say it was good priorities," I mutter. Leo sighs with a grumble underneath. "He was always like that."

"You don't need to explain his actions," Leo practically growls. "Although I'm sure you'll tell me I'm not allowed to touch him. Play *nice*."

I purse my lips, somewhat thinking about it. My mind flicks to many moments, those not just of the last week, but also from years ago. Every order, every demand. Sure, he was the 'good guy', but it never really felt like that. Back then, he was all I had though.

Leo leans back, making me look up at him as he furrows his brows again. "Are you considering *not* telling me that?"

"Don't ask me important questions before breakfast, such as who to put under cement or what to paint the bedroom floor."

"It's carpet."

"See? My point exactly."

Leo snorts. He smooths back my hair, and I hum at the touch. "Fine, we'll discuss after food and a shower."

He begins to get up, but I stop him as I hold onto his arm. "I can't tell you I'm completely fine," I whisper. "You've dealt with my panic attacks and shit in the past, but this is…not quite the same. I don't want to be coddled though. I want to try feeling normal and happy again. Even though I'm sure there's no way of going back to that same normal again. With us, I mean."

Leo takes my hands, bringing one to his lips. He kisses each knuckle and prompts me to look into his eyes. "You're right, we won't be able to go back to that normal again." My heart begins to sink. "A few things will remain the same though. One of those is me helping take care of you. Another is that I love you, and that shall never change." He kisses my wrist. "And I will *always* help protect and safeguard your happiness, because it is one of the most wondrous pieces of this world, especially in mine."

A sudden giggle comes out of me. Mr. Smooth Line Leo strikes again. I try to bring my hand up to my mouth to stop it, but he doesn't let go. He smiles faintly, bringing his face close to mine. "There she is."

I lean forward, kissing him gently. "I love you, Leo," I murmur against his lips.

"I love you, dear Watson." He lets go of my hands as I wrap my arms around his neck, pulling him back into a deeper kiss.

The core of me warms as his tongue sweeps over my lips, and I open to allow him in. The taste of Leo almost makes me whimper, relief flooding me as I clutch him and hold onto the joyous feelings. My body and brain chase after the desirable emotions, shunning the other awful feelings. Tingling sensations run up my spine, not for danger, but of bliss and pleasure. My legs move around his waist.

Leo quickly pulls back, and I groan at the loss of contact. "Slow down, Autumn."

"I'm fine."

"You've had a long couple of days and nights. You barely ate last night."

My hands move down his chest, touching his skin and how it expands with every breath. Loneliness of the past week, fuck, past three years, is like a heavy blanket over my shoulders. "Leo, I said no coddling—"

"Red."

I freeze at the word. My hands going still as I stare at him. There's a calm about his disposition, and his expression is neutral. "There's a difference in coddling and being responsible about your health. In all aspects. And trust me, I would love nothing more than to already be deep inside you." I blink at his words, breath shallow. "I won't chance triggering you. We have time. I promise. Do you understand?"

I nod, and he quirks a brow. "Yes."

"Good girl." He kisses my cheek, keeping an arm around me as he starts to get off the bed. "I'll offer a compromise."

"You're offering one first?"

He pauses halfway off the bed. "It can happen."

Oh, yeah sure after his arm has been twisted and he has to choose between my favorite Nick Cage movies to watch. Otherwise, smooth sailing.

"Both of us need a shower, so *that* can be our next activity together." I raise my brows at him, and he chuckles as he steps off the bed. "No shower sex."

I groan dramatically, hanging my head back to make him chuckle again. "You're annoying when you're being responsible Leo, but okay."

He kisses my neck, making me chuckle and he smiles as I bring my head back up. "It's my specialty."

"And you did safe word," I mumble under my breath.

"Thank you for listening."

"I've been trained well."

"Is that so?" He smirks, walking us into the bathroom.

"Uh-huh."

The bathroom is huge, not a surprise, but the décor is. It's a light amber hue with cream tiling and wooden walls. There are two sinks with bronze piping and the shower to the left is a large walk-in with sandstone tiling and walls. It's very spa-in-the-mountains.

Leo sets me down on the rug next to the conjoining sinks, which is soft under my bare toes. "Go ahead and start the shower. I'll be back."

He walks out, closing the door behind him and I shake off the odd feeling of being shut in. I pull off my shirt and sweater, putting them aside next to a wicker hamper. As I begin to pull off the leggings, the fabric catches on two band-aids. I hiss a little. Quickly, taking them off, I sit on the toilet and freeze just before I peel away the other band-aids.

I don't remember there being so many.

On the inside of my calves is where I cut. In the past, doing it on the thighs it only worsened the wounds from chafing and outside of my legs were prone to being bumped into. Slowly, I peel one off, trying to remember every time I'd done it. There's nine all together. Four on one calf; five on the other.

I don't remember each one.

Glancing up at the shower, I reach within my mind of when last I showered. Nothing. I *had* to have showered at least once, right? Or had I only used it for *that*?

My stomach tightens, making me feel sick as I gently tug off the rest of them. They're not extremely deep, but they're long and too straight. Not to mention some have crusted blood and look infected. My gaze flits to the door, heart pounding as I realize Leo will see them.

Excuse. I need a damn excuse.

What had I used before? Falling against brick? Someone's cat? Hopping a fence?

My thoughts ramble on how to spin this, feeling guilt if I lie to him again. My stomach clenches, already wanting to vomit. Frozen with bandage in hand, I stare at the ground trying to keep my thoughts from unraveling in fear that interweaves them. How disgusted will he be? Or will be horrified and finally admit I'm broken?

The door opens and my head jerks up as Leo enters. He glances at the empty shower, pinching his brows together as he looks over at me and stops. I watch his eyes move to my legs and my heart plummets.

No emotion flits over his face. No pity. No disgust. He just stares at the cuts on my legs.

"I..." the excuse won't come. I swallow hard, standing and dropping the bandages into the waste basket. I stare at the tile beneath my feet, trying not to look at the multiple wounds.

He still won't say anything.

Shame begins to fill me, and I try to push it away, and ask, "Are you gonna pull a Mr. Grey on me?"

"Would I pull off James Spader?"

"Maybe," I half-heartedly laugh.

"Would it work?"

"I don't know."

My eyes meet his, and he turns away to start the shower. Water falls from two large showerheads, covering most of the space. He brings his attention back to me, holding his hand out.

"Leo, I—"

"I understand all too well," he states, and my throat tightens. "Craving pain in hopes of relief."

I flick my gaze over his bare chest and arms; at the tattoos covering so much of his body.

"Let's get cleaned up," he says softly.

I step toward him, putting my hand in his as he guides me into the water. He keeps back to strip out of his pants and enters the steam filled space. The water rushes around me, and I lean my head back as it falls over my skin. The heat strikes over my skin. Briefly wincing at the hot water running down my legs. I then sigh, breathing in the steam deeply. Eyes closed, I hear Leo step around me and the water splashing on the ground. My eyes jolt open when a soft washcloth moves over my shoulders. I look up at Leo as he begins to wash my skin, scrubbing lightly as he concentrates helping clean me.

"Stand still," he whispers, taking one of my arms to scrub it and then the next one. I just stand there as he washes me, watching him as he goes. Peace begins to fill me, keeping my attention on the man whose entire attention is on me.

As he moves the washcloth down my side, he kneels before me as he goes to scrub my legs next. My breath hitches as he pauses at my thighs, his gaze down toward the cuts. Minutes seem to tick by as the water rushes over us. Finally, he carefully moves the cloth over the wounds, and I bite my lip to not make a sound. It hurts a little, tender from not being properly taken care of the last few days.

When Leo speaks, each word is deliberate and slow. "I want you to never cut yourself again."

I look down as he looks up. Calm hazel eyes are all I see as I nod my head stiffly. He finishes washing my legs, and then he kisses my skin. He places a kiss over every self-inflicted wound with a tenderness that makes my heart clench.

"I'm sorry." My voice is quiet as I stare down at him, hands beginning to shake.

Leo drops the washcloth as he stands, clutching my face with his hands. "No, don't..." he swallows harshly, eyes becoming softer, "...

I'll help clean your wounds, but I'd rather help stop your hand. You're not alone."

Tears that are somehow still left, leak from my eyes. He kisses my cheeks before I wrap my arms around his chest. I listen to his heartbeat, a bit faster than it has been before. His arms fold me into him as he takes a long breath in. The only sound is the falling water as we hold onto each other with much needed reassurance that we're both alive and not alone anymore.

Leo puts two plates on the table, sitting next to me in the kitchen nook. The kitchen itself is smaller than his other ones, but it does have an island in the middle. The table can sit up to six people and is off to the side wall of the open floor plan downstairs. The entire living room and small bar can be seen. Sunlight streams in from the vast windows of the patio doors. It's quiet and quaint.

We were in the shower awhile, which included Leo washing my hair and I did his. It only seemed fair. Leo also helped fully clean and bandage my cuts. We came downstairs for breakfast soon after, barely 7:30 AM. I smile at him as he sits with his mug, nodding at me to eat. Hunger pangs hit me as I look at the eggs, pancakes, bacon, and coffee he made. A moan leaves me as I take the first bite.

"Just hungry or missed my cooking?"

"Both," I mumble. He smiles then goes to eat.

Breakfast is silent for a bit before questions start to rattle in my brain. The fog is still there, but I can think a bit more clearly. And I'll take anything to distract myself from the other thoughts.

"Sooo, question?" I ask, and he raises a brow. "Not mob-related... yet." He snorts and then nods his head. "Why is this place different from the other two? It has more personal style, including pictures." I nod toward a painting of mountains above the fireplace.

"Remember how I keep my businesses separate?" I nod. "I've done the same with my living quarters. The apartment and penthouse reflect one, while this reflects another."

I hum, tapping my fork. "Basically, keeping it safe *from* the mafia?" He pauses, then ever so slowly nods. "Let's be honest Leo, one of the things that's gonna change is approaching *that* topic. It's gonna come up."

"Yes, but I'd prefer not talking too much of it today. Take a break."

"I'm okay, Leo, I swear. Groggy and tired and in need of some fuzzy socks and a cartoon movie or Nick Cage, but okay."

"I know, but there are some things I'm not ready to talk about yet. Even though I'm why—"

"I'm such a jerk," I groan, hitting my head against the table. Leo catches it before I do it again. Realization slams into me like a ton of bricks.

"What?"

I pull away, flinging my arms out. "I've been caught up in my own shit, worrying and… I didn't think about how hard this has been for you. I have, for moments, but then get all self-guilty over here and…crud muffins, I'm sorry Leo, I should've been better and not self-absorbed."

"Alright, enough of that." He pulls my hands down from their angry interpretive dance.

"I should've paid attention. How you are."

He practically gapes at me. "My dear Watson, I am trying to tread carefully to open these new doors for you and me, but there's no need to apologize. You've been through a lot this past week you don't need to—"

"That's no excuse," I cut him off. "If I came back for you, for *us*, then that means I've got to take care of you, too. And not be so selfish or even—"

He shuts me up with a searing kiss. My breath comes in quick at the suddenness and I grab his shoulder to steady myself as his lips press hard against mine. I taste him through the coffee he's had, moaning at *that* wonderful taste.

Leo breaks away. "The time will come to help care for me. Not now. And you're not self-absorbed or even selfish for trying to figure out your emotions and pain. All I want now from you, need, is *you* near me. That's how you can care for me. We'll talk more details another day, discuss everything. But right now, today, we're going to forget that side exists, alright?"

"Uh-huh." I blink quickly, mesmerized.

"Stunned you?" He chuckles under his breath.

"I'm out of practice."

"Hmm, perhaps I'll do it again when you panic ramble."

"Good tactic." He smiles before giving another quick kiss.

"Alright, no talk of it today."

So, we talk about everything, but the mafia. For the first time in almost seven days, it feels normal again. Breakfast with Leo. The quiet moments and off-the-wall conversations about movies or whatever. Once finished, he lets me help him clean up, during which I hear other doors in the estate open and close.

I walk over to the patio doors, staring out at the vast countryside. Sunlight fills the place as I look out at the unfamiliar view. I've gotten so used to buildings and city life; it was odd waking up to trees again. Leo wraps his arms around me from behind. I lean my head against his chest, listening to the faint thumping. An idea pops into my head as we look out together.

"We're free all day, right? So, options are open?"

"Depends, but mostly yes."

I stare at the shiny blue sky, no more grey clouds. "Seems like a nice day for a ride, don't you think?"

His grip tightens around me and nuzzles his face against my neck. "Yes, it does."

Chapter 10

Leather Vests & Patches

I'm wearing real leather.

Leo helped me into a pair of jeans, checked if they caused discomfort over my wounds, and put me in leather chaps. He's wearing leather pants with boots similar to mine, along with a long-sleeved shirt and dark jean jacket. Next, he pulls on a black leather vest. On the back is an image of a red and black devil creature with *Forgotten Demons* across the shoulders. Below the image is another patch which says *California*. I tilt my head as he pulls out another vest, smaller than his and holds it out to me.

I take it, noticing the same devil patch on the back but across the shoulders it says *Property of The Spartan*. Must be an extra vest.

I glance up at him and as he starts to help me into it. The front of Leo's vest has patches that say *President, Founder, Forgotten Demons,* along with an American flag. On the other side of his chest, one says *The Spartan*. There are some with numbers or maybe years on them. I glance down at my vest, noticing it only has the American flag.

"Not only a mafia boss, but the president of a biker gang, too?" A small smile rises on my face.

He chuckles. "Not a gang."

"Right, MC, club. Pretty sure Jameson told me some of that stuff, too."

"Such as?"

"He and you are the ones who created the club." I point at the *Founder* patch.

"Basically. We're not official in any capacity, but for some reason 'president' was slapped onto my name for our crew."

"Since you didn't wear this last time, does this mean we're not riding alone today?"

His hands grip mine, thumb stroking over my skin. "Due to current circumstances, it's safer to ride as a group, not solo. They all need a club ride anyways, otherwise they'll start itching for other outlets."

"How come this vest doesn't have patches like that one?" I nod toward his. "This your stealthy vest?"

"No, it's yours."

"Mine?" My brows shoot up. He watches me carefully as my face scrunches up in confusion. Why do I get the feeling the shoulder patch doesn't mean the vest itself?

Leo keeps a hold of my hand and explains, "It's a biker, MC thing. Women aren't usually allowed into MCs as full-patch members, but can be associated with one through whoever they're with. They're called 'Old Ladies,' and are…loosely a member's…"

"Property?" I raise a brow.

"Partner. It's also for protection. No biker is gonna touch or come near you unless I give permission." Leo places a hand against my jaw, stroking his thumb. "I've never met a biker who'd harm a woman or child, but there are still assholes out there. It's our way of showing respect to you…and who you're with."

"Ah," I say, nodding along. "So, basically if they fuck with me, they fuck with you?"

"And the rest of the club."

Well, that doesn't sound too bad. And I get a leather vest.

"Okay." I smile, and he gives me one back. Keeping hold of my hand, he leads me out of the bedroom and toward the stairs. "So, how many are there in this…*Forgotten Demons*?"

"Eight of us are here. There's more in California, Oregon, and a couple in Florida. They keep watch over…legal affairs."

"These guys here are part of what we're not talking about yet?"

"Jameson and I founded the MC back in California, before any of them knew my family's business. The original crew followed me here. Gave them all an out, keep their hands clean, but they're loyal pricks and stubborn assholes. Wouldn't leave."

"You're a hard man to leave," I murmur. We stop halfway across the catwalk. His gaze softens in a loving way. I squeeze his hand and he does it back. "Anything else to know about them? Other than being pricks and assholes?"

Leo begins leading us down the stairs. "Jameson's the Vice Pres, Isaac's the Sergeant of Arms, and Rudolph is my Road Captain."

"Gonna explain all that in the future, right?"

"Yes, don't worry," he laughs lightly as we make it to the foyer. "You've not met the others, even though I'm around them a lot, but…" Leo pauses, and his jaw works a little as his brows furrow, "…I'm particular who meets them. They've known about you though, helping to keep an eye on you. I've been waiting for the right time for you to meet them, probably now will be best as we figure things out."

I look at the front door. "So, they're your family?"

He shrugs. "In a sense."

Huffing and shaking my limbs out, I say, "Alright then, let's go meet the *gang*."

Leo puts his hand against the small of my back, leading me outside. Blinking against the sunlight, the driveway's vast space is covered with motorcycles and men in leather vests and rugged attire like Leo. Boots and all. None of the bikes appear to be from Leo's garage, and I wonder where *these* all came from. Searching amongst them, I finally see three I know.

Isaac and Jameson have a different air about them as we approach, more…relaxed?

Jameson folds his arms over his chest, glancing at me briefly with a grin, "Looking good in leather there. Wondered if you had it in you."

"Watch it, Sombra," Leo warns as we stop before the two. Isaac smirks at them, winking at me next.

"Come on, it's a compliment and it's been a long fucking week," Jameson mutters. "You had a good idea to go riding."

"Wasn't my idea." Leo kisses my check. "Stay." He walks away toward the garage, calling back, "It was hers."

Jameson swings his gaze to me. I smirk, noticing Isaac lean against a bike I presume is his. I glance at their vests, noticing the title patches on them and other names. Curiosity guides me back to the motorcycles, staring at the differences of the models.

Isaac asks, "Want to know what they are, Miss Autumn?"

"Sure. I remember the bike Leo and I rode was a Harley heritage classic, none of these look like that."

"You remember the model?" Jameson asks.

I shrug. "What's yours?"

"Harley Bobber, Iron 883." He cocks his head near a bike with red sides that appears sturdy with shorter handles.

"Mine's a Harley soft tail standard," Isaac says, gesturing at the brighter silver chrome of his motorcycle.

"Someone better explain what the numbers and names mean later," I mutter as I glance between the bikes.

Isaac laughs, and starts pointing at the others and more confusion fills me as he talks. "Iron Buffalo usually rides his custom-built chopper, it's the very dark metal looking one. Chesty rides what's called an Indian Larry Knucklehead Chopper, that one with the wooden look to it. Animal rides a Harley sportster, also an Iron 883, and then Enigma there rides an Indian scout bike. Lastly, Ringer rides that big ole' custom built Road king."

I stare at Jameson in deep confusion, and he just starts chuckling. He's no fucking help.

"Isaac, were you speaking in code?"

"Fucked up there, Pretty Boy," Rudolph says, walking over with a smirk. He's clad in leather like I am, seemingly larger than I remembered in how he stands. He stops a few feet from me, and he crosses his arms over his chest, scrunching his vest a little. "You evaded me at the station, *bärchen*."

I adjust my stance and give a somewhat guilty look. "Yeah."

"Impressive."

"Thanks...Rudy."

He smiles, grey eyes shining as he opens his arms. I go into them, becoming engulfed by the large man's embrace. He squeezes me a little as I do it back as he whispers, "Good to have you back, *bärchen*. Worried about you."

"Feeling better being...hold on," I say, stepping back and tilt my head back at him. "Did you just call Isaac *Pretty* Boy?"

Rudy starts laughing and Isaac shakes his head. As I look up at Rudy, I notice patches that say, *Ringer, Road Captain,* and *Original Crew.* I look over at Isaac where he has an *Original Crew* one, along with *Sergeant of Arms* and *Pretty Boy Bond.* A few things start to click.

"Biker nicknames?" I ask as Rudy steps back, while the others start coming over.

"Road names," Jameson answers.

"Biker thing?"

"Basically, each of us has one. Sorry, thought he told you about that," Isaac says.

"Not yet." The others come over and one of them, I think Enigma, swears, I think Spanish, under his breath and then Jameson does the same. I look to where they're staring, finding Leo rolling out a different bike from the first time. This one has higher handlebars, mostly black with shiny silver chrome. Not to mention what looks to be a bigger backseat. It gorgeous.

"I'll be damned, he really does trust her," one of the men mutters.

"Told you," Rudy replies.

"Is that bike special or something?" I ask.

"Yeah, it was a gift," Jameson answers. "But his most prized is a chopper made specially for him years back."

"Why didn't he choose that one then?"

"Cause it doesn't have a bitch pad." The one who spoke is shorter than Isaac, but he has a large wide chest and gut. He's got piercing green eyes, and a long goatee beard that's braided with metal beads. He has light brown hair, an undercut, and the ink on his hands seem faded against his tanned beige skin. Lastly, he's clad in leather and a vest that has a patch which says, *Chesty.*

He honestly looks like most bikers I've seen depicted in movies.

"Bitch pad?" I ask.

"Seat behind the driver," Isaac explains. I raise a brow, glancing at the other bikes. Some have it and some don't. "You can ride the fender, but you're still pretty new a rider and it's gonna be long ride."

Leo parks the bike near us. I look straight at him. "When do I get to graduate from bitch pad to fender?"

He pauses, narrowing his eyes at the others. All the men chuckle low.

Leo places his arm around me, and says, "Leave you alone for five minutes with them."

"So…awhile?" He snorts, then juts his head at the others I've not met. "That's Waylon." Viking, weightlifter biker, got it. "That's Drew." He's a bit taller with a smaller gut, and black hair braided down past his shoulders. He has a dark beard, longer than Waylon's, and has olive undertone skin. And he may have the warmest brown eyes I've ever encountered. "Julio." Similar height to Drew, the man has large, wide shoulders and a strong gut much like Rudy's with ochre skin. His black hair is faded on the sides and his beard is cut short. He has lighter brown eyes than Drew, and like Waylon, has tattoos on his hands. "And finally introduce you two, that's Owen."

I look over at Owen, who inclines his head. "Nice to formally meet you."

Drew lightly shoves Isaac and juts his head at Leo. "That's how you do it, instead you just confused the woman."

"She asked."

"About what?" Leo asks.

"The bikes, but Pretty Boy Bond here used all their road names," Jameson smirks.

The frustrated look Leo gives Isaac makes me giggle. I try to hide my laughter behind my hands, but he pulls them away as his expression softens before he kisses my cheek.

"Helheim must be melting," Waylon mutters, and Rudy elbows him.

Leo brings his attention back to them, and they all straighten. None of them give off even a hint of being a threat, no matter how terrifying they look with their leather, tattoos, and rough skin. Those I was around in the clubs years ago appeared not much different, but they always had a horrible glint in their eye. Not them.

"Must really trust her, if you introduced us as our real names," Julio says.

"He does," Owen comments. "And if he does, we will, too."

"Wait, hold on." I bring a hand up to halt them, and they all stare at me. "There's no reason to introduce myself, since you all know who I am, but there's still something I wanna tell y'all...I want to apologize to all you."

Leo's arm tightens around me. Eyes widen in shock, flicking between me and Leo. Isaac clears his throat and Jameson goes to speak, but I interrupt him, "Whether you're angry with me or not. That you understand why I ran or whatever, I still need to apologize."

Jameson's jaw tightens, folding his arms over his chest.

"Leo can put all his trust in me, that's his decision, but what I did jeopardized you all. So, I expect none of you to give me that kind of trust. Not right away. I understand. Don't even have to be okay with me being around, though I'm sure *someone* would have something to say about that." I glance up, finding as if on cue, Leo's furrowed brow. "I do apologize for any harm I may have caused or will for leaving. And if it'll make you feel better, I'll use your road names instead. Practically already have name tags." Waylon and Drew snort loudly, while Isaac smirks. "But I promise to earn your respect."

They're all quiet, exchanging looks with the other. Julio nods towards me. "Call me Enigma or Julio. You earned both when you scrambled my cameras."

I raise my brow. "So, you're the ex-FBI guy?"

He grins wide. "You and I should talk sometime."

"Noted."

"Prefer Chesty," Waylon speaks next. "Faster response." I nod.

"Animal." Drew raises his hand, smiling. "Drew is for formal occasions."

"You already know what I prefer, *bärchen*." Rudy pats his chest.

"Got it, Rudy." I do a mock salute, and Animal and Enigma raise their brows.

"Nothing's changing for us, Miss Autumn." Isaac inclines his head, and Jameson agrees with Isaac for himself.

"Stick with Owen, but if you wanna be formal it's Iron Buffalo." The tall black man winks at me, gesturing at the bikes. "We should get going, and maybe she is ready for the fender."

"Snake Eyes knows we're coming sometime today," Rudy speaks. "Just don't go messing up his bar…again."

"That was Pretty Boy and Chesty last time, not us."

All the men go to their bikes, talking low with each other as I turn toward Leo. He grips my face suddenly, giving me a bruising kiss, which makes me gasp. My hands clutch his vest. "You're perfect," he says.

My brows shoot up. "For that?"

"For being you. And you earned their respect when you came back last night, putting a gun on my desk instead of shooting me."

"Well, that's a different rom-com, I think," I say a little flustered from the kiss. Leo laughs under his breath, walking me over to the bike. "Which one is this?"

"Harley classic soft tail. Engine was rebuilt and the frame reinforced," he explains, handing me my helmet, then puts his on. "First club I rode with, the founders gifted it to me before I left for New Mexico."

"This…this was that bike?" I ask as Leo straddles the bike.

Now I know why the others were shocked. Leo gestures for me to get on behind him, and I settle into the seat as he checks my leg placement. I give him a thumbs up and he nods before he turns on the engine.

The ground rumbles as they all start their motorcycles. The quiet countryside is obliterated by the loud noise of engines vibrating under the ground beneath us. A small laugh escapes me as I smile, feeling the bike rumble between my legs. A peaceful feeling runs through me as I wrap my arms around Leo, breathing in the smell of leather and metal.

Rudy starts off the pack, riding down the path with Leo and Jameson close behind, and then the others. We ride out from the estate and onto the road, engines revving as we speed up and take over the road. Beautiful autumn landscape surrounds us as we ride down the winding road, heading north. I squeeze Leo a little, and I can practically feel his entire body relax as the bike picks up speed.

Scenery passes us in a blur. The only thing I hear is the engine, a constant noise, as I look out at the landscape. Bright oranges, reds, and a few greens speckle the countryside. All I can do is smile as I watch it all pass us, and it widens more as I see glimpses of the bikers behind us. Around one of the curves, one of them pulls up, Animal, and I see him smile broadly at me before we round a hillside.

All thoughts in my head eddy out. My full concentration on the feeling of the Harley under me, the sight of the countryside, and the freedom it brings. I've no idea where we're going, but I couldn't care less. Signs for Ithaca and other cities flash past as we go deeper into the upper north of New York State. The sun is high when we start coming upon some small towns, and then pass through one before we start to slow down. Ahead, there's a long building surrounded by trees.

Leo pulls in, backing into a space as the others do the exact same. All their bikes line down the far-left side of the building. There are other bikes parked, backed into spaces. Once the engine is off, I ask Leo while dismounting, "Why do you back up?"

"Easier to leave in a hurry." He gets off, taking his helmet off and then mine. "Only use the road names in here, including mine."

"What about me?"

"Your name is fine or just Spartan's Old Lady." He winks, and I roll my eyes at him as his hand goes around mine. We walk into the bar with the others.

The place has a long bar at the back, with a door to the kitchen and another hall to the bathrooms. There's a couple of pool tables and other tables scattered with most against walls, and there's more people in leather vests and jackets. Blues music plays from a jukebox. People look at us, while a few look to the bartenders.

A tall, large black man, walks around the counter with a stern expression. He wears a leather vest, like the rest and blue jeans. Rudy walks right up to him, clasping hands with him and then Owen does the same.

"Told you we'd make it," Rudy says.

"Took your time."

"Had a new rider, Snake Eyes," Owen comments.

Snake Eyes nods, glancing at Leo and then at me briefly, then says, "Been a while since you've been up here, Spartan."

"Busy," Leo replies. They shake hands quick.

"Better lay down that *busy* on the bar." Snake Eyes glances over at me, a half grin coming over his face. "Never thought I'd see an old lady on your arm. *Busy*, huh?"

Owen's face becomes rigid as Rudy flicks his gaze to Snake Eyes. Even Jameson tenses on the other side of Leo. I almost hear Leo growl, hand tightening around mine.

"I'm Spartan's Old Lady, Autumn." I hold out my other hand, hoping to diffuse Leo before he gets snappy. The man looks at my hand and then at Leo. I'm about to rescind it when Leo nods and Snake Eyes takes the offering. He grasps me tight as his hand completely engulfs mine. I'm beginning to think that all bikers look like wrestlers or MMA fighters with grips of steel at this point. I smile, eyes meeting his deep brown ones. "Good to meet you, Snake Eyes."

A smirk comes over his face as he drops my hand. "You seem too nice for him."

"Eh, just balance." I shrug, and he chuckles.

"What do you drink?" He folds his arms over his chest.

"Water." He raises a brow. "Unless you got coffee back there."

"Might…and given you're brave enough to ride with this riff-raff, and shake my hand in front of The Spartan, I'll even make you a fresh pot."

"That's awfully sweet of you, thank you." My smile doesn't falter, and the man gives me one back.

We're soon all sitting with two tables brought together near the wall. Each of the men end up with a drink in front of them, while I get water and coffee. Leo keeps me close arm draped over the back of my chair. More bluesy, rock music plays in the dark atmosphere with the neon lights and beer advertisements. The other bikers in the bar keep to themselves but glance our way from time to time. Otherwise, the place is pretty relaxed.

Even with the smell of smoke and liquor, no anxiety ticks up my spine. The worry is far gone. As I drink my coffee, I catch the eye of a couple of bikers who stare at us from a pool table. They turn away when Waylon and Rudy give them a look.

"They're just curious. We don't come around here much," Animal says, leaning in from across the table.

"Not scared," I say.

"Eh, fine if you are," Julio reassures, taking a drink from his beer. "New people, new space, new culture."

"Definitely not made for everyone," Owen adds. They all grunt in agreement.

"Not that new," I mutter. "I'll take a biker bar over a drug infested club any day." Leo tightens his grip, and I give him a half smile. Worry flits over his scowling face, which probably is the other reason why everyone has stopped looking at our tables. "Green," I whisper.

Leo relaxes.

We become silent, while I people watch. Most of the bikers sit and drink, while some play darts or pool. A few dance on the open floor, moving slowly to the slow rock music. There's a woman bartender behind the bar who keeps yelling at some men, laughing as she does. The change of atmosphere is a relief, reminding me of a very old memory of sneaking into a bar growing up.

"Since, I'm sure you all know about me," I start off. "Why don't ya'll tell me about yourselves?"

Every single one looks at Leo, who nods once. His gesture of approval prompts the first conversation, and from there we go down the rabbit hole that is the *Forgotten Demons*.

Waylon was in the Marine Corps. Enlistment ended due to an injury after he survived a couple of deployments to Afghanistan and Iraq. Nowhere else to go, he stayed in California where his last station was and met up with Owen who'd just gotten out of the Army. While Waylon specialized in Motor T, a military trucker essentially, Owen had been in communications and analytics, along with finance. They met during a contracting job, hanging out at a tavern where they met Drew.

Drew was a mechanic at heart, him and Waylon connecting on that, but he's one of the few of their little crew who wasn't in the military or government beforehand. He rode out to Nevada first, leaving college after one semester. His family had been a prestigious one of some sort, kinda like Leo, and he left them behind. Haven't heard from them since after his father disowned him, close to fifteen years ago. All three have been in MCs before the *Forgotten Demons*.

Julio came into the picture shortly after leaving the FBI. He didn't speak much about it to anyone, even the club. All he alluded to was his career was cut short, and ever since then he's been more aware of the 'justice' within the judicial system. Julio started riding after he met Jameson as a consultant for security systems for one of Leo's hotels. He never left after that.

Finally, I learned about Rudy. He's from Germany and the Ukraine, used to be a wrestler and was good. Until the drugs. I can only stare at who I considered a gentle giant as he mentions the number of drugs he did, which got him kicked out of the wrestling ring and partly why he's in the U.S. He was hired by Leo to work on his choppers, he rebuilt some of the engines and then he just stuck around. Few times almost went back to the drugs, but it seems all of them here have helped him stay sober for years now.

None of them had family outside of one other. They either left them behind or *were* left behind. Club name fit. Whenever they spoke about the other, they referred to themselves as the Crew, given all of them are the Original Crew of *The Forgotten Demons*.

During the conversations we have lunch, and some move away from the table to play pool or hang out at the bar. Leo at some point is waved over by Snake Eyes, and he walks over with Rudy close behind. I'm left with Waylon, Drew, and Isaac.

"You know after all that, none of y'all said where the road names came from," I say, picking at some fries.

"Well, those are stories may be for another time," Isaac answers. "And road names are given."

"Like something you earn?"

"More like what a club thinks you're like. A descriptor," Drew explains. "Take mine for example, cause I don't give a shit if you know why, and these fuckers are why I have it." I start giggling, and Waylon rolls his eyes. "But you gotta ask first."

"Okay, *Animal*, why that name?"

"Cause I fight and fuck like one."

I almost sputter out laughing.

"Don't go lyin', you scraggily pirate," Waylon scowls at him, then looks over at me. "It's cause he's always drumming on our bikes with shit, sounding like he's part of the Electric Mayhem."

"Not to mention the chains," Isaac says, pointing at the two thick chain necklaces around Drew's neck. My mind flashes and I press on a smile to keep from seeming suspicious as my stomach plummets.

"All good reasons," I reply.

Julio calls Drew over, who gets up and winks at me as he walks away. Isaac watches me closely, and I notice him exchange a look with Waylon. The goateed biker leans in next to me, and asks, "You good?"

"Yeah." My eyes flick over the silver beads in his beard, and then down to the rings he wears, and I notice one of those remembrance black metal bands veterans will wear. "This may sound abrupt, but you mentioned you were in combat?" He nods his head steadily, keeping inquisitive eyes on me. "Do you…what I mean, does it feel like…um…"

"Over ten years and still hate crowds." He glances at the bar, grabbing his beer. "Fucking hate loud noises, that popping shit, ya know?" I nod. "And don't get me started how nervous I get if I don't have a weapon on me." He pats his boot, where I see a knife stashed and another under his vest. "Sometimes I forget I'm not there anymore."

"Really?"

He puts his beer down, leaning in closer. "Don't know much of your background, just pieces, but I know enough, sister. You've been smart to get therapy, regularly, hopefully to help with that shit. Except…that stuff ain't ever gonna really leave you. It shapes you."

"Two years ago, I'd have fought you on that. That it wasn't that bad."

"The Autumn now?"

I snatch a fry. "She wishes she could just fucking sleep." Among other things.

He nods his head. "Been there, still am some nights. What helps?"

"Watch movies, it's sucked lately without them." A tightness moves around my throat, anxiety beginning to rise up my spine. "Really wish I had my movies. They're…important to me."

"I getcha. Same with my knives. Freak out with'em." He pulls one out, it's handle has the USMC emblem on it. "Should know, the name Chesty comes from me blabbering about my time in the corps. Never shut up about it. Know who Chesty Puller is?"

"Decorated Marine, right?" He smiles, and I notice one of his teeth is gold. "After watching *Sands of Iwo Jima* and *Back to Bataan* found out about him."

Shock covers his face. "What kind of movie collection you got?"

"80s action flicks, children's movies, cult classics, rom-coms, and whatever I find in cheap movie bins."

"Pretty Boy Bond." Drew walks back over, and…Chesty juts his thumb at me. "You knew about her collection and didn't share?"

Isaac shrugs, "In my defense, so did Ringer."

"You know how hard it is to find those movies?"

"Like *get to the choppa*?" Drew says in a terrible accent. I start laughing at how serious he was in saying the line. "Hey, not that bad!"

"Pretty bad," Isaac mumbles.

"You do it."

They all start trying to mimic Schwarzenegger, and none of them really succeed. They even try to get Rudy to do it, and he just glares at them with a snarl. I about drop my coffee, trying to keep in my laughter as they argue about accents and attempt other classic movie lines.

I'm still laughing when Leo comes over with Jameson and Snake Eyes. I grin at Leo, and he leans down to kiss the side of my neck. "There she is."

He steps back and Snake Eyes says, "Spartan here says you dance."

"Yeah, I do." I flick my gaze to Leo.

"Wouldn't know west coast, would you?"

I scrunch my face together. "Yeah, I do actually." My brows lift. "Wait…are you asking me to dance?"

"Sure, as hell ain't asking them. Probably make my toes bleed." Chesty and Rudy snort.

The idea of dancing, especially a style I haven't in years, makes me giddy. I've not danced blues or west coast since before…

"Okay." I start to get up, pausing to look at Leo. I'm not sure how etiquette works in the dancing arena. I'm not even sure if I almost crossed a line earlier shaking Snake Eyes' hand.

Leo's expression is passive as he nods. I quickly join Snake Eyes, taking his hand to lead me out into the middle of the open space. A few couples are still swaying to the slow music as it ends. Snake Eyes nods at one of the bartenders, who starts a new song with a Michael Jackson classic. I grin at my dance partner, easily being able to follow him as he leads.

"Come on, girl," he sings along, pulling me forward and easing me back. We move around the dancefloor at a quick pace, which makes it easier for me to follow him. I'm rusty, but he makes it easy to catch up and create moves as we dance. He begins to smile near the end, spinning me as my boot almost catches on the floor.

When Michael Jackson finishes, a slower paced song begins to play. He croons a little with the singers, "Wade in the water..."

"Good dancer and singer there, Snake Eyes." I grin at him.

"Call me Ikemba when it's just us." He winks at me. "And I was right, you're too nice for The Spartan."

I glimpse over my shoulder at the others and Leo who's not taken his eyes off me.

"Well, Ikemba, don't we all deserve some compassion from time to time?"

"Won't argue there," he says spinning me and bringing me back. "Even if it's towards the *infamous* Spartan."

I try not to read into his last comment as I become distracted by the music and dancing.

⸻

Leo

Leo leans against the wall, watching Autumn dance. An easy smile on her face. After this morning, he thought he'd watch her crumble again, fall into that painful abyss. Somehow, she's showing signs of herself again. Of course, his dear Watson has a spine of steel and the fortitude of a fucking warrior. Refuses to stay down. *Won't* stay down.

His stomach twists, eyes flicking to her legs where the cuts are.

Never cut yourself again.

Fist clenching, his jaw tightens as wrath travels up his spine.

Jameson leans close. "You've never been the possessive type," he comments low. "But even I was surprised you agreed for her to dance with him."

"He needs to like her. Trust her," Leo responds harshly. "Needs the attachment."

A few of his Crew shift in their positions. Jameson swears under his breath. "Cabrón…you want this to be another safehouse, don't you?"

"Careful, Sombra," Leo warns. "Better to be prepared."

"And how many back-up plans are you going to make?"

"As many as I fucking want." Leo flashes a look at his oldest friends. "This shit has only just begun. Every damn side will drag her back into their claws if they find out how deep her involvement went. Imagine if Matteo knew and that she was alive." Jameson swears again, grabbing his beer and letting out a sigh.

They all become quiet in the loud bar. People are lively as more begin to dance. This bar has always been a safe haven for them. It would be for her, too. Although Snake Eyes knew nothing about the *Forgotten Demons* mob involvement, he's kept the place open for them to stop at. He only knows that Leo is a hotel mogul, who helps keep this place afloat as a "favor" to being able to stop through his territory. Snake Eyes kept prying eyes out, which makes it safer for Autumn if shit hits the fan.

"Think that detective will rat her out?" Jameson asks.

"No," Julio answers instead. "Feds aren't gonna let him. They'll get bad press if it gets out that the NYPD used a civilian for undercover work."

Owen snorts, "He was ready to wring her out, use her again. That's what they want. Another in."

"Exactly. She's more valuable keeping this identity…for now," Julio exchanges a glance with Leo. "Unless it's worth selling."

"*No one* finds out about her past." Leo orders. He finally rips his gaze away from Autumn. He passes a hard look with every single club member. "Sarah Marie died years ago. *End of.*"

All of them incline their heads as the music changes into the third song. It's a country two-step and Leo watches as the burly biker teaches Autumn a few basic moves. Her smile is bright, but he still can't get the image of the horror on her face or the fear on it.

"Start finding every single fucker that came into contact with her undercover," Leo instructs as his gaze darkens. "I want every single damn name that worked with her ex. *Everyone.*"

"Then what, boss?" Rudolph asks.

Leo's chest concaves, heart aching as his mind's eye plays back the tears. The cuts. Her screams at him to hate her. The flinching. The pain in her eyes. He'll never be able to take away her scars, but there were certain things he could do. With burning vengeance and a coldness in his voice he answers, "Make them wish it was the devil who found them first."

Chapter 11

Halls and Walls

I jolt awake. Swallowing past a dry throat, the cold sweat on my skin makes me shiver. Eyes blinking to see through the darkness, I glance at the windows to the balcony. I wipe away at the sweat on my brow, slowly getting out of bed to keep from waking up Leo. He sleeps soundly as I tiptoe to the bathroom, and quietly keep the door cracked open. The lights hurt my eyes and I adjust them to be dimmer. They illuminate the room in a faint glow. Water is splashed on my face, and it drips down my jaw as I stare at my reflection.

It was another nightmare I can't remember, but can feel the lingering terror. A memory. They seem to keep finding me lately. Dr. Wilson always said sometimes it can be like a domino effect. The brain remembering finally what we locked away.

"Not back at square one," I whisper to myself. "Healing isn't linear…it'll pass, just a hitch."

Nightmares coming back more frequently wasn't a bad thing. Just temporary. Just for now. Though I wished it'd move along faster and the guilt and shame covering my skin would just leave.

Pesky feelings.

Yesterday afternoon and evening had been fucking perfect. The ride back from Ikemba's bar was beautiful, even as we rode a bit into the twilight. Think I'm starting to understand the appeal in just finding freedom in riding, even if I am Leo's 'backpack'. It was peaceful thinking of nothing else but the motorcycle, scenery, and the rumble of the engine. I'd hoped it meant no nightmares. Guess the Harleys couldn't chase them away just yet. Neither could Leo.

I grab a towel and wipe my face, pushing my hair back. Well, sleep ain't gonna happen. Could pull a Belle, go exploring. Maybe he has a secret west wing. Almost convinced to do so, grunting and groaning comes from the bedroom.

"Autumn?" Leo's voice is rough and worried. "Autumn?"

"Bathroom."

The door practically slams open as Leo rushes to the doorway. He stops, holding onto the frame as his chest heaves. The tattoos ripple over his bare chest and shoulders, and there's sweat covering his skin. Leo comes forward suddenly, pulling me into his arms with a trembling force. I hug him back as a shudder goes through him, and any worry of my nightmare is gone.

I whisper against his skin, "Check in."

Leo presses his face into my hair, breathing deeply as a hand moves up to the nape of my neck. Finally, he responds, "Yellow."

I'm not certain what he needs. He's said all he needs is me, but what else do I do? Do I get him scotch? Call Jameson? Put him in the shower? Questions swirl in my head, colliding with what he's done for me, but me cooking may give him a stomach ache.

Leo inhales deeply. "I thought you were gone," he says softly. "Yesterday was a dream and you never actually came back. Or that…"

My heart aches, tightening as I hear the worry in his confession. I blink harshly, getting rid of any tears that threaten to come. "I love you, Leo. I'm not going anywhere. I promise."

He pulls back enough to look into my eyes. One of his hands cups my face, and I lean into the touch. His forehead comes to mine. "I love you, my dear Watson."

As we stand there, an idea forms in my head. I grab his hand.

"Follow me." He looks at me incredulously, and I faintly smile. "Come on, mister…follow me."

He grips my hand, trailing behind as we leave the bathroom and I dig into one of the dressers a moment. I find the jackpot, maybe knowing him more than I think. I grab two pairs and have him follow me through the quiet estate. A few lights are on as we go downstairs, and I look around the large living space. It's perfect. Leo keeps his hand firmly in mine as we stop in the middle. A bit of dawn begins to peek through the windows. I face him, holding up two pairs of fuzzy socks in my hands. He looks down at them, and his eyes brighten a little.

"Fuzzy socks make everything better." I place a pair into his hands.

"Are you going to run into me again?"

I feign a gasp, "One time." I start to put mine on. "Put them on."

"You want me to join?"

"Wanna play bumper cars or regular race?" I smirk and he snorts. "Plus, you said I didn't go that far. Put your money where your mouth is, mister."

A soft chuckle is his answer as he puts them on. I smile at the purple fuzzy socks on his feet. He quirks a brow at me. A giggle escapes me next, doing my best not to bring my hand up to cover my mouth. The small grin on his face grows just before I turn and sprint, stopping to slide across the wooden floor. I spin, sprint, and do it again. Then I slide back to him, grabbing his hand to try to pull him across the wood.

My heavily muscled tattooed biker mafia boss boyfriend doesn't budge. Damn it.

He kisses me quickly. I'm flustered from the contact; he breaks away and smirks wickedly. Promptly, he moves and slides across the floor.

Further than me.

I gape. "No fair!" He shrugs. Oh, he is *not* winning this!

Quickly moving, I slide past him and skate around the furniture as he tries to catch me. Giggles erupt as he goes the other way, sliding as his face scrunches in concentration. He races with me, both of using the couches and chairs to slingshot ourselves further or help with tight turns. Sunlight fills the room as we run out of breath. Coming around a corner, I breathe hard just before I run into Leo, and he grabs me.

We fall, landing on the couch as we both laugh softly. He snuggles me closer against his chest, kissing me as I hum. "See? Fuzzy socks help."

"They do, especially with you," he whispers.

I bury my face against his shoulder. Something deep within me, hidden within all the shadows and worries, there's a fierce need to protect him. He worried about my happiness, but I worry about the fragility of his.

<hr>

Noon has just passed as I follow Isaac toward the back of the estate. Vineyards and woods surround the place, although there's a good open backyard. There are smaller buildings to the left and more to the right near the helicopter pad. One is a safe house, while the others are where people can sleep, a garage, and for whatever else they have on property. I look up at the balcony that's part of the primary bedroom.

"The vineyard goes on for about another two and a half miles, so don't go too far without an escort."

"Any safe houses out there?"

"Not really," he smirks. "Just an old barn."

"Hmm."

After Leo's and my morning 'tryst', we had an early breakfast. As we were finishing up, his duties as boss walked into the door in the form of Jameson and Owen. He'll be in meetings all day and on the phone, catching up from the past couple of days. I'll be trailing Isaac most of the day, I guess, becoming familiar with the estate and land.

I search through the vast landscape of grapevines, trees, and greenery. It's odd seeing so much green. A small sinking feeling comes. Anxiety pricks at my neck, but I brush it off easily. The rest of the emotions don't rear their ugly head, staying in the far back reaches of my mind as I continue to push them away.

It's easier to feel safer, convince myself I am. It's not like I was with Roger or undercover, where there was no plan or back up. Always on my own. I'd grown used to a new kind of loneliness over the past three years, and this felt better.

Leo and the Crew were careful. Detailed. I wasn't alone, which felt odd and unfamiliar.

"Miss Autumn?"

I come out of my thoughts. Isaac's blue eyes wrinkle with concern. "Sorry, last few days catching up with me. Week, I mean."

"We can take a break."

"No, it's fine. I'm good to learn more, probably best to know now than later. Just in case. Maybe, I just…forgot that with this life things move quickly? Got used to the nothing ever happens daily life."

"Military was like that, too. Always on the move, hurry up and wait kind of living. In the wait period now."

"Did you get used to it again? Joining Leo after leaving?" I start walking toward the other end of the house where the garage is.

"Somewhat," he responds, following. "You readjust from expecting life to be slow. Learn it's okay when it is, too. Can't always control what happens tomorrow."

"There's so many precautions in place, I doubt y'all could be surprised."

He comes up beside me. "We have them in place *because* we don't know what the next day brings. Events can escalate quickly, within moments, and we've seen them in a manner that could make rockets appear slow. We do this, knowing we can be surprised, but will have more than one solution to have an outcome we desire."

"So…just controlling the outcome no matter what? Very Leo."

"If I hadn't known he was never in the military, I'd have guessed he was. A few military outfits could take notes from him. He was trained well." From the tone of his voice, I have a guess of who it was that trained Leo. "He's good at it; over the years he's learned even those you trust can fall through. Given his large *empire*, you need multiple avenues to control situations. Apart from his abilities to achieve what he wants through this; he understands there's one thing he can't control."

We come around the garage and look up at the windows of the bedrooms where the Crew live. There are rooms for each, apart from Jameson, Rudy, and Owen who live in the main part of the estate upstairs. Isaac leads me toward the graveled driveway.

"Please, don't say me."

He chuckles shaking his head. "No, Miss Autumn. It's humans in general. Each has their prerogative and objective. We've all learned that lesson harshly."

"Tell me about it," I mutter as Isaac opens the garage.

"It doesn't mean he won't try. He has an uncanny ability to end up on top still." We head into the garage, where tools lie on the ground near the far side, and there's a couple of motorcycles without some of their shiny tubes and a wheel is off one. Oil splotches are underneath, along with towels flung to the side.

My hand trails over the handlebars of a chopper. "Hey, Isaac?"
"Yes?"

"Maybe not today, could be another house to explore, but since I'm sure we're gonna be stuck here for a bit, could you or one of the Crew explain the bikes to me?"

He raises a brow, folding his arms over his chest. "Are you that interested in them?"

"Grew up watching bikers at this bar I'd sneak into. They always looked cool, and the times I've ridden with Leo were fun. Why not learn a new hobby?" And anything to get my mind off the fact I don't have my movies. Or books. A smile comes over my face at another idea. "And could we not tell Leo?"

"You want to surprise him?"

"I need to get *one* surprise on him." Isaac raises his brow. "Past week doesn't count. Besides, he loves this, and I saw how much by riding with him. Given everything he's done for me, I can return the favor in sharing a passion."

Isaac's lips purse, looking down at the ground. "He's not doing this as a favor. He's doing it because he—"

"I know, Isaac." My interruption causes him to go still. "I can still show appreciation in my own way. I want to learn about bikes and riding, too. Could become the next *Forgotten Demon* and get a road name." We both chuckle. "Ever gonna tell me how you got your road name?"

He snorts, rolling his eyes. "The Crew thinks they're funny."

"Oh?"

Isaac sighs, running his hand through his short hair. "Used to be London Maniac in my old MC, and then with this Crew I became Bond, cause of the whole military intelligence thing and Animal swore I was MI6."

"Were you?" He gives me a half-smile. "You know what, I don't wanna know."

"It's also because I do kind of resemble Daniel Craig."

Ha, so not just me then. "Why the Pretty Boy add on?"

"Cause I'm the *prettiest* out of the group." I let out a sharp laugh. His unimpressed voice cinched it, along with the boredom across his face. "If you could refrain from…"

"Don't worry, your regular name is just fine with me."

"Or just call me Bond." He smirks, glancing over the long line of motorcycles. "You'll need to learn how to ride, too."

"By myself?"

"We've got bikes you can start with, less torque that won't throw you off," he teases. "Best way to learn is to just ride, know how they handle and what their quirks are. We've got a few more weeks before it gets too cold. We'll ride anytime, but not great for newbies."

"You're serious? You'll teach me how to ride?" My face lights up at the idea. Get out and feel the wind.

"Chesty or Animal would be best to teach you, along with Ringer. I'll talk to them. They'll be on board to surprise Leo, too."

"Yes!" I almost start hopping in joy. A vision comes over my mind of being on my own, riding freely next to Leo and the Crew. If he's going to be busy with work, I can come outside and practice with the others. Could surprise Leo before we head back to the city of what I learn or later down the road. I'll finally be able to keep my hands busy again.

"How long does it take to learn?"

"Depends. How long did it take for you to drive?"

I bite my lip as I avert my gaze. It's been a while since anyone has asked me about driving. Isaac makes a noise, and I watch as recognition comes over his face. He asks quietly, "You don't know how to drive?"

"Almost 29 years and never been behind a wheel."

"I understand with living in the city, but…" he looks out as an SUV comes into the drive, "…you grew up in a smaller town. Not somewhere like New York or L.A."

"There were buses, bicycles, and…overbearing parents who only drove." Another vehicle joins the first. "My trauma comes in layers like parfait. Or an onion."

Isaac's jaw tightens as the vehicles park near the main entrance. He places a hand on my shoulder, leading me toward the entry within the garage. "Well, perhaps we can break that streak of yours."

My stomach clenches, not liking Isaac's changed demeanor. "Thanks, and I do know how vehicles work and such, just never got a license or fully learned. Don't tell Leo, just yet, pretty sure he thinks I can."

He pushes the door open for me, pressing on a smile. "We'll keep it a secret. For now."

"Never know when I may be part of a car chase, huh? If that happens, can I pick the car?" I try to joke as we walk through the small hallway.

"Not sure if this is a subject we should laugh about," he warns. "Given it's not far from happening in reality."

"All the more reason to laugh, so I don't scream."

"Why are we screaming, and why was I not invited?" Animal asks as we come into the foyer, moving toward the back hallway.

"I'll send you a reminder. It'll be in the vineyards, but it's BYOB," I reply promptly.

Animal chuckles. "One tour of this place and already know the best screaming spots?"

"Specialty. Along with knocking out guards." I peek over at Isaac, who doesn't seem as amused. I giggle at his serious expression, while Animal grins.

The front door opens, and Isaac ushers me down the right hallway. Animal stays where we were, and I hear more footsteps and doors open. I glance over my shoulder, noticing a gathering of people. There are men who wear dark suits. At the front of the group is a taller woman with a pixie cut of dark hair and lighter skin with a golden undertone. She wears a button-up, tight around her broad shoulders and chest. The woman captures my attention with her no bullshit stance.

"Let's go over this area next." Isaac takes us further down, leaving all of them out of sight.

"We already have."

We've been through the entire estate, except where all those people were beginning to gather. I've been down this way knowing it leads to a study, small movie theatre, bathroom, and a stairwell that connects to the upstairs.

"Could just test you—"

"Isaac, what's going on?" I wondered of being like Belle, investigating the place, except now I'm feeling like another part of the story. "If I'm not supposed to be in that area, fine, but tell me. Or at least who those people are."

"Nothing for you to worry about."

"Really trying that?" I halt, causing him to jolt to a stop just outside the study. "Just tell me."

His jaw muscles tighten while his blue gaze narrows. I wait for a proper answer, unmoving from my spot. He breaks the eye contact, then looks back to where the voices emanate from. That sinking feeling comes back, stronger than before.

"Are they mafia?" I ask in a low voice.

"Yes."

My heart rate kicks up and my hand begins to shake. The fear and terror pushed to the far reaches of my mind creep back slowly, climbing up my spine.

It'll only be a few months. Bringing you back—

"Miss Autumn, they work for Leo. No one knows the exact location of this place, unless they have explicit security clearance," he quickly explains. "Those who do, will not *dare* come without invitation. Precautions, remember?"

"Then who are they?"

"Leo will determine when it's time for you to know or meet them." Yeah, really not liking this change of behavior.

"He give you orders?"

"Yes."

I watch him, waiting for anything more. His gaze keeps flicking from the foyer down to my shaking hand. "Will you tell me what they are?"

"No." The answer is swifter than the others. "What you need to know is that you're safe here. All those you've already met are who you need to know. Apart from an occasional housekeeper or groundskeeper, don't mingle with anyone else. Do you understand?"

"Stay away from the guards. Keep your head—"

I swallow hard as an ache in my chest blossoms. Panic starts to form, twisting its way through me. The look in Isaac's eyes tell me to listen. I blink harshly, uncertainty flicking through my veins.

He says my name, and I shake my head, gripping at my hair. The cuts pulse, pinching under the bandages, making me want to rip at them.

Not the same. Not the same. The words are repeated in my head, except I'm slowly losing the battle. Fear of history repeating roaring in my head.

"Talk to no one unless it's a biker, got it. *Leo* approved." My tone is surly, filled with venom.

"That's not what I meant."

"Isn't it?" I glare at the floor, hands clenching.

The voices disappear down the opposite hall. Wish the ones in my head would shut up, too. "You *are* safe here. The only people he trusts with you is the *Forgotten Demons*. He's being careful. We can stay in the study until they're gone or I'm sure we can find a movie—"

"They're not *mine*," I blurt, beginning to rub at my chest. The walls are closing in. "Just hide whenever someone comes? Don't go outside unless told? *Always* have an escort? I don't like being alone, but damn...y'all take it to another level."

Isaac takes a small step back, eyes going wide at my own change of behavior.

I didn't mind him being my shadow in the city, I still had space. Here it was beginning to stifle me. That was the feeling creeping up from the depths. Being watched. It felt like the freedom I'd gained was slipping away, having to ask permission and kept in certain areas. Panic rises at the idea that I'm being punished warps my mind, telling me I'm being an insolent child. My hand rubs harder against my chest. It's like I'm breathing in through a small tube, not enough oxygen.

Suddenly the walls of the hall look like Roger's living room. I smell the burnt, fucking coffee and the cheap liquor. I smell the musty shower and hear the water drip from the faucet. My heart pounds as fears from three days ago bubble to the surface.

Had I gone from one cage to another? Had I been wrong? *"His type always—"*

A headache pushes at my skull. My breathing becomes more erratic as Isaac tries to speak to me. I push him away, stumbling back as I try to decipher the past from the present.

"I won't lose my freedom again," I rasp, trying not to dig my nails into my chest. "I can't...I can't—"

"That's not happening," he tries to reassure. "You still have—"

"Not if I'm being followed all the time! Told where or who to speak to!" I yell, feet tripping backward and my back slams against the wall. A choked gasp comes out of me as I keel to the floor, falling to my knees. I clutch myself, swearing, "Shit...shit... shit..."

"Breathe, Miss Autumn." Isaac tries to calm me, kneeling before me. "Recite your poem."

Everything closes in and the need for a knife comes throttling back. "Red," I choke out. "Red…red…"

"Fuck."

I rock, holding onto myself as footsteps rush down the hall and soon there's more. People yell in the distance, but everything is a haze as I continue to mutter the word. My hands skim over my calves where the cuts are, and I choke out a sob. No. No…

The voices come closer.

"What happened?" Leo asks in a harsh tone, and someone kneels before me.

Isaac speaks, but his voice trails off from my ears as I try to concentrate. My eyes open, finding Leo watching me with an intense gaze.

Would he lie to me? Has he this entire time, and I've fallen for the same trap? Old fears, ones I thought I'd gotten a handle on, come crashing through like a broken floodgate.

"Can you hear me?" Leo's voice pierces through the haze of swirling emotions. I nod slowly, tightening my arms around me and my vision feels a bit clearer as I continue to focus on him. "You're not a prisoner. You're free, I promise you."

I start shaking my head, closing my eyes with chin quivering as I try to believe him outright. I *should* believe him, but thoughts fight and thrash inside. *"His family—"*

"Look at me, dear Watson," Leo instructs gently. Head stopping, I slowly concentrate on him again. "Good girl." I exhale with some relief. "You are safe, my dear Watson."

Keeping my gaze with his, I nod my head. I swallow hard, loosening my arms around me and stop rocking as the fog in my head thins.

"Check in," he asks.

"Yellow."

"I swore I'd protect you, I meant it in every capacity." His voice is gentle, the tone he only ever uses for me. He brushes back a few strands of my hair, barely touching my skin. "Only love and care from me. No matter what."

"I know…" there's a strain in my voice, "…I know, but everything is screaming at me to run. Get out."

"Do you want to?"

"No…no." The thought of going on without him wounds me. Scares me. It pierces down through my heart, worsening the sick feeling inside. Flashes of the past are exchanged with him from this morning. Yesterday morning. I shudder a breath, and whisper, "I'm scared."

"I know." He moves closer, brushing a hand over my hair. "I love you, my dear, dear Watson whatever you need or want, I'll make it happen."

A coldness sweeps over my body, needing a familiar warmth. "Hold me."

Leo takes me into his arms, bringing me into his embrace to help chase away the cold in my bones. I clutch to him, burying my face into his suit jacket as his hands stroke down my back. He kisses my temple, whispering against my ear, "Only for you would I ever repeat this morning's ventures. Again. And again. Only you."

Chapter 12

The Long, Long Road from Home

Leo hands me a glass of water, touching the side of my head as he walks to the door. The downstairs study has dark paneling with built-in shelves lined with old books; there's even some small Roman statues. Two black leather couches face one another, and there's a large desk near the back of the room where a small window up high brings in sunlight. There's a wet bar on the other side, and the room smells of leather and whiskey.

It reminds me of his first-floor office at the *Italian Lily*.

It's been a few hours since my breakdown. Once I was able to compose myself, I apologized to Isaac for freaking out. He kept reassuring me it was fine, but apprehension was on his face. Don't blame him. Even I scared myself on how untethered I became in a few minutes.

Trauma thing sucks.

Leo cancelled his meetings, which frustrated Jameson to push him to finish one or two. Even Rudy and Owen weren't happy, especially since there were 'guests' here. One cold, harsh look from Leo and they shut their mouths. To appease them, he met with someone and came back quickly to me, where I've just been staring at the books with Animal and Isaac close by.

Leo opens the door, revealing Jameson and Owen. They whisper low, both with disgruntled looks on their faces. Jameson crosses his arms, shaking his head. Oh, that's gonna help the guilt inside me.

I stand, but Leo closes the door and locks it with a heavy sigh. His gaze finds mine, flicking it to the couch as a silent request to sit. I do so as he pours himself a glass of scotch.

"I'm feeling déjà vu," I murmur. "Except less wet."

"And less pepper spray."

"Right, I'm losing my touch, but the panic attacks are leveling up." He pauses, looking over his shoulder. "Sorry."

"Don't be. Your humor is coming back." Leo leans against the desk, unbuttoning his jacket and taking it off. He shaved this morning, giving him a more refined look again.

"Pretty sure the uptick of meltdowns is, too"

"Yes, but perhaps settling a few things will help mitigate them. I know I won't be able to concentrate unless we have."

"Such as?" I shift in my seat, putting the water down.

He catches the small movement, and his facial expression softens. "You did nothing wrong, but there is a long overdue discussion between us. I do not think you'll feel comfortable or safe enough until we do."

"But I do feel safer, Leo. It was just…just Isaac mentioned to stay put, keep out of sight and it brought up old shit, igniting everything."

"All the more reason to talk, so it doesn't happen again."

"It will though, you know that," I argue softly. "No matter how many precautions you take, my PTSD, the depression, and trauma will rear its ugly head. I learned how to control it mostly, but…I don't know how now. I can't pretend it never happened anymore…"

Leo walks over, sits next to me and grabs one of my hands. "I know these anxiety attacks may never go away, but it doesn't mean I can't help you find a balance. Perhaps, knowing *my* side of everything will help. Especially when I'm not around to ease those worries. And trust me, I wish I never had you out of my sight." I snort at him. "Just a little protective."

"Only a smidge," I tease.

He smiles, brushing some of my hair back. "You need the whole truth. You've given your story, it's my turn."

I reach for my water, drinking some and nod. "Green."

He takes a few sips of his scotch, placing it down on the coffee table. "Time to address the elephant in the room..." he pauses, staring at the books across from us and then fidgets with unbuttoning his shirt a little, "...although I'm not sure where to begin."

I squeeze his hand, and ask, "Why not at the kidnapping? Because something tells me that was mob related."

His brows furrow, looking at me with confusion. Realization falls over his face.

"Of course, you remembered," he says, reaching for his glass again. "Yes, it was due to a...scuffle with another mafia family. I'd been taken, held for ransom as my father took days to respond. Through their phone calls, he'd tell me to stop worrying and crying. I was five." He stares down at the glass. "I remember hearing my mother's cries in the background."

Leo stops, swirling the scotch in his glass. I remain silent, keeping my hand in his as I wait patiently. Thought my parents were awful. His father created his own subgenre of bad parenting.

"My relationship with my father was never good. When my mother died, I was eleven..." there's a drop in his voice as he grips my hand, "...and things changed, my father focused on his prodigy, Gabriel, the eldest. I was left on my own with staff or bodyguards. It became easy to befriend the bikers I told you of, my father was disappointed, but he always was or otherwise didn't care what I did. Gabriel was his successor that's all that mattered."

"So, Matteo is your half-brother?"

He nods. "Born 12 years apart, after my father remarried a younger woman. They were killed, I think, by the same mafia family who'd captured me years before. Explosives in their cars during a drive."

"Oh, how *Godfather*," I mutter. Leo huffs, taking another drink. "Sorry, continue."

He brings my hand up to kiss it, leaning back into the couch. "I was seventeen. Gabriel about to be 21, and Matteo was five. Gabriel took over as the head Mafia Don, obliterated the family who killed our father, and everything was in an uproar. Perfect time to escape. I hated leaving Matteo behind, but I couldn't bring him with me. All I could do was hope for the best that his mother's family would take care of him."

"That's a lot to go through." All before even being a legal adult.

"The hardships of my childhood haunt me from time to time, but they've lessened in the past month or so." His eyes catch mine in a tender gaze. I smile softly, kissing his hand in mine.

Leo finishes his drink, getting up and pouring another, talking as he does. "Riccardo Marchetti was my father's name. I changed mine to my grandmother's maiden name, I thought it was the best path to keep my mother's memory alive and to distance myself from his family. His side refused to acknowledge my mother's lineage, her connections…who she really was."

"You've never told me her name."

Leo pauses, his back still turned to me. "Giovanna Maria Luciano." He takes a moment, clears his throat and comes back to sit down. "Everyone called her Gigi. My parents' marriage was arranged. Details as to why are scarce, most likely money, but her family hated my father."

"I'm not the only one who used an old family name, huh?"

He snorts, shaking his head as he leans back. "You know what happened next. I met Jameson, built the hotel franchise, and so forth. I used the tools and skills I learned from watching my father. Although some things he did I couldn't quite do, wanting to keep some honor, but then my past caught up with me."

He suddenly stands again, pacing next to the desk as he sips his scotch. Oh, a great sign. Not.

I steel myself for the part I'm not quite sure I'll ever be ready to hear. "What happened, Leo?"

He stops before the desk. "You were told about the blackmailing?" I nod. "Gabriel fucked up. Broke a major rule; don't use your own product. He became addicted to the drugs he was selling. Every business under my father's name was going under into bankruptcy and being sold off as collateral to other crime families. Gabriel was losing his social standing, money, connections, and the feds were on his heels. The other families could've tried to take him down, but him being high all the time, made it easier for their control."

"Skim money off him, and then have him take the fall when there's nothing left."

"Basically. Corrupt bosses are easier to manipulate. Fake what you want because you need the product they're using. They'll do anything to have more of it." Leo's brows furrow, staring down at the glass in his hand. "Matteo was barely in his teens when Gabriel attempted to blackmail me. Swore he'd make Matteo take the fall."

"Did you stay in contact with Matteo?"

"Scarcely and secretly. I'd find ways to check on him. He's my half-brother, but with my father's blood, he has some claim to the family business and to be the next head. Potential rival to Gabriel. I knew Matteo had a clean record, ignoring the initial blackmail…" Leo quiets a moment, frowning at the drink before clearing his throat, "…and then when that didn't work he put a hit on him."

I gape at Leo. "What?"

"Gabriel is stubborn and wanted money. *My* money. He knew my weak spot was our younger brother. He attempted to kill Matteo the same way our father was. Car explosion. He barely got out alive. Julio used his connections to connect the hitman were hired by Gabriel. Force my hand to come back. Revenge."

"Revenge?"

Leo's gaze becomes distant as he stares at the amber liquid in his glass. "My brother knows me, even after all these years."

I swallow hard. "He wanted you to find out."

"More likely, or I'd come back and stir shit up with the other families. I'd go after them for him." He puts his scotch down, jaw muscles flexing. "I came back to New York to warn Matteo. He didn't believe me. I offered for him to come back west with me, but he refused. He wanted to save what was left of the family business, honor our father, only believing Gabriel was an addict. Believed our brother would stop. He was a fucking teenager. Nowhere near ready to take over. So, pieces fell into place for me to."

I stare at him, and say quietly, "You came back into the mafia to protect your brother."

He nods stiffly. I sink further into the couch, some of the pressure on my shoulders disappearing. I hadn't forced his hand to stay, but someone had.

"I did what I did best; curated relationships and flipped businesses. Gained favors from every person Gabriel screwed over." His business-like tone is jolting, changing from his previous passiveness. "I worked to regain what was lost under Gabriel's nose. He almost got himself killed, along with Matteo. Someone shot up his apartment, while both were inside. Gabriel's position was questioned more, and many were ready to throw him under a fucking train, but that could've meant Matteo's demise, too. He'd be forced to be the boss at such a young age or die if another took control, I couldn't let that happen. He was too trusting, too naïve, and overly emotional. I took over without Gabriel's knowing, others didn't argue given I helped raise profits and nothing sways men more than money."

I rub my forehead, trying to get some things to make sense. What I'd known back then versus the truth. "The police swore Gabriel was still boss four to five years ago, but it was…you?"

"He was boss by name. I worked in the shadows, as it were, having meetings without him, conducting deals with other underbosses without him knowing. All behind the scenes. *Every* underboss, major crime lord, and captain saw me as their…Don Supreme. The rest on the food chain still presumed nothing had changed, including Gabriel himself who was lost in his own world of drugs. He still had his clubs and imports, people loyal to him, but I had to wait for the perfect opportunity to remove him completely."

I rub at my chest a little, fighting off the anxiety. *He* was the Mafia Don Supreme the entire time. Who the feds wanted. Not Gabriel.

"Then someone stepped into the picture," he says quietly. "Sarah Marie Mitchell did." My hands stop and I keep my gaze with his. "Although I didn't know your name at the time. I knew someone had outed people I was having trouble with. We thought it was an under-cover cop. All the trash I was trying to take out, you did in a single sweep. Some of those who weren't arrested, lost money and territo-ries, but they were afraid of losing more. *They* needed protection and I had the means to offer it. Those arrested and gone deserved it. And even the money you cost me; it wasn't something I was concerned with. My accounts weren't on those lists, but Gabriel's were."

Leo knocks back the rest of the scotch, placing it on the coffee table as he sits across from me. "Gabriel lost everything that was attached to his name, mainly the Marchetti name. He was taken out of the picture, leaving me to fully take over without a hitch. I was their saving grace. Matteo was sent to Italy, making it seem as though he'd run away to preserve the family business. He's been there ever since, under close watch by a few contacts and my uncle. Maybe, one day, he'll take over if he still wants it." He clears his throat, lounging back. "But that's my side of the story."

The room is quiet.

The information sinks in. I helped take down a good portion of the mafia, but ultimately helped Leo. Somehow all that work I'd done seemed for naught, but then I wonder how much worse it would be if Gabriel was out and still dealing. How much longer would Leo had have worked to keep Matteo safe? Would there have been another attempt on Leo's life, too? Could it be worse now without Steve being in jail? The others?

I mull over his words, realizing he left out something. My gut begins to wrench, warning pricking at my neck.

"Where's Gabriel?" My voice is soft. Leo shifts in his seat. I hear his knuckles crack as his hands clench. "Is he in prison?"

"No."

"Where is he?"

"Florida."

My breath shudders. The 'issue' he flew down for.

"After what he did, you didn't..." I can't seem to get the word 'kill' out of my mouth.

Leo sighs, shaking his head. "Matteo still loves him. Begged me to save him. I couldn't bring myself to ignore his pleads. Take away someone else from him."

There's a bit of shaking in my hands, and I clutch my thighs to make them stop. "Does Gabriel know I'm alive?"

"No." His answer is quick. "No one knows that you're alive. Or even here for that matter, apart from Nancy."

I exhale shakily. Right, I've been so caught up with shit I've forgotten to check in with her and the others. Leo adds, "Leanne and Trix know that you're safe."

I laugh emptily. "Why hide me then if people don't know who I am?"

"I won't take any chances, not until some precautions are in place and the dust has settled," Leo speaks in a harsh tone. "There's no guarantee *anyone* even knows Sarah was why the mob was almost obliterated. I won't take that chance. You've hidden well the last few years, but there's no telling if someone else will connect the dots."

"Plus, you may be the only one to forgive me," I whisper. Leo watches me as I lean back in the couch, exhaling sharply. "What *are* the chances of the mob finding out?"

"Depends how curious they get. New partners or girlfriends always peak interest as a form of control, but your backstory is quite ironclad. I'd have never known if you hadn't told me snippets of your past or mentioned Steve. Unless he or Detective Caltz decide to out you, a ploy to—"

"Roger won't. If it's revealed I never died…that opens a whole other can of worms for the feds and police. That kind of PR? Not good. Trust me. They want 'Autumn Watson' alive and well. Nothing helps by saying Sarah Marie never died, it'll jeopardize any current operations, not to mention…" a small smile pulls at my lips, knowing how much trouble I could put the police in, and maybe why Roger tried to hold onto me so tightly, "…what they allowed me to do."

Leo's brow furrows, the line on his forehead becoming deeper. My smile becomes tender, seeing it and its comforting familiarity. "How much *do* you know?"

A voice in my head tells me to be careful. Hold my cards tight. But

I didn't want to hold them. I wanted them out of my damn hands and in the open.

"Everything," I whisper. The hard lines on his face disappear. "Routes, offshore accounts, venues, people...where meets were conducted, who was in deep cover, politicians. I can tell you—"

Leo raises a hand, stopping me. "Unless someone plans to point a gun at my head or yours, I will not use you like that. I won't be like them."

"At the end of the day, Leo, you're still a mafia boss. I get it." His eyes darken. "I could help you. Give what I know about operations, protocols, how to get in—"

"No." He gets up from the seat across from me and sits next to me as he grabs my hand. "I have people whom I've had hired and paid well to do all that for me. You were an innocent victim they preyed upon for their own damn gain. I wouldn't let Gabriel use Matteo, and I will not have you be used in a similar manner. *You* are my love, who deserves far better than being a pawn in a fucking game of chess for cheaters and manipulators."

I smile faintly, stroking back some of his hair and touch his freshly shaved face. A flurry of emotions flash in his eyes. "Okay, but uh, given I *did* cause an uproar and you were technically the Mafia Don back then, how did you keep the position? I would've thought they'd turn on you, even if you *could* offer protection, they didn't blame you?"

"As I said, nothing sways men more than money." I raise a brow. "I came in already with a multi-million-dollar revenue and self-sustaining businesses. A gold rush for them. They thought they'd get a profit from it. Over the past few years money has been far more lucrative than when Gabriel was in charge."

"Wait, how would their profits get higher? Your businesses are separate."

"They don't know that."

A small giggle escapes me, and a smile tugs at his lips. "They think the money is from your hotel and real estate businesses?"

"Yes, but in reality, it's from importing goods and *other* real estate that myself and Matteo have integrated under the Marchetti name. Including conducting a few deals that allow certain operations to continue, such with my uncle in Italy."

I raise my brow. "Let me guess, Italian mafia?"

"Yes. My mother's brother." Oh, I'm not ready to touch that yet. "A good deal of profits come from those deals. Hopefully, it'll satisfy a part of the mob organism that evolves. And I'll walk away. For good."

"Really?"

"It's the plan for myself and the *Forgotten Demons*. Everything has to be handled carefully, keep everything apart, and there's a shit ton of moving parts."

"Well, I'm relieved I'm not the only one who wants to get out." I fall back against the couch. Leo moves his arm around my shoulders, tugging me against him.

Shit ton of moving parts was an understatement with the complexity of it all. It wasn't just hiding so police don't follow you, but the rest of the mafia or other past mistakes. A flickering hope does spark deep inside me. We could leave this all behind. Together.

Yet, everything can change overnight. Hell, my life ten days ago… four, even, was completely different.

"I saw your old photos." His voice breaks the silence, and I look at him. "Not just the ones you photoshopped yourself, although you even impressed Julio with those."

"Leanne knew a guy."

"There were ones with you beside…*her*. You don't really look like her anymore."

"Surgery."

"They gave you plastic surgery?"

"No, well, kind of," I start, adjusting a bit out from under his arm. "There were surgeries they *had* to do." Clearing my throat, I bring my legs up and wrap my arms around them. "My face was so battered, I needed it to just breathe properly. They basically did a, um, masculine facial reconstruction."

"Masculine?"

I nod. "Straightened my nose, gave it a higher bridge to help me breathe, cause it was crushed. My jaw was fucked up, so they realigned few things and made it more angular. And they did something with my forehead. They used skin grafts for around my eyes, which is why I have a slightly different eye and brow shape naturally. Lastly, they gave me Lasik." I clear my throat. "Roger and a few other agents thought it was best to make me look more masculine, so I'd be less...pretty."

I peek over at Leo, who has a dark look in his eyes. "Bullshit."

I shrug. "At the time, I didn't want anyone near me. So, I agreed."

His rage radiates from him, jaw tensing as his hand clenches. Well, at least they didn't make me pay for it. Or my funeral.

"Kept my hair short and dyed it. It rarely grows in blonde anymore; think I grew out of it."

"You changed everything."

"It was that or be sent somewhere else. Even, like you said, no guarantee I'd be recognized, but I couldn't leave Nan or Leanne. I was a wreck. Not a chance was I going to survive without them. And only they cared that Sarah died. No one else came to the funeral."

"Your family never came?" I shake my head, swallowing past the sob in my throat.

I still remember Leanne's face as the phone dropped from her hands. My mother had told her good riddance. Pretty sure the tears in her eyes at my "funeral" were from the pain she'd seen in mine.

The first months were awful, and the pain felt never-ending. If it wasn't physical from all the damn surgeries, it was mental or emotional. I was in and out of precincts at late hours to keep from being caught, hospital rooms, and de-briefed so many damn times I lost count.

"I promise you'll see and speak with Nancy and Leanne soon," Leo says.

"I know."

"What can I do to make this easier for you?" He asks, and I sigh as his eyes search mine. "Whatever else you want to know, I'll tell you."

"Leo, this can't just... just always be about me. I know I cry a lot, especially lately, but you need reassurance as well. We've both gone through hell the past five or so years."

"All I had to do was change my damn name. Most states. I had Jameson and the Crew, and money and power to fall back on."

"Leo."

"I will do *anything* to protect you. Even if word gets out about your past, I can't guarantee I'll stop the onslaught that will come, but I will protect you. My methods can be controlling and unorthodox at times, but please tell me what I can—"

I grab his face, making him stop. "I know you meant it, every bit of it, I know. From time to time, I struggle to remember what's real or not. That's something I need to work on, not you. You have done nothing wrong." His face falls. "I trust you, really I do, and I hold onto that trust when my mind feels like it's slipping. And remember that…that I need you."

His lips crash against mine. I let go, reaching around his neck. His hand snakes up to the nape of mine, keeping my mouth against his. I breathe in deep, inhaling his scent as a moan leaves me. The kiss is almost bruising and exhilarating as the core of me ignites.

Leo breaks away, putting his forehead against mine. "You have broken through every single one of my defenses, my dear Watson. No one else has looked at me like I'm the light in their darkness. I never want the hole in my heart you've filled to be empty again, and I will do all I can to ensure that burning light inside you doesn't die. You are the most precious, wonderful, beautiful woman I've ever met. Not even the demons of hell will keep me from loving you."

I'm frozen at his proclamation.

There's a heavy look on his face, lines across his forehead that trace over his brows. Eyes flecked with gold peer into mine.

This man before me with a multitude of layers. All that people seem to overlook, finding only the strict and controlling boss. They only see the mobster from the destructive family and his cold demeanor. He is willing to be the monster to protect who he cares about most, including me. All the words of warning I'd gotten from others evaporate. The fears of the past and repeated hurt. When I see his face, it's easier to remind myself and hold onto the truth I know.

I reach up, touching the hand that presses against the nape of my neck.

These hands will never harm me. *Ever.*

His promise from weeks ago is what I will hold onto whenever the voices get too loud. When I get lost in memories and pain. Although he's screwed up, there's one promise I know he will never break. And it's the single most important one to me.

"… where there was pain, there will be pleasure; where there was fear, there will be comfort. I promise you everything that I have, your body will never be harmed by my hands, only protected."

I climb onto his lap, straddling him as I cup his face and I stare into his eyes. "Mafia boss. Biker. Hotel mogul. Businessman. Dom. Whatever title you're given, I don't care. Who I care about is the man I see before me, who loves and cherishes me, who makes me want to be alive." A glimmer passes his gaze. "I'm not scared of you. I trust you with everything, and *that* is what keeps me from screaming into the void because I know you're right there holding my hand. Fighting for me."

His breathing becomes ragged. Eyes flicking to my lips. Gently, I kiss him as he inhales harshly against the tender touch. My fingers thread through his hair. I revel in the beauty of him, staying in this moment, before I pull away and tell him, "Promise me you'll protect yourself, too. Cause if you do all this for me, and if I fucking lose you, I'm gonna find you in the afterlife and make you watch *Reefer Madness* endlessly." He chokes out a laugh. "You are mine and I love you. I'll follow you."

The hand against the nape of my neck squeezes slightly, while his other skims down my side. A shiver runs through my body as I close my eyes at the affectionate touch. A burning begins to blossom, heat trailing from his skin. He takes one of my hands, kissing every knuckle.

His eyes smolder, meshing with greens, golds, and light browns. He speaks with a low, deep tone, "You'll be given a schedule every morning, it'll detail who will be here, and then *you* may decide where you want to be. If outside, someone will be with you. If inside, you can choose to be alone. You'll be informed of where I am at all times." He kisses my neck and my breath hitches. "You'll have more decisions without being controlled, while I know where you are and are safe. Do you agree?"

Leo's hot breath falls over my skin, causing shudders throughout my body. I hum as he kisses my neck again, his fingers trailing down my spine. "Yes, Leo, yes."

"We'll rediscuss when we go back to the city. Understood?"

"Yes," I say breathlessly. I swallow hard as his breath sweeps over me. My skin tightens, anticipation of the blissful feelings that could follow. The need in my core deepening and wanting him. "Please…"

"Please, what?" He murmurs against my ear, tongue tracing the edge. "Or do I need to reteach you how to tell me what you want?"

I mean, our first lesson was kinda fun.

Fingers drift back up my spine, sparking my heart rate to pick up as he kisses down my neck. My chest rises heavily, clutching his shoulders as he drives my body insane. I cling to the pleasure and desire building. As his other hand moves up my thigh to my waist, a whimper escapes me.

"Fuck me," I moan. "Leo, please fuck me."

"Good girl." A shiver travels down my spine, ease washing over my bones. He kisses the underside of my jaw, and places another above my clavicle. "We'll go nice and slow."

I groan at the idea of being on the brink. It already feels like it's been years since I've had him this close to me, inside me. Just us. A wicked chuckle rumbles in his chest. He agonizingly, slowly starts to raise my shirt. "You're still vulnerable, my dear Watson. And responsible Leo has reached his limit." He brushes his nose against mine. "We both seem a little too impatient and in need. So, we'll take this slow."

Leo whips my shirt off, while I unbutton his all the way and tug it off, then his undershirt. I'm met with his tattooed torso—dark lines of ink in all their glory. I trace the designs, over the fires and vines and skulls. I'm entranced with the colors and lines once again, barely noticing him taking my bra off.

"Check in."

"Green." My eyes snap to his.

"Good girl," he murmurs, tracing his fingers down my breasts.

"I've missed that." I close my eyes, skin tingling in the gentle caress over my body. His hands move over my breasts, and I moan as he massages them, rubbing his thumbs over my nipples.

I gasp, breath catching as he fondles me. One hand remains there as the other slides down, then around to my ass. He grips me through the leggings, mouth enclosing over the breast he left at the same time. Leo moans as he sucks, tongue circling and causing my nipples to stiffen. I press further against his mouth in an attempt to gain more of the wet heat of his lips. Suddenly, he pulls away and I whimper at the loss of contact.

"And how I've missed you," he murmurs. He kisses me fervently like a man needing water.

He wraps an arm around my waist, while the other stays underneath my butt, lifting me up against him as he stands. I cling to him tightly, feeling the heat of his skin against mine. It's almost scorching as I grip my legs around his waist. The desk hits my butt as he puts me down, moving his hands down to pull off my shoes and starts peeling my leggings off. I help him, kicking them off along with my underwear.

Leo pauses, lifting each of my legs to check my bandages before he goes any further. A small smile pulls at my lips. A bit of the shame being chipped away. He kneels before the desk I'm sitting on, pushing open my legs to kiss the inside of each knee. His fingers trail over the bandages, checking them and kisses my thighs. My breath hitches, clutching the desk as I lean back, trying to keep my balance.

Rising to his feet, his eyes roam over my body unhurriedly until he meets my gaze. One hand holds my knee, pushing it further to open my legs. A harsh swallow moves down my throat, arms shaking at being so open and vulnerable in front of him. The shame that's been chipped away trickles back, aware of scars and marks on my skin. Not just the new ones.

"Check in." He stops, flashing his eyes to my trembling arms.

I pause a moment, before answering, "Green."

"Autumn…" he warns gently, stroking his hand up my thigh, "…tell me the truth."

My breath shakes a little, reminding myself to be truthful. He won't be mad. "Yellow."

"Good girl." Some of the stiffness in my spine relaxes. "Do you not like this position?"

I look down at how open and naked I am before him. Frowning at the scars and lines that cover me. Something about being fully nude, while he still has slacks on feels very…I'm not sure. I don't think I'm scared, but unsure. Leo towers over me, his head tilting a little in question.

"It's very, um, revealing."

"How did I describe you?"

I blink up at him. He nods for me to speak, moving closer as he slides his hand up my thigh, thumb caressing my skin. "Uh, precious…" I start slow, the words feeling heavy, "…wonderful. Beautiful."

He steps between my legs. "How would you describe me?"

A giggle comes out abruptly, and he smiles gently. I place a hand on his chest, my breathing slows as he takes a sharp intake of breath. My fingers trace the harrowing designs, finding the beauty in them. My eyes flash to the scars on my body, and I smile faintly to myself. "Precious. Wonderful. Beautiful."

Leo leans in close, kissing my forehead, which makes me sigh.

"Check in," he asks.

I place a kiss over his heart. "Green."

"Place your arms around my neck." I do as he instructs.

He keeps a hand on my thigh, while the other moves toward the apex of my thighs. He slips a finger through the folds of my sex, lightly and teasingly. He strokes ever so fucking slowly and my breath quickens. It feels like forever before he pushes his finger inside me, thrusting carefully. Another finger is added to the first, and his thumb circles my clit.

My arms tighten, holding myself up as he continues the slow movement. He grips my thigh, holding me in place as my legs start to shake and try to squeeze harder from the sensual torture. The heat deep inside my core builds, grasping for the release that already seems to have me on the brink. Muscles convulse within, gripping at him as I concentrate on keeping my arms in place. The tightening coil spreads up through my spine and travels down my muscles. I try to push my hips closer needing more.

"Leo," I whimper, feeling the crest of an orgasm. "Please."

"Almost there, sweetheart." He kisses my neck. His fingers hook, pressing upward as his thumb circles upward and harder. A shout catches in my throat, gasping for air. All my muscles begin to tighten now, feeling it up my spine as my toes curl. Leo dips his head, and orders quietly, "Come for me."

An explosion of tension releases. I let out a soft shout, gripping him as air catches in my lungs. He strokes slowly, caressing his thumb lightly over my clit as pleasure trickles up from my lower back as my legs involuntarily squeeze around him. I shiver as the climax runs its course. He puts his arm around me, helping me sit up as he pulls his fingers out.

"Good girl," he whispers, massaging at my lower back. I close my eyes humming, moving my arms down around his waist.

"Already done?" He asks.

"No." I sit up quickly, wide awake. He chuckles and then looks down at his hand. Silently, he brings his hand up, putting his fingers in his mouth to clean them. My heartbeat kicks up. Core tightening all over again and ready for round two.

Noted. That's hot.

Leo steps back to take his shoes and slacks off, moving around the desk. He opens a drawer as he drops his boxers, erect cock springing free. He pulls out a condom.

I grip into the desk.

Fuck, I didn't tell him. I had the perfect opportunity with the surgeries and didn't tell him. Now does not feel like the time. I swallow hard, trying to keep an enthusiastic expression and focus on the present.

Leo rolls the condom on, coming back over and pauses. He raises a brow. "Check in."

Quit noticing my tells! Crud muffins!

"Green." He gives me a look, and I reach for him. "Just nervous."

"You're safe," he says, and he comes close to clutch my face. He kisses me deeply. I taste me on his lips, tracing my tongue over his bottom lip. I let the pleasure override the worry, making it go back into the far reaches of my mind as I caress my hands over his chest.

Breath catching, he moves his hand down where it was before, notching his dick at my entrance. Steadily, he pushes his cock inside. I grip his arm that holds me. His cock stretching me as he works his way in at an easy pace. He pulls back and then completely thrusts in, filling me as he comes to the hilt. I break the long kiss, gasping.

"Check in."

"Green."

"Lay back." My eyes fly up to him, then glance at the hardwood behind me. He kisses the side of my mouth. "Trust me, dear Watson."

My chest squeezes and I inhale sharply. I begin to lean back, fearful of what will happen when my back touches the hard surface, but I never reach it. A strong arm crosses behind my back, holding me up enough to keep from touching the wood completely. Leo uses his other to pull me until my ass hangs off the edge a little.

He demonstrates this new position with a small pull out, and then swiftly thrusts back in, causing us both to moan loud.

Bracing himself against the desk, he moves his hips and begins to pump inside me. I gasp as his cock goes deep, hitting my inner walls with a vibrating force. I cling to his shoulders, flinging my head back as I moan. Each thrust causes sparks to fly up my spine, clenching to him as my legs spring up and wrap around his torso. The angle changes, and he grunts against my skin. The heat feels like it's going to burst again, sweat forms on my body, and it drips down his brow.

Suddenly, Leo lifts me up against him, standing fully. He pulls out of me, and I make a sound of protest as he puts me on my feet. He turns me around, placing my hands on the desk and spreads my legs. My heart thunders as he trails a hand down my side and around my hips, running it under my ass cheeks.

"Check in." His voice is hoarse.

"Green," I gasp.

My hips are slammed against his as he enters me. I whimper and moan, gripping the desk as he does it again and again. I struggle for air as he continues the pounding force, an arm snaking around my waist to reach up and clutch one of my breasts. My legs shake as he rubs at my nipple, thrusting into me. A warmth develops over my back as his chest meets my skin, engulfing me with the sticky heat. He clutches me, driving forward as the tingling sensation over-whelms my body enough for it to shake. My muscles strain, trying to stay standing as my head becomes fuzzy. Each breath I heave, strug-gling to catch my breath in the best way.

The desk becomes slippery, and I hold onto it the best I can. His other hand comes around, pressing his thumb against my clit and circles it as his cock fills me.

"Leo!" I'm near the brink, sensations washing over me with ecstasy.

He kisses my shoulder. "Come for me."

I scream as he thrusts once more, pressing his thumb up. My orgasm explodes through my body, every muscle locking as I clench the wood. Leo grunts behind me, holding onto me as he comes and buries himself inside me. Breathing heavily, he presses his face against my neck, laying kisses along my skin. "My dear Watson."

He stands us up, keeping my back against his sweaty chest. He caresses my skin, moving his hand against my neck to place a gentle hold. I reach up, grabbing the back of his head while I clutch the arm around my waist. I'm completely engulfed by him. Just him and I. Quiet bliss. "Yours. All yours."

Chapter 13

Morning Rides

My eyes snap open.

I jolt forward with erratic breaths and stare out into the darkness of the bedroom. Gulping against my dry throat, I clutch at my chest and throat. An ache runs over my body, tensing like it's tired from a run. Pushing my hair back and shaking off the sudden heightened nerves, I look over at Leo. He sleeps on his side, body rising with each long breath.

Carefully, I step out of bed and head to the bathroom to splash water on my face. Chest feeling less constricted, I turn off the sink and wipe my face. Scratching at my head, I walk back out to the bedroom and suddenly I feel sick to my stomach. I stop to stare at Leo in the bed.

Broken. Worthless.

"Stop it," I whisper.

My arms wrap around myself as I look around the room. There's no way I'll be able to sleep. I'll spend the next few hours staring at the ceiling, and the feelings creeping up my spine will get worse. Once again, I debate exploring the house as I had the morning before, but I knew where everything was already.

My gaze flicks to Leo.

I can't disappear again.

I begin to pace, rubbing my arms as my breathing picks up again. I wish I had my movies. My books. Fucking anything that used to help these long nights. There was the movie theater downstairs, but I have no idea how to work it and…and it's not *my* movies. Nerves kick up, anxiety pricking at the back of my neck as my stomach clenches and hands feel itchy.

"Crud muffins," I mutter, rubbing my head as I continue to pace. My gaze keeps flashing to Leo sleeping, wondering whether to wake him up, but then the guilt builds. It evolves from the root of why I woke up. The self-repulsion, self-hate, and brokenness turn into this thing that chokes me.

I should've told him. I should've *fucking* told him.

What if he thinks I trapped him? Will he hate me? Will he think I'm broken, too? I said I'd told him everything, and I lied. What if it's a dealbreaker? No, wait, there is no leaving is there? Or what if—?

Get out.

I stop, holding my head with fingernails digging into my scalp. A quiet, whimpered groan leaves me as I go to my knees. As I settle down against my legs, I feel the cuts and wince. Breath shaky, I bring my legs out from under me and run my hands over the bandages. My body rocks as I attempt to regain control, clutching at my knees to keep from scratching at the healing wounds.

"I want you to never cut yourself again."

Stomach plummeting and twisting, I begin reciting *The Raven* under my breath. I grip tightly as I rock, going through every stanza quietly. It seems forever before I get to the end, tripping over words. Once I complete it, I keep repeating: "Nevermore… nevermore…nevermore…"

"Autumn?" My head snaps up. Leo eases himself up, looking towards where I should be sleeping.

"I can't get pregnant," I blurt out, surprising myself. Leo snaps his attention to me. My voice trembles, even as relief fills me to say it again. "I can't get pregnant."

Leo gets out of bed, soon in front of me kneeling and grabbing my hands to stop me from scratching against the bandages. When did I start that? They begin to shake violently as I squint against the darkness to look at his face better. One of his hands cups the side of my face.

"I'm sorry, I'm sorry…I should've told you, I wanted to—"

"It's okay." He kisses my hands, keeping them against his lips. "You're okay."

"Don't leave me," I whisper, clutching him as he goes still.

His hand against my cheek tightens just before he kisses the middle of my forehead. "Deep breath, dear Watson. Breathe."

I do as he says, taking in a large gulp of oxygen. I do it again as he does it with me, murmuring pieces of *The Raven*. After some time, I calm and the shaking stops. The voices in my head quiet as I concentrate on him.

"Good girl," he murmurs, stroking my hair back. The pressure on my shoulders loosens, and my body slumps slightly. "I'm not leaving you."

"I know, I swear I know, but the voices…crud muffins, it felt like I was slipping again. And I felt guilty lying to you. You'd hate me."

"You hadn't lied." I search for his eyes in the darkness. "I never asked if you could." I nod, and he kisses my hand again. "Will you be able to sleep?"

"No, that's why I wasn't in bed. Go, um, go back to sleep. I'll distract myself with something."

Leo turns toward the patio doors, where a hint of dawn begins to show. "I've a better idea." He pulls me up to stand with him. "Although it's not fuzzy socks."

A blue haze covers the landscape of the early morning. Thin clouds spread throughout the horizon, creating not a glow, but a smoky look. The breeze whips past us, and I cling closer to Leo's leather clad back. Even in my jacket and chaps on, it's still chilly enough I almost shiver. We ride his heritage classic bike again, the engine rumbling underneath us as he takes a curve. I concentrate on the vibrations of the cylinders, keeping my head against his back to watch the trees whip past.

No voices in my head. No screaming. No shadows.

Just the land, motorcycle, and Leo. Thank fuck. It's the calmest I've felt since the last time we went riding.

Leo takes us around another turn, and then begins to slow down as we approach a scenic overlook. He parks the bike near one end of the parking lot and cuts off the engine. I hear the other motorcycle behind us rumble and then shut off next. I glance back at Rudy with his large bike, who's been following us since we left the estate. A big, burly shadow for our morning ride.

We get off the bike, and Leo takes both our helmets to set down. The blue morning catches my attention, and I gaze at the changing trees of fall. Leo wraps his arms around me, leaning me against his chest as I shiver a little from the breeze.

"Didn't think it'd be this chilly," he says.

"It's fine, more reason to snuggle." I wiggle against him, and he flexes his arms gently. "Pretty good way to wake up." Much better than puking.

"Used to ride in the mornings out in California, before it got too hot."

"Yeah, leather doesn't seem like it'd be fun to wear in the heat."

"Not especially," he muses.

I glance over at Rudy, who sits back on his bike looking all scary bodyguard like. He was already up and volunteered to go riding with us, and Leo didn't want us to go riding alone. It was that or waking up Animal or Chesty, which Rudy suggested wasn't the smartest idea since they were grumpy men in the morning.

"Feel better?" Leo asks.

I exhale a long breath. "I keep hoping I've got control again, and then it just…finds the cracks. Seems like I can't stop it. I swear I'll wake up like a normal person at some point or another."

"You're relearning how to be in a world that hurt you, Autumn. Not to mention the new environments and people. A heavy past that's made it hard to perceive what's real or not won't make it easy."

"Is that how it felt when you came back?"

"Me being a control freak and acting paranoid wasn't your first clue?" He muses when I snort slightly. "I get it. It's why I can't give up the riding. The bikes. Only thing that felt real."

"Felt? Past tense?"

He kisses behind my ear. "Then you came into my life."

I let out a choked laugh, knowing he's being serious. The sun peeks over the hills, streaking its rays through the thin clouds. The pit in my stomach hardens. I've got to tell him the rest. I clutch his arms a bit tightly. "Why I can't, it's because of the assault."

Leo's body tenses, hardening around me as if he's a snake ready to strike.

"There was so much damage that, uh, it was causing internal bleeding," I explain quietly. "I don't remember much of the conversations with the doctors, I was drugged and in pain. But, Roger kept telling them I needed to stay alive. And, I guess, the conclusion was basically a hysterectomy and stitch me back up, but I never got a real say." His hand strokes over my arm in a tender manner. "Never thought of having kids, but suddenly I didn't have the choice anymore. But that's it. You know everything now."

His face presses to the side of my head, murmuring, "I'm sorry, Autumn."

"I didn't think it'd bother me, until someone said I was worthless and broken. I taught myself to shut up. Already felt broken, and it just, dug that well deeper. Torn between knowing it wasn't true and believing them."

"Is that why you were worried about telling me?"

"A little, but mostly…that I couldn't give you that if you wanted it. And I guess, when I realized who you really were it'd be something important for you to have." Leo pulls back, causing me to look up to see his furrowed brow. "Maybe I've watched too many mafia movies, but heirs are usually a big thing."

A humming sound comes from his throat. He lifts a hand,

catching a few strands of my hair that's fluttered in the wind. Concentration flits over his face as he brushes them back.

"Not for me," he says softly, and my face falls listening to the quietness in his voice. "I could never bring a child into this world, knowing what it could do to them. Too many shadows from my father. Dangers from my own family. I've barely kept my younger brother alive; I'd be a fucked-up father like mine."

"Bullshit." I turn to face him.

The line above his brow disappears. Eyes becoming gentle. He kisses me tenderly, cradling my face with such gentleness I could cry.

"All I need is you, dear Watson," he speaks against my lips. "But if it is something you ever want, then we will figure it out together."

I nod in response, then wrap my arms around his neck and kiss him again. As a cold breeze passes through, another shiver rattles my body. Leo holds me close, providing the warmth I need as I clutch him. I lean my head against his chest, watching the blue smokey sunrise. All I hear is the sound of his heart underneath the leather jacket, the rustling leaves, and morning calls of birds.

"You're not broken." A faint smile comes over my face.

"We should head back. Get some breakfast."

"Feeling omelets today?" I ask, stepping back with the same smile.

"Perhaps." He starts to turn away, but not before signaling something to Rudy. "I'll be right back."

"Showing off the bathroom skills again, huh?" I say deadpan, and he chuckles before heading toward the line of trees. Must be nice.

I look over at Rudy, who's watching me diligently. Flicking my gaze to the ground, I notice some dandelions that have made it this far into the season and pluck a couple. It may seem a bit childish, but it's all I got currently. I walk over to Rudy, who raises his brows as I approach.

"Thanks for the shadowing," I tell him, holding out the dandelions. "I don't have jackshit right now that's mine, but here. And apologies again for the whole train station thing."

"Would've done the same, *bärchen.*"

"Yeah, but pretty sure I made you look bad."

"Did that to all of us."

"Touché," I smirk, keeping the dandelions out.

Small lines form at the edge of his eyes as he smiles, taking the yellow weeds and putting them carefully into his saddlebag. "Pretty Boy Bond mentioned you wanting to learn about motorcycles."

"Yeah." My face lightens. "You wanna help teach me?"

"Better than spending all hours with the other numb-nuts." I giggle at him, and his smile broadens.

"Okay, but you can't tell Leo." Rudy winks at me. I look at the bike behind him. "Can I ask a favor?" He inclines his head. "Can I ride back with you?"

He looks over at Leo's bike, and then back to me. "Long as he's alright with it."

I turn just as Leo comes out the tree line, and I meet him back at his motorcycle, grabbing my helmet. "Alright if I ride with Rudy back to the estate?"

Leo pauses, full-on furrowed brow. "One condition."

"Oh?"

"You ride with me again tomorrow morning."

"You drive a hard bargain." I kiss him quickly. "But okay, mister." I pull my helmet on, practically sprinting back to Rudy. The giant ex-wrestler gets onto his bike, helping me on behind him. He has a back-rest on his that I can scoot up against, while only getting a very small portion of his body between my arms.

Leo's engine starts, rumbling before it gets drowned out by Rudy's. The motorcycle vibrates through my body, and I adjust a little to get a better grip around Rudy.

"You can let go, long as you're secure against the backseat. Keep legs in," Rudy calls back as we start to pull off.

We ride onto the road before Leo. Rudy's bike makes more noise, thundering through the countryside as we start to wind back on the country roads. After a few minutes, I loosen my hold around his torso and lean back. I'm going nowhere, stuck between the giant biker and the backrest. Grinning, I look back over my shoulder to Leo.

He looks absolutely stoic and hot on his motorcycle. He revs his engine, coming up closer until he's practically beside us. My breath hitches, watching him ride and handle the motorcycle between his legs. Leo flicks a look over to me, grinning and pulls back as we come to a curve. I continue to stare, entranced by the man riding the Harley easily next to us. The roar of the engines thunder as they speed up. All my worries disappear as the sun rises.

Chapter 14

Blue Skies

Leo

"You are not putting off another meeting," Jameson warns, scowling at Leo.

The mafia boss flicks his cold gaze to his best friend. He grunts, grabbing another file from the top of the desk that Owen placed down moments ago. Leo can barely concentrate, scanning the page of numbers and statistics for the new hotel that's supposed to be operational in a less than a year.

"You act as if you can't handle the board," Leo retorts.

Jameson snorts at him, lounging in one of the soft chairs sitting across from the desk. The upstairs office is a light grey and dark blue with two computer stations on the left side where Owen and Julio usually work. Monitors line the right side, showing different images of the hotel and live feeds from several warehouses. It's not gigantic, meant to only be temporary. Apart from the fluorescent lights above, sunlight streams in from the window behind the main desk.

Leo tosses the report onto the desk. "Everything's in order. They shouldn't fucking worry because I miss a few board meetings."

"Tell that to the blonde hurricane pain in my ass," Jameson mutters. Isaac snorts, skipping through the video feeds of the hotel. Jameson glares at him. "You don't have to deal with her."

"Carrie will settle when the new hotel is up and running," Leo says. "And she should be focused on the media about the Italian Lily right now. Distracting reporters and the police. If she complains, tell Chiari to use an excuse to keep her occupied."

The door opens, and in walks Julio with a couple of manilla folders and a grim expression. Leo furrows his brows as the man doesn't fully approach his desk.

"What is it?" Leo asks.

Julio exchanges a glance with Owen, and then Isaac and Jameson, who stands up and reads the top of the folder. He swears in Spanish, muttering something to Julio.

"What the fuck is it? Don't make me fucking ask again."

"I found the hospital records," Julio answers, keeping a tight grip on the folders. "Wasn't easy to get the real shit, and some paperwork has disappeared. Even with my connections. But..." Julio clears his throat, and places the folders on the desk before Leo, "...gonna warn you, it's worse than we thought."

"What do you mean?" Isaac asks.

"Found out why it was easy for everyone to believe she was dead." Leo reaches for the folders, and Julio puts his hand on top of his. The mafia boss' gaze becomes menacing. "I've seen some fucked up shit. From serial killers to fucking psychos, this is up there, you sure you want to see this?" Leo growls low, warning Julio. "I warned you."

Julio lets go, stepping back as he exchanges another look with Jameson.

Leo flips open the folder, staring at the medical report of *Sarah Marie Mitchell*. His eyes scan over the details, going over every injury that seems to span on for pages. She was hooked up to machines, couldn't breathe on her own because they'd crushed her ribs. Internal bleeding. Concussion. Broken bones. And only in the ICU for five days before she…died.

Leo's hands almost tremble as they flip over the pages to reveal the pictures taken of her. Blood is everywhere. Bruises. Her head half shaved because of the injuries. As he keeps flipping the photos, each shows close-ups of the damage she'd taken. He swallows hard knowing where each scar comes from. Up close images show her fingers, bloodied and destroyed from fighting back. And lastly, what was left of her lower—

He chokes, slamming shut the folder, and breathes heavily as he tries to keep from hurling from the images. His chest shakes, anger writhing through him as he curls his lips. Through the last few years, he's done some heinous shit in "interrogations" and obtaining information, but that was…

She'd been fucking tortured.

"Should've strung those three men up by their intestines," Isaac mutters.

"I *want* the last three men," Leo orders in a cold tone. "Especially her fucking ex."

"We know where they are," Owen answers, voice steady as he swallows harshly. All the men in the room shift on their feet, staring at the folders filled with the horrific images. "We need to wait."

"I want them *now*." Leo turns on Owen, fury raging behind his eyes.

"We're playing the long game, boss," Owen assures him, unflinchingly. "If we go after them so shortly after dumping the other bodies, we're fucked. Not to mention two of them are in prison already."

"They'll be ours," Julio adds. "Just need time. Trust me, I'll want in on cutting the pendajos into bloody shreds."

Leo stares at the folders, beginning to pace behind his desk. "Fine. Just make fucking sure it's absolutely safe to go back when its time. If I find out *anyone* tries to touch her, I'm ripping their hands off myself. Understood?"

"Want help holding them down?" Owen tries to joke, but only gets a cold look from Leo.

"Breathe," Jameson says. Leo snaps his head to Jameson, who juts his head toward the window. "She's fine. Look outside."

Leo flicks his gaze to the backyard, quickly finding Autumn laying in the grass. Next to her, by some miracle, is Rudolph, hands folded across his chest. His breathing calms, remembering the ride with her earlier this morning. She's fine.

"Also, Nancy's back in New York," Isaac says softly.

"Did you get everything?" Leo asks, still watching as Autumn points at the sky. Isaac sighs, and Julio mutters under his breath. "If you fucking tell me something's happened—"

"Nancy's fine, but she's the most stubborn woman I've ever met." Leo snorts. "She wouldn't let anyone into the apartment."

Leo turns to Isaac. "Why?"

"Won't let anyone in or near it unless she gets explicit permission from Autumn to grab her stuff. Didn't say why."

Leo scrunches his brows, confusion flitting through him. Nancy knew Autumn was with him, why the fuck wouldn't she let his men in? She's also met Isaac, which is why he sent him to collect some of Autumn's things.

"Autumn made two calls on the phone we gave her," Julio adds. "One of them soon after Sombra left the diner."

"Thought she could only call Leo," Jameson murmurs. Leo and Julio exchange a glance. "Course you fucking did." Jameson sits back down in his seat, and Owen smirks.

"Take care of the board," Leo says, grabbing his phone and walking out of the office.

"Are you fucking serious? After I just—"

"Just threaten to buy out their positions."

Jameson swears, words mixing between English and Spanish. Owen attempts to reassure him, "He's kidding."

Leo stalks down the hall, punching in the phone number as he tries to calm himself down. Phone ringing, he holds the phone to his ear and pauses on the catwalk. He shoves the images he'd just seen out of his head, trying not to allow them to warp with others.

"Hello?" Nancy finally answers.

"Nancy, you agreed to give your cooperation—"

"And what is this regarding, Leonardo? I just got home and have a bookstore to open in a day. I've already paid my rent."

"This isn't about that."

"Well, then we have nothing else to discuss, do we?"

"My men came by for some of Autumn's things," he says, heading down the stairs.

"Oh, *that*. Autumn didn't tell me."

"That's because it was meant to be a surprise," Leo argues.

"Well, I gave my promise to ensure her things were safe, and that includes everything in her apartment. Unless I hear permission directly from her, then no one, even you aren't getting in. Perhaps you should respect her wishes." He stops, rubbing his temple.

"I am trying to help her, Nancy."

"By barging into her apartment? Taking her things while she's gone?"

Leo scowls, letting out a huff of frustration. Although Nancy's been helpful, she had a way of driving him over the edge. "As I said, surprise."

"And I'm sure she's had enough of those—"

"Nancy, I am about to put her on the phone with you to give permission in gathering her things. I do not care what *you* think, my priority is her health, and right now that means bringing a handful of her movies and books to where she is to help her relax. Do you understand?"

Silence is his answer. Suddenly she asks, "How is she?"

He looks out the patio doors, which are open, letting in the cool breeze. Autumn and Rudolph stare up at the cloudy sky. "Better."

She clears her throat. "I assume that detective didn't help in anyway. Never met anyone so self-absorbed and narcissistic," she mutters. "Even after everything, thought he'd have some sympathy."

Autumn points up at the sky, swirling her hand around like she's drawing what she sees. "How long was she in the ICU, Nancy?"

A few moments pass before she answers, "Weeks. Healing took longer than it should've. They took a lot from her, but not her fight."

Leo pushes his hair back, wiping away the sweat that's collected on his brow. "Given your *resources*, I'm assuming you found the hospital records?"

"Yes."

"Then you know why she ran. They broke her."

"She's not broken."

"No, but at the time they *had*. She had every reason to run. You and I both know that."

He stands fully, walking over to the bar, and pouring a quick drink. "You knew who I was. Knowing what she'd gone through, who attacked her, why didn't you warn her? About me?" Leo asks.

She's quiet a moment, before answering, "She wore a dress for you." Leo stops. "Finally started living again. I didn't have the heart to ruin it."

He knocks back the drink. "Were you hoping I would?"

"That's between you and her, not me."

Leo brings his voice down low. "I'm not the bad guy here, Nancy. I want what's best for her."

"We'll see," she murmurs. "Now, you'd best put her on the line, because no matter who you are *Leonardo*, I'm not breaking my promise. Otherwise, you bring her home."

He mutters under his breath, heading outside as Autumn lets out a soft laugh. "I'm telling you, it's a double dick dinosaur," she says, waving her hands in the air.

Leo clears his throat, and both sit up from the grass. Autumn smiles when she sees him, and his anger from earlier vanishes. "I need you to talk to your stubborn Nan."

Her face scrunches, standing up. "Is she okay?"

"She's fine, back in the city, but she won't let anyone into your apartment." Autumn stops, smile and mirth disappearing. "Isaac and Julio went to find some of your things."

"Why?" Her tone is quiet.

"To bring them here," he says gently, noticing her defenses rising. "Thought to have some of your things brought here. Your movies."

Her shoulders relax, and she shakes her head. "I was going to surprise you."

"Right, yeah, uh, thank you." Autumn gestures for the phone, and he hands it over. She moves past, talking quietly to Nancy on the line. She'd spoken to her earlier this morning, but her greeting sounds like it's been forever since she had.

Leo moves toward Rudolph, who gets up and brushes himself off. His shirt appears too tight again, clinging to his bulging muscles and gut. Both men cross their arms over their chest, watching Autumn talk on the phone.

"How long you been out here?"

"Lunch," Rudolph answers. "Meeting?"

"Jameson's handling it." The big biker snorts, shaking his head. "Wanted this taken care of."

They stand there silently as Autumn paces, grinning before going inside. A stiff breeze passes them, and Leo glances up at the sky. It's filled with clouds, moving and changing in shape. The cold part of fall was approaching fast.

"Hardest point in sobriety was the second time trying to detox completely," Rudolph says, breaking the quiet. "Everyone thinks it's the first time you try, nah, it's the second time. Cause you thought you had it the first time but you didn't. Just feel shame. Stupid. Guilt. Failure." The older man stretches, rubbing the back of his head. "She's detoxing again, and it's gonna suck more this time around than the first."

"Advice then?" Leo murmurs.

"Whatever the fuck you've been doing seems to work." Rudolph shrugs. "Or do what you did with me." He clasps Leo's shoulder.

"I don't think throwing her into a mechanic shop is gonna do the trick," Leo says. Rudolph snorts with a mischievous look, walking into the house as Autumn comes back out. Leo narrows his gaze at his Road Captain, settling his expression when Autumn approaches and hands him his phone.

"You can now storm the castle, successfully," she says.

He stares down at her, noticing the few freckles along her cheeks.

The light amber brown of her eyes, and how her short hair falls to the side. At the roots, it's a light brown, fading into the darker auburn. Not a hint of what he'd seen in those photos, yet this was the same woman.

Leo strokes his fingers down her jaw, shoving all those images from his mind, but not the anger. Not the need of vengeance to destroy every single person who's touched her.

"Check in," she whispers.

His gaze flicks to hers. "Green."

He wraps his arm around her waist, pulling her in against his body as he kisses her gently. She's safe. She's alive.

<hr>

Autumn

I hold onto Leo, feeling him tense as he presses his face against my hair. Something isn't right. He feels rattled, and more than just from a phone call with Nan. I mean, she can shake you up, the rascal, but not this much.

He clears his throat, moving away as he strokes my hair back. His face scrunches. "Did I hear you say double-dick dinosaur?"

I shrug. "Or dragon."

Leo quirks a brow, and I chuckle. "You busy?"

His gaze flicks up toward his office window. "Not at the moment."

Taking his hand, I lead him back to where I was lying next to Rudy. He follows my lead, lying in the grass and I sidle up against his side. He allows me to use his arm like a pillow, lounging back. Searching the blueish, grey sky I find a cloud and point.

"Airplane with Godzilla."

He snorts a laugh. His hand strokes the side of my arm, and he asks, "What else do you see?"

"Well, what do you see?" Leo turns his head, gaze becoming tender. "Nuh-huh, no smooth line, mister. Look at the sky."

"I'd prefer to look at you."

I groan, "Still did it."

A breeze blows through, and Leo holds me close. I kiss his cheek and begin pointing out more cloud shapes and what I see. He's quiet the entire time, listening to my every word and the anxiety in my chest vanishes.

Chapter 15

Handprints

"You're wearing a helmet right?" Leanne asks again.

"Every time, promise," I tell her over the phone. "Pretty sure one of my *teachers* would tan my hide if I didn't. Or Leo would have an aneurysm." Chesty and Rudy snort near the motorcycles they're working on. Drew chuckles, walking his bike out of the garage.

She sighs, "Okay, okay…even though I don't know *who* these men are."

"They're good guys, don't worry," I murmur, stepping out of the garage and into the warm sunshine.

It's been a few days since my morning ride with Leo. Within that time, Isaac and Julio were able to get an encrypted phone to Leanne. Nan had hers since she arrived in the city, and she finally let them bring up the movies I asked for. A shit ton of my anxiety has calmed once I saw the box of DVDs, clutching a selected few, including *Howard the Duck*. I've had a few nightmares, but not nearly as terrible as when I first got here. Not to mention, I can go back into my routine and go watch a movie if I can't sleep. Only difference is that Leo insists to be with me every time, no matter the hour. He makes it down to the movie theater and about twenty minutes into any film, he passes out again until morning.

I caved within fifteen minutes on the phone with Leanne, though. Told her *everything*. It was a long, long phone call and I wanted to tell her in person, but who knows when that is. She doesn't trust Leo or any of the *Forgotten Demons*, and I don't blame her. She hasn't truly met any of the Crew and saw what the mob did to me. I could never keep secrets from her. I'm surprised I did as long as I had when I was undercover, only breaking when I couldn't keep lying to her as to why I had to stay homeless. Besides, she's only threatened once to come find my ass up in the countryside. If it wasn't for Nan telling her she believes I'm safest with Leo, Leanne would've found me quicker than anyone.

I'm not sure what Nan knows. Apart from the conversations we've had daily, and at one point I know Jameson and Isaac went to see her after getting my things. The FBI and police had apparently knocked on her door and the *Luna Stella Women's Center*. They'd gone there next, and I worry Trix may be caught in the middle of this mess. Leanne tells me she's fine, but I hate not being able to talk to her. It's not safe yet. I can't have done all that work of keeping my friends safe to have them dragged into this now.

"But no driving today?" Leanne asks.

"They call it riding, but nah. It's nice out, but I gotta stay nearby." While Leo spends a good amount of his afternoons working, I spend mine with Chesty, Rudy, and Drew. They take turns teaching me about engines, build models, and riding in general. Yesterday I was able to ride for the first time on one of the back roads with Chesty. I swear if he wasn't on the bike with me...I'd have fallen over.

Got a long way to go.

For now, my favorite thing are the rides I get to have with Leo, whether early in the morning or late afternoon. The past week has been like this mental retreat full of motorcycles, movies, and hearing stories about the Crew. It all must be working, cause the panic attacks have been minimal.

"What're you doing this weekend?"

She sighs, and I hear papers shuffle. "Working. Semester has been chaotic."

"That bad?"

"Miscommunication honestly might be my nemesis. Or people just not doing their job," she mutters. "So, you better get back here soon so I can have a bashing session over coffee...or alcohol."

"Well, I'll try to be back soon, but for all I know you may be too busy for me."

"Me? Never, hun," she says as I smile softly, staring at the changing leaves. "Do you have any idea when you'll be back?"

"No. And even when I'm back, who knows if I can even walk around the city without being targeted."

"Don't say that."

"Not by the mafia," I say, glancing over my shoulder at the men with tools in hand. "Honestly not *that* worried about them. Pretty sure my back is covered, it's Roger I'm worried about. He doesn't give a shit about the rules if it's in the name of justice or the 'right thing' or whatever."

"Do you..." she clears her throat and then says more quietly, "...you think he knows what you did?"

"No," I respond quickly, stepping further away from the garage. "Too self-absorbed. But I'm really thinking I should've never gone to him."

"You were scared, hun. Can't blame you after what happened."

"That's what everyone keeps saying."

"Because we're right," Leanne says. "I might like these guys after all, great minds think alike." I snort at her. "Look, Roger was a dick, but...he was still your handler. The only one you were connected to for a while. For months even I didn't know where you were. At some point you trusted him, it's a complicated relationship."

"Yeah, but is cutting off *normal* ex's this complicated?"

Leanne snorts. "What's this criteria for normal?"

We continue talking for a bit before I hang up and go back into the garage. The next few hours I learn more about engines, and their differences. Chesty tells me more about his time in the Marine Corps,

Rudy grunting at the guy whenever he says a really dirty joke. I about fall over laughing every time Rudy just shakes his head disappointingly at the veteran. Drew comes over to sit on a bucket next to me.

"Hey, Ringer, you tell her about your road name yet?" Drew asks Rudy, who pops his head over one of the choppers he's working on. He gives me a look, and I shrug nonchalantly.

"If he wants to tell me, sure," I say.

"German for wrestler," he answers.

My brows raise. "That's it?"

I look at the other two, Drew shrugging and Chesty waving it off as he grabs a wrench.

"Eh, they don't always have to be so inventive," Drew chuckles. "Sometimes just straight to the point."

"Okay, so I now know the origins of Ringer, Animal, Chesty, and Pretty Boy Bond. Someday I'll collect you all," I muse. Chesty laughs and Rudy snorts. "Think the others will ever fess up?"

"Gotta catch them first." Drew bumps his shoulder against mine. "Those fuckers work all the time, which somewhat plays into their road names."

"Only Sombra," Rudy grunts. The other two make sounds of agreement, and I decide that I definitely want to 'catch them all' one day.

We move into conversation about the motorcycles again, Chesty and Rudy arguing about torque or something. I smile at the two dudes practically growling at the other, while Drew goes to check one of Leo's bikes. I listen to them, moving closer to see what Chesty is talking about and he pats my shoulder. Rudy gives that disappointed look again, and I see there's a greasy handprint on my shirt. I laugh at the mark as Drew brings over a rag, trying to wipe it way, but only makes it worse. I fall over laughing, directly into more grease and Chesty laughs with me.

Drew tosses the rag to the side, brown eyes lighting up as he grins. "So much for that clean streak."

"Never last long, and now she's taken the next step to being a biker," Rudy comments. "Grease and oil."

"Oh, yeah gotta get oil smeared on you at some point, otherwise we'll all look like Pretty Boy Bond." The men laugh, and then Chesty promptly takes his dirtied fingers, swiping them over my nose and temple. I scrunch my face, giggling at the odd sensation. "There. Much better."

"I might prefer this over makeup," I giggle.

"Want a smokey-eye?" Drew asks.

"Maybe another time, Animal." I get up, wiping at my face and the look from Rudy and Drew tell me I made it worse. Whelp. I do it again, and Chesty starts bursting out laughing again. "Not a good look?"

"Worse, you're beginning to look like a coal miner," Animal muses, and Chesty smacks the man's leg. Rudy grunts.

"Oh, gee well, I better go shower then. Whatever would I tell Leo?"

"Careful not to get that shit in your eyes, stings like a bitch," Rudy warns.

"And don't eat it," Chesty comments.

"Darn. Hoping for a midday snack." I wink at them, heading into the house.

It's quiet in the estate as I head upstairs. During my time here, I've only met one groundskeeper, a mechanic that regularly and exclusively checks Leo's motorcycles, and a grocery guy. They appeared surprised meeting me, then quickly schooled their expressions whenever Leo or one of the Crew looked at them.

Keeping hands to myself to not get grease everywhere, I glance down over the catwalk to see Isaac and Owen in the kitchen with devices in hand. Quietly, I slip down the hall and into Leo's bedroom. I begin to pull my shirt off until my gaze catches the view. Long streaks of orange and yellows fill the sky as the sun begins its descent. I walk toward the balcony, opening the doors and peer out at the autumn scenery. Elbows placed on the railing, I peer out at the colors of browns, reds, and oranges.

"Favorite season," I murmur.

I inhale the fresh scent of the outside. Chills run over my skin, remembering the scent of cheap cigarettes, burnt flesh, and smoke.

I listen to the quiet, filled only with chirping birds and rustling leaves. My stomach tightens, remembering the scratching of rat claws, clicking locks, and the phone ringing.

Ringing. Ringing.

So many nights I spent alone curled up on couches, telling myself it'd be over soon. I'd get out. It would be enough. All of it would be enough.

Blinking harshly, I shove off the memories. I concentrate on what's before me; the gentle breeze, the changing leaves, the smell of grass and flowers, and the fresh feeling it provides. I take a few more moments, allowing myself to be present. I rub at my face, realizing what I might've done and look at my hand. Yeah, probably just smeared the oil more. A laugh escapes me, turning to head back inside, but I stop short.

Leo leans against the patio doorway, hands in pocket in a leisure manner as he watches me with a soft composure. He's wearing only his slacks and undershirt, the sun making his tattoos stand out. He moves before I do, meeting me at the railing.

"Anything you want to tell me?" He strokes a finger across my forehead. Black grease is all over it.

"I'm Batman."

He snorts, moving his hand to the nape of my neck and pulling me toward him. Tender lips press against mine into a long sensual kiss. I struggle to keep my hands at my side. He pulls away, and there's some grease on his nose now. A giggle comes out of me. I put my hand over my mouth, then laugh harder, knowing I just made it worse.

Eyes shimmering, Leo picks me up suddenly and I squeak in protest. "Leo! I'll get grease all over your clothes!"

"Fuck the clothes." He carries me through the bedroom, and I throw my arms around him. I nuzzle my face against his neck, smearing the grease. His chest vibrates with laughter as he carries me into the bathroom.

We get each other out of our clothes, peeling them off as he turns on the shower. Before we get in, Leo takes a washcloth and wipes off my face. His hazel eyes become gentle, and for a few moments it seems that he's not entirely here as his hand stills against my jaw. The moment passes, and we go into the falling warm water. Leo grabs the washcloth, and orders gently, "Stay still."

My breath hitches as he kneels before me, opening my legs slightly to check over my cuts. They've healed fine, and I've not needed to bandage them since yesterday. His hands lightly touch my skin, pushing against the water that streams down my legs.

Heat blossoms inside me, pulsating down through my sex. My body becomes aware as Leo continues to gently wash my legs, following up over my hips, and then my ribs. I can't take my eyes off him as he stands, then steps around me to wash down my back. Breath catching again, my hands almost reach back to grab him.

We've not had sex since the study. There were times we were close, but not like this. My body feels wholly aware that Leo is right there, moving his hands over me and I want him. Even as my chest shakes, still having trouble asking for him. The words don't come, fumbling on how I should ask.

I swallow hard and go the route I know. "Check in," I whisper.

Leo's hands go still over my hips. "Green."

Focusing on keeping myself from trembling, either from uncertainty or getting aroused, I tell him, "Put your hands on the wall."

Leo grips my hips a moment, releases me and steps to the side. His back to me, he places his hands on the wall, straightening his arms wide above him. Anticipation rushes through me. I focus on the want to keep exploring, to fully being vulnerable with him.

He still has a washcloth in his hand, bunched up under his fist. I grab another, soaping it and approach his backside quietly. My gaze falls over the stark imagery; wings, flaming sword, and hell across his back. I continue to look down, realizing I've never seen how much further the tattoos go. His ass is even fucking tatted.

I tentatively touch his hip, and he inhales a sharp breath. Just as gently as he had with me, I wash him. His breathing escalates as I move my hands over his ass cheeks, moving down to his thighs where I'm met with motorcycle parts tatted in disarray. There are even Roman helmets, feathers, spears, references to his family's lineage. My fingers press against the muscled calves as I crouch behind him, breathing deeply as I move myself back up his body. I stare at the flaming weapon on his back, tracing a finger up his spine to the hilt of the sword. His entire body tenses as I lean up and kiss the hilt next.

His fingers dig into the shower's wall as I place another kiss down his spine. Another. Then another. I can hear his breaths become jagged as I continue, stopping just above his tailbone. My hands skim over his waist, wrapping around him as I press myself up against his body.

"Dear Watson," he rasps.

"You don't need to use a condom if you don't want to," I murmur against his skin. His heart pounds wildly under my touch, chest expanding with every deep breath he takes. "And I've never had shower sex before."

"Tell me I'm allowed to move." His voice is hoarse, rough with need. I step back, flicking my gaze down to see he's hard.

I drop the cloth as I take another step back, watching his body tense as his hands fist against the wall. The shower continues to pour down over us. Heart rate kicking up, I watch him struggle to not move from the wall. I wait a few moments, believing he's just going to turn and take me, but he doesn't. Still, I keep waiting.

He doesn't move.

Leo's breaths are heavy, almost as loud as the water that splashes against the tile. Every one of his muscles tenses as he presses against the wall. I swear I hear it creak under the pressure. My entire body heats, arousal traveling up my spine and over my skin. I practically vibrate, realizing he's not going to move unless I tell him he can.

Power. Control. For a flickering moment it's intoxicating, but then fear rears its head.

The worry of taunting him too far makes me finally say, "Move."

The washcloth drops as he spins, and my eyes widen at his smoldering gaze. I'm frozen by the feral look. He prowls toward me, lifting me into his arms. One arm under my buttocks, he places his other hand carefully against my neck as I grip his shoulders.

My body tenses. Worried I've pissed him off. Maybe I'd gone too far. Or he doesn't want to be told what to do, isn't that the Dom's job? I took too long. I should've—

He murmurs against my lips, "Good girl."

"What?" I ask as he turns off the shower and walks us out.

"Told me what you want." He kisses my cheek, then again at my jaw just above where he cradles my neck. "And being brave in telling *me* what to do."

"I'm allowed to do that?"

"Always."

He walks us out of the bathroom. "Shower sex another time. I want to take you bare the first time without that hassle." He kisses me briefly. "Water's a terrible lubricant."

"Oh," I gasp, clutching his shoulders as I try to make sense of my emotions. Although I'm still aroused, ready and wanting him to continue, another part is confused. I should just keep my mouth shut, it's fine. He's not mad.

Right?

My mind wars with thoughts as he sits me on the bed, kneeling on the ground with his hand still against my neck as he grabs my thigh. He kisses me, and that should be enough for me to know it's fine, yet anxiety pricks at the back of my neck. It's too harsh to ignore.

"Yellow," I murmur against his lips.

Leo snaps his head back, brows furrowed deeply as he frowns. Within seconds his face falls, and the hand against my neck is snatched back like he'd been touching fire. His always in control mask while during sex…slips.

Fear flickers over his eyes suddenly. My own breath catches seeing the sudden change as he looks down at the flexing hand that was against my throat.

"I scared you." His voice is rough as he moves back from me. "I shouldn't have done that."

Wait what? My gaze flashes to his hand, that's now fisted and white knuckled.

"No, no, no, no," I say, reaching for the hand in hopes to stop whatever miscommunication is happening right now. "That's not why. That's not…shit."

Leo's gaze reaches mine, and his other hand on my thigh moves away. No. Don't stop touching me! I snap my other hand out, keeping his hand on my thigh. I want his touch. I *need* his touch. Leo goes still.

"You didn't scare me," I begin to ramble. "It was trying something and starting up sex and thought to see if it could work. I wasn't expecting you to…okay, listen and not move, but you did. Listen. And you've listened all other times, but I thought you'd move. You'd give in and just…*move*. But you didn't, and I thought I went too far, and you were mad…please don't stop touching me." My eyes clench shut, clutching his hand on my thigh.

"Look at me," he speaks softly. I do as he says. Hazel eyes search mine.

"I trust you." My hand brings up his, putting it back in place against my neck. "You'd never hurt me." I press his hand against my neck, making him take hold again in a gentle manner. The touch is reassuring, helping remind me I'm safe. "Replace every touch. *Every* touch."

My hand drops and his remains.

The worry on his face disappears. He strokes his hand down my thigh, and I sigh against the familiar gesture. Leo comes in closer, brushing his lips against mine. My eyes don't leave his, focusing on the swirling colors of greens and flecks of golds. Only when he kisses me fervently do I close my eyes, leaning into the affectionate kiss. Heat rushes over my skin as I whimper. The touch of his hand trickling excitement in its wake. I reach up, weaving my fingers through his hair. He breaks away to begin moving me further up the bed and lays me down with him on top. I can feel his erection against my leg, and I blink up at him as he adjusts to keep from crushing me.

"What worried you about me not moving?" He asks in a gentle tone.

I swallow hard, trying to think of what I'd felt seeing him like that. "Not sure."

"Were you scared? Be honest." His hand leaves my throat, skimming down my torso to my hip. I nod tentatively, moving my hands up his chest. "Of me?" I shake my head. "Of you?"

My eyes widen as I go still. He doesn't stop caressing my skin, rough hands tracing and stroking, which somehow helps me concentrate. "You wouldn't move until I told you."

"Correct."

"Why?"

"The same reason when you look at me when I tell you." I wet my lips, slowly connecting the dots. His chest expands as he breathes in deeply, moving his hand up to my breast and massaging me carefully.

"I'm not sure if I…what you do, that I…um." The words come out jumbled, not sure how to even say it. What to even say. That I don't want to control him? The idea of having power over him is daunting. It felt terrifying. But what scared me the most is that deep down, I think…I liked it.

I don't want to.

"It's okay." He kisses my jaw, and then my neck. "You don't have to. But do know, my dear Watson, that I will do whatever you ask of me. So, if you get worried, just tell me."

My arms wrap around his neck. "I'm not scared of you."

Leo kisses me, deeply and lovingly as he squeezes his hand around my breast. I moan against his mouth. We continue to kiss, hands moving over each other as the pleasurable tingling comes back.

"Green," I say against his lips.

"Green," he repeats, giving a quick kiss before he gets off me. I sit up, trying to follow him, until I realize he's only going to the bedside table. "Better lubricant." He shows off the small bottle and starts to coat his dick.

My sex tightens as I watch him. It sinks in that he's not using a condom, and the little guilt that comes before the start never arrives. I smile up at him as he crawls back onto the bed, engulfing my body with his. He kisses me, fingers trailing through my folds below. My body jolts at the touch, and my legs open with invitation. Leo strokes the lube left on his hands onto me, rubbing as he kisses my neck.

He holds my hip down, notching his cock at my entrance. Slowly and agonizingly, he enters me. Filling me with easy, sliding short thrusts, I grip the sheets and my muscles tighten around him. I notice only a slight difference in how much smoother it feels. He practically fucking glides while…well, fucking me.

Leo groans, pressing his face against my shoulder as he pulls back and pushes back in again. "Fuck, Autumn…you feel divine."

I blink at the verbiage, finding it odd, but alluring. My fingers dig into his back as he continues to thrust at a leisurely pace and then finally buries himself all the way, filling me completely. He groans, clutching the sheets.

He thrusts his hips, continuing the long strokes and driving his cock into me, every time feeling deeper and deeper. I wrap one of my legs around his waist, pushing my hips up against his to gain more. He growls low, grabbing my hand and intertwines our fingers together as he pumps his hips against mine. My muscles clench around him, feeling him hit inner walls and create flurries of sensations up my spine. Tingling runs down my legs and to my fucking toes, curling as he rams inside me again. Pleasurable bliss travels over my body.

"Check in," he grunts.

My breath catches as he pushes forward. "Green," I gasp.

Leo pulls out completely and the loss of him makes me involuntarily whimper. Grabbing my hips, he turns me onto my stomach and pulls my hips up. I'm completely on my hands and knees, legs shaking already.

"Put your shoulders onto the bed," he instructs in a strained tone.

I do as he says, feeling his hand stroke down my spine and around my ass. I breathe out, calming more as he runs his hand back up my spine again and presses his fingers against my scalp in a caressing manner.

Oh, fuck me.

I moan at his touch and gentle words, and then lose my damn breath when he pushes back inside me. I clutch the sheets as he hits deeper, his cock brushing against other nerve endings from the position change. He then moves his other hand over my clit, fingers stroking over it, slowly and easily. His other hand remains in my hair, massaging my scalp as he fucks me from behind.

Between the soft caresses and the harshness of his thrusts, my body becomes overwhelmed with sensation. Fire trickles through my veins, making my muscles pulse around his cock. The sparking ecstasy before an orgasm flourishes, running up my back and exploding down my legs. I moan against the bedsheets, my entire body tensing as I come, and Leo doesn't stop the continuous thrusts of his hips.

"Leo," I plead. His thumb presses against my clit, moving upward and I lose my breath. Another fiery explosion hits as I come again, and I struggle to find breath as I cling to the blankets, finding release as he touches me.

His fingers don't stop.

I swear I'm starting to see stars. My body begins to tense again as *somehow* another orgasm feels like it's going to crest, following the others. How in the bloody hell—?

"One more time," he grunts, thrusting his cock inside me. "Come for me one more time."

"Leo."

He leans down, whispering as he thrusts again. "You can do it, sweetheart." My eyes widen. It's almost like an electric jolt went straight to my core.

He circles his thumb on my already sensitive clit, and I cry out against the sheets as he drives his cock deep. His hand engulfs one of my mine, intertwining our fingers again as his thrusts become harder and harder. My entire body shakes, legs barely able to keep my hips up any longer as I come one last time. Leo gives a final thrust, groaning against my ear as his fingers stroke me below. I moan as the orgasm hits, feeling everything at once and as if I'm not in my own body anymore. Every thought in my head is gone, only focused on the warm touch and breathing of the man on top of me.

After what seems like forever, I catch my breath and my legs finally give out. Leo remains inside me, careful not to crush me as he kisses my neck. His hand takes mine, gently holding it the same way as he does with the other and presses his hips gently against mine. I gasp, loving the feeling.

"Check in."

"Emerald."

He kisses behind my ear. "Something you've never had before?"

"Honestly didn't know my body could do that." I turn my face, and he kisses me deeply. I hum against his lips in complete bliss. "Learning new things today."

Leo murmurs gently, "I love you."

There's something too soft and fragile about his voice, suddenly worrying me.

"I love you, Leo," I whisper, tightening my grip in his. "I'm not scared of you."

He exhales a long breath, burying his face against my neck. We stay there in silence, him wrapped around me as he presses me into the bed. He stays inside me, oddly comforting that he's not moved at all. Minutes tick by, and I almost start to wonder if he's fallen asleep. I wiggle gently, and Leo moves silently as he pulls out of me and off me. I start to get up, but his hand lashes out to grip my arm.

"Bathroom," I whisper.

He nods once, letting go and I quickly use the restroom, then come back to bed. Leo tugs me against his chest, cuddling me with arms wrapped around me and my head tucked under his chin. We lie there together in peaceful silence.

Chapter 16

Our Shadows Remember

Darkness greets me as I joke awake, head throbbing. A shiver runs over me as the sweat on my skin hits the cool air. Rubbing my head, I groan and pull my legs in as I concentrate on bringing my heart rate down. Old nightmare. The kind I used to have while undercover.

I shudder and the images slowly drift away.

After I feel calm and a bit more aware of my surroundings, I realize the bed is empty. My stomach drops as I feel for where Leo should be, panic driving me as I get out of bed. I scramble for the bathroom. Empty. My heart starts pounding. I stumble into the hallway.

He *has* to be here.

Don't let me wake up in Roger's house. Please. Don't let this—

I check his upstairs office. Empty. A scream claws at my throat, fearful I'm stuck in another nightmare. Or if something happened. *Wake up, wake—*

Quiet voices drift from downstairs. And there's crackling from the fireplace.

I move toward the noise and crouch near the catwalk. There's clinking and it sounds like a bottle is being opened. Another creaking sound and there's muttered voices. Carefully, I move further across the catwalk, hands gripping at the railing as I peek down at the quiet scene, hidden in the shadows.

The Crew is spread out, either sitting or standing in the large living space. Leo sits in one of the chairs, lounging with a glass in his hand. Jameson is near him, along with Owen. Chesty and Julio share a couch, while Drew stands near the bar with Isaac. Rudy is in the last chair, elbows propped on his knees. They all have a drink, and Chesty and Owen have cigars they're smoking from.

I glance at the clock. It's just past two in the morning.

The pounding of my chest lessens, allowing myself to calm when I see Leo. I remain in the shadows, putting my head against my knees as I bring them in close. Not sure what to do I remain hidden. Definitely can't go back to sleep. I could go to the theater, but that means sneaking past them. I don't want to interrupt. Can't even go to the study downstairs to snatch a book. Should've stashed things in the bedroom.

Maybe they won't mind if I just pass through. Or they will if I interrupt whatever is that bikers do late in the night. A sense of guilt pangs me, not wanting to interlope on their conversations. I'm half tempted to just keep watching the fireplace, but their conversation catches my ears.

"She fits in really well," Drew comments.

"You'd have known that earlier, if we'd told you what she did to Isaac," Jameson chuckles.

"How about we don't reminiscence?" Isaac asks. "Besides, I was *ordered* not to touch her."

Leo's dark, low laugh cuts through the air. Jameson joins him.

"Admit it, Bond," Chesty, says around the cigar. "She surprised you. Knows how to take care of herself in a fight."

"We all learned that when she disappeared to Jersey," Owen mentions. "You ever figure out how she scrambled your cameras yet?"

"No," Julio answers, sipping his drink. "Gonna try a few more things, then *maybe* I'll ask her."

"If she tells you to fuck off, you listen," Leo warns. There's a small bit of silence, and Julio nods in reply.

I scoot over more, catching more of the scene below me. The fire casts long shadows, and there's a slight chill with a patio door open.

"Certainly, a fresh of breath air, and not just one who keeps us on our toes," Drew says.

"Yes, she is." Leo's voice is barely audible. Doesn't help he's facing away from me. Although, I can imagine the furrow between his brows.

"Oh, she probably will, cause it ain't gonna be easy keeping her hidden," Chesty comments.

Leo grunts, and I notice Jameson and Owen exchange a look. "Some point we have to go back to the city," Owen says. "Can't stay out here forever and placate *certain* people that she's safe."

"Most don't actually give a shit if she's safe," Rudy growls.

"Unless you count wanting her for info. Inside man, again," Chesty adds.

"Safe or not, they want her," Julio speaks next. "We've played their game before, we can do it again. And as much as you want her out of harm's way until the coast is clear, boss, that may never happen. And the longer she stays here, the harder it'll be to stop their snooping. We're too far away."

"And Chiari can't keep covering our asses," Jameson adds.

"She knows what she's doing," Leo says. "And every precaution has been put in place."

"May not be enough," Owen warns.

"It *will* be enough." Leo's movement stills as he slowly turns his head toward Jameson and Owen.

Jameson starts to speak, "Look, Leo—"

"I don't fucking want her in that city until I have that *fucker* in my hands."

"Which fucker?" Chesty asks. "Got an entire roulette table of them." A few of the men grumble.

"You know which ones."

"One of them we'll be able to get out, just gotta play nice and carry out favors for a judge," Julio says. "The other has been spotted near Queens, but in order not to start a little curb war, we need him handed over."

"Find an excuse," Leo states.

Drew cracks his knuckles. "Oh, with pleasure. Got a book filled with them."

"Say he owes us money," Rudy suggests, and few snicker. "It fucking works. No one asks questions; look the other way."

"Finally got eyes on the last one," Owen adds. "He's in max. Could try swaying it to put him in general pop, but that means easing his sentence."

"Won't matter to the other prisoners, he's been labeled as a murdering rapist," Rudy grunts. "He'll be dead within a week without our help."

"Could put a hit out to leave him be or give him a taste of his own medicine," Chesty adds.

"No." Leo leans onto his elbows. "I want him alive with *all* working nerves when I get my fucking hands on him."

A shiver runs down my spine, hearing the warning in their words. Although they're speaking jovially with each other, there's an ominous tone. I clutch my knees a bit closer.

"Any word on the feds?" Isaac asks.

"FBI is backing off," Julio answers. "For now. Got nothing to go off, ain't gonna waste money or chance of the media getting hold of it. But a little birdie may tell them about this *operation* down on Staten that'll pique interest." Owen grins along with Julio, exchanging a glance. "Two birds, one stone."

"That wanker of a detective was poking his head around Nancy's place, though," Isaac comments, and my breath hitches. "She told him to fuck off, basically, but that won't stop him for long."

"Contact is working on it, has to tread lightly since Caltz is investigating another case. Wasn't supposed to have it, but…" Julio looks over at Leo, "…*someone* didn't listen. That detective never been on a short leash apparently. We'll take care of it."

"I want him gone," Leo orders, standing up to pour another glass.

"Out of the fucking state if it's possible. Send him to South Carolina or some bullshit."

"Trying, but he's got some good connections, probably cause of the mob undercover work he took credit for. He's a..." Julio's words trail off, turning into Spanish. The only ones who seem to understand are Jameson and Leo. Both tensing.

"Well, shit don't need a translation for that," Chesty comments.

"He's a loose cannon. Find a way to take care of him," Leo states.

"We will, boss," Drew answers, and a few others grunt in response. "If we're lucky, we can drag him by your chopper all chained up. Maybe he likes chains like me." He lifts up his chain necklace, smile glinting.

"Oh, good Animal's volunteering tools already," Julio comments.

They all chuckle and another shiver runs down my spine. A cold feeling spreads over me, making me feel numb. Something pricks at my neck, nagging. My body starts to lock up as my heart pounds.

They're not talking about you. They're not—

"Sounds like a good time." Rudy finishes his bottle, tossing it into the fireplace and shattering it. "And we fucking destroy whoever else gets in your way, Spartan."

Suddenly, I'm not here.

I'm back in a dark room, lit by burning cigarettes and neon signs from outside. They pulsate, casting obscure shadows of hunched figures over lines of drugs. Steve tosses a bottle on the ground, shattering over the linoleum floor.

"*Our* way," Leo states.

"Anything your way *is* our way," Jameson argues. "Made that deal years ago, pres."

"Which includes protecting our own," Chesty comments, blowing smoke out.

My head would always hurt when they smoke too much. Steve's voice echoes, telling me it was just cause I'm a lightweight. No, it wasn't cigarettes. It always burned and made me choke from the awful stench. I can taste that air again; stale alcohol, burning drugs, mold.

"About damn time we had fun kicking in heads," Rudy mutters.

Drew chuckles, "Getting bored over there?" Rudy grunts, snapping open another beer.

"Can't have that, huh, Ringer?" Leo muses. "He'll start rewiring everyone's bikes again."

Rudy chuckles, while Chesty and Owen groan. "Worse if Animal joins him," Isaac mentions.

"Hey, we fixed all your shit four times over and then some," Drew argues.

"Tell that to Iron Buffalo's—"

"One fuck up, that's it."

"Careful, Animal may steal your tires, Pretty Boy," Jameson chuckles.

"Needed a damn spare, and he wasn't using it," Drew argues, which causes more of them to laugh.

"No, but Enigma sure was using that old seat of his before Chesty swiped it," Owen adds in.

"Don't call me a Coastie, and you're shit will remain intact," Chesty says around his cigar.

"Mechanics and their pranks," Jameson mutters, then takes a long drink and juts his head at Leo. "What we get for creating a Crew filled with maniacal mechanics."

Chesty counters, "Those *maniacal* mechanics are who upkeep your bike, so be careful Sombra, we may—"

"If you threaten my bike again you demented devil dog—" They all begin laughing and taunting the other, not a sound of animosity in any of them.

It's not enough to separate the past from the present.

I grip the railing, body beginning to shake as the past melts into the present and my vision becomes blurry. The smell of that fucking apartment sticks inside my nostrils, making me feel sick.

I'm not there. I'm not—

Suddenly, Drew pauses with his drink and my entire body becomes frozen as his eyes meet mine. Isaac hesitates next to him, following his gaze. Terror invades my mind, not seeing the men I've been spending time with. It feels like my chest constricts into a tinfoil ball.

All I see is Steve's haunting blue eyes. The drug dealer's brown ones. And the smell of the smoke, drifting from the crime boss.

"Wanna join us, sister? Got plenty." Drew asks above the laughter. All the men stop, moving their attention to me.

My vision blurs, muscles aching as they shake. I can barely make out Leo as he places his glass down. The terrifying feeling worsens as three of them stand, someone speaking about me coming down again, but the past drowns them out.

There's only screaming.

The clicking of a gun safety.

The smell of burnt skin. Wood cracks loudly from the fireplace, striking the final match. And I forget where I am completely.

I run.

Instincts scream at me as I scramble up, bolting down the hallway. There's thudding behind me as people follow, voices calling out that are familiar and warped. My shoulder slams into a wall, and I whimper, thinking I've been thrown. Remembering being struck. I continue racing down the hall, heading for the back stairwell. My feet catch the carpet and I fall forward, barely catching myself.

"Autumn!" The fog closes in, surrounding everything. My hand touches a railing for the back stairs. "Check in!"

Something about that voice and word, makes me halt as I clutch the railing with both hands. Older voices, those from years past, shriek. Shots of gunfire echoing. Loud music and the bass drowning out my own screams. A hard wall, slammed against it again and—

I can't breathe.

I'm almost choking as I crouch, hugging myself and rocking as the onslaught I once forgot comes back. My body flinches, knowing I've been caught and readying itself for the blows. It always hurts. Just get through it. Just close your eyes and it'll be over.

"Autumn," a soft voice drifts through the landscape of the screaming chaos. I'm falling into a chasm of darkness again, sweat running down my head as silent tears fall down my cheeks.

I can't breathe.

A hand touches my shoulder.

"I won't tell!" I scream. "I swear I won't tell! I didn't hear anything! Please!" The words I'd pleaded once before come bursting out.

"Autumn—"

"*Please!*" I shriek, bracing myself for the punches. Everything shakes, hurting and aching through my body. "I wasn't spying! I swear! I swear I won't tell! Please don't kill me!"

There's silence in the hall, but the roaring hasn't relented inside. Terror tears its talons through me, pushing forward horrific images as I try to fight them. A whimper escapes me.

A chair is thrown. Bones snap. Gunfire goes off.

"Don't shoot!" I beg. "*Please!*"

"Autumn, listen to my voice, you're not there," someone with a deep voice speaks to me. "Just bad memories. They can't hurt you. You're not there. You are in control. They're only faded bruises and scars, deep breath." I choke out a breath, shivering violently. "That's it. Again, deep breath in and back out."

"Please, don't hit me," I plead.

"No one's gonna hurt ya. Breathe, sister."

Rocking back and forth on my haunches, I slowly open my eyes. My vision is blurry from the tears now. I see the outline of a large man in front of me. I blink more, trying to focus as I listen to the calm, steady sound.

"Deep breath in. Doing good. I know those shadows are scary, but they can't hurt you. No matter how hard they try, they can't anymore. You're not there. You survived."

Finally, I recognize who's speaking to me.

Chesty sits a few steps down from me. Beyond him are two more figures, illuminated by faint light. I flick my gaze to the side, catching sight of more feet. My trembling worsens again, and I brace myself, feeling cornered.

"Hey, hey, hey, keep your eyes on me, sister," he says softly. I do as he says, body still tense. "There you go. You're not alone, no one here is gonna hurt you. Not there anymore, just pesky shadows. May seem pretty real, but they ain't. Just memories."

My arms clench around my legs, holding tight as I continue trying to stay in the present. I swallow hard, nodding as he gives me a half smile. Chesty…Waylon settles forward a bit, tilting his head. "Wanna hear a story?"

The roughness in my throat is too much, so I just nod my head.

"Whenever my memories haunt me a bit too much or seem real again, I think of funny stories," Waylon says, and my eyes widen slightly. "Yeah, it happens to me, too. Got some of those…forgotten demons, you know? Little fuckers like to remind us they're there."

Someone shifts behind me, and I flinch at the movement. One of the figures behind Waylon holds their hand up, and there's another scuffed sound. My eyes squeeze shut, bracing myself again out of instinct.

Waylon mutters something and everyone goes still. I open my eyes again, finding him holding his hands up, waving off the others. He brings them down so I can watch him do so, placing them between us. Fear keeps my body immobile and every lungs ache.

"Alright, funny story," Waylon says, leaning against the wall. "Okay, so this one time, me, Spartan, Animal, and Iron Buffalo decided to go for a ride. Without Ringer, mind you, which was a dumb idea. He always helps us map out routes and knows the best places to ride through. Must've been a wily day for us, anyways, we get almost a seventy miles into the desert of California when this thunderstorm hits. Before we know it, we're soaked to the bone, leather and all. By the time we made it to this motel, it took about two people each to peel the leather off. That shit squeaked in places it shouldn't have. Not to mention how much baby powder we used, thinking it'd help get it off us."

A giggle escapes, and I stop with a hiccup. Waylon smiles at me. "Nah, you can laugh. Pretty funny image. Four bikers hiding out in a motel, and before that it was an underpass, but the wind was so strong it didn't help our situation much. It took Leo growling at the receptionist to get a hold of Ringer to find a way back home. Cause, uh, we'd no idea where we were. Had better luck in Afghanistan finding a convoy than getting our asses back to the city. Caught out in the rain like stuck cattle in a river, lost at this random motel, and covered in baby powder."

Yeah, that's a funny picture.

A part of my mouth pulls up into a small grin. "Whenever we try to ride without Ringer, he reminds us of that mistake," Waylon glances over his shoulder at one of the lingering shadows, a much bigger one than the others. Another giggle comes out of me. "And nothin' will make Leo surlier than being caught in the rain with his good leathers on, cause he looks like a 1950s cartoon cat dumped in milk."

"His brows furrow," I barely whisper. The fog around me is beginning to lift, reality sinking back in even as my head pounds.

"What?"

I inhale shakingly, letting out a short exhale and loosen my arms around my legs. My muscles ache from the trembling, but it won't stop. I swallow hard, trying to get my dry throat to work. "He furrows his brows. When he gets confused or frustrated. And there's a line above it."

"Permanent landmark on his face, huh?"

"No." I shake my head. "It disappears when he smiles."

Waylon hums, moving up a step to me. "Well, he's been doin' that more since you arrived."

My gaze flashes to the side, seeing someone crouched nearby. I can't see their full profile, but I know who it is. Memories fade, falling like sand into the ocean being swept away with each long breath.

"Got a funny story?" Waylon asks.

I bring my attention back to him, chest feeling heavy as the nerves ease, but now the aftermath begins to plague me. I shrug, feeling tired and depleted. Grogginess replaces the swirling confused, fearful emotions.

"How about I tell you some more?"

"Okay."

I lose track of how many stories Waylon tells me, ranging from those when he was in the military, the *Forgotten Demons*, or other shenanigans while they were out in California. Tears on my face have dried, and the trembling finally stops. My chest remains heavy, weary from the panic and flashbacks.

Waylon finishes another, and asks, "How ya feeling, sister?"

"Like I was hit by a truck." He snorts a little. "Better. Thank you."

"We all battle our own shadows, just gotta remember they're only that. Can't hurt you. Can only follow you. Don't mean you can't smack'em around."

My eyelids feel heavy. I nod again, shifting where I sit and finally look over at Leo. He sits against the wall, knees brought up to give me more space.

"I'm sorry," I choke out.

"Nothing to apologize for." My jaw quivers a little at the softness of his tone. "Do you want to go to bed?"

I shake my head. "Nightmares."

"Movie?" Isaac suggests from behind. "Bad chick flick sounds good."

"More of a Disney guy myself," Waylon comments.

"Softies," Drew teases from down the stairs.

"Coming from the Muppet," Rudy mutters. "And shush, *bärchen* chooses."

I look at Rudy, smiling faintly and he gives me a wink. I nod in agreement, beginning to stand. Leo swiftly gets up, offering me his hand. I stare at it a moment, and then up at the towering man before me. The dim lights of the hall cast an odd shadow over his face. He doesn't smile, but there's no furrowing of his brow either.

Passive. Masked.

I take his hand and am lifted to my feet. Leo doesn't touch me anywhere else, keeping his hand in mine as we go down the hall. I fold in on myself a little, embarrassed and sleepy. The others get up and follow us down to the movie theatre. Leo puts me on the sofa I usually sit in and comes back with several movies in hand. I point to one, and he puts the movies back, handing my pick to Isaac to put into the player. Leo sits beside me, still not touching me.

The others take their seats, settling in with their drinks from before.

It Could Happen to You begins to play on the large screen, and I glance at Leo's hand near my thigh. His fingers flex. His gaze remains on the screen, and it feels like I wanna hurl. A tightness wraps around my chest, completely different than what I was feeling before.

Quietly, I reach over and place my hand over his. He stops flexing it, flicking his gaze to me in silent concern. I thread my fingers through his, moving our conjoined hands to my chest in hopes the warmth will get rid of the anxiety.

I fucked up. It was too much. I'm too—

"Check in," Leo whispers for only me to hear.

A sob catches in my throat. Unable to speak, I squeeze his hand twice.

He swiftly brings me onto his lap, cradling me against his chest. His arms wrap around me, holding me firmly as I listen to the steady beat of his heart. The horrible emotions dissipate, vanishing as I breathe in his scent. Everything still aches while my mind tries to catch up with what happened, feeling confused and lost.

Leo kisses my temple, stroking my hair back as the rom-com plays. He whispers against my ear, "My dear Watson…you're safe."

Ease washes over my tired bones. The tension erased as my brain finally realizes I'm not there anymore. It was all just…

Forgotten demons.

Chapter 17

Love is Patient, Love is Freedom

Something caresses my face, waking me gently as I flutter my eyes open to the dimly lit bedroom. I touch the hand against my cheek. Leo sits on the edge of the bed next to me. He must've carried me back up after I fell asleep during the movie.

He strokes his hand down my jaw, then holds my hand tightly. "Go back to sleep, sweetheart," he whispers roughly.

I shake my head, beginning to sit up. He remains in place, staring at the ground as I hold onto his hand. "Leo, I'm sorry if I scared you—"

"Do not apologize for what those monsters did to you." His voice is strict and clipped, and his hand flexes in mine. "Do not—"

"Leo." I touch his shoulder, and he shudders. Unsure of what to do, I start to take my hand away, but he holds it in place. "Talk to me, Leo."

The grip he has on me tightens, clutching my hands as he shakes his head. He clears his throat as I feel his body practically vibrate. Leo stares at the closed bedroom door, jaw working. Slowly, he faces me with anger in his eyes. Anguish covers his hazel gaze, hurt peering through them.

I know that look. I've seen it in my own. And my heart constricts at the sight.

"A question kept repeating in my head last night," he murmurs, neck muscles tightening. "All I could think was 'what the fuck did they *do* to you'? Again and again, I asked it."

I swallow hard, hoping he won't actually ask me that. I never want him to know certain parts, see the photos, or hear of what I'd done to survive. I cling to him, trying to stop the feeling of my chest caving in.

"I've been in some extremely fucked-up situations," he continues. "I've done things I'm not proud of. While others, I'd do again in a heartbeat. I may have nightmares, doubts, and some shame in shit that backfired or didn't turn out well, but...I knew what I was getting into. I *knew* what those decisions would cost me, where they would take me. Every ounce of blood, broken bone, life taken, everything...I knew the cost. But I regret *none* of it. I did what I had to. I can live with it."

He caresses my face, stroking his fingers down my jaw and stopping. He curls his lip, an expression filled with wrath, completely opposite of how tenderly he holds my face.

"*What the fuck did they do to you?*" He growls.

My chin quivers. Don't make me answer.

"I was the boss. Even if no one knew, including you, those people belonged to *me*. They were under *my*..." he sneers, breaking eye contact, "...they conducted such cruelty to a young girl, overpowered her, and tortured her to be in the ICU for weeks."

A gnawing pit forms in my stomach. How does he know that?

"Leo—"

"You didn't answer me last night," he continues, like he can't hear me. "You ran from me and the Crew. You forgot where you were, *begging* me not to kill you. To not shoot *you*. *Hit* you. You were fucking pleading for mercy...begging us. You didn't answer me."

"What they did wasn't your fault, you probably didn't know who they were. You can't control—"

"Fucking hell, Autumn, myself or *someone* should have done

something long before they...they..." he swallows hard, breathing hard, "...we should've known. And it wasn't just that night, was it? It was more than you becoming homeless or your ex abusing you, wasn't it?"

I clutch his hands in mine, but he begins to pull away. "I blocked a lot of it out. It's been over a year since I've had a flashback that harsh, well, apart from at the nightclub. But I've learned to move on. Forget." Mostly.

Leo shakes his head, digging his hands into his hair as he stands up and begins to pace. He stops, his face a mask of frustration and anger. "Did Caltz know what they were doing to you? How bad it was?"

His questions jar me, and I'm afraid to answer, knowing it will only piss him off more. Or land Roger in deep, deep cement underwater. I hate the guy, but not to the point of wishing him death. My silence is enough of an answer for Leo. He snarls, hands shaking as his hands flex at his side. "You were beaten. *Tortured* for over a damn year. And he did *nothing* to help you? Why didn't he get you out earlier? Fucker kept you...*son of a motherfucking cunt.*"

I blink at his language, startling me at the harshness of it. He continues to pace, breathing heavily as I try to think of something to say. I've got nothing. What is there to fucking say? I've come to terms that I was basically left to die, mostly, but Leo hasn't. He reminds me of me years ago, angry and muddled.

I sit on the bed, watching him as I pull my legs up against my chest to hug them. He's not angry at me. I know that. Yet, I have to keep reminding myself that as he takes each heavy step. My eyes don't stray from him as he stops suddenly, staring at the floor with hands still flexing. His jaw tightens and the furrowed brow of his worsens. He's honestly...scary.

This was the anger he'd mentioned. What I think the others were trying to warn me about. And then I remember his road name. The Spartan. I have an inkling it's connected to what I'm seeing now.

Leo won't look at me, but he speaks with a dark and dangerous tone, "I want to kill every single one who touched you. *Hurt* you."

My breath hitches, holding my legs closer. "That'd be a very long list," I murmur low.

He looks over at me, loosening a long breath as he fists his hands and unclenches them. Some of his rigidness eases, exhaling sharply, and stares up at the ceiling.

"You didn't understand why I wasn't mad at you," he says in a softer tone. "Why I wasn't angry that you were the catalyst for a lot of things. For leaving…Autumn, how can I be fucking angry at you when they hurt you so badly? How can I when I was partly to blame? If I'd just replaced Gabriel sooner…shut down his damn clubs and warehouses, checked—"

"No," I state. I will not have him take the blame for Steve's asshole actions. He *will not* take the burden for my trauma. No.

"I should've known."

"No."

"Autumn."

"What's done is done. No changing it."

"Except—"

"No," I repeat, getting off the bed. "I'll live with my decision, no matter how much it hurts, just as you have with yours. What you witnessed last night, I'm sorry—"

"Stop saying sorry for what *they*—"

"Then stop taking the blame for them." For a brief flash, he glares at me, but it quickly passes. "Boss or not, you had no control over their actions. I stopped blaming myself for what they did to me almost a year ago, and you don't get to take the reins now." I point at him, and he hangs his head, scrubbing at his hair. "You cannot control everything, Leo, or take the fault for my damned ex and what he did to me. Or Roger. I won't let you."

"Someone needs to take responsibility."

"*They* will. Some day." His hands drop, staring at me. "Whether I think it will truly happen, I *have* to believe it, so, I don't take the blame for what they did. Neither will you. Do you understand me? *You* get to be the reason I heal. To love. To find happiness again. And none of them get to take that from me again. Don't you *dare* let them take you from me."

"Autumn. I am no different. What I've done—"

"I don't give a shit what you do behind closed doors or have done." Tears form in my eyes, while confusion and fury mix within his gaze. "As long as you keep your promise of letting me decide their fate…do whatever you need to. I know you'll never hurt me, even if my anxiety and fears scream at me, I trust you. I'm struggling and fighting to not fall back into the dark chasms of my mind, but I love you and trust you. I trust those hands more than anything. Whatever you need to do to get the job done. Fine. Do it. Except from this moment forward, you will *not* take blame for my pain. None of it."

Anger diminishes from his eyes; hands going lax. The tense muscles along his jaw go slack, staring at me as though I'm not real. I shake a little, mainly out of anger. I've had to live with my decisions and past hounding me, seeping into every little crevice of my life. It's threatened to douse every happy moment with pain. I can't let it creep into Leo next.

I will not let my past take away what could be good. That good was Leo.

I know what that kind of hatred can do. It consumes and destroys.

Breathing heavy, I say, "Check in."

"Red," he rasps.

"Come here." I open my arms, and he comes and clutches me to him. I stroke his hair back, placing his head into the crook of my neck. Leo shakes as I hold him, and I grip him tighter. We stand there in silence as the sun begins to peek through the window. A small bit of relief finds me as I hold him, pressing my face against his head.

I whisper, "How did you know how long I was in the ICU?"

"Nancy." Sneaky old woman.

Leo picks me up, wrapping my legs around his waist as he sits on the bed again with me in his lap. I settle against him, keeping his head cradled against me.

"You shouldn't have lived through that," he murmurs.

"On paper, I didn't," I snort.

He huffs, "I don't know how you do it."

"Spite." A small laugh leaves him. "Can teach you. Does wonders."

Leo kisses my neck, and then my cheek. His forehead settles against mine. "I love you, my dear Watson."

"I love you, my mister…Americano."

He pulls back to look at me. For a few moments, he strokes back my hair concentrating on my face. Those eyes search over my features, like he's memorizing every little thing. Or remembering.

"I hate seeing you in pain," he says. "And I can't do anything. I feel helpless."

"I know."

"Of all the things I can't control, it's the one thing I wish I could. Take it away for you."

"You do more than you think." I kiss him briefly, giving him a half smile. My gaze darts out to the sun rising. "There's one thing that helps that only you could do."

"Hmm?"

"Wanna go for a ride?"

A faint smile on his face grows. "You're perfection."

"Shhh, don't give me a big head," I say, getting off his lap and pulling him toward the closet.

Thirty minutes later, Leo's riding us out onto the country roads. The chopper he chose rumbles beneath us, engine revving as he speeds up into the sunrise. I lean against the backrest, keeping my hands loose on his sides. I've gotten more comfortable with some of the motorcycles to not fully hold onto whoever is driving. One of my hands move up to his shoulder, rubbing it a little against the leather. His head cocks to the side, tapping it and I smile as the wind picks up.

Leo takes one of the backroads, heading for a curve and I hold on tight to him as he takes it. For a brief moment, I glance over my shoulder to see Chesty and Julio close behind. Smiling, I settle into our morning ride and hold onto Leo. Both of us finding that small bit of freedom.

"Who betrayed me?"

I roll my eyes. "Really?"

"We're miles from a grocery store."

"And the Crew thinks I'm adorable," I retort, pushing the bowl of marshmallow cereal toward Leo. He quirks a brow at me as I lean forward on the counter, putting my hands under my chin as I grin. He glares at the "atrocious" bowl he named earlier. "You said you'd let me make breakfast."

"I did."

"And the Leo I know, and *love* by the way, wouldn't go back on his word...would he?"

He narrows his eyes, tossing his leather jacket onto one of the chairs with mine. "You learned how to be conniving from Nancy, didn't you?"

"Maybe." I shrug as he stiffly picks up a spoon.

It's just past eight thirty. We came back from our short morning ride, dropping the chopper off with Ringer in the garage. It was a good ride and definitely needed for us, but my morning is slowly getting better than how it started as I watch Leo scowl at his "arch-nemesis." Pretty sure he's never gonna forget what my brand of cooking is.

He swirls the spoon in the cereal, then puts it down. I roll my eyes again, starting to giggle as he glares at me. It only makes me laugh more at how much he detests the sugary goodness.

Mister Americano indeed.

"It's not gonna bite you," I say between giggles.

"Autumn."

"By the way, I'm *definitely* laughing at you now." The laughter keeps coming as I hold onto the counter for support.

"I'll make you a deal, dear Watson." Although he's being strict, there's amusement in his voice.

"Trix Rabbit can't bail you out." I smile large. Leo attempts to keep his furrowed expression but is slowly losing the battle. I straighten myself, inhaling deeply to stop the giggling. "Yes, mister?"

"I'll take a bite of this—"

"Three bites."

"One."

"Two."

"One."

"Two." I cross my arms.

"*One* bite and then I'll make breakfast," he counters. "With pancakes." Oh, I'm beginning to see how he wins his deals. I won't break that easy. Grabbing the spoon, I get a mouthful of the cereal and chew the sweet, flavored cereal with a grin. He frowns. "For *both* of us."

"I don't know, this is pretty good, and I've missed it," I say with cereal still in my mouth. Annnnd back to full-furrowed brow Leo. I take another bite, and he taps his fingers on the counter. "Three bites and I'll agree."

"One."

"Really not budging huh?" He shakes his head.

I ponder how to add more. You can't judge cereal with only one bite! One is for the cereal taste, second is for the marshmallows, and the third is for the combo. Basic science.

I glimpse past Leo, listening for any movement in the house as a wicked idea pops into my head. Grinning and feeling mischievous, I suggest, "Two."

"Autumn—"

"But you only have to take the second bite if I surprise you."

"Surprise me?" I nod. "Such as?"

"My dear mister Americano, I think you've forgotten what surprises entail."

He sighs, folding his arms over his chest and after a few moments nods his head in agreement. My grin widens as he grabs the spoon and takes a bite of the cereal. Leo narrows his gaze, chewing and raises a brow in question. I step back and then quickly lift the hem of my shirt, showing my bare breasts.

Leo's eyes widen, shock covering his face. And then almost knocks over the bowl when I say, "Hey, Jameson."

Leo spins as I keel over laughing, pulling my shirt back down. We're alone.

I'm laughing so hard, I don't notice Leo stalking me until he's a few inches away and grabs my waist. I yelp as he hauls me up his chest, but I can't stop giggling. He gently grabs the nape of my neck, tilting my head back to look up at him.

"I don't remember you having brat tendencies, dear Watson," he whispers.

"Usually not, but I really wanted you to have another bite. And…" I lean up, kissing him briefly, "…to stop the scowling. Even if it's adorable."

What's left of his hardened expression vanishes, becoming tender as the line above his brows disappear. The hand on my nape relaxes, massaging into my skin. Leo kisses me filled with affection.

"And don't worry. I don't plan on being *bare* with anyone else. Only you," I tell him.

"You're cheeky this morning," he smirks.

"Had a pretty good morning ride." I wrap my arms around his waist. "And behind this really hot biker."

"Oh?"

"Yeah, blonde hair, blue eyes—"

Leo brings his face up against mine. "Autumn," he warns.

"Okay, okay." I kiss him again. "Since I've not been the nicest, one bite will suffice." I step away and grab the bowl of cereal, taking it to the kitchen table to eat. "But this is my appetizer."

Leo walks over, and I prepare to fend off for my marshmallows. Instead, he grabs the spoon and takes another bite of the cereal. He holds off a grimace, eyes shining.

I eat, watching him cook as the smell of eggs, bacon, and pancakes fill the air. He places a mug of coffee in front of me, then goes to finish the pancakes when Owen comes down.

"We've had a security breech."

"Shit," Leo swears as the spatula clacks against the counter. "When?"

"6 AM."

"Why this long to report?"

"Gathering intel now." Owen holds up his digital pad. "Sombra's making calls and Bond is on the phone with Mila."

"Office. Ten minutes."

Owen nods, disappearing up the stairs. Leo grumbles under his breath, finishing making up my plate. I watch carefully, unsure if I can do anything as I clutch my mug. He places the food in front of me. "Eat."

"What about you?"

"I'll be fine," he says briskly. "I'll be in my office all day, most likely, to settle this. Please stay within the house, but if you go outside, take one of the Crew with you."

"Okay," I murmur. He kisses me once more, grabbing both our jackets and leaves. Suddenly, even up against the corner of the large space...it feels too large and empty. I stare at the food, not feeling hungry anymore.

My mind clutters with a number of things that could be wrong. Mafia? Hotel? In New York or somewhere else? I lean my head down, lightly tapping it against the table.

Yeah, that's not gonna help.

Unable to eat, I leave the food he made me and start to clean up the kitchen. As I begin to run the water, I pick up the iron skillet he was using and grab the dish soap. "Don't use soap!"

I screech, jumping from the sudden voice and look up with hands up, still clutching the two items. Chesty stands there, eyes wide. "Shit, didn't mean to scare you."

"Not the first time, but it is over soap," I say, putting it down and hold up the skillet. "Is there something special for this?"

"Don't know how to clean iron skillets?"

"Do I look like someone who would? My specialty is finding the nearest *good* takeout place that's still open past midnight."

"Pretty good talent for the city," Chesty says, joining me at the sink as I hand him the skillet. "Parents never used an iron skillet?"

I shrug. "Maybe. Never was allowed to cook. And told not to touch my mother's dishes." Chesty hums. "My cooking skills make sense now, huh?"

"Don't know what you don't know. Why don't I take care of the iron cookware? You eat." He nods toward the food on the table. "Been told you loved his cooking."

"I do," I murmur, staring at the lonely plate. I scrunch my brows in thought.

"You good, sister?"

"Yeah, fine," I shake my head, grabbing other dishes I know I can wash with soap.

"Sure? Seem a little out of it, besides me scaring the tar outta ya."

"Kinda lost my appetite." I put some of the leftover pancakes on another plate, and then pile the bacon into its own bowl. "Want some?"

"Will you eat if I do?" I glance over at Chesty, whose green eyes meet mine. Silence stretches between us as he waits patiently for my answer.

I clear my throat and nod, putting a plate together for him and setting it down on the table. I sit, taking my mug of coffee to drink. Chesty pours himself a mug, sits next to me and waits again. I'm beginning to think he's more stubborn than Leo, and that's saying a lot. Maybe cause he's not talking.

I start to eat, stomach not fully repulsed by the idea of food, especially as I taste the practically perfect pancakes Leo made. Once I've taken my third bite, Chesty starts to eat. We eat quietly, until I'm about halfway done and can't take it any longer.

"There was a security breech and Leo had to leave."

"Yeah, I know."

"Not sure I can do anything, and just felt bad he left before eating." I stare at the food before me, pursing my lips. Damn it, I was fine after our morning ride, and we were laughing again. We were fucking fine and then some son of a biscuit ruined it. My fork pushes around at the food, knowing I'll feel worse if Leo learns I didn't finish while he was gone. And then I'll feel guilty he made breakfast after I teased him so much.

"Need to talk?" Chesty asks.

"Just frustrated." I shake my head. "But, uh, thank you for helping last night. I appreciate it. Been a while since an episode that bad, probably why I lost my appetite."

"It happens. And I get it. When shit like that happens to me, it just flips shit around a bit in the head."

I snort. "You ever run screaming down a hall thinking someone's gonna kill you?"

"Nah but have woken up almost strangling Enigma or Animal thinking they were cutting my throat. Or another time I almost shot up some bikes because one backfired. Fucking things sound like IEDs going off."

I blink at him. His face is passive as he takes another bite of pancakes. "I'm such a fucking dick."

"You always this colorful in the morning?"

"You've *literally* been deployed, and I just acted like—"

"Hold on, didn't say it to make you feel bad or guilt ya." He taps my hand to get my attention. "It was to help you realize you're not alone. Trauma is trauma. No matter how it occurred or fucked your brain up. Your shit ain't any less than mine cause I was deployed and saw shit. You saw shit, too. Fuck, all of us Crew have."

"That why you all go to therapy, too?"

He smirks. "Yeah, helps us remember not to punch a guy for popping water bottles."

I breathe easier. The guilt drifting away as fast as it came. Damn. Forgot one of the first lessons I was taught at the women's center. Don't compare trauma. Spectrum and all that jazz. "Sorry."

"Don't gotta apologize. And remember, you've got brothers at your back who understand."

"New concept for me. Not being alone."

"Well, you got time to get used to it. And if there's anything you can't tell the boss..." he salutes with his coffee mug, "...come find me."

"Thanks. Waylon." He smiles, going back to finishing his pancakes. I start to follow suit, glancing at the still messy kitchen. "So, we know *I* don't really know how to cook, but can you?"

"Pretty good, why?"

"I wanna do something, but worried I'll burn down the estate by washing a skillet with soap." He snorts, almost coughing up his coffee. "Wanna help me?"

"Sure thing, sister."

Chapter 18

Autumn's Song

Even with Chesty's help the place smells of burnt pancakes.

It's been determined my best talents don't lie in the kitchen. I attempted to make breakfast for Leo, but in the end Chesty had to take a more hands on approach. Bless Leo because Isaac still brought back empty plates. So, it was edible at least.

Give me ten minutes to find a shop at 6pm that delivers within twenty minutes. I'd have *conquered*.

I sit in the living room, switching between reading about motorcycle maintenance and *Pride and Prejudice.* I'm a sucker for Mr. Darcy apparently.

Chesty sits across the room, fidgeting with some pieces of metal while Julio works in the kitchen. The counter and table are filled with paperwork, and I can hear him typing on a laptop. The house is quiet otherwise. I keep trying to focus on Elizabeth, but my mind wanders on its own. I put the book down, staring out at the vineyard. It feels like five different tabs are open and pretty sure two of them are playing music that don't blend. And one of them keeps flashing lights.

I rub at my head, trying to push away the odd unease that's beginning to creep along my spine. This would be when I'd go work at the coffee shop or the bookstore to distract myself. Numb out. Or go watch a film, which I've thought about, but not sure that'll even help. I continue staring outside at the hazy, grey clouds and darkening colors of fall. Putting the books aside for good, I get up and pull on a cardigan.

"I'm going outside, Chesty, but I'll stay near the patio."

"You good, *hermana*?" Julio asks.

"Just need some fresh air." I glance over my shoulder at him, and then notice Chesty's knowing look.

I walk out into the brisk outside, instantly smelling the changing leaves, grass, and cool hillside air. I stop at the edge of the patio. The colorful landscape captures my attention. I close my eyes and concentrate on the breeze. The warmth of the sun. The fluttering of the grass.

It should be relaxing and give me ease, but a shiver runs down my spine. Anxiety pricks at my neck. "Come on, you're fine. Nothing's wrong."

I open my eyes and let out an aggravated huff. I did *not* want a day of anxiety. Already tired enough as it was. Chewing at my cheek, I look around the patio and notice the stereo near the wall. Quickly, I head over and find the MP3 one of the Crew connected to it days ago and start scrolling through music. Song after song, I veto, humming until I find one worthy enough.

I hit play, turning up the volume and step out past the brick of the patio, bare feet hitting the grass. My toes wiggle into the soft ground and bristling blades. John Denver's voice carries through the wind, singing of mountains in springtime. I start to dance, waltzing like I'm back in one of the hotel's ballrooms. My arms swing out as I spin, allowing the easy music to fill up my senses. A patch of sunlight shines through the clouds. My face lifts up to the warmth as I move in circles, pretending I'm Julie Andrews in the mountains. Away from the worry. Away from everything.

The grass scrapes under my feet as I twirl, kicking a little as I gain momentum and sway to the music. A small laugh comes out as I continue and make up quick foot movements before falling into the grass as song ends. I smile up at the sky, breathing hard as the anxiety and chaotic thoughts fade.

"Having fun?" Chesty calls out.

I sit up, grinning. He leans against a chair, while Julio grins next to him with his arms crossed over his chest. "Ever dance in the grass before?"

"Not recently," he snorts, and Julio chuckles.

"Highly suggest it."

"Want another song?" Julio asks. "Or do you want some privacy dancing?"

"Let's be honest," I say, brushing myself off as I stand. "I know y'all have seen me dance and slide around in my socks by now, no point hiding it. I could start doing cartwheels and none of y'all would bat an eye."

Actually, that doesn't sound like a bad idea. Could I do a cartwheel?

Chesty snickers, sitting down as Julio goes to the stereo. I tilt my head at the guy, wondering what he'll play, when the speakers start playing a salsa song. He turns back to me, wiggling his brows. "You can dance blues, but what about the rhythm of salsa?"

"Is that a challenge?"

"Maybe, *hermana*." He takes my hand, spinning me and says something in Spanish I don't understand, until he asks, "Can you keep up?"

"Challenge accepted!"

Julio starts to dance with me, spinning me in the grass. Laughter erupts as we dance, Chesty chuckling along with us. I dance with Julio, breathing hard and tossing my cardigan off before the next song. Julio smiles along with me, both of us having fun under the slow-moving clouds and autumn breeze.

Leo

Leo stares out the office window, watching her dance and smile with Julio. Leo's own expression is stern, not at all showing the relief he feels watching her. Mila had been rambling off numbers when he'd heard *Annie's Song* playing outside. He looks out, watching as Autumn spins in the grass. Her entire face lights up as streams of sunlight catch it, and the constriction around his chest, the pressure on his shoulders subsides. The bubbling anger from all morning, apart from when she sent him breakfast, fades as he regains control.

Safe. She's safe.

"Boss?" Jameson asks.

He tears his gaze away, bringing his attention back to the office and its occupants. Jameson, Isaac, Owen, and Drew are here, along with Mila, who stands before the desk, phone and papers in hand.

Leo clears his throat, nodding for her to continue.

"You need to come back to the city," she states.

"All fail safes went into play," Owen retorts in a cold tone. "Our firewalls stopped them from getting too close. NYPD doesn't have the resources."

"And the FBI?" She argues.

"That's why we got Enigma," Drew comments. "They were rerouted to another site."

Leo flicks his gaze at his Crew, grateful for the quick responses and handling the small breech successfully. Just another fucking weekday for them.

"All cameras near the warehouses associated with that company have been scrubbed," she says, keeping her attention on Leo. "For *extra* precaution, we're looking into what they were searching for."

"We've pinpointed who the hacker was," Isaac adds, holding up his digital pad. "Small server a few blocks from a police precinct." Leo exchanges a look with Isaac, who nods once. Roger Caltz. Son of a bitch may become a bigger problem.

Jameson catches Leo's attention next, both knowing *who* he was looking for.

"Keep tracking him," Leo orders.

"You can't be serious—"

"He is," Isaac interrupts Mila. "We've got a tail on him already. We'll try to bug his phone or computer next. Then maybe his house."

"Careful with any technology swap, he may get suspicious if he gets bumped into," Jameson advises. "Might be easier to get into his house. Maybe Autumn can—"

"No," Leo growls, and Jameson snaps his mouth shut. He gives the mafia boss a look, but Leo's hardened gaze makes the subject drop immediately. Mila adjusts her stance, while the rest of the Crew exchange glances.

"All footage inside, outside, and near the Italian Lily was saved, outsourced to private servers," Mila continues to report. "Everything has been replaced with mock setups and looped images. If anyone tries to hack into security again, they won't know a difference of today, three weeks ago, or five months ago."

"Who has access to the old footage?"

"You, Bond, Iron Buffalo, Enigma, and Chiari."

"I want *all* that footage to be accessed only by Enigma, Iron Buffalo, and myself. I want *no one* to get a hold of that footage until we get rid of it completely, are we clear?"

Owen nods his head once, along with Isaac at Leo's demand.

"Yes, sir," Mila answers. "Even with this little *bug* that has been taken care of, we still have the rest of the families to deal with. They're getting restless, including Rossi and DeLuca—"

"I don't give a shit. It's been a few fucking weeks. No revenue has been lost or impacted. And no one's knocking on their doors or trying to hack into it." Leo sits in his chair, lounging back. "Caltz isn't after them. They can fucking take care of their own shit."

"Except with this detective—"

"We'll handle him."

"FBI agents came and questioned hotel staff at the Italian Lily, it makes *you* look bad," Mila speaks back in a harsh tone.

"Carrie took care of the PR for it. People think a client did something shady. We're secure," Leo argues.

"That's not good enough for—"

"It is. Because I say it is." Leo's frown worsens.

"That's not the only issue here, sir."

"Then what is?" Jameson asks, crossing his arms over his chest.

"Those agents were asking about Ms. Watson's whereabouts. Chiari reported that staff had been asked if they'd seen anything, and she mentioned that the questions seemed pointed as if they thought Ms. Watson was kidnapped or held there against her will."

"Did anyone talk?" Leo asks.

"No."

"Have those agents come back?"

"Not after those first interviews."

"Have they issued warrants?"

"No, due to lack of—"

"Then *why* are you pressuring me to go back. Chiari has it handled, including yourself."

"Why are so hesitant to come back, *sir*? If there's suspicion of you kidnapping a woman, then you should return said woman to the city. Is there a reason you are breaking your *own* protocols and rules?"

Leo's face gives an expression of warning, and Mila takes a small step back.

"Tread lightly, Mila," Drew warns from the doorway. She glances back at him, skimming her gaze over the others before landing back on Leo. She rolls her shoulders back, jaw tightening as she adjusts her stance.

Leo cocks a brow at her.

"I'd like to know why after years of working for you, you've changed your schedule and patterns *now*. Breaking protocols we've established over the years, halted communications with Matteo—"

"My brother started that. Not me."

"Because you left the city," she argues. "You left the city abruptly, and I'd like to know *why*. Why go to such great lengths for this woman? Because I've never known you to care much about the women you fuck."

Wrathful heat grows inside Leo's chest. He glares at the head of his security within the mafia. Mila has been a great asset and is damn good at her job. She's helped keep underbosses and captains in line, ensuring his name stays out of certain mouths. He had a lot of respect for the woman, since she was one of few in his secondary inner circle. Except right now, she was towing a very, *very* dangerous line.

The other men freeze, fixating their attention on Leo as he glowers at Mila. Slowly, he stands with a menacing aura. Jameson goes to take a step toward him, but a single curl of his lip makes the man back off. Mila visibly swallows, fully stepping back from him. Leo's nails dig into the desk as his anger flourishes, reigning it in the best he can.

"Have I *ever* had to explain myself…*to you*, Mila?"

"Never, sir."

"Do you think I'll start now?"

"No, sir."

"Will I *ever*, do you think?"

"No, sir."

"Then I will return when *I* am good and ready, not you. Do your damn job, whether I am there physically or not. If others are getting restless, tell them they can answer directly to *me*, or I will *personally* remind them who the fucking boss is and who controls most of that fucking city. Are we clear?"

"Yes, sir."

Warning fills his voice, "And until I say you can, *never* speak of *that* woman in front of me again."

She swallows harshly. "Yes, sir."

"Get out before I lose my temper over your blatant disrespect. Bond and Sombra will keep you informed. Animal."

Mila swiftly turns, walking out with Drew following behind her. Leo's hands unclench from the desk as the door shuts. Owen continues typing into his computer, exchanging a glance with Isaac and then Jameson.

"You're all going to agree with her, aren't you?" Leo asks, straightening himself.

Owen answers, "We can practically handle everything here

surveillance wise, but… she's right. Gonna need your presence back in the city."

"If you and Miss Autumn stay here too long, the FBI may knock on more doors than the Italian Lily or Nancy's," Isaac adds. "Worse if that detective pushes, using them as ammo against us if she doesn't show up soon. Who knows what protocols they have if she goes missing for good."

"Probably none from what we've seen, but better safe than sorry," Owen says. "If Caltz wants her that badly, who knows what he'll do."

Isaac pinches his face. "You think he'll break laws or something?"

"Possible," Jameson mutters, watching Leo closely. "Sent a civilian in to do his work for over a year, no one batted an eye."

"Except now, he's out of his jurisdiction while she's here. That's why she needs to stay," Leo states.

"But it doesn't keep him off his *current* case," Owen retorts, giving Leo a long look. "We don't know what that cop knows. We've regained ground and feds have backed off, but we stay any longer like Pretty Boy said…they may come back and find a hole to wiggle into. If he oversteps or go past his jurisdiction that'll be our way in, but until then, hands are tied, boss."

"Not to mention keeping up appearances with outside companies," Jameson says. "You're still the CEO, and we've pushed off too many meetings. They want to see you, not me."

Leo moves back to the window, watching as Autumn twirl in the grass with Julio. It's hard to believe she was the same woman begging for mercy last night. The same woman who has cuts on her legs. The same one he's found on the ground crying. She bounces back easily out here. Worry yanks at him, unsure what will happen if she goes back.

Protect her. Don't let them near her. "They broke her."

"It'll never be perfect timing to return," Jameson tries to reassure him. "We don't have our hands on certain individuals, yet, but we will."

"We're close," Owen adds.

Leo continues staring out the window.

"Julio and I can come up with a new security schedule, revolving around her with all of us involved," Isaac adds. "New protocols for the hotel and outside of it."

Jameson sighs when another beat of silence goes by. "Leo, you can't hide her forever."

Leo stares at her short auburn kissed hair. The smile on her face brightening as she runs and then tries to do a cartwheel. "Bring her up here."

Autumn

I fall into the grass, groaning as I land hard. Chesty and Julio laugh, and I flail my hands in the air. "Hey, I did it twice already. You do it next time."

"But you're doing good enough for the both of us," Julio calls out. My middle finger is my response to him. They laugh and I join them, holding my stomach as I do.

"Miss Autumn," Isaac calls out. I sit up and he gestures inside the building, "Boss needs to see you."

I get up, brushing myself off and walk over as the other two exchange a glance. "Ominous, don't you think?" I mutter as I follow Isaac inside.

"Don't want an air of mystery?" He smirks, leading me toward the stairs.

"Think I'm done with those for a bit." I scratch my head, flicking off a couple strands of grass.

We reach the second floor and worry suddenly hits me. Isaac keeps walking to the office, and I look down over the catwalk to Chesty and Julio still outside. Shit. Leo's office is upstairs just above where I was being loud and playing music. Not to mention cartwheeling like a kid. I groan inwardly, feeling like a dumbass as Isaac opens the office door.

I walk in apologizing, "I'm so sorry. I forgot the office was right up here, and you probably heard my shenanigans outside. I didn't mean to disrupt anything. I'm—"

I stop.

The room is a mostly empty space with monitors on the wall. Somehow this office is *worse* than his apartments in bareness. Even with Owen and Jameson in here with Leo, if feels quite stark.

"Autumn." I shake myself and look at Leo. "Whatever are you—"

"I totally forgot you were up here. Don't worry. I'll go to the theater, cause havoc in there. Or dance on the helicopter pad. Or go back to wrecking the kitchen, which you owe Waylon like a raise or something for saving your iron skillets."

Leo stares at me, brow fully scrunched in confusion. I swallow hard, beginning to back out of his office. Why is he looking at me like I became latte art again?

He looks past me to Isaac. "Did you tell her why I wanted her?"

"No. Probably should have." Isaac quirks a brow.

Jameson begins to speak, "Autumn, the reason—"

"Leave us," Leo states. The others all walk out of the room without another word, closing the door behind them. "Come here."

I approach skimming past the plain, dreary desk and stop in front of him. Leo flicks his gaze out the window, and I follow suit to see a perfect view of where I'd been dancing and doing cartwheels. I groan, covering my face. What am I, a teenager now with no regard to privacy?

"I'm sorry—"

"Stop."

He grabs my hands, bringing them down and a small smile tugs at his lips. "Leo?"

"I was going to tell you I had the perfect view of your dancing. Better than on camera, but I do prefer being the one to dance with you."

"Oh?" Really thought I was in trouble there. Well, that can be a topic for therapy later.

"You were not too loud and never will be. In fact, you were a good distraction from me almost shooting my head of security."

"What did Isaac do?"

"Not him."

I scrunch my brows, trying to recall who he's talking about. I then remember the back doors were being opened and closed, and Leo hasn't used the front entrance for any visitors since I had my panic attack. "Mila's here?"

"She's already left."

Well, at least she's still walking. "Why did you almost shoot her?"

"Because she was questioning my decisions and authority." He strokes his fingers along my jaw gently. "You know how I feel about that, especially pertaining to you."

"It was about me?" I grimace, and Leo's jaw tightens, not quite stopping his frown. "Leo, I don't want to cause more trouble. Or be a reason why you shoot one of your security."

"That's my decision, not yours." Oh, yeah, cause we *love* that answer.

"If it's something I've done…"

He shakes his head, kissing me to stop a potential ramble. He then kisses my knuckles, exhaling a long breath like he's been holding it in. "It's been handled, don't worry."

"Coming from the one who just kissed me to distract me. You're getting very good at that."

He smirks, brushing back a few wild hairs of mine. "I wanted to speak with you, because I have to make a decision that I won't make until I know your answer."

I'm not sure why anxiety pricks at my neck again, fear crawling up my spine at the tone of his voice and firm hold. Mila was here, so whatever happened was mob related. Maybe something is really wrong, and he has to leave. Fuck, is he gonna leave me? No, wait he hasn't decided yet. Crud muffins, why is it getting hard to breathe?

"Check in."

"Yellow," I rasp.

Leo moves his hand to the nape of my neck, massaging his fingers into my hair. Everything about him becomes affectionate, his voice filled with sudden calm. "What is it?"

"Anxiety."

"Why?"

"Are you leaving me?"

"No. Look at me." I do as he says. "I'm not going anywhere without you."

I nod, swallowing hard. "Mila was here, meaning it was mob stuff that happened with the breech?" Leo nods his head in reply, continuing to stroke the back of my neck and his thumb mimics the movement over my wrist. "Does…does that mean the mafia…it…?"

"You're safe, my dear Watson," he murmurs, kissing my forehead. "You're safe."

Inhaling deeply, I grab the front of his shirt. One simple conversation about the mob, barely, and already I feel the pressure closing in. Damn. I thought I gained better control than this. Sometimes *I'm* not sure how I survived over a year undercover.

"What do you need my answer for?" I ask quietly, concentrating on his soft movements.

"I meant it that I'm not going anywhere without you, so…" he tilts my head up, the lines are above his brow, "…I need to know if you're ready to go back, Autumn. Back to the city."

Well…fuck.

Chapter 19
Rocky Roads

"And Nan?"

"There's a patrol for the building, since the boss here practically owns the entire block, hand-picked security will be in place at the other stores nearby," Isaac answers. "It's now under the…" he pauses, glimpsing at Leo then back to me, "…under Marchetti protection."

Never thought I'd hear that.

"Can I go to my apartment?"

"Yes, but first couple days it'll be best to stay the night at the Italian Lily," Julio answers. "Better eyes on you, easier to handle any disruptions until we've got everything covered."

"So, first few days is like a…see if they move period?"

"Yeah, unless you're itching to run away again?" He teases.

I snort. "No. Can't let you take another hit to your ego."

"Oh, he'll survive," Drew chuckles. "But Iron Buffalo and Pretty Boy Bond may feel it personally if you evade procedures…*again*."

A few others laugh under their breath, until Leo clears his throat.

The fire crackles in the fireplace. The past hour we've gone over security details, schedules, protocol, procedures, and basically how I fit into all that. Julio, Isaac, and Owen compiled an entire portfolio for once we get back into the city.

I told Leo yes to going back. Although I was terrified, unsure how these next steps are going to be taken; I missed Nan and my friends. I've not been able to contact Trix yet, worrying about her. Not all that including my uneasiness with Roger and what he may do once I'm back in city limits. He's part of the reason why everything is in such detail.

"In the hotel, you can be by yourself," Julio continues. "Just inform us, Chiari, or Oliver the receptionist you've met that you'll be roaming."

"Oliver?"

"He doesn't know about the mob part, but he specializes in privacy for our guests. Also oversees security when myself, Isaac, or Chiari aren't there for…certain hotel clientele."

"Gotcha." I hold my mug of tea close, glancing towards Leo who stands off to the side with Jameson. Julio and Isaac sit on either side of me on the sofa, papers spread out on the coffee table before us. The others all sit in other various chairs in the living room area.

"One of us will be with you at all times, unless you request privacy." Isaac pulls forward a paper with a time schedule. "We'll do 8-hour shifts. If you leave the hotel past a certain perimeter or enter an area we know is being watched, you'll have two of us. Including, when you see Leanne or Trix. For your protection and theirs."

"Got you another phone." Julio holds it up, putting it in front of me. "Top of the line, has all the numbers you'll need, and you can make any phone call without being tracked."

"Embedded scrambler?" I ask.

"Yeah."

"By how far?"

"Give or take ten blocks." I nod, and he continues. "Boss is your first speed dial. Isaac second. Jameson third. You can add more, but important to note is this button." He shows me the side of the smart-phone, seemingly looking like any ordinary phone. "Punch this twice, it'll delete everything on the SIM card. No trace, no nothing. So, no more switching cards."

"Alright," I laugh lightly.

"We'll also know you're in danger, pinging your location to all of us one more time before it goes dark," Isaac says, tapping the phone. "Memorize one phone number, in case that happens. The code we gave you is what you'll give if you ever have to call us from any other phone, and we'll know it's you."

"Okay."

"Lastly, weapons." Isaac puts a Smith and Wesson 9 Millimeter on the table. "When you leave the hotel, you can choose to have this on you. We already got you a permit. Keep it on your person, wherever you feel comfortable."

"Got a smaller .22 and ankle holster if you want something easier to handle," Drew suggests.

"*Bärchen*, will be good with that," Rudy muses over his drink.

"Just saying." Drew shrugs.

"Animal has a point," Waylon chimes in. "That'll be more dangerous if she doesn't know how to—"

His voice cuts off as I start to take apart the gun. It's not much different than the others I've handled, maybe it's more common throughout the mob or something. I take it apart down to the springs and pins, laying them out on the coffee table. Picking up the firing pin, I hold it up to Isaac, who shares a smile with me. He takes it, and smirks, "Where's mine?"

"Bedside table on the left, second drawer, and in a container of thumbtacks." Isaac snorts, handing it back to me as I quickly put the gun back together.

"Holding out on us, sister?" Waylon asks, and I give him a small grin with a shrug.

"Well," Julio clears his throat. "Chesty also has a new k-bar for you, since you've got a fondness for those as well."

"Got it." I stare at the gun as I place it down, flicking my gaze over the paperwork as I try to keep my thoughts in check.

Although I feel like I should be more terrified, like I was this afternoon, perhaps feel stifled or overwhelmed, but I don't. I feel numb more than anything and a bit resentful.

Relief hits me, seeing all these back up plans and guarantee of security. They have backup plans to backup plans, for me and for them. None of it dismissing the reality that I *could* be taken or be compromised. Not once have any of them mentioned "this won't happen" or "you'll be perfectly safe the entire time" or other bullshit I was given years ago. All of this is *if* it does and help prevent it. There'll be a way out as long as I'm patient and trust them.

They're not lying, gaslighting me, or pretending everything will be fine.

And that makes me angry for my past self.

Meeting after meeting, and phone calls with Roger and another agent giving me sparse details to contact them sporadically. Always telling me nothing will happen so long as I followed their plans, kept my head low, and didn't bring attention to myself. Yet, shit always happened. Excuse after excuse would be given, usually pertaining to how *I* fucked up. Never them. And with all these "fuck-ups" they supposedly said I did, they never cut me loose. I was still too valuable and too deep undercover that I couldn't leave.

Deep down, I think that was Roger's plan all along. Get me in deep enough, I couldn't leave, and they'd get all the intel, technology, and evidence they wanted. Fuck. With all of this, I *could* disappear again, and far easier.

"Miss Autumn?" Isaac asks. I blink, looking up and realize I've spaced out longer than I thought. All the Crew are watching me. "If this is too much, we can take a break."

"No, it's fine."

"Questions, then?" Jameson asks.

"Not really," I laugh under my breath and finish my tea, getting up to pour another cup from the kitchen. "Honestly, it's all stuff I kinda wished I had years ago. Kind of jealous, even if it's for me now."

If they'd been quiet before, the only noise now is the crackling of the fire and wind outside. I pause, looking back at the dangerously silent men. They're faces are severe, eyes averting from me as they frown. Leo's own forehead has that line above his brow.

Really wondering how much they found in my past, cause the look on their faces tells me they went digging. They know more than they're telling me.

"Alright, kiddos, we need to have a talk, cause I don't know how much you know, and I don't need to. But you're gonna listen and listen to me carefully before we do more of…this." I gesture to the paperwork with my hand, putting my mug down on a counter.

Crossing my arms, I lean against the counter and look at every single one of them. I ignore the anxiety creeping over my skin, remembering how they all tried to help me last night. How they treated me like a teammate, instead of an asset. And if any of them tries to hurt me, Leo may shoot them with the gun on the coffee table.

"I've already spoken to my grumpy boyfriend, so now it's y'all's turn. None of you, *none*, will take the blame for what happened to me. No pity or any of that bullshit, and all this we just went over better not be because you *do* feel guilty."

"It's cause we care about ya," Chesty says.

"I know. After last night, I know." Our gazes meet momentarily before I continue talking. "The only people to blame are those who *did* hurt me, whether it was me being beaten, interrogated, abused, forced to drink and take drugs, assaulted, or the long ass grocery list of shit. But it was those fuckers. Who I *know* you have tabs on, or at least a handful of them." I flash a look at Leo, who's unmoving with a stone-cold expression. "Business is business, whatever, but no guilt from any of you for not knowing. Not stopping it."

Jameson clears his throat, "Autumn, those were still our people. Our responsibility, it only makes sense for us to right our wrongs."

"It wasn't your wrongs," I state. "Besides, I was undercover, *deeply* undercover. None of you were supposed to know I existed. Since none of you did know, not even until *three years later*, be impressed or something that I did so well."

Jameson tries again, "Autumn, what happened—"

"What happened to me was shitty. How I was treated was beyond fucked up, but I do not regret *what* I did, because I do not regret taking out key players. And scaring most of New York's mafia families, including you all."

They remain quiet, shifting in their seats. Some of them knock back their drinks, pouring another or opening a bottle.

"I'll follow every protocol and do what you need me to do. Just don't coddle me. I know I've had some, uh…hiccups, but I don't want to be treated like a porcelain doll or something. And y'all will make me feel worse if you start feeling guilty, overcompensate, or whatever in response to what I deal with in my head."

"We worry about you, *bärchen*," Rudy says.

"I get that, but…would you coddle Chesty after one of his flashbacks? Have you ever?" Most shake their heads, others murmuring "no." "What about Iron Buffalo or Enigma?" More shaking of heads. "If any of you had a bad day or moment because something reminds you of a bad memory or the pressure got too much, would you treat any of the Crew like that? Fragile and handled with care?" Throats are cleared. "We have low moments, but we get back up. I have mine, just like the rest of you. I'm healing from my shit and learning how to live with it along with the consequences of *my* decisions. Not yours."

Leo starts, "Autumn—"

"Dragged into it or not, it was still *my* decision, Leo." Some of the men stare at me with wide eyes, flicking their gazes to Leo. He meets mine with a hard gaze, but keeps silent, the lines above his brow softening.

No one interrupts Leo in public unless you wanna lose a hand, except me apparently.

"I'm not broken," I state. "I know none of you will treat me like I am, but that means you can't treat yourselves as such, punishing yourselves over something you had no control over." Oh, gee I'm starting to sound like Trix and my therapist. "If I don't get to feel broken or at fault, neither can you."

Silence hits the room again, until Drew whistles low and Chesty exhales sharply.

"So," Jameson starts with a bit of amusement. "Not just Leo

you've learned to pinpoint behaviors in, huh?" Leo scowls at him. "Am I wrong?"

There's a collective, "No."

Leo's jaw works a little, scowling at them.

"Hey, quit picking on my grumpy boyfriend, that's my job." Isaac and Chesty chuckle, Owen smiling a little. I cock my head at Jameson, "And I'm not done. You're getting the whole ass speech now."

Jameson's brows raise.

I hold onto the counter behind me, knowing I need to say this out loud. Get it out into the open. Be honest with them. With myself.

"I don't want to go back." Leo starts to come toward me but stops as I continue. "I want to be far away from the police, the mob, and everything in between, but I can't keep running. I'm terrified, but neither myself nor Leo can keep hiding. I'm scared, cause I know how bad it can get and that it can always get worse, but..." I breathe in deep, glimpsing at the paperwork and gun, "...I trust you to have my back. Not just Leo. I'm certain none of you will leave me like others have. This past week, I know you're all good men. You haven't failed me so far, and I doubt you ever will."

The Crew exchange a look with each other, some of them with small grins and others nodding their head. Chesty stands up, holding his glass up, "Til Valhalla, sister."

Those sitting, stand up, raising their glasses and doing a similar salute before knocking back their drinks. Leo inclines his head, finishing his drink. I give them a little, wiggling finger salute, and Chesty and Owen laugh.

"Will have to teach you how to salute properly," Chesty suggests.

I blow a raspberry at him, and a few others laugh. Jameson pours himself a drink, sitting down. "You not listening to authority, such a surprise."

I cross my arms. "Give me someone worth listening to then."

Owen and Julio spit up their drinks, Rudy letting out a loud bark of a laugh.

Leo catches my gaze, his eyes smoldering, and I swallow hard as I feel everything below the waist tense. Isaac pours himself another drink, all the men replenishing their own before sitting.

"If we're done going over protocols and procedures, I say a movie is in store." Drew winks at me. "Dibs on picking."

"Shit, gonna have to watch *Muppet Treasure Island* or another kid film," Julio mumbles.

"Hey, you like 'em."

"Yeah, like *Goonies*."

"Nah, *Aladdin* is where it's at," Chesty adds, lounging back. "Better yet, *Shrek*, now that's a hell of a film."

"Pretty fucking funny," Rudy comments. They all start to bicker over favorite movies. I grin at them before Leo interrupts their little argument.

"We still have more to discuss. In two days, we'll head back, and everything needs to be set before we leave."

The conversation changes to business once again. It's almost astonishing how quickly they can go from joking biker club to serious mafia men. All of them sit back with ease, discussing how to handle certain people or checking other venues. Slowly, confusion begins to trickle over me as they speak candidly about...*everything* in front of me. Maybe it's how they're talking about it, being professional and not fully cold-shouldered, but I feel odd.

I try to decipher my emotions, filling my mug with more hot water for tea. It feels different, hearing them talk. Was it from my little speech or whatever? The fact they seemed to listen and respect me? Or perhaps they have *actual* plans, not some half-assed bullshit? I swirl honey into my tea, watching them in earnest.

No yelling. No actual arguing, but discussions instead. No fake shit. Succinct with answers. Not cruel, but realistic and understanding. Relaxed, but not lazy. Aware of who they are and what they can do, no hot air blowing. They speak to each other like equals. Even to me.

"Want to join, sister?" "Til Valhalla, sister." "Got brothers at your back."

Forgotten Demons before anything else, even the mob.

My heart squeezes, guilt from running weeks ago which had endangered them all makes my stomach twist. The self-blame I won't let them have falls over me instead, hating that I could've potentially hurt these men. Not only weeks ago, but what could come. That inner hate comes flooding back. Guilt tears at my gut. There's no point for them to take the blame when it was clearly all mine.

Unexpectedly, my fingers itch to scratch at my legs. Peel and dig.

No. You just told them you've got your shit together, don't bend now.

Instead, I try to focus on Leo as his brows furrow as he listens to Jameson and Owen's discussion. He scowls like he always does when he's concentrating. Guess I could go watch a movie by myself, not exactly needed for this. The twist in my stomach becomes harder at the idea of being alone. More guilt and shame hitting me.

Almost like he can sense my inner dilemma, Leo turns his head toward me. Once he catches my attention, he gestures with his hand to approach. Silently, I grab my mug and walk over and sit across his lap when he inclines his head to do so. I lean against his chest, keeping my mug close as he adjusts easily to put his arm around me. He strokes my arm, pressing his face against my hair and breathing deeply. Leo kisses my cheek briefly before going back to the conversation.

None of the Crew give us a second glance.

I frown deeply as the garage closes, shutting away the motorcycles for the winter. Isaac chuckles, leading us toward the helicopter pad. "We'll be back, Miss Autumn."

"I'm gonna miss them." Along with my daily rides with Leo and making a mess of the gravel.

"We'll find time to keep teaching you. Surprise the boss." He winks, and I grin as Leo and Rudy approach. The rest of the Crew left earlier this morning. Only the motorcycle mechanic and housekeeper will be here for the next few days, then it'll be empty again.

Rudy nods at Leo, walking away with Isaac to help with checks before flight. Leo speaks briskly on the phone with whom I'm guessing is Jameson. The helicopter starts up in the distance, and I pull my jacket closer as the wind picks up. Leo wraps an arm around my shoulder, hanging up.

He kisses my head as I watch Rudy and Isaac inside the helicopter. "Check in."

"Green." I look at him with a smile.

The past two days have been a blur. We've practiced my memorization of a few names, codes, and numbers. Isaac even went over some territories and routes that could come in handy, which was easy to know from my own past escape routes. It seems my anxiety was helpful in some cases these past few years. I'm still anxious but try to concentrate on who I get to see again.

I almost talked to Leanne for three hours the day before when I told her I was coming back. Nan for one. We've set up times to see them, starting with Nan tomorrow. I've kept telling myself I'm going home, but it's been hard to believe it. I'm not sure where my home is. My apartment feels too distant. Empty and like a dream. Questions swirl in my head, trying to grasp the situation I'm in and how this is all going to work, but…my thoughts just eddy out. Blank. Numb.

Even with all these churning emotions, I tell Leo green. I'm afraid if I say anything else, he'll usher me right back into the estate and never leave. Running away isn't going to help right now. Gotta face the music sometime.

Rudy gives a thumbs up, and Leo walks us to the helicopter, helping me get strapped in. Headsets are all placed on as Isaac goes through radio checks. I hear a little banter as Leo gets in beside me, shutting the door. He smirks, and I press the button to talk to him. "What?"

Leo pushes a button above us, and I hear Isaac and Rudy. They talk to others on the radio, someone in the city I think, but using phrases I don't understand. A few I catch such as "The Spartan" and "The Raven" within their lingo. I give Leo a confused look, and he switches off their chatter as we begin to ascend.

"We have signs for each other." I scrunch my brows, thinking as the scenery moves below us and I make the connection.

"Your road name is The Spartan." He nods. "So…I'm The Raven?" He nods again, squeezing my knee.

"First time them using it."

"Was that your idea?" I ask, and he shrugs. "Well, Chesty and Animal did say you have to be given your road name."

"Will have to make it official at some point." He rubs my leg, letting his hand stay there.

"Hey, Leo?" I ask, looking out the window to the changing season below. "Why The Spartan for you?"

He flicks his gaze to the front, then settles back as we turn in the air. "Road name used to be King Leonidas."

"Wait, really?"

He nods. "It was changed to The Spartan or Spartan for short to continue as a tribute to my family lineage to Sparta."

"Why change it?"

"Too similar to my real name, but they wanted something connected to the original as well for being their founder and President, among other things."

We turn in the air again, and I grab Leo's hand. I smile at the vast landscape and hills, knowing I'll miss it. "You got the name for your leadership, then?"

He's quiet, and I'm unsure if I heard him over the headset. Facing him, his face concentrates in watching me with deeply furrowed brows and all. The smile he gives me doesn't reach his eyes, it's barely one. "Yeah."

I keep my eyes on his, noticing his mask hides something underneath. His hand grips mine for a moment. Almost, I want to ask him if the name means more than that. If there's another reason why. But I decide not to push. Not now.

I grin. "Pity, you seem like one of the few people on earth who'd pull off Leonidas."

Leo snorts, kissing my hand. The rest of the flight is quiet, apart from the engine of the helicopter and the spinning blades. There's occasional talking up front. Leo doesn't remove his hand in mine, keeping hold throughout the flight. Soon, I see the city skyline, skyscrapers coming into view through the late morning clouds. As we get closer, a sense of relief comes over me, realizing how much I've missed it and happy to see New York City again.

Flying over the buildings, we start to descend to the top of the *Italian Lily*, landing softly. Jameson and Owen are near the door on the roof, both on their phones. Leo helps me out of the helicopter as the blades die down above us. He keeps his hand at the small of my back as we approach the two waiting. Jameson gets off his phone and hands another to Leo.

"Mila and the first team are in the office. Chiari has…" Jameson continues to talk through his 'welcoming spiel' as Leo pockets the new phone, not stopping our pace as we approach the elevators, "… Enzo Rossi is in the main conference room…"

Something shatters in my chest as I hear that name. My footsteps falter as the elevator doors open and my entire body tenses. *Run.* Leo stops us as I gulp and feel my hands begin to shake. Rossi.

Jameson continues to talk, walking onto the elevator, "The apartment is set and—"

Leo holds up his hand, completely turning to me as Jameson holds the elevator doors. It takes me a minute to realize Leo's hand is on my face, urging me to look at him. "Check in," he repeats.

"Yellow."

"Isaac. Rudolph. You'll stay with her in the apartment. Jameson, tell them I'm taking an important call. Owen stall Mila." Leo's stark directions make all of them move onto the elevator. It closes, leaving us alone.

Leo cradles my face as I start to shake as names echo in my head, staring past him to the closed doors. Flashes comes back. Cocaine. Guns. Loud music. Yelling. Rossi. Not this soon. So close—

"Look at me, dear Watson," Leo orders softly. His eyes are gentle again. "Good girl." I reach up, gripping his arms. "Your name is Autumn Watson. You are *my* girlfriend, protected by me and my people. No one will touch you. And *he* will not see you."

My eyes widen, realizing he knows what's causing this. I swallow hard, nodding just barely.

"You're safe," he says, kissing my forehead. "Breathe."

I do so, relaxing more into his hold. I loosen my grip on him, taking longer breaths. Safe. I'm safe. *Not that vulnerable girl anymore. Not alone.* I repeat those words in my head, until the elevator comes back up with a ding. Leo doesn't move.

I nod toward the doors. "You should go. I'm okay."

Leo presses his mouth against mine, kissing me gently, yet deeply. His touch melts away the last of the anxiety crawling over me, and I sigh against him. I focus on the consuming touch until he pulls away. He places another on my cheek, leading me onto the elevator where only Rudy remains inside.

"Unless on the approved list, no one gets in," Leo orders as the elevator descends.

"Got it, boss."

Leo kisses my temple as the doors open, revealing Jameson and Owen waiting on him again. "I'll have you informed when he's left the building," he whispers.

"Thank you." And just as fast as it came, Leo's calm, loving expression vanishes. His usual passive, stern one comes back as he walks out and veers to the left. The doors close again, and Rudy pushes the button for the apartment.

I loosen a breath, and he pats my shoulder lightly. "Does that apartment have ice cream yet?"

"What kind you want?"

"Rocky Road seems on brand."

He pulls out his phone. "No problem, *bärchen*."

"Ever gonna tell me what that means?" He shakes his head with a smirk. Figured.

Chapter 20

Throne

R udy's my favorite.

He hands over the small pint of Rocky Road, winking before he walks out of the penthouse. They can all call it "apartment" all they want. It's a penthouse.

I grab a spoon as Isaac picks up our mugs of British tea, putting them down on the coffee table. I sit on the couch as he turns on the fireplace, then joins me. After a few nibbles of the ice cream, I'm feeling far better than I was about thirty minutes ago.

"You ever come in contact with them? The other bosses?" Isaac suddenly asks. I pause with the spoon in my mouth. He shrugs. "May be good to know, just in case."

"Only Rossi, once at his club. Even if I looked the same, I doubt he'd recognize me anyways."

Before Rudy delivered on the ice cream, I rambled to Isaac about what I knew of Enzo Rossi, Nicholas (Nicki) DeLuca, two mafia bosses I've dealt with in the past. Technically, I've dealt with all of them at some point, well…more like dragged to meet-ups and witnessing exchanges. Steve was a *personal* runner for Gabriel, so he'd get into places to grab merchandise. I remember Rossi the most, always harassing women or making them do vile things. He had a creepy streak. Unfortunately, he didn't make the cut when others were being arrested. Strangely, he wasn't the worst compared to others.

"They don't remember the whores that came into their clubs," I mutter. Isaac clears his throat.

"Tell me if I'm out of line, but were you ever…*that*?"

"Prostitute you mean?" I say around a spoonful.

"Yes."

"No." I shake my head. "Came close, and others tried to make me, but no. Doesn't matter in those clubs or places, all women were just…whores."

"I've been through those clubs occasionally. We don't spend much time there, allowing the other bosses to control their own territory. Keeps them compliant. Although, the mob *you* grew to know, is far different than the one we've dealt with. Still bloody, but not as…"

His voice trails off, clearing his throat again as he sips his tea.

"You're at the top of the mountain is why, and thank goodness for that now," I explain, putting the ice cream down and having some of the tea. "Like Leo, none of you can control every aspect of an empire, especially when there's parts of it you don't own, technically. That's like expecting to know the workings of the cleaning staff at the hotel, but you visit once every three to four months. You'll never know what's truly going on or ever ask. Job is being done. Who cares about the rest?"

"Or managers who hide what's happening behind closed doors. Such as your ex-handler."

"Yeah," I scoff. Or your manager who doesn't fire the barista who fucked someone in the backroom. Seems like forever since *Blue Java Café*.

"No matter what, boss will make sure they don't see you."

"I know. And I know I'm in a better position than before, but just really annoyed about being back not even an hour and already…" I blow a raspberry and flip my hand up, "…not sure what's worse. Getting a panic attack from a damn name or grass."

Probably grass. It's everywhere.

Isaac shifts in his seat. His piercing blue eyes catch mine, then become distant. He concentrates, and I give him a minute for his attention to come back to reality. He blinks, and then says in a stern, but soft voice, "The day you ran in the park, you told me it was just a normal panic attack. That wasn't the case, was it?"

"No."

"You kept looking behind you. Around us. Did you believe you were being followed by them?" I nod. "Even though I was shadowing you?"

"Couldn't see you and I thought they'd gotten you. I'd been found. Kind of why I kicked your ass in the first place." He snorts, and I grin a little. "I've barely gone to Central Park by myself in the last three years. Steve used to do some of his drops there, and Roger would make me tail him. Tiny parks aren't too bad, easier to get out. Find a subway or alley."

"I know you said not to coddle you, Miss Autumn, but if you'd like that all transportation avoids the park, we can do that. And thank you for telling me, I can update the others."

"Not a bad idea."

"Your open mindedness about a bodyguard is clearer now."

"Hey, the 'I'm a woman in the city' spiel *totally* worked on you and Leo," I smirk, taking a large bite of ice cream. Isaac snorts, leaning back. "Unfortunately, not wrong either."

We're quiet as I eat a bit more of the ice cream before I take it to the freezer to keep from melting.

"It's commendable how long you survived on your own," he breaks the silence as I sit down. "Developing your own survival habits and tactics. You should be proud of yourself."

"Thanks...Pretty Boy Bond."

He snorts, putting his tea down as his phone buzzes. He starts typing on it as I stare outside. Maybe I feel off kilter because it's been so long since I've been here and how, well, empty this damn place is. Seriously, just *one* painting.

The phone rings next and Isaac gets up, talking in a low voice in the kitchen. He's on the phone for a bit, and I get up feeling restless and head into the TV room. Drew and Julio brought my movies from the estate. They're stacked neatly near the television, and I bop them with my toe.

Safe and sound.

Isaac hangs up, and I head into the kitchen. "According to protocol, I can make plans to leave the hotel, correct?"

"Yes. You're not a prisoner, Miss Autumn," he responds quickly.

"Easy, I know. No panic attacks. Promise." My attempt at a tease works, and he relaxes. "Just wanna make an appointment with my therapist. Maybe that'll help me transition back. Should've called a few days ago but got caught up with everything."

He nods, moving to pick up his mug and speaks as he does. "Nancy called the women's center that you were on vacation. It may be good for a cleaner narrative for your disappearance, and of course, best for your mental health."

"Thanks. I'll call and set up an appointment."

Isaac pauses. "What do you think her reaction will be about you disappearing so suddenly? If she believes it *was* for vacation?"

His face lines with apprehension, and I wave him off. Dr. Wilson will listen, and I won't tell her everything. I trust her enough with some subjects, and my worry about something new is right up her alley. Since she did push for so many weeks for me to be out more anyways. Just no dragging her into this world. She didn't deserve that.

"She'll understand that I needed to…figure things out. If it wasn't for her, I don't know where I'd be. I trust her to listen that I needed a…break. Thinking retreat."

He goes to say something, but his phone chimes and he checks it. "All clear. He's left the building."

I slump against the counter. Fight or flight that was warring inside disappears. A bit of exhaustion hits me, and I turn to put my forehead on the counter. Barely noon and I'm ready to finish that Rocky Road. Isaac's phone rings again, and he disappears into the small office.

I grab my mug and look around the penthouse. I'm wondering if I could convince Leo to at least repaint the place. Put in a plant. Macaroni art. Tiny figurines that'll sing I'm not in love. Pursing my lips, I wonder what could make it better than this *American Psycho 2.0* look.

Okay, maybe it's not Patrick Bateman bad, but come on!

Boredom starts to set in, and I'm not in the mood for movies. Humming, I pick up my phone and dial. I'm greeted by Oliver's familiar, warm voice, "Good afternoon, how may I assist you?"

"Hey, Oliver, it's Autumn."

"Good afternoon, Miss Watson, it's wonderful to hear from you. Was the ice cream delivered before melting?"

"Yes, thank you, should've known you had a hand in that," I smirk.

"It's good to have you back. Is there anything else I can assist with?"

"Yeah, you know more than the ice cream guy?"

"Depends. Try me."

"Does the hotel have a go-to florist?"

"We do."

"Great, I'd like to place an order."

I wave at the delivery guys, both smiling at me as the elevator doors close. "They were nice. I'm surprised you even let them up here."

"All employee backgrounds have been thoroughly checked," Rudy replies.

Isaac walks out of the penthouse, shaking his head with a laugh. I grin, standing in the foyer with Rudy, who grins wickedly with me. "Come on, we know the place needed it."

"Ja," Rudy agrees. "Boss' taste was always dull."

I smack him lightly, and he looks down at me. "Is not."

"Well, I'd like to see his face when he does see this," Isaac muses.

"He's a romantic, deep down, just like Rudy the Gentle Giant here." Isaac's eyes widen, clearing his throat as Rudy glares at him.

The sweet biker puts his hand on my shoulder, gesturing between us. "Our secret, *bärchen*."

"Got it, Ringer."

Hopefully the bit of change I brought into the penthouse will bring a smile to Leo's face. Or I'm gonna find out *real* quick if he hates flowery perfumes. Which may be funny given the hotel name.

We're about to walk back into the penthouse when the elevator dings and the doors open to reveal Drew. He flicks his gaze over all three of us. "Boss wants you," he says directly to me.

"Me?" He nods. "Now?" He nods again. I narrow my eyes. "Does he know about the flowers?"

"The what?" Isaac and Rudy snicker. "Uh, no, something else."

I glance down over myself, wearing only jeans and a plain shirt. "Should I change?"

"Said to come as you are, unless you were naked." A bit of a grin pulls at his lips.

"Everyone?" Isaac asks.

"Yup." I get on with all three men, standing in the middle. "We're all set."

I scrunch my face at them, who seem sneaky and conniving as we ascend. "Should I ask what's going on?"

"Not yet, but only talk to Leo," Drew says. "Do what he says. And remember that no one can touch you without *his* orders."

"Just some shitty coworkers again," Isaac smirks. "But don't dump coffee on them."

"That was a *little* accident," I argue, crossing my arms.

The elevator arrives, revealing the quiet hallway and closed doors of Leo's office. There's some murmuring within. Drew gestures for us to wait in the hall as he slips inside. My lesson was learned a couple days ago—quit barging into Leo's offices.

Rudy leans down next to me. "Just formalities."

I'm not sure what Rudy is getting at, but Drew comes back out and gestures for us to go in. I shake myself a little, loosening a long breath. I step into the office with the other two close behind. There's over a dozen people inside—men and a few women scattered throughout, and I recognize some from the estate, especially Mila. The rest of the Crew are here, near the walls and keeping watch on the others. Quickly, I scan through everyone until my gaze lands on Leo standing behind his desk. He stands casually, yet there's an air about him that's commanding.

"Autumn, this is Mila. She's the head of security outside the hotel." Leo inclines his head toward the woman. I start to walk toward her, but stop when she frowns, and I flick my gaze to Leo. The harsh lines on his face don't move.

Didn't wanna shake hands anyway.

Unsure of what else to do, apart from hiding in his bar area again, I move towards him. My hands start to tremble, and I bring them in front of me to stop. There's a stillness in the room as I pass everyone, joining him behind the desk and I swear someone gasps. I go to look back, but Leo pulls his chair out for me.

"Sit down," he orders smoothly. I do as he says, and someone *definitely* makes a surprised noise that time. Leo places his hand on my shoulder, leaning down next to my ear. "Good girl."

I suppress the hum I want to give, instead, keeping my expression neutral. His thumb strokes over my shoulder as he stands to his full height. His own face a mask of resigned control. I look away to find the rest of the room watching me with wide eyes and shock.

Oh, shit, what did Leo just do? What did I just do? Their stares make me adjust in the seat uncomfortably.

"This is your *formal* introduction to Miss Watson," Leo states in such a harsh, cold voice that it catches me by surprise. How the fuck does he go from that affectionate tone to *this* so quickly? "You've all been updated about her position. I suggest you inform others of her significance and of the consequences one will face if ignored."

Leo practically growls the last bit, a stark contrast from how his thumb casually strokes over my shoulder. My breathing picks up, stone frozen as the unknown faces in the room stare at me. They're frozen, too. All their eyes flashing to Leo and then to me. His hand moves to the nape of my neck, settling there with a gentle caress. The rest of him isn't as friendly. Leo's entire demeanor is threatening, practically suggesting they try defying him so he can strike. My gaze flicks to the gun sitting on his desk.

My stomach drops, unsure why he's doing this.

"You can't trust—"

Shut it old voices.

I glance at Jameson, who's just as stern in expression, but…bored? Oh, well good for him. Just another fucking workday.

Leo keeps his hand on me, leaning forward to flip open a folder and move some papers. I peek at the desk again. The picture of him and Matteo is gone.

"Mila, continue with your report," Leo instructs with a bit less threatening tone.

Some feet shift and someone mutters under their breath. My gaze meets Mila's hard stare. Kind of wanna crumble beneath her grey gaze, feeling the weight of it across my shoulders. A part of me wants to shrink into the shadows, hide under the desk like a fucking lady. Instead, I straighten a little and repeat in my head that she's just another bitchy customer. I give her my pleasant customer service smile and think, *would you like cream with that?*

Her brows pinch together.

"Mila."

Removing her gaze from mine, she begins talking. My mind blurs as other voices join hers, each going through report after report. They collide as I steady my breathing, concentrating on Leo's hand at the nape of my neck. The air feels thick with his menacing aura, causing everyone to reply quickly or stumble over words if they don't answer him right away. Only after it feels like forever sitting there, that reality sinks into my bones. As if suddenly, I'm waking up.

A mafia don's meeting.

I'm sitting, listening to a mafia meeting with every main underboss and captain of Leo's. The Crew uses different verbiage, but that's who these people are. Leo doesn't prefer being called 'Mafia Don Supreme,' but that's *who* he is to these people. Their words whirl in my head about clubs and warehouses and business fronts. Imports and exports. There's mention of cash flow numbers, which are fucking stifling and I see how much I *didn't* infiltrate while undercover.

Automatically, my brain starts to decipher the numbers and I realize how good Leo is at separating his businesses. All I'd collected, *everything*, seems next to nothing compared to this. Is this what he's created in just *three* fucking years? Or was it always these numbers? How did he do this? I'm spiraling, understanding more of the 'empire' I've joked about him having.

Leo leans down, placing his mouth next to my ear. "Breathe." Someone talks about exports to Italy, names I don't know. He kisses the underside of my jaw. *"Upon a midnight dreary…"*

I murmur the first few lines with him, while he acts distracted in kissing my neck. I continue, concentrating on each line and the tender kisses over my skin as his captains keep talking. Leo pulls away, but I keep going in my head. Repeating the poem.

"Your cooperation is appreciated for any more changes I make," Leo finally speaks, bringing me out of my thoughts. "I'd hate to remind *any* of you when that appreciation is taken for granted. I want any brain worth a dime to understand *how* serious I am with my decisions after today. No further discussion. That's all."

Everyone starts to file out, disappearing into the hallway or the side door to the left. Mila is one of the last to leave with some of the Crew right behind her. Jameson and Owen mutter a few words to each other, the last left in the office aside from Leo and me.

"He's in the garage," Jameson states.

Leo nods, and orders me, "Stay. I'll be right back." He walks out with the other two, door clicking shut behind them.

Once fully alone, I melt into the chair like a test dummy after impact. I groan in relief, rubbing at my face. "Holy crud muffins, I like watching *The Godfather*, but never wanted to be in it! Guess I've got not choice…"

My words trail off, wondering if this is going to be a normal occurrence or one-time thing. Not sure how I feel about it being a commonality. I press my forehead against his desk, groaning again and not sure what I've gotten myself into. I told him I didn't care about him being boss, don supreme, crime boss, whatever the hell title he's given, but that was…intense.

Straight up lamb in a lion's den.

I shake myself a little, and start to stand, but stop. Did he mean stay in the actual chair? Or just the office? I glance down at where I've been sitting for over an hour. Well, it is pretty comfortable, surprising given how the décor of Leo's spaces have been chosen to emulate coldness. Huffing, I decide to remain put, figuring he's not going to take forever anyways and fold my legs up underneath me.

After about five minutes, I groan as I poke at the papers on his desk. I stop. Didn't go so well the last time, not ready for the next round. To keep myself from poking around at things, I spin the chair. I do it again. It has some great spinning ability, and I pick up speed, careful not to knock into his desk. Once I'm dizzy, I laugh a little and shake it off.

"Of all the things, the *chair* is the best thing in this office?" I snort laugh, spinning again and allowing the bit of joy to wash away the weariness of the past hour.

Nothing like getting dizzy to make you forget astronomical numbers you just heard.

Worked in college.

I roll myself toward the window, spinning to face the city. Bringing my legs up, I put my chin on my knees as I stare at the beautiful place. There're more clouds than earlier this morning, blotting out the sun a bit. Sparkling lights from the buildings flicker off windows. Not sure which I prefer: Upstate New York or NYC.

Distracted by the outside, I sway a bit and the chair moves with me. I spin again and tilt my head back, while my stomach does little flips from the sudden movement. I giggle at the sensation, peeking over my shoulder.

Still empty.

Staring at the very thin carpet an idea pops into my head. A game Leanne and I used to do back in college. The dorm halls during midterms at 2am were great for chair racing. Helped with the nerves back then. And to not freak out about another set of numbers.

I scoot myself closer to the glass, turning to face the window and slip my shoes off. I plant my feet on the window and look over my shoulder again at my pathway. I got this. Adjusting and folding my legs up close, I push off and send myself flying backward. The chair doesn't roll as far as I wanted, and I groan at the lack of distance. Resetting myself at the glass, I push off and barely get any further.

Window ain't doing it, I need more wind-up.

Determination fills me as I move the chair to the front of Leo's desk, planting my feet on the edge of desk. "Racers…start your engines." I wind myself up. "And may the best chair…win!"

I slam back into the office chair, rolling at a faster pace and further than before. It goes twice the distance, and I start laughing as I spin at the end. "Oh, that was good."

I set myself up again with feet on the desk and get as close as possible to propel myself back. Just as I shove off, the side door opens as I let out a screech of delight. I'm too busy giggling as the chair rolls to notice the three men enter. Once I've stopped and spin a little, I come face to face with them and clam up.

Leo, Jameson, and Drew all stare at me. Each of their gazes' flash from the chair to the desk and back to me. Not sure what else to do and I've already been busted, I say, "You said stay. I did. Never left the chair."

"Not exactly what I meant," Leo answers.

"Well, be more specific next time." I fold my legs underneath me. None of them move, just staring. "What? Never seen how far a chair can roll?"

"Miss the bikes that much, huh?" Drew asks with a smirk. "Hasn't even been twelve hours. I think she's addicted to the rush." He tries to keep himself from laughing.

"Leave." Leo doesn't take his eyes off me. Jameson locks the door they came in, then he and Drew leave through the main doors and I hear it lock next. "Before you begin apologizing…" I gape at him, "…you were about to."

I cross my arms. "Fine."

"Allow me to explain what happened," he starts, then pulls his jacket off in a smooth manner. My heart thunders in my chest as he lays it over the back of a couch. "I was being questioned from *my* people about you. Wondering why I was spending so much time and effort on you. I'd rather not have others speculate about our relationship or automatically assuming you're just a good fuck I'm keeping around." He unbuttons his shirt sleeves, rolling them a little to reveal his tattoos. "I could send a message to them that you're worth more than that. Warn them who their rumors are about, but actions speak louder than words. They are *especially* louder when they *see* how important you are. How *vital* your protection is."

Each empathized word strikes through me, causing my insides to burn and tense. I glimpse at the chair I'm in, watching him come to me with a, well, cocky confident air. He stops, leaning over me to place his hands on either arm of the chair, rolling me back toward his desk slowly. The heat in his gaze makes my skin tighten, breathing in his warm breath at his closeness.

"There's significance in how I've placed things in my offices. They represent positions my people have earned of where they're allowed to enter or touch. One of those significances that *all* my immediate people know is this chair. Because only *I* sit in it."

He rolls me past the desk.

"But I'm sitting in it," I murmur.

"Correct." His tone is assured and smooth. "You are the only one who can question me, interrupt me, or speak to me without permission. No matter where or in front of whom. So, you are the *only* person allowed to sit in this chair, besides myself, because you are *that* important." He brings his face close to my neck, inhaling deeply and kissing my jaw. "Now they know. When tomorrow morning comes, my *entire* organization will know not to even look at you unless I give them permission. Or I'll take their eyes and hands."

The chair stops, bumping into the window as his gaze meets mine. "The chair symbolizes your authority and control. Your power."

"Yes."

"Basically, your throne."

"Yes." He looks over his shoulder at the office. "And you were just rolling around in my office in said throne like you were in a derby."

"I—"

He grasps my face, placing a searing kiss against my lips that causes me to gasp. I breathe in deep, moaning as his tongue traces over my lips and explores my mouth as he deepens the kiss. My toes curl and the heat that has been building for the last few minutes starts to flood my veins. I grip his shoulders, pressing forward as he continues the dizzying, breathtaking kiss. His fingers trace down my jaw, hand landing gently against my neck.

"You are *absolute* perfection, my dear Watson," he says against my lips. "I love every piece of you, fuzzy sock moments and all."

I smile against his lips as he kisses me again. Leo hauls me up, sits on the chair, and straddles me over his lap. His hands go under my shirt, lifting it over my head in a swift action. I start to unbutton his shirt but stop when I realize where we are.

"What if someone comes in?"

"They won't." He trails his tongue up my neck and I shiver. "The windows are tinted; we can only see out of them."

At his reassurance, I continue to take his shirt off. I practically rip it off him, tossing it to the ground as he grasps my breasts, circling his thumbs over the bra's fabric. My breath catches. My body involuntarily bends toward his touch as I grip onto the back of the chair. He then unhooks my bra, flinging it off as his mouth descends onto one of my nipples, sucking lightly. I let out a soft cry as he continues to knead the other and my sex pulsates.

"One last thing about this chair," he rasps, releasing my breast and carefully grips my hair, making me look into his eyes. "I've fucked *no one* in it…until today."

A spike of pleasure hits me, spreading over my body like a tidal wave. I feel hot and heavy, wanting to suddenly grind against him. Okay, add that to list of things Autumn didn't know she was turned on by.

Leo strokes his hand over my side and then unbuttons my jeans, skimming his fingers over my underwear, and pressing where my clit is. I whimper at the touch, trembling as he lightly traces over the fabric's seam, and then dips his fingers under to make direct contact. He barely loosens his grip on my hair. His chest rising with long, deep concentrated breaths.

"Check in."

"Green," I answer. "Fucking green."

"Good girl," he rasps, plunging two fingers inside me. I gasp loudly, panting as I press my head against his shoulder as he carefully pumps his fingers. His thumb circles my clit, pushing up at a leisure pace. My hips start to grind with him of their own accord as the heat inside me rises, engulfing me with pleasure.

"You did so well in that meeting, absolutely perfect listening to me," he praises against my ear. A jolt of pleasure strikes me, causing my body to tremble at the praise. "I'm so proud of you."

I whimper as relief overflows at his words and pride.

He pushes his fingers harder, then hooks them as he circles my clit lightly. The groan I give pleads for more. I feel like I'm on the brink of coming, desperately trying to keep myself still for him to work me. But I keep grinding against him, wanting more as he scissors his fingers and plays with me below. I whimper, feeling the base of my spine tingle and racing up toward my neck while my legs tremble.

"My beautiful, wonderful Watson," he whispers reverently, kissing my chest and then moving back down to the breast he'd not had his mouth on yet. Breath hitching, his hot mouth encloses around my other nipple. His hand grips my hair, fingers moving inside me, and his mouth sucking and biting in a teasing manner. He knows he's driving me insane, working me carefully like a puppet along with the praise and recognition. And I fucking love it.

The pleasure builds and the orgasm I was on the brink of comes over me like a damn storm. It breaks through and my head flings back in ecstasy as the pressure explodes like a thousand stars.

Leo expertly continues to ease me back down, releasing my breast and stroking me in a calm manner. I'm brought down slowly from the high, breathing hard as he takes his fingers, covered in my cum, and sucks them clean. I stare at him, legs shaking as he maintains eye contact with me as he finishes licking them.

Whelp, yup, still hot. Fuck me, please.

"Take your pants off," he instructs, and I get off him quickly to do so. Except, I'm slightly wobbly and he grabs my arm to make sure I don't fall over like an idiot. He smiles, and I glare at him. "Problem, dear Watson?"

"Shush." I take my pants and underwear off as he removes his own. He opens the bottom desk drawer, squirting lube onto his fingers. Does he just have the stuff stashed *everywhere*? Is this a Dom thing? Not complaining, but seriously?

"How long have you wanted to do it in here?"

Leo smirks, coating his cock in the lube. "Do you honestly want to know?"

I nod as I watch him stroke his dick, lounging back in his chair. He gestures with his finger for me to come to him, which I do, and straddle his lap again to hover over his cock. He strokes a lubed finger over my sex, and I shiver at the touch. Leo slips a hand into my hair again, aligning his dick to my entrance.

"The first night I made you carbonara." He thrusts his dick into me, and my breath hitches as he fills me, causing my body to shudder. My body tenses, clenching to him. He pauses a moment, and my muscles begin to relax again. "Check in."

"Green."

He nips at my ear, breathing hot breath against my skin as he thrusts into me again. "Move your hips, sweetheart." I start grinding on him, gyrating in small circles as I ride him in the chair. I pull back up, slamming back down onto him and tighten my muscles around him. He groans, gripping into my thigh. "Good girl."

My thighs burn as I move my body up and down, breathing erratically as he holds onto me. The burning in my muscles become hotter, tightening as pleasure fills me once again and overwhelms me with a scolding passion. Leo moves his hips up, and I gasp as he buries himself deeper.

"Did you like it on the desk before?" Leo suddenly asks.

"Yes."

"Good." He pulls me down onto him, holding me close as he stands and puts my ass on the edge of the desk. Leo quickly shoves off all the paperwork and folders, scattering them to the ground. I gasp and a giggle comes out of me. Quickly, I slam my hand over my mouth to keep from laughing any more than that.

"What have I told you?" He asks, removing my hand and thrusting into me. Leo moves both my hands to the desk, helping me stay upright as he pushes himself back inside me again. "Don't hide your laughter with me."

"Trying to be…to be serious." My words are short with gasps as he continues to move his hips.

"Sex doesn't need to be," he grunts, placing a kiss at the base of my neck. "It can be fun. Enjoyable. Invigorating. Or pure bliss. But not *fucking* serious."

The way he says it makes me giggle again. I bite my bottom lip, looking up at him and he pauses with his strokes. He grins, kissing me fervently and desperately. I wrap my legs around his waist, tilting my hips back to bring him in deeper. We both moan loudly against each other's mouths. Leo breaks the kiss to pull his hips back and slam back into me again. Pleasure writhes through me as I struggle to breathe, holding myself up with locked arms. He does it again and I bite back a louder moan.

One of his hands presses down onto my pelvis, thumb moving to circle over my clit again. I gasp, staring up at smoldering hazel eyes. He pounds into me as I do everything I can to remain upright and bite my lip to not scream.

"I told you," he grunts, driving into me with a force only he can do. "You're never too loud." He clutches the back of my head. "So, you better scream before I give you no choice, my dear Watson."

He drives himself completely to the hilt, pressing his thumb down. I can't hold back as the sensations zap through my body, making me shake as I try to fling my head back. As Leo holds on, keeping me in place, I let out the loudest scream I've ever given during sex with him. My throat burns as I let out another as he buries himself again, ecstasy writhing through me, exploding up through my back as the orgasm takes hold. It hits all over again and reality sways as I hear Leo grunt and tense up through his neck muscles. My vision blurs as I watch him come, feeling a pulsating sensation from his dick and my entire body locks up.

I gulp for breath, trying to collect my thoughts as my legs fall against the desk. My body becomes lax as Leo pulls his hands away, cleaning his thumb with his mouth, and then puts his hands on either side of me on the desk. His tongue brushes over his bottom lip, eyes dark and smoldering.

I smile, falling back toward the desk.

Leo goes to catch me but doesn't make it in time before my back lands against the hard cold surface. My eyes widen as he reaches to pull me back up, but I stop him. I stare up at his concerned face as the cool surface of the wood presses into my sweaty, hot skin.

Neither of us move.

No panic. No fear. No anxiety. None of it comes creeping up my spine. There's no flash of memories or worry. My body feels liquid against the chilled surface, warming under my back. A smile grows on my face, and I wiggle slightly, feeling Leo still inside me.

Well, looky there. Made progress somewhere.

Leo kisses the middle of my chest. "Good girl."

A giggle escapes me, and he smiles broadly. He pulls me back up, wrapping my legs again around his waist as he carries me tightly against his chest. He presses a button on the phone, that somehow is still on the desk, and then begins to walk out of the office leaving our mess behind. I tense, keeping my front pressed against his as he unlocks the office door and goes to the already open elevator doors. He keeps an arm wrapped around me, locking me in place.

"You're gonna make someone else clean our mess?" I'm not sure whether to be embarrassed or amused.

"Uh-huh, including having someone scrub the cameras in here." I almost shriek as the doors close, but close my mouth when I see a wicked smile on his face. Hold on, no way my overprotective, controlling boyfriend is gonna let anyone see me naked.

"I'm sneaking marshmallows into your food," I warn.

He chuckles, kissing me briefly as I laugh a little and he groans. Oh, right, he's still inside me. His problem, not mine. That is, until he adjusts to pull himself out as the elevator doors open. Leo carries me across the foyer and to the door of the penthouse, it barely closes behind us before he freezes in the hallway.

My nostrils are slammed with the scent of fresh flowers ranging from lilies to roses. I look at all the bouquets of flowers that are scattered in their own vases in the living room—short hallway, kitchen counter, and those even in the bedroom. Leo turns his stunned expression to me.

"Surprise."

His face softens to such a tender, loving degree that my heart practically melts. He rests his forehead against mine. "I love you, my wonderful dear Watson."

"I love you, mister Americano." He hugs me closer, walking us through the flowery ambiance and into the bedroom.

Chapter 21

Cuffing Season

Leo sets my plate on the counter. I chew on my bottom lip, concentrating on the coffee mug. Yesterday I'd been able to get a hold of Dr. Wilson, who quickly made sure she was open this afternoon for a session. I asked about Trix, but she wouldn't say anything about her. Really not liking being able to know how Trix is.

"Autumn?" Leo asks. I shake my head, coming back to reality. He watches me closely. "What is it?"

"I'm just worried about Trix and going to the women's center today. I'll probably feel better when I talk to Dr. Wilson, and maybe, by chance I'll see Trix."

"I hope you do as well." He goes back to the stove, and I dig into the eggs and toast. The penthouse smells of breakfast and flowers. The multitude of colors help brighten the place a little, although there's still a slight cold shoulder feeling to it. But the flowers help.

"I'll be busy most of today. I'm certain Jameson double-booked us on meetings," Leo mutters as he sits beside me. "Dinner with Nancy later, correct?"

"Yeah, I'll be at the bookstore after therapy."

It'll be a relief to see Nan. When I called her yesterday that I made it safely back into the city, she told me to check her security cameras after Leo's guys have 'tinkered' with them. I could only snort at her as I watched Leo cook dinner.

"Hopefully I'll be there on time," Leo murmurs. His calm demeanor isn't that relaxed with his brows already pinched together for the day.

If he had any meetings or work yesterday afternoon, he didn't give voice that he'd brushed them off. We spent the rest of the afternoon and evening together. I didn't have any nightmares, but Leo tossed and turned in his sleep. I've never seen him have them before. Worry clutched at me as I tried to help him settle, holding him and he'd calm in a few minutes mumbling my name. When I woke up this morning, he was already in the kitchen on the phone with our clothes left in his office cleaned and folded on the counter. Before 8am, he must've taken at least five phone calls.

We were barely back for 24 hours and already he's being hounded for "normal" work and the *moonlighting*. I'd been unsure about his busyness before, but this was a freaking tidal wave. And on top of it all, I can tell he's trying not to disappoint me.

"Autumn?" Leo's voice carries through my thoughts. I blink and find hazel eyes watching me intensely again.

"Sorry, I keep disassociating."

"What is it?" He places a hand on my thigh, rubbing his thumb. I shake my head. "Autumn."

"I'm just worried." Common constant feeling of late.

"Isaac can go back over procedures if you want. I know it was originally planned for you to mostly stay within the hotel for the first couple of days, but you'll be fine. There's been no movement to cause concern. Things have gone smoothly. I can even send Rudolph or Waylon with you."

"Not worried about me." I put my hand on his. "But you."

"Me?"

"Yeah, cause—" His phone starts ringing. We peer at the vibrating contraption on the counter.

Leo sighs, checking it and declines the call. He brings his attention back to me. "You were saying?"

I almost laugh. Leo isn't perfect, but damn, some moments he was close.

"There's a lot on your plate and I don't want you getting overly stressed. I know you say you have it all handled, and juggling all of it seems impossible to me, but I'm worried about you. You're doing a lot. I don't want you to break."

"I won't."

"You know there's this thing with people not admitting their faults?" I tease a little.

He rubs his hand over my leg, squeezing softly. "I won't because I have *you*. Long as I know, my dear Watson, that I'll hold you every night then nothing will break me. That's all I need."

His similar answer to other questions. *I just need you.*

I stare at him a little flummoxed at his tenderness, feeling like I should be used to his little declarations of affection and adoration, but they astonish me still. And a part of me is unsure that I really am enough. There has to be more…right?

"You're gonna give me a big head or whatever someday."

He half-smiles, kissing me with fondness. Placing another at the corner of my mouth, he points at my food. I roll my eyes at him. "I'm still allowed to worry about you," I say.

"Of course, dear Watson."

"It's in the fine print of loving you. Part of the terms and conditions."

"I'll check this *fine print* for future discussions," he muses. We laugh lightly, going back to breakfast and some of the unease disappears.

<hr>

The car stops half a block from the women's center. I glance at Rudy and Isaac upfront. Pain in the ass bikers wouldn't sit in the back with me, and now I feel like Miss Daisy. "Y'all good to sit out here the entire time?"

"We'll be fine, but still think Pretty Boy should go up with you," Rudy says. "Since you left the gun behind."

"I don't need to bring a weapon with me into therapy," I retort. "He can walk me to the door. I'll be fine after that. The center is safe. And I don't want to make anyone uncomfortable bringing someone in who isn't a patient or works there." Isaac gets out, and Rudy still eyes me through the rearview mirror. "I appreciate you caring." I lean forward, placing a quick kiss on the man's cheek. "Try crocheting."

He chuckles at me as I get out of the car and walk to the center with Isaac.

"Phone?" He asks. I pat where it is in my back pocket. "Text when you finish, and I'll meet you at the door."

"Thanks." I get up on my tiptoes to kiss his cheek next, quickly going up the stairs. I hear him snort with laughter. "Don't tell Leo!"

"Of course, Miss Autumn."

As I head into the building, I go up the stairs and check where my phone is again. It eases me a little as I approach the floor I've been coming to for three years. I take a deep breath, feeling a bit jittery. It *has* been approximately six weeks since I've last been here.

I walk through and I'm met with a new receptionist with short blue hair, brown eyes, and light skin, piercings along their ear. They smile as I enter, glancing at the computer monitor. There's a pin on their shirt that says *they/them*.

"Hi, I'm Autumn Watson. Been a while since I've been in," I say leaning on the counter a little. "What's your name?"

"Dex," they say, shaking my hand. I smile as they type on the keyboard. "Dr. Wilson is on her lunch break but should be coming back soon."

"All good. Like I said been a while. Been gone."

"Sometimes we don't always need as many visits." Dex shrugs, adjusting one of their piercings. "Been over six weeks though, quite a bit of time there. Vacation or something?"

"Uh, yeah, for my mental health of all things. New environment and all for a bit."

"Tell me about it," they laugh lightly, grabbing some papers to staple. "After I got this job, it was a relief after the last place. Call center. Love helping people, but can take a toll on you."

"Nowhere near that, but I was a barista. Heard all kinds of problems. I get it."

I walk over to one of the chairs I used to always wait in. After a few minutes, I lean forward and ask, "Hey, do you know Patricia Fuller? Has she been in lately?"

"Oh? Trix?" I nod. "Her office was moved up a couple of floors. She's working today, do you want me to tell her you're here?"

"Would you mind?"

They shrug. "Sure. No problem."

I sink back into the chair, a bit relieved. Minutes tick by, and the doors open suddenly with Dr. Wilson walking in. Her hair is pulled up into a bun, a jacket in her arms. She pauses when she sees me, staring for a moment and then plasters on a grin.

"Hey, Dr. Wilson."

"Autumn, it's good to see you. How are you?" She walks up, squeezing my shoulder as she searches my face.

"I'm okay." She gestures toward her office door, hanging back to whisper something to Dex and then follows in close behind me. I sit down in my regular spot, hearing her lock the door and sit across from me.

"I was extremely worried about you." She lets out a sharp exhale. "Not hearing from you for so long, and then being contacted by Nancy that you'd left the state. Thought the worst, but you're here and not hurt, I hope."

My legs rub together, and I force a smile. Yeah, not at all hurt. Peachy.

"I'm okay. And I'm sorry if I scared you at all. Just some panic attacks that caused me to, well, you see—"

"Autumn, you don't have to explain yourself to me." She holds her hand up. "I was relieved to get *your* phone call yesterday and to hear *your* voice." Something twists in my stomach on how her voice changes. "I tried to speak with Nancy multiple times, but she kept insisting you were fine and would call when ready. Then explained you were with your...boyfriend."

Throat going dry, my stomach sinks lower as my neck begins to prick. "Yeah. He's been helping take care of me. Somehow, he's gotten even sweeter with how much he cares. And he *really* does care about me."

Her lips purse and the prickly feeling worsens. Warning signals run down my spine as her fingers tap the armchair. I adjust in my chair. It's fine. She's just worried. You disappeared for weeks, come on.

"I apologize for scaring you. Making a ruckus. I had a panic attack, freaked out, and had to get some...clarity for myself. Everything has been worked out and now I feel good enough to talk. I think it would be good if we talked."

"Do you?" She cocks her head. "Do you think you need to tell me? Perhaps the truth...*Autumn*?" I swallow harshly. "What is the truth, *Autumn*?"

"Why are you saying my name like that?"

"To help remind you who you are. How far *we've* come. Who you are now."

Get out.

"Dr. Wilson—"

"I'm very worried about your health, especially after your disappearance. It's very easy for you to fall back into old habits, and I think you may already have." *Run.*

"I haven't." At least not the ones *she* knows about. I never told her about the cutting.

Her fingers keep tapping on the armchair, and I notice her eyes flick to the clock behind me. "From what I understand, you went back into a dangerous environment when you shouldn't have. You know better. Those are some signs of slipping back into damaging habits, such as relinquishing boundaries. And let us not forget about *how* your relationship began with Mr. Luciano in the first place."

"What? We already discussed—"

"I'm afraid you've given your autonomy over to someone too

easily. Another old habit. Abandoning control out of fear, self-hatred, lack of self-esteem." Her voice is calculated and every single word whips at me. "Perhaps it was self-loathing or loss of confidence."

"That is *not*—" I stare at her as she folds her hands in her lap, taking a long breath. "I never told you Leo's last name. How do you know it?"

She clears her throat. "You have a tendency of staying in dangerous relationships, Autumn."

"What are you doing?" I reach back for my phone.

Celine is calm. Her movements small and short, but her eyes keep flicking to the clock. Her voice is like someone chastising a young child, demeaning. "I thought we had overcome those patterns, but sometimes others will restart those tendencies. Much like an alcoholic going back to drinking when around those who do. Is that what happened, Autumn?"

My chest trembles as I clutch my phone, keeping my eyes on her. "No."

"Are you sure? Being back in a...*familiar* environment may have influenced your decisions. But given you called, I believe a part of you knows that you needed honesty and stability."

"Stability?"

"Yes, I've spoken to the police, who firmly believe you may have been caught in—"

"What?" My heart pounds in my ears. "No, no...that's not...what are you—?"

"Were you not kidnapped? Taken against your will outside of the city *and* state?"

"Wait, *what*?"

"I had hoped from what you told me about this *relationship* with Mr. Luciano, it was a good thing, but it appears I was wrong. I apologize. I should've stopped it sooner, listened to my instincts and not advised such a relationship so soon. Clearly, you weren't ready yet."

My mind spirals as I stare at her in horror. This can't be happening.

Everything crashes into a thousand pieces as I listen to someone

I'd trusted for *years* about my trauma. My pain. Every word pierces and cuts at me. She told me to try with Leo. She *pushed* for me to get out more and have relationships. To *try*. Celine had been supportive, fucking impressed with our communication even.

How the fuck is this happening?

My chest tightens, and I narrow my eyes at her. "Why did you talk to the police?"

"They came to me."

"When?" Get out. *Get out.* Racing thoughts slam into me as I go through every exit in the building I've memorized, scrambling through the protocols I went over with Isaac this morning. "When did they contact you?"

"A week after you left New York."

"I was *back* in New York. I was fine and…" *gone from Roger,* "… Nan knew where I was. There was no—"

"You didn't contact me though."

"As *helpful* as you've been, you don't need to know my whereabouts at all times."

"I do in concerns of your mental health." Why does she keep looking at the clock?

"I'm a fucking adult and don't need to be watched. If I decided to leave, then that is *my* decision no one else's. Given I'm sitting in front of you, it's obvious I wasn't fucking kidnapped or taken against my will. Nan nor my friends reported a missing person. Who gave you that idea? What police officer—?"

"Detective Caltz."

Mother fucking asshole!

Anger boils in my gut. My hands shake, standing up as she does and continues to talk. "He contacted me after you disappeared from his care. He was worried, had every right to be, knowing your history. How many times did you disappear undercover? Or that final time which led to—"

"Shut it!" I point at her. "Don't you *dare* pin that on me."

I was watching three years of work, private sessions, intimate talks go down the drain. Every piece of advice crumbling to dust.

How much of it was real? Was *any* of it real? The cracks I've fixed the past couple weeks re-shattering.

"Detective Caltz believed you'd been pulled back into that world again, and that you may have been caught in their net. He was asking for help and information that could—"

"What are you talking about?" My hand trembles pulling my phone out and tracing my thumb over the button. "Why would he…" my heart clatters in my chest as she watches me with a calm, passive, sickening expression, "…*Roger* told you his name. He wanted information on Leo, which means you…did you give him my medical records?"

"It was life or death, Autumn."

I'm seconds away of puking up my breakfast. "You gave *my* medical records and information, private *fucking* information, to the police without my consent? That is against HIPPA—"

"Not if I believed you were in danger."

"To myself or others, which I wasn't!" I scream, stepping away from her. "Disappearing has *nothing* to do with that, especially if a family member or guardian, which is Nan, on record, knew where I was. And if he contacted you *after* I left his place, then you were *completely* in violation…you had no right to give them my personal information!"

I've been ratted out. Used.

My therapist of three years easily just gave over my private thoughts, ramblings, anxieties, fears, and more to the police. Worse, to Roger, whom she *knew* what he'd done to me. Made me do. On top of that, the one thing I wanted to remain private—Leo's and my relationship was no longer private. It was all in possession of *him.*

I didn't give him what he wanted. So, he played dirty, pretending he cared about me. *Again.*

"I did what I thought was right." Her voice is strict and awful. "You have a pattern of disregarding your own safety for others, giving in to those who may mean you harm. At times you can't tell the difference. You are self-destructive, and it is quite plausible you believe someone who means you harm and do what they say—"

"Did you even think I was healing? That I was better at all?" Emotions whirl, trying to make sense of all the hurtful betrayal flooding me.

"Of course." Celine crosses her arms. "Except you were… well, I couldn't stand by and let you destroy all the hard work we've done, ruining what we've accomplished."

"You just did." A sob works up my throat, but I push it down. No remorse is in her eyes as I move closer to the door.

"The police are on their way. You won't get—"

"Fuck you." I press the button twice on the phone and unlock the door to get out. Celine chases after me and I spin on her. "You gave over vulnerable pieces of myself to a man who pushed me to almost commit suicide multiple times while in *his* care." Her eyes widen. "But no, you can't *possibly* think that because he's a detective. You didn't do any of this cause you give a shit about me. It was for your own damn conscious. *Your* practice and *your* reputation. Not for me."

I head for the stairs, hoping to make it out before the police show up. Dex watches with wide eyes, gaping at us. Celine calls out just as the office door opens, revealing Trix. My friend doesn't pause to hug me close, and I freeze.

"I was so worried about you, Leanne said that you were—"

"Did you know?" I pull back, gripping her arms.

Her joyful expression falls away to confusion. She flashes her gaze at Celine. "What's going on?"

Celine starts, "Patricia, don't let her—"

"Shut up, Brutus!" I turn, pointing at her. My outburst makes Celine step back. Even on my harder sessions with her, never did I raise my voice at her, but I was beyond hurt now. I look at Trix, hoping she wasn't in on this. "Did you know she gave my medical records to the police? Without my consent?"

"What?" Trix clutches my shoulders, moving us away from the doorway. "Did they have a warrant?" She asks Celine.

"It's complicated—"

"So, no." Trix's voice drops.

"Detective Caltz—"

"I am speaking with Autumn right now, back away before I call the police on *you*," Trix warns Celine. She guffaws. I concentrate on Trix's warm brown eyes. "Hun, were you in danger of hurting yourself? Did you…we haven't talked, but Leanne never said—"

"Trix, please listen to me." I take her hands, hearing noise outside the doors and the elevator dinging. Fuck. I'm not sure if it's Isaac or the police. "I am safest with him. With Leo. Roger is trying to use me again. Please. You have to believe me on who to trust—"

The doors open and Trix puts herself between me and who walks through.

Roger's eyes lock with mine.

His dark eyes are ruthless. The room becomes tense as Dex presses themselves against the wall, and Celine becomes frozen. Trix keeps her hand in mine, unmoving.

"Do you have a warrant to be here? We have policies for our patients' health." Trix's voice is calm. Leveled. A memory flashes back from the hospital.

"Autumn Watson you need to come with me," Roger says, ignoring Trix.

"Warrant?" I ask.

"I don't need one to question you."

"And what would those questions be over?"

"I don't need to answer that."

"Then am I under arrest? If you don't have a warrant or paperwork—"

"You need to come down to the precinct with me." He takes a step toward us, cuffs coming out and Trix pushes me back. Roger flicks his gaze to her, scowling harder. "Ma'am, move aside."

"Warrant, *detective*. If not, then I suggest you state why you're here for her. She has a right to know," Trix speaks succinctly. "But I should have *you* know, I've already been informed her medical records were compromised, wrongfully placed in police hands without her consent or by court order. That is grounds for Miss Watson to sue Dr. Wilson *and* you. I'd be *very* careful in what you say next."

"Patricia, let the Detective do his job," Celine says. "You don't know what you're defending or—"

"I know *who* I'm defending. Do you?" Celine gapes at her.

I flick my gaze to the door. Where the fuck is Isaac or the others? Then again, I don't know who came with Roger.

"Fine." The cuffs jingle in his hands and he locks eyes with me again. "I believe she's involved with a homicide case, which gives me reason to take her in for questioning. You're correct I don't have a warrant, but she has a habit of running."

Homicide? He glares at me, and I glare back. Either he really hated the last note I gave him or he's trying to corner me to get me to talk.

Trix looks back at me. Determination flits over her gaze with some fear. She'll go down with me. She's always done everything to defend innocents, from the law or not. She'd sacrifice her own job to help me, and I can't let her do that. I can't have her dragged into this mess next.

And Roger knows that.

Fine. Celine's right. I'll self-destruct or whatever, but it's only due to not wanting those I care about getting hurt. Not if I can do anything about it.

I step around her, but she pulls me back and spins toward me, whispering low, "He doesn't have a warrant or even evidence from the sound of it, but they can keep you for up to 48 hours for questioning until they do. I don't know what's going on, but if it's about you disappearing and he has your records...he may find *something* to charge you with."

"I'm not letting you get in trouble for helping me."

"It's *my* job to help you," she whispers harshly. "You are my friend. And I promised you that night in the hospital. I meant it."

"Trix."

"I won't let them break you again." I stare at her, surprised at the ire in her voice. I grip her hand, mind scrambling on what to do. Roger isn't going to leave unless I'm in those cuffs. He'll forcibly arrest me if he must. Warrant or not.

The door opens again, and I relax a little when I see him, adjusting his suit.

Jameson moves past Roger, ignoring him as he approaches Trix and I. He nods to her, and she takes a step back for him to come close. "Miss Watson, are you alright? We noticed you were running late and then police cars showed up downstairs."

That's why they hadn't come up. Roger brought friends.

"I'm alright."

He looks at Trix, giving her an easy smile. "Trix, good to see you again."

"Nice to see you, too, Jameson." When did they get on a first name basis? "We're having trouble with Detective Caltz, who seems insistent on taking Autumn in for questioning, concerning a homicide case."

Jameson straightens, looking at Roger like he's just now noticed him. He adjusts his cuffs, expression much like Leo's when he's concentrating and barely showing emotion. He's cold with an air that's menacing.

"Detective, I don't believe we've met. Jameson Vasquez. I'm a friend, may I implore you for the reason why you're insisting on this matter?" Roger straightens at Jameson's stern and calculated tone.

"I don't have to answer that. I need to question her for multiple matters, Mr. Vasquez."

"Do you have a warrant?"

"No."

"Evidence that she's connected?"

"Confidential."

"Is that so?" Roger grinds his jaw. "That does cause a bit of a problem, doesn't it?"

"Let's not forget him convincing and lying to my *ex*-therapist to get my medical records without my consent," I add.

Jameson's eyes snap to Celine, who flinches and takes another step back. Dex moves down the hall of offices, staying out of the line of fire. Jameson clears his throat. "Guess we'll need to help you find a new therapist."

"Apparently," I scoff.

Roger takes a step forward. "She needs to—"

"Do nothing. If you don't have reasonable cause, evidence, or a fucking warrant…then I wonder what the *real* reason for taking her is? Because if you take her without just cause, I could have a judge decide your current case to be dismissed. Is that understood, *detective*?"

Roger's expression darkens as he frowns deeply. Suddenly, he straightens more and then looks at me without any emotion. Fuck. It's the same look he'd give when he wanted something. Something was up his sleeve, some fucking trick to get me to do what he wanted.

Get closer to Gabriel. Stay longer with Steve. Hack into their—

"She was one of the last people to see three men alive." My stomach plummets. "Three men she knew *very* well and could be connected to their deaths. I fully have reason to believe it's *why* she came to me weeks ago."

Homicide.

Jameson goes still next to me. Any worry ticking up my spine, stops. It gets yanked into nothing as a chill sweeps over my body. His words drip venom. All of me goes into a full defensive mode.

"Unless you want this to get messy, *Autumn*, you should come with me," Roger says in warning. "Or I could knock on someone else's door."

Time stands still as I glower at him.

He smirks smugly. My hands flex at my sides. He wants to play? Fine.

He's not touching Leo for doing something the police failed to do. Get rapists off the damn streets.

"I'll go with you." My voice is distant.

"Hun." Trix grips my arm.

"Autumn," Jameson whispers.

I look at him and he stares at me, searching my face for answers in what I'm doing, and then realization passes. Jameson's muscles tense along his neck and he puts his hand on my shoulder, whispering against my ear. "Juanita Hernandez is your lawyer. Ask for her. Don't give them anything, understood?"

Trix starts to protest, "You can't possibly—"

"I'll be fine." I force a smile.

She bites her lip as I walk toward Roger, but not before dropping my phone into Jameson's pocket. Roger doesn't notice as he gestures for the door, leaving right behind me. He grabs my arm, and I flick my gaze over my shoulder to see Jameson touch his pocket and nods. Roger pulls me into the elevator and pulls out a piece of paper, shoving it into my hands as we descend.

I smirk when I notice what it is.

"Really had to do all that? Embarrass me? After everything I gave you and helped you with? *That's* how you pay back what I've done for you?"

"All you ever gave me was a self-destructive complex, trauma, and pain." I growl back. "And maybe, *just maybe*, you'll think twice now before using a woman to do your filthy work."

He glares at me. "We'll see soon enough. Face the wall."

I turn and he slams me against the elevator wall, pinning my arms behind my back as he cuffs me. A shot of terror hits me, warring with memories as I feel the bite of the cuffs. I crumple the piece of paper in my hands. My chest constricts as the elevator hits bottom, and he leads me out of the building. There are two cop cars, and a handful of officers.

I glance down the block, noticing Isaac and Rudy with concern etched on their faces. Both their expressions betray their terror as they see Roger lead me to his car, handcuffed. They start for me, but I shake my head once and hear Jameson leave the women's center. I can barely hear him swearing in Spanish, most likely from seeing me in the cuffs. We get to the car and I push the paper back to Roger. He takes it as an invitation, slamming me against the car and I grunt as pain blossoms through my torso.

"Careful, you're under arrest for being involved with a homicide case," Roger warns against my ear.

"Hey!" Isaac yells.

"Police business, stay back!" One of the officers' yells, and then I hear voices collide behind me as Jameson intervenes.

"Keep the note. It's yours," I mutter back to Roger, looking over my shoulder at him. I can smell the cheap cigarettes on his breath. He shoves me into the car and the door slams shut. I notice him gripping the last page I wrote, hidden underneath the pages I concocted for him. A simple message meant only for him.

SARAH MARIE MITCHELL DIED FOR YOUR EGO AND PRIDE
NEVER AGAIN

Chapter 22

Forty-Eight

The fluorescent lights in the interrogation room hums. I sit back, looking up to where the cameras are. None are on.

When they searched me, Roger grumbled that I didn't have a phone. Got an odd look from another police officer for not having anything on me. Well, they took me away from those who have that shit. And may have dropped my wallet into Trix's hands without Roger noticing, too, just before I dropped the phone into Jameson's.

Pick pocketing skills stick with you.

I'm unsure how long I've been in here, trying to count the minutes in my head, but there's no way to tell. The room is grey with dark carpet, and the only color outside of that scheme is the darker grey door. Across from me is the viewing glass.

It's the same damn room Roger put me in to debrief for over ten hours. Wonder how long I'll be here this time?

I shift in my seat, tapping my fingers on the large metal table. No warrant. No evidence. Either I get out in 48 hours or Roger finds something that keeps me here longer.

I will get out.

The door opens and in walks Roger, slamming the door and then throwing a folder onto the table, making me involuntarily flinch. I glare at him as he leans over me, flipping open the manilla folder. I keep my gaze on him. His flicks down to the table, spreading out whatever was inside.

"Lawyer. Detective."

"I don't have to give you one until about 24 hours." He flicks his gaze to me. "Or until arraignment, but that means—"

"You have to charge me with *something*. Need more than just your 'hunch' or whatever." His eyes harden, frowning harshly. "Or you afraid that a judge will learn how you usually get some of your...evidence?"

He ignores the question, walking around the table to sit down across from me to push the pictures toward me. "Odd coincidence these men were found dead soon after you saw them." If he thinks his interrogation tactics are going to work on me—they won't.

"They're brought in on drug charges, suddenly released and then...boom, found dead a week later."

I look down to the photos. Three men. Bloated and covered in cuts. Their skin pale and discolored from being in water. And in the last photos of them laying on the morgue table, each has a bullet hole in their head. All naked and without their dicks.

An odd stillness settles in my bones. Deep inside myself a part of me closes like a book you know you'll never read again. Done. Gone.

Leo told me the truth.

"You came to me, panicked and worried, and then disappeared again. Peculiar, don't you think?"

"Why'd you tell Dr. Wilson you thought I was caught up in trouble? Maybe even kidnapped?"

I look directly at him. He licks his lips quickly, leaning back in his chair as he attempts to act like he owns the room. Yeah, after sitting in a mafia meeting yesterday, he's not that fucking scary.

"You were under my protection, then was gone. I was worried."

"Bullshit. You knew you lost me and wouldn't be able to use me."

"Using you?"

"To do your damn job. *Again*." I curl my lip at him, flashing my gaze to the pictures. "And it seems like someone *else* did your job for you, too."

"Did you know they were dead?" He asks suddenly. I scoff. "Not a no, so I guess you did and never reported it to the police? Another peculiar thing."

"Seriously? Using *that* on me?" I scoff again, rolling my eyes. Sitting back, I cross my arms and focus on keeping my heart rate down. The cameras are still off.

My anxiety spikes, pricking at my neck, but I know I can't break. Don't give him *anything*. There's no telling how much within my medical records he's sniffed through. He'll use any of it against me. Make me either give myself in or Leo. There's no evidence connecting me to the murders. Perhaps, none for Leo either, but I can't be certain. Roger will do anything to bring down another mafia boss, and unfortunately, he knows who those three men were, what they did to me, and who I ran back to. For Roger and me, it's not hard to connect the dots. But he needs paperwork, confessions, evidence to get what he wants.

We stare at the other, neither breaking. As the quiet stretches, an old version of me begins to crawl to the surface. A sinister, conniving side that was cultivated while undercover to survive. It creeps over my skin, and I let that take over to diminish and block out every emotion in my body. Unfeeling. Angry.

I'm numb. *Sarah.*

"Most would be disgusted seeing these," Roger says, pushing the photos closer. "Yet no reaction from you."

A cruel, empty laugh leaves me. I point at one of the photos, leaning forward. "Photos of three dead men who raped and tortured me for over twelve hours? You think I'd have *any* emotion in seeing them dead? How privileged are you, detective, to *not* know how it feels to have parts of you taken? I didn't kill them years ago. I haven't now. Whoever did, I'll give my thanks for the rest of my life. And so would every other woman they touched after me because *you* released them."

"Careful."

"What? Afraid whoever is beyond that glass is gonna learn how you made a deal to let them go?"

"That case was bigger than all of us," he scorns.

"Bullshit."

"Really? After *everything*?"

I shove the pictures back at him. "You endure what me *and* Sarah did; then you can tell me how to react. Which emotions to show. They're dead. Good. Least I can sleep easier and every other woman who fell to their hands because you…let…them…go."

"You have no idea what you're talking about. You think you knew *everything* that was happening? What was needed?" He leans closer, practically snarling at me.

"How much information did they get you? Was it worth it?" The darkness in his eyes and frown tell me he got jack shit. They probably disappeared on him. That's why they were in a club still selling drugs. "Were *they* your last informants and that's why you're pissed?"

"That's classified—"

"So, they *were*." I lean back, giving him a maniacal half grin. "That why you pressured me to help you? To come back?"

"No."

"Sure, about that? Because we both know how good I was at being your informant. And you lost me. *Twice.* No more connection to the underworld and now you're trying to get me to do what you want because you fucking suck at your job."

"Watch it."

"Are you seriously holding me for this?" I shove the pictures off the table casually. "That I had *anything* to do with their deaths? You're a real piece of work. I went to you for safety, instead you're planning to make me your sacrificial lamb. *Again.*"

He slams his hands on the table. "*You* came to me."

"And I will regret that decision forever."

Roger's eyes search my face, shoving his chair back as he bends down to grab the photos off the carpet. He thrusts them under my face, but I don't budge as he crowds me. "This kind of behavior is mob related."

"Do I look like the Joker to you?"

"No, maybe Harley Quinn with the route you're going."

"Well, you're no *fucking* Batman or Robin."

"Don't you mean that detective or whatever?"

"Detective James Gordon. But, of course, you'd forget the name of an *actual* good detective."

Roger's lip curls, pointing at the dead men in the photo, and says, "Mob is known to mutilate bodies. To send a message."

"Then why are you—"

"Or *maybe* it was a vindictive—"

"Watch it," I warn.

"It's something a victim would do." He drops the photos on the table. "Revenge for their *good* friend, who died at their hands." My eyes flick up. The cameras are on. "Justice in their head or not, this kind of retaliation is against the law. Murder that is. So, either you're gonna help me get whoever did this or I lock you up in their stead."

"Not sure what's more sickening. You trying to make me help admonish whoever killed those men or trying to punish the woman they assaulted and almost beat to the brink of death for it instead. You tell me."

"I want answers."

"No. You want an easy route back inside the mob again."

"You ruined that. Not me." Stupid prick. I want to fucking elbow him in the side, kick him like how he made me feel for a week. I've made a lot of dumb decisions but running back to him was the worst.

Unless I do what he wants, he's going to keep me in here. Try to torment me. Get me to out Leo or *anyone* to get him closer to what he wants.

"Time of their death?" I ask. Roger adjusts himself, standing up straight and walks back in front of me.

"Where did you go when you left my place?" He evades.

"New York." He scoffs at me. My expression remains neutral.

"How'd you get back into the city?"

I shrug. "A friend."

"Who?"

"Why?"

"May need them for an alibi."

"For what?" I gesture to the room. "You arrested me without charges or even giving me a full understanding of *why* I'm here."

"You're involved with those men's deaths."

"Am I?"

"Yes. You are involved with the mob, who killed them and perhaps even did it yourself," he states, pointing at the pictures. He's talking in circles, trying to get me to slip up.

"*When* did they die?" I ask again.

"Before you came to my house," he finally answers. "So…you got an alibi or not…*Ms. Watson?*"

My mind starts to scramble. I try not to show anything on my face, knowing that Leo probably pulled the trigger while I was on the ferry or evading Rudy at the train station. Shit. I can't even say, pull this footage, because I scrambled so many damn cameras in the city that Roger could hit me with illegal shit for messing with public security cameras.

Almost, I begin to panic, and then realize the timing. *While I was on the ferry.*

"Depending on their time of death, how would I have disposed them *and* gotten to your house when I did, then?" I throw back. His smugness falters. I lean forward, keeping my gaze on his. "Charge me if you're so certain. Come on, throw that physical evidence at me. Anything besides a hunch?"

His lip begins to curl. He arrested me without a warrant or without sufficient evidence, which means in the next 44 hours if he doesn't come up with something…it's more than just the case that can get thrown out. He didn't just put this homicide case in jeopardy, but his career and precinct, too. He's grasping for straws, trying to shake me, and I've got to shake him back. Roger thinks he's cornered me, but I could corner him instead.

"You were supposed to be a safe haven for me," I say. "But you weren't. I said I was done. There was no obligation on my end to tell you anything. I was *done*. Why would I *ever* help you again after what you cost me?"

"You knew what you were getting into back then."

"No. You used a young girl to get into the worst parts of the city because you were too damned scared to do it yourself. And then you continued to use her because you have a fucked-up hero-complex."

Roger frowns about to say something when the door opens. An older gentleman with a bald head and tanned skin comes in. His eyes dart to Roger. "Detective. Outside. Now."

Leaving the photos on the table, he stalks out and slams the door behind them. I can barely hear the harsh words coming from beyond the door and flick my gaze up to the cameras. Off.

Minutes tick by as I steadily stack the photos and place them back into the folder. One last look I see the face of the one I saw. The one who'd smiled at me at the club. Looked at me like I was a piece of meat. Something to devour.

"I'm left broken because of them…"

"You're not broken."

Less than 24 hours. That's all it took for Leo. While the one outside that door helped them walk. Gave them freedom to do it again, and it sickens me, knowing they probably did.

I shut the folder.

The door opens and the man from before walks in. "Miss Watson, I'm Captain Walton. I apologize for any—"

"Am I being charged?"

"Excuse me?"

I remain seated, looking up at him. "Am I being charged?"

His brows pinch together, deep lines appearing over his forehead. "No, unless you're going to give a confession."

"Yet…right?" The Captain's eyes flick to the glass. "That's what *your* detective wants, isn't? Or proof to who killed those men?" I follow his gaze to the emptiness. "*Anything* to warrant an arrest?"

"Miss Watson, given the nature of your arrest—"

"Did a judge sign anything that fully dismisses me?" I ask. The lines get deeper. I speak slower. "Have I been recused from this case? Or will your detectives just show up again to arrest me on a *hunch*? Will I keep being dragged here for that evidence Detective Caltz so *desperately* wants?"

A flicker of fear moves over his gaze. "I will handle Detective Caltz, Miss Watson."

We stare at each other. He gestures toward the door, trying to get me to move.

Handle him? No, he won't. Roger did things *his* way years ago, he'll do it again. Long as he plays by the rules, and he knew how to do that. This wasn't the same Captain from years ago, and from the way he keeps flicking his gaze to the glass...someone's watching.

"How long since I've been arrested, Captain Walton?"

He sighs deeply, jaw tensing harshly as he drops his hand. "Four hours."

I put my hands on the folder, pushing it across the table toward him. "I will not leave until his forty-eight hours are up in finding *real* evidence that connects me to these men's deaths."

"Ms. Watson—"

"Your detective wants to play games, Captain. I think it's time he deals with the consequences of them. So...you tell him he has forty-four hours to find *sufficient* evidence of my arrest or obtains a confession from me that proves he didn't just put your precinct in jeopardy by falsely arresting me. Let's be honest...if I was anyone else, you would have let him throw me in jail without cause."

His eyes widen, and he fully looks over at the glass for a beat longer than before. Uncertainty. Unless it's his boss on the other side, I have a dark feeling on who it is. Why else would he come in here trying to get me to leave? I wouldn't put it past Leo to pay him off. Except, if I leave now, Roger will probably only get a slap on the wrist. No, my bastard of an ex-handler deserves to lose far more than that. I just need to outlast him.

Whether Leo is on the other side of that glass or not, this was between Roger and me. And that fucker isn't laying his hands on the men who helped me this past week.

"Miss Watson—"

"My lawyer is Juanita Hernandez." I push the folder closer to the edge, not moving from my seat. The captain stares at me, bewilderment covering his face. I lean forward and whisper, "Forty-four hours, Captain. You tell Caltz his badge is on the line, so he better start proving how *good* a detective he is."

A beat of silence before he finally walks out. I sit back in the chair. My gaze moves to the glass. Deep down in my gut, I can almost feel him like an oncoming storm that's pissed that I didn't just walk out; take the 'get out of jail free' card.

Don't bail me out, I plead inside. I'm not leaving until I'm certain he'll think twice before coming after me or Leo again. So, fucking help me by the end of these 48 hours, while Roger tries to pin me with evidence, I'll have enough of my own to bury him without the help of a mafia boss.

I say loud enough for whoever is beyond that glass to hear, "Green."

Roger has come in to interrogate me twice. The first time he kept trying to get me to say anything incriminating that would involve me with the three men's deaths. The second was to try shaking me up, saying things like "he's going to hang you out to dry" or "you'll take the fall for him" and all the classic lines.

And I thought *I* watched too many bad movies.

It feels like hours as I sit in the interrogation room, becoming accustomed to the bright humming lights. I keep myself busy, tapping on the table and counting lines between the ceiling tiles. Every once in a while, panic tries to force its way up my spine. I quickly shove it down, reminding myself that I've been in worse than a closed off boring room.

Wait it out. Just wait it out.

I'm drawing invisible images on the table when Roger comes back in. He places a coffee on the table and sits down across from me. I glance at the swill then back up at him.

"Trying for good cop, now?"

"Figured you'd be tired."

"Is this coffee from your place?" I pick it up, smelling it and I swear the police need more funding just for coffee.

"Like it black, right?" He asks, sipping his with a passive expression. I give an amused look, sipping the stuff and swallow hard. Somehow the coffee at his place is better than this. Didn't think that was possible. "Whoops. Forgot."

"Giving me crappy coffee? Really think that's gonna get me to say something useful? Come on, Roger," I taunt him, leaning onto my elbows. "Decorated detective like you? You can do better than that."

"You're not as calm as you think you act. I know you." He puts his feet up on the table, causing it to jerk and the coffee to spill a bit. "You hate being alone. Right?"

I cross my arms. "Read that in the records you illegally obtained?"

"You were in danger."

"No, I wasn't."

"Tell me why you weren't then."

"I don't have to. You lied and manipulated my therapist to hand them—"

"She gave them willingly. Fully believing, as I did, you were a danger to yourself and others. Which is why we're in here." He takes a long sip, and I continue to glare at him. Silence ticks by as we sit.

I shove my coffee cup to the side. It's probably been hours since I've had anything to eat or drink, but it's not worth ruining that streak. My stomach tightens, being reminded that I haven't eaten since breakfast and then my lower abdominal area begins to hurt.

"Gonna keep me in here the entire time?" I ask.

"Like I said. You don't like being alone. Put you in a holding cell, for all I know you may make another *friend* like you did to get back into the city."

"Some of us aren't dicks, Roger. You should try it."

He puts his cup down, getting up and slapping his hand against the desk. I flinch without being able to stop it. My heart rate spiking at the sudden noise. Bastard. He leans down onto the table, coming in close. "You really just willing to sit in here, ready to rot for *him*? Go through this torment when you could just..." he snaps his fingers in front of me, making me jolt, "...get out? Do the *right* thing?"

My hands clench, one of them moving down over my lap and pressing my nails into my thigh. How much trouble would I get in if I punched him? "What do you know about the right thing?"

"More than you. Part of the job."

"Doubt it."

Roger walks around me, whispering near my head as he places his hand back down on the table. His breath smells like burnt coffee grounds, making my stomach tighten more. "No one will remember you," he whispers. "I mean, no one even remembered your *friend*... Sarah Marie." A pang hits my chest. "What makes you think they'll care if you disappear next? To jail? To the harbor like those men? Does he even know? What you did...to his *brother*?"

My eyes stay locked on the table before me, unmoving from the awful cup of coffee.

"Family is family for them, when do you think he'll get tired of you? Weeks? Months?" He continues to walk around me, trying to get me to look up. "Come on...Autumn. You *really* willing to waste it all for Gabriel's *fucking* brother? Or perhaps that's it?" He stops next to my ear and hisses in a dark tone, "Is that why, cause he's *fucking* you?"

My fingers dig into my thigh, spiking pain through me.

"Became his *whore*, huh?" He taunts. "Cause that's all you'll be to him."

I can feel my nails burrow into my skin, fisting my other hand. I continue staring at the coffee. All I see are hazel eyes. Tattoos. Furrowed brow.

"He's fucked a lot of women," Roger continues. "Come on, you're better than just some notch on a bedpost." He leans in closer. "Sarah."

"I need to use the restroom, detective," I say in an even tone.

For a moment, Roger doesn't move. Finally, he does and grabs his coffee. He leaves without another word, slamming the door behind him. My hands unclench and I rub at my thigh, taking a deep breath and start reciting *The Raven* under my breath.

***

F uck grey walls.

Somehow they're worse than Leo's penthouse and offices.

My fingers continue to tap on the table before I get up and pace. My stomach hurts, especially my bladder from Roger not allowing me to go to the restroom. It pinches at my sides, and I quickly sit back down again.

"Hey, I need to use the bathroom," I say out loud. Someone is beyond that glass. No one answers and the door doesn't open.

The intercom clicks. "We're short staffed. Someone will be along momentarily to escort you."

"If you put me in a holding cell, you probably wouldn't have to—"

"Just wait."

I cross my arms, glaring at the glass and wait. And wait. And wait.

"Mirror, mirror on the wall…won't you let me go down the hall?" No one responds. "Not a nursery rhyme crowd, got it."

I adjust in my seat, the pinching feeling now fully aching and it's like someone is stabbing at my lower belly. Roger is screwing with me. Trying to make me uncomfortable, but usually the police are smart enough to be in the room with you to question you during such time. Or he thinks I won't…

"Hey, ya'll ever see the movie *Secretary*?" Slowly, I put my elbows on the table, laying my hands down flat and sit straight up. It's quiet as I stare at the glass. My body shakes and my muscles clench, making it hurt even worse. From the waist down it's like every muscle is being pressed and pulled at the same time, down to my damn toes. It hurts to breathe as I continue trying to hold my damn bladder.

I wait, and no one comes.

"Fine."

My body revolts, anxiety telling me to hold it in from pure disgust. I ignore it all, and let loose, completely pissing myself. My pants become warm and wet, seeping down my thighs and into the plastic chair I've been sitting in. Once I've released my bladder, relief fills me as the pain subsides and I feel like I can breathe again. Every muscle that was taut becomes lax as the warmth moves under my legs and I hear it drip onto the floor.

A part of me screams at the wet warmth. My mind flashing back to other things, but I continue to force myself to go numb. Go back to other memories that are less harsh and demeaning. Focus on the relief and then the pang of hunger that follows.

The door slams open, and I only jolt a little. Roger and another stand at the door, staring at where the urine drips under me to the carpet. Both give looks of horror and the one I don't know gags a little. I would feel more disgust with myself and feeling dirty, but I'm too relieved with my empty bladder to fully care. And Roger's face is almost worth it.

He gapes at me, appalled and repulsed.

"I said...I needed the restroom."

A female officer walks me out of the interrogation room. Apparently, it's late, and it took them about thirty minutes to find someone to walk me into the women's bathroom. Roger had me stay seated in my own piss for that length of time.

Being covered in hot coffee and whipped cream was still worse and far stickier.

We head down the hall to the bathroom, just past the main hall to the bullpen of the precinct. The officer keeps me walking as I glance across the scarce night shift. My eyes flick to the clock. 2:30 in the morning.

Just as we're about to walk into the bathroom, I see the captain's office. Door closed and blinds open. Leo meets my gaze before the police officer moves me forward.

———

They replaced the chair.

Figured they would've changed rooms for me, but no, Roger had other plans. It doesn't smell like piss anymore, just cleaning supplies and there's leftover powder where they vacuumed when I changed.

I'm wearing sweats now. They even had me change out of my shirt. They're kind of scratchy, but comfortable enough. My head lays on my arms, sleep overcoming me when I'm woken up by the slam of the door. I jerk up, breathing heavy as Roger stands there with the door open and someone walks in with a coffee cup, water, and a plate with a bagel and pastry. They practically drop them onto the table, both disappearing through the door.

I groan, rubbing at my eyes and pushing my hair back. I shake off the uneasy feeling, traveling up my spine and pricking at my skin. Giving myself a few minutes to wake up, I stand and stretch. I walk around the room, rolling my neck and shaking out my limbs next. My eyes flick to the table, hungry, but not sure if I'm hungry enough for that nasty coffee.

The coffee cup isn't the same as before and the bagel is wrapped in plastic like it's fresh. Scrunching my brows, I move back toward the table and look at the bagel. Cinnamon raisin.

That's my favorite.

I stare at the pastry next, realizing it's a chocolate croissant.

My gaze moves to the coffee cup. *Blue Java Café* is printed on the sleeve, and I recognize Mabel's writing. *Miss you* with a heart.

Slowly, I grab the cup and smell the coffee. Once I've taken a deep breath, the fresh scent of properly roasted coffee beans fills my nostrils. It mutes the musty and overly clean smell within the interrogation room. I clutch the cup, taking another deep inhale and for the first time since I've been in here, I want to cry.

Americano.

I don't know if this is a ploy by Roger, meant to shake me. He could've found out about the Americano from the sessions I had with Dr. Wilson. Not sure if I ever told her about Leo buying me the croissant though.

I sip the coffee, not finding the overly bitterness of the drink, but a hint of sweetness at the right amount. Five sugars. There's only one person who knows how I'd drink an Americano.

In the quiet of the room, I take another small sip, smiling faintly and feeling a bit less alone. There are four knocks, quick like a heartbeat. Tap-tap. Tap-tap.

No other noise comes as I look over my shoulder, finding only my reflection. The knocks come again. They're coming from the other side of the glass. My brain scrambles through its tired fog and lack of food. I continue staring at myself, searching in my own eyes for the meaning. Protocols, procedures, numbers…finally, it hits me.

Check in.

Leo.

I lift the cup a little. "Yellow."

———

After this, I may make Leo paint his penthouse hot pink. Maybe fluorescent orange. Neon blue?

"Violet." I put my hands up, gesturing toward the walls. "And there can be velvet, too. Fuck it."

I've been talking out loud to myself for…I have no idea how long. Afraid that reciting

The Raven wasn't going to help much after the hundredth time, I just started rambling. Whoever

was on the other side of the observation glass has been getting my inner most chaotic thoughts.

And Roger gets bits when he comes by to wake me up, whisper crappy things, and remind me

that I pissed myself.

Yeahhhhh, don't care.

After having not found a bathroom in time while homeless, I've been in soiled clothing for hours. If he wanted to taunt me with how terrible this was, he shouldn't have forced me to be somewhere that was much worse. Like his house.

I've lost track of time, but know that Leo is probably counting the damn minutes. I'm surprised that a lawyer hasn't popped in yet. Or Captain Walton to come back to try dragging me out to save his ass and precinct. And then I remember how controlling Leo is. If I'm going this far to stick it to Roger in the end, then he's going to make sure everything out there is set. Make Roger dig his own grave.

Not to mention I can practically feel Leo's own wrath through the observation glass. Otherwise, it's the random taps on the glass to "check in" with me that I know he's frequently there. Leave it to my mafia boss boyfriend to communicate with me while I'm in interrogation.

Such a cutie.

Okay, maybe the isolation in the boring grey room, boring sweats, and humming lights are getting to me.

Maybe I could act out *The Room*.

"Violet room," I say out loud, pacing around the table and chair. "Oh! Soft ass bed and those rugs that look like something from Cosmo. The plush ones that you can sink your toes into." I laugh to myself, thinking of a 70's room filled with shag carpet. "Yeah, cause he'd totally go for that. Well, I could do that for *my* room. Apartment needs a pick me up. And some shelving. And…" I click my fingers in the air, and gesture at the floor, "…resin floor! That's it! The stuff people started doing making things look shiny and shit, but it could be like a galaxy. One far, far away. With silver. And stars." I lean against the table, staring at the ground as I try to imagine it. "Just one of those opulent rooms, you know? Makes you think of a bad romance novel or 90s film. Yeah, those."

I purse my lips, staring at the glass. Silence.

I scrub at my head and begin to pace again. The odd thing with this kind of isolation, is that it feels different than being normally alone. There's nothing in here apart from a table and chair, water sitting on top and a trashcan. In rooms or buildings with stuff, there's so much to occupy yourself with, yet you can feel paralyzed by it all.

Something has to make you happy. Anything from paintings, treats, movies, books, people…what's the point of feeling alone when all that is around you? Here? There's nothing. Just you. Like being homeless. Just you.

Okay, *definitely* sounding like the room is getting to me.

The grayness crushes me, surrounding me in nothingness.

I let out a long sigh. Rubbing at my head again, I then squint at the glass window. "Was I talking out loud or in my head?" No answer. "Fine keep your secrets, in the meantime, ever hear of *Reefer Madness: The Musical?*"

R oger slams the door behind him.

Same old, same old. *Stop protecting him. He's left you. He fucked other women—*

Blah, blah, blah.

I roll my head back, slumping into the chair that's beginning to make my back ache. Whatever tactics he came close to of getting me to snap with, he's overused at this point. Not sure when, but by the seventh or eighth time of him coming in, trying the whole 'good cop turned disappointed father' I realized I didn't talk about my father issues enough in therapy. Then again, I shut that entire life off when Sarah died.

Sarah.

That name keeps tumbling around in my head as I numb out every time Roger leaves. With the numbness, comes old memories and I have to clutch to the recent present. Not her. Not her anymore. She died. She—

The door opens, and when I look to see who it is, I can't help but stare.

The woman walks in with a pressed suit, dark curly hair around her shoulders that compliment her copper toned skin. She puts down a briefcase, opening it as she sits down and the door locks. I check the cameras. Off.

"Juanita," I say.

Her brown eyes flick up to meet mine, then back down to the papers she starts to take out. No recognition. No notice of who I am. She works for Leo, and by the way her face is now stone cold, I wouldn't be surprised if she knew *who* he was aka Mafia Don Supreme.

Huh, Mafia Don Supreme kinda sounds like an ice cream flavor.

"Mr. Luciano has provided me with everything to represent you," she says, putting a pen and paper before me. "We're building a case currently, and—"

"Do you even remember me?" I blurt out. She stares at me, searching my face and features, nose wrinkling a moment. Yeah, doesn't smell like roses in here. And even though they've been quick about getting me to the bathroom now, the sweats don't help much. "Never mind. How long have I been in here?"

"I don't think that's—"

"Tell me."

She inhales sharply. "Twenty-Eight hours."

"Huh, reached the halfway point. All downhill from here," I say, leaning back in my chair.

"Miss Watson, I need you sign this."

"Why?"

"Mr. Luciano has explicitly—"

"Or you can just tell me what it is."

Another sharp inhale. How exasperated would she be if she realized I'd been the one who spilled coffee on her boss' Italian leather shoes?

"This makes me your attorney, so that I may represent you and file against the precinct for their misconduct."

"Misconduct?"

"I've been informed you soiled yourself due to them not allowing you to use the restroom in a timely manner and that you were not given food for over eight hours or water for that matter," she states. "It is one of the reasons why I've not been here earlier. We've been building a case for you, which includes the police illegally obtaining your medical records, arrest without a warrant or sufficient evidence to sustain such arrest, and lastly, that Detective Caltz has a personal bias that has impeded his judgement, which he should've recused himself earlier on this case for. My job is to make certain he will *never* bother you or Mr. Luciano again once you walk out those doors."

I stare at her as she keeps a straight face. Oh, so this is who Leo was referring by saying he has *very* good lawyers.

"All that enough to strip him of his badge?" I ask.

"It's a start."

Ignoring this unexpected twist of fate, I take the pen and sign my name. As I hand the pen back over to her with the paper, I lean forward to tell her what I've kept quiet about since the women's center. She tilts her head at me as I gesture a finger for her to come closer. She does, raising a brow.

"Detective Caltz stated I was under arrest after he cuffed me, but never read me my Miranda Rights," I whisper, covering my mouth so those watching can't see.

The slow smile on her face is the best thing I've seen in 28 hours.

The floor isn't too bad to sleep on. Makes me miss my apartment's.

I sit cross legged, looking bored as Roger sits at the table. His chair is turned to me, lounging back like he has all the time in the world. He stirs his coffee with a stick. The one he brought me was from the breakroom again, I'm guessing. Certainly, isn't the Americano that Leo was able to smuggle in for me.

I tap my fingers on the cup sitting directly in front of me. I concentrate on every ring that's created from the tapping and creating ripples, while imagining it's a lake…river…Roger drowning.

The lights continue to hum. A constant white noise for me at this point. And they don't hurt my eyes anymore, especially if you stare at the grey walls long enough. Which I probably have.

"What happens if you leave?" Roger breaks the silence.

"When." He clears his throat, gesturing for me to answer him. His cocky air reminds me too much of the 'olden' days. "Probably go get better fucking coffee."

"And then?"

I eye him, unsure where he's going with this. "Take a shower." His dark eyes don't leave mine as he sips from his cup. "Change clothes. Take a damn nap. Watch a movie."

"Back to *his* hotel?"

"Maybe."

"You stay in his personal suite?"

"Maybe."

Roger snaps his fingers, banging his hand against the table and I flinch. Crud muffins, every damn time. "Wait, are the rumors true then?" I cock my head at him. "That he has a *fuck* suite that he uses?"

Don't show him anything. You know Leo. You know—

"You didn't know that?" He continues, leaning back and sipping his coffee loudly. "Hell, half the precinct knows that. Leonardo Luciano, the hotel mogul with rooms to spare to fuck and leave those women in. He doesn't go to events often, but when he does, he always leaves with women. Never the same one. All beautiful. Heard he was like that out in California, too."

The folder Roger had brought in is flipped open, and he tosses copies of newspaper articles to the ground in front of me. They're articles about Leo. Dressed in tuxedos. Women barely wearing anything. Auctions he was a part of to promote the opening of the *Italian Lily*.

"Get a date with a hotel mogul!" "New millionaire bachelor in town!" "Millionaire with ALL the assets"

I stare down at the headlines. My gaze flicks over the dates. All of them are within the first couple years he'd come back from California. I come across one of the pictures of him standing with others at some charity event. No smile. Uncompromising expression while everyone else has a smile plastered on their face. And I swear there's no emotion in his eyes.

My mind flicks to the shimmer of his hazel gaze. The breeze brushing past as the Harley rumbled beneath us. The smell of leather. His hand squeezing my leg. Blue hazy morning. Every bit feels far away, like a distant memory, when it should feel fresh.

What comes easily is staring at the date.

I'd been near there. The hotel. And…I remember that suit. My face in the window. I slipped and fell, and someone held their hand out. A concerned voice had followed me as I kept walking into the winter wind. I reach down, tracing my finger over his face.

"You're apologizing for falling?"

Realization slams into me. That was him. He'd been attending a charity at his hotel and must've been outside when I fell.

Abruptly, I start laughing. I throw my head back, laughing for the first time since I was brought here. My hands scrunch the papers, wrinkling them. There's a piece of me that snaps as I continue to laugh and point at Roger with the papers in my hands. "You knew, fucker. You *knew*, didn't you?"

Roger frowns at me, face pinching in confusion. "Knew what?"

"You knew," I continue to say. "You fuck. Less than a block away. That's not a fucking coincidence."

"What are you talking about?"

"The drops," I sneer through delirious laughter as more of myself cracks. More of Sarah snaps. "Under their nose. Under their nose you *always* said. You *knew*!"

Roger gets up, shaking his head at me like he's the one who's disappointed. I stand, shaking throughout my entire body as I accidentally knock over the coffee cup. It spills across the carpet as I stalk toward Roger as he moves toward the door.

"You pompous, manipulative, motherfucker! How much did you lie to me about?!"

"Calm down!" He yells into my face.

"No!" I scream back, coming closer. "I will *never* calm down!"

The doors slam open, and a couple of officers start to come in, but

Roger holds his hand up as he watches me. For a split second I see glee cross his eyes, and the moment I do, I realize he's getting through my defenses.

Quickly, I step back. My laughter has stopped and now I seethe. My entire body quivers, vibrating with years worth of anger.

We remain staring at the other in a silent showdown.

He knew about Leo before I came to him.

Perhaps not that Leo was boss or pulling the strings, but he knew that Leo was involved. He knew about Leo being in town when I went to him. He said it himself, that he wondered if Leo was involved. Roger's been waiting for the last three damn years to find something on him. The last Marchetti brother. Not caring about my safety if he was right.

He put in the recommendation for *Blue Java Café*.

He recommended the *Luna Stella Women's Center*.

My handler had put me right back into the fire without me knowing for *three years*. The case never ended for him. Bringing me back was always the plan.

Used me. Manipulated me.

Tears begin to stream down my cheeks as not a lick of emotion comes over his face. And in a broken voice I whisper, "I *trusted* you."

He steps forward, bringing his face close and I feel sick smelling his breath. Dim brown eyes lock onto mine. "*You* failed me first."

My lips curl in a snarling expression as I practically growl. Hate fills me. Betrayal. Everything I'd done, I'd given, forsaken, and lost. Gone because of the sanctimonious man in front of me that I should've slammed the door to years ago.

I'm not sure who I hated more. Him or Steve.

"Try not to keep spilling *shit* in my interrogation room," he says, turning to leave with the other officers.

The door shuts and locks, leaving me alone in the grey room once more. I turn slowly, still seething as I look down at the papers. I get on my knees, spreading out the papers and stop as my hand comes over his face.

"You're not broken."

I fist my hands, crumpling the pictures as tears stream down my cheeks. I want to scream. Flip the table. Throw the chair. Punch the walls. Dig my fingernails into my hair. My skin. Cry. Yell.

All I do is kneel on the coffee-soaked ground, concentrating on the wrinkled picture of Leo's unsympathetic face and furrowed brow.

* * *

I'm slowly snapping apart.

My legs feel numb as I sit in the chair, staring at the metal table. Roger has come and gone twice. I've refused to speak with him. The rest of me feels deadened from simmering anger. It swirls around and around.

I've tried to sleep, but the screaming thoughts won't stop. The betrayal. The feeling of worthlessness. The returning emotion of it all being a lie scratching at my skin. How much of my life was never truly mine? Every so often, I can feel those old cuts pulse and remind me how worthless I've believed it to be true.

I'm not sure I can do this. I don't want to play this fucking game anymore. I want out.

I want out.

The lights hum. Silence. Until…

Tap-tap. Tap-tap.

I look up at the window. It happens again, faintly.

I want to scream "red" and allow Leo to get me out of here.

My gaze moves to the newspapers on the carpet still, wrinkled and stained. Suddenly, I see those hazel eyes I've clung to in my dreams. How emotionless they are in the pictures. Were they that empty when he tried to help me that night?

Tap-tap. Tap-tap.

My reflection stares back at me as I look up once again. Even though all I can see is me, I know I'm not alone. That small piece knowing Leo's on the other side, twists my anger to not give in. Not yet. I *will* outlast Roger, no matter what lies are uncovered.

"Yellow."

"Tell me why," I whisper to myself, laying on my side on the table. "Ain't nothing but…" I continue singing the song softly as I stare at my reflection in the glass. I shiver a little from the cold table, scrunching my body up as I continue to sing the Backstreet Boys.

Roger hasn't returned. No clue how much longer. Could be hours or minutes.

I'm left alone in the interrogation room with the fucking grey walls and my thoughts.

After three more songs, I stop singing. Just the low hum of the lights.

Silence.

"Did you know Nicholas Cage bought this…pyramid to be buried in?" I say quietly. "New Orleans. Inscribed with 'omnia ab uno'. Also owned a haunted house. New Orleans again."

I continue talking, moving on from random facts to movies he's starred in. I just keep going, laying back on the table, even as my body stiffens at the hard surface. The dark thoughts creeping towards me in the quiet are held at bay as I tell whoever is on the other side about Nicholas Cage.

The door opens, Juanita and Captain Walton entering.

"Forty-eight hours, Miss Watson, you're free to leave," she states, then flicks a cold gaze to Walton.

She continues talking about paperwork, suing, restraining order, and more but my mind starts to fuzz out. My legs feel wobbly as I stand. My throat is dry as I walk out next to Juanita, who speaks succinctly with the captain as we head into the bullpen. It's late afternoon. Roger sits at his desk watching as we pass, heading for the captain's office. Our eyes meet and his gaze darkens, frowning.

Checkmate, bitch. I made it.

We enter the office and the last 48 hours almost crush me right then and there. Leo turns, his hardened features making him terrifying with an irate look in his eye.

A shaky gulp goes down my throat as I move toward him. My hands are trembling as all the pressure on my shoulders loosen. Leo barely takes two steps before he yanks me into his arms, surrounding me in his warmth and safety. He breathes heavily, chest expanding in sharp breaths as he strokes my hair back. I grip onto his suit, not giving a shit if I'm wrinkling it. Leo kisses my head as the door shuts.

Walton starts to speak, "Miss Watson, I'd first like to—"

"You don't have the privilege to speak with her." Jameson's voice comes out of fucking nowhere.

I barely turn my head, seeing him in the office as well. He's wearing a similar suit to Leo's, pristine and clean.

"Then, Mr. Luciano—"

"Him neither," Jameson states, moving forward and adjusting his jacket. "All of this could've been avoided if you'd just taken care of that loose cannon out there as we discussed weeks ago."

What?

"I understand that, but—"

"But nothing, I've had to disturb several judges for your incompetence," Juanita intervenes. "Not to mention, while under your leadership, the mistreatment that Miss Watson endured. Or do you always treat potential suspects as you have with her?"

"Or he just allows a low grade, detective run his precinct," Jameson joins.

"Mr. Vasquez, Caltz is a decorated detective and well known for his contribution to the...downfall of numerous crime bosses. He's been awarded multiple times since I've come into my position here. To the others here he's a...well, hero."

"Then it's time for your *hero* to fall," Leo finally speaks with disdain and menace. "Or we may rethink certain arrangements, *including* your future with the NYPD."

I can practically hear the captain swallow hard, and my body starts shaking for a different reason. He's actually under their thumb. Roger works within a precinct controlled by the mafia. Well…fuck.

At this revelation, my stomach plummets and I shake more.

Leo nods. Jameson takes that as his cue, and gestures for Walton to sit down. "Let us talk about your *future* in general, Captain."

Gently, Leo turns me around and keeps his hand at the small of my back. We walk out of Captain Walton's office. One more time, I look over at Roger. He sits at his desk, glaring at me with two other officers next to him. I yank my gaze away from him as Leo and I approach the elevator and get on. Once the doors close, my knees buckle, and Leo catches me. "Almost out."

He hugs me close, and a sob catches in my throat. My stomach churns and anxiety moves up my neck, waiting for police officers to be there when the doors open. For them to take me away again. Back to the damn grey room.

"Leo," I murmur.

"Almost there. I'm getting you out, dear Watson." He kisses my temple, helping me stand on my own again. His hand massages into the back of my neck, and I want to whimper at the soft caress. Fuck, I feel with each step away from the interrogation room the more I feel like I'm tumbling into a familiar dark abyss. Just before we get to the bottom, he bends next to my ear, "Good girl."

I straighten at the honorific as the doors open. His hand remains at the small of my back, guiding me down the hall and I see Isaac at the entrance. "Nancy is waiting at the bookstore. Perimeter is secure," Isaac says, eyes staying on me even as he addresses Leo.

"Double the watch. I won't be long."

"What?" I ask, turning toward him as terror fills me. Oh, fuck no, I did *not* just go through my own fucked episode of *Criminal Minds* for him to leave me. "Leo."

"You're going to the bookstore," Leo says, turning me toward him as he cradles my face. "Make it look normal going home. Nancy already knows all that happened. Stay there until I come. Do you understand?"

I swallow hard as I stare into those hazel eyes. The ones I kept seeing randomly in coffee cups. Bagels. Newspapers. Grey walls.

"Yes," I whisper.

He brings his face in close, whispering against my lips, "I love you. I will take care of the rest, my dear Watson. Wait for me." He kisses me and a sob gets caught in my throat. I hold onto his arms as he kisses me, relief and anguish hitting like a truck.

Leo pulls away, placing one last kiss on my forehead and then nods to Isaac. His features become stone again, menacing as a darkness covers him. I stare as he steps away and the small crowd parts for him as he stalks towards the elevators.

"Miss Autumn." Isaac touches my shoulder and I jerk at the contact. I stare up at him, loosening a breath and grab his hand. "We've got your back. Never stopped."

"I know."

He leads me out of the building, and I take a deep breath of the fresh air. Isaac lets me take a few moments to inhale the outside, smelling every city scent that was absent from the staleness within.

Out. I made it out. I fucking did it.

Yet, with every step I take toward the car, my stomach twists and my body shakes. All the nerves built up, overwhelming me at once and I feel lightheaded. Without much warning, about twenty feet from the car with Rudy and Julio next to it, I puke. It spills out onto the pavement, burning my throat as my chest heaves. Isaac tries to stay beside me but is quickly pushed aside by Rudy who sweeps my greasy hair back.

"We got you, *bärchen*. You're safe. We've got you."

"He can't come for you again, *hermana*," Julio says from the other side. "You made sure of that."

I puke the last of my stomach's contents, breathing in through my nose as Rudy rubs my back. All three men help try to soothe me, finally getting me to stop dry heaving and get me into the car. Rudy takes the wheel, while Isaac sits in front with him. Julio remains in the back with me, putting his muscled arm around me. He hums something of a lullaby when I start to finally sob freely as Rudy drives away from the precinct.

Chapter 23

Our Sharp Shadows

Nan embraces me as I cry against her shoulder. She rocks me slightly, shuddering a long breath. "Oh, my dear, you're home. You're okay."

I grip onto her as sobs wreck through my chest, trembling as she hugs and soothes me on the sidewalk outside the bookstore.

"Let's get you inside. Proper food," she says, keeping me close as we head through the bookstore to her apartment. I sniffle as she brings me into her warm home. The colors are a relief from the drab grey of the last 48 hours. Rubbing my shoulder, she sits me down on her comfy sofa and pulls a blanket over me. She moves to the kitchen, coming back with tea and small sandwiches before sitting.

"Well, don't just stand there. Sit down yourselves, no point in looming."

"Ma'am—"

"Don't disagree with me, Isaac. Nothing wrong in sitting down for a spell. Besides, you've got enough guards around this block to scare off sewer rats. Sit. Been a long couple days for us all."

A stifled laugh comes out of me, hearing her order them around. Isaac and Julio sit across from us. I hear a door close, and I presume

Rudy decided to stay outside. Each breath I take is longer than the last. Nan gives me a tissue and starts to put a cup of tea together. She then places a couple sandwiches directly in front of me.

"Eat, dear."

I do, almost moaning at the taste of her simple sandwiches. My stomach clenches feeling a bit better as I drink some tea and look around the old familiar space. Seems like forever since I've been here.

It's only been a damn month.

Her apartment has light yellowish orange wallpaper, trimmed with dark wood and some floral designs. The living room is filled with trinkets from around the world, including a glass cabinet with porcelain statues and china dishes. Her furniture is soft and old, plush like a stuffed animal you've had forever. The small alcove that leads into her kitchen has pictures along the wall of her family down south. She has a short hallway that leads to the bathroom and bedrooms, and the window near the back is covered by her lacey curtains. Her home emulates what I always thought grandparents' houses should look like from movies I'd watch growing up. Purely warm and smelling of fresh herbs, tea, and candles. The candles were always Finn's thing I was told.

As I eat my third sandwich, Nan gets up and starts to play some jazz. Holding my tea close, I sit back with a shaky breath. I catch a glimpse of Isaac and Julio exchanging a look, watching me. They faintly smile, but I can see how forced it is.

Nan comes back and rubs my thigh. "I'd hoped to see you again under better circumstances, but I'm very glad you're out of that dreadful place finally."

My gaze flicks to the other two, now both stone faced. "Nan, how much did they tell you about what happened?"

"Well, everything. I had to help sign a few things to testify against Dr. Wilson, and whatever else that Juanita woman asked me to do."

"Wait, Nan, they involved you in…y'all weren't supposed to involve her." I turn toward Isaac and Julio. "No one—"

"Shh, dear, as I said, I know *everything*." I pause, bringing my gaze back to her warm, brown one. A guilty smile begins to pull at her lips, but my face only falls and cracks.

"Oh, dear, did you really think that I wouldn't find out eventually?" She folds her hands in her lap, but fidgets.

I set my tea down carefully. "Nan?"

"I had to be sure what I knew about Leo in the beginning, including his intentions, but I think he should've—"

"Hold on, hold on…I've barely slept and must be hearing things. *What* do you know about Leo?"

"We should wait to tell her, Nancy," Isaac says.

Nan looks at the other two, who adjust in their seats.

Not liking the guilty looks and tone of their voices right now, and Nan acting weird. Perhaps, I'm dreaming and I'm lying on the interrogation floor, drowning in crappy coffee. Yup, that's happening.

Isaac clears his throat, "Miss Autumn, we can wait to discuss with you—"

Nope this is real.

"I should tell her now," Nan interrupts.

"Nancy—"

"Tell me what?" I ask again. I try to stand, but Nan gently pulls me back into my seat. Julio clears his throat. "Crud muffins, just say it."

"I know that Leonardo is a mafia don." Nan's collected tone makes me stop. "*Before* you disappeared."

I stare at the coffee table. What?

Isaac and Julio grumble under their breath. My head shakes. "No. No, even I didn't—"

"I thought you knew who he was and was trying to hide from me again." Another crack splits my heart. The words seem to echo in my head. "When you disappeared, I thought he hurt you. But then he called me, worried sick and then he offered a way for you to contact me. And then you called, and there was so much confusion in your voice and fear. You sounded so much like…when you first moved in. Fearful of the police. I hoped you'd come back, and you did, but then

Leonardo took you out of the city. I'd have come up myself, but he insisted you needed space."

I whisper, "How did you even know?"

I had no fucking idea, and I'd been undercover for over a year with the mob.

Her smile becomes sad, squeezing my hand a little. "Little things. I wasn't quite certain at first, but when I was, I warned Leonardo to tell me the whole truth and his reasons with you. Especially, when his *men* tried to come get your things without me hearing from you, yet." She eyes the two across the way, and Julio clears his throat.

"Just doing our jobs," Isaac answers.

"Yes, I know. A little too well I think at times. The girl can make her own decisions."

"We are well aware of that, Nancy," Isaac intercedes, his facial expression becoming firm. "We've never forced—"

"Well, given Leonardo's status, and he seems to—"

"Wait, wait, wait," I say, getting up and beginning to pace, feeling just as caged as I was in the interrogation room. "Little things? What do you mean...?"

My words trail off as I look at her. Faint guilt lines her face as she averts her gaze from me. "Nan...how did you know Leo's a mafia boss?"

She picks up her tea, trying to act nonchalant as she releases a deep sigh. I begin to realize how much of the truth I didn't actually know these past few years.

"It never felt like it was needed for me to tell you everything. It's been done a long time. But while you were away, Leonardo said that I should tell you. Something about us all being guilty with our secrets, and you deserved the truth. I needed to tell you everything, which I planned to do when you returned, and well, no point dragging it out anymore. Apart from knowing who Leonardo is..." she sighs exasperatedly, "...but my Finn worked for his father."

Julio starts to speak, "Nancy, the boss wanted to wait—"

"No point spreading it out like thin butter on toast. Or wait for someone else to do it. We're not always going to be on *his* schedule.

And he doesn't have to be around for *everything* when this is between her and I."

At some point I'm going to wake up surrounded by humming lights and grey walls. Right? I pinch myself. Nope.

The sandwiches I just had feel like stones in my stomach.

"Now, dear," she says, and pats where I'd been sitting. "Let me explain. What we need is to get it all out and clear the air now."

I'm half tempted to tell her what I needed is a nap. Ice cream. Different fucking clothes to wear or at least those that are mine. To give me a fucking minute as the fog in my brain thickens. Except I'm too exhausted, parts of me falling away as I sit down. Any anger in me is shoved so deeply under the exhaustion, I can't feel it.

I'm just so...tired.

She waits for me as I close my eyes, reciting a few stanzas in my head. And then a couple of bad lines from Nick Cage movies before I nod for her to talk.

"I knew that I was bound to lose the bookstore due to that 'interest' rate I'd been given," she starts, averting her gaze from me again. "I never told you, because I couldn't bring myself to tell you the truth, knowing what you went through. I never meant to keep secrets but was trying to protect you. You've always been like a daughter to me since you...wandered into that bookstore." She squeezes my hand gently. "When we had that first dinner with Leonardo, it was the way he spoke, his demeanor, and words were very much like...well, his father. Suddenly, my 'landlord' was gone, and I knew for certain." Nan shakes her head as she swirls her tea, voice becoming distant. "You never forget the Marchettis. Never."

I swallow hard.

"The boss knew who Finn was," Julio adds softly. "Soon after he bought most of the block, Jameson was pissed, cause of the random buy and that it kicked out who originally *owned* the block. But then he told the rest of us, and we made the connection that her late husband had worked for Riccardo. He remembered."

Julio nods toward one of the pictures on Nan's mantel. It's of her and Finn from years ago, long before I met her.

Elm Jed

"Leo was never going to out Nancy," Isaac tries to explain gently to me. "For several reasons, but definitely not until he told you who he was. But when you disappeared, it became clear why she was so secretive, especially with you. We were all just trying to protect you, Miss Autumn." I meet Isaac's blue gaze. "Promise."

"Were you gonna let the bookstore get taken?" I ask her abruptly.

"I'd have figured out something," she answers solemnly. "It was pure fate for Leonardo and you to bump into each other." She pats my hand again, trying to be reassuring. "But you and I would've made it work if needed."

"What uh, happened to the guy?"

"Advised to move out of town," Isaac answers. "Small bit mobster from another family and was giving some of the cut to them. Until Leo bought the block—"

"It became *his* territory," I finish. Oh, gee more white lies. I've been living in an apartment owned by the mob *before* Leo. Just couldn't shake'em, could I?

"Leo didn't kill him," Julio reassures, and I give him a bored expression. "May have taught him a few lessons, but the guy's breathing."

"She's had a long day and night." Nan waves them off, but shudders when she says, "No need to discuss…*that*."

Oh, yeah, cause this is *so* much better.

I sigh, trying to keep from screaming or just completely numbing out. I know Nan is trying to be honest, but this timing sucks Spaceballs. My brain is already filled with fuzzy noises and the fog feels heavier and heavier.

"How long was Finn in the mob?"

"About fifteen years," she answers, and I gawk at her. That long? "We were small potatoes, well, he was. He did stuff for passports, identification cards, carrier, and, well, we were comfortable. He took care of us. Made enough to open the bookstore and retire, and then Riccardo died. Finn got out soon after."

Well, I guess now Leo and Nan can swap stories around the fireplace.

"That's how you were able to help me change my name. The little details I hadn't thought about," I tell her.

"Learned from my Finn." She still won't meet my gaze.

Pulling my hands away from her, I place my head into my hands. The weight on my shoulders gets worse and I'm beginning to feel sick. Suddenly, the sweats I'm wearing feel too scratchy. I can smell the urine on me again.

"I'm sorry if you feel like I deceived you," she says. "I was doing what I could to give you a safe home. And you had nowhere else. Besides, the old owner never came around, long as I paid. For those past three years, I thought we could put it behind us, but then Leonardo came around."

"Yeah," I mutter.

Behind us, sure, until she was sucked dry of money and the bookstore.

"And now may not be the greatest time, but I don't know what that detective may have put in your head or made you believe. I've always wanted to help you, and to make sure the air is clear."

I pull my hands away. Finally, Nan meets my gaze and there's the full guilt. Pity. Except, there's relief on her face, too. This insidious voice in my head says, *she's only clearing her conscious, not because she loves you.*

"Who'd care if you disappeared...again?" Roger's voice mixes with the other.

I shake off the thoughts, tugging at that piece of numbness again. I clear my throat, "What happened to Trix?"

"She's fine," Isaac answers. "Everyone presumes she was only doing her job."

Anger blossoms. "Because she *was*."

"Meaning, no one suspects of her being involved."

"*Because* she *isn't* involved in this fucking mess," I scoff. "And I swear to everything, if you involve her or Leanne next, I am putting ink in all your motorcycle engines."

Their eyes bulge. Yeah, I'm pissed off enough I'll fuck with the bikes. In reality, I'd never, they're too precious, but they don't know that.

My chest constricts, hurting at the thought of Leanne or Trix being arrested next or framed for bullshit reasons. Or worse. And the main denominator for whose fault it is— me.

"Autumn," Nan whispers, touching my lap and I press my legs together, feeling where the old cuts are. "I'm...I'm sorry. But if I did it over again, I wouldn't change my decisions. You needed peace."

Which meant lies.

"I...uh, I need a minute, actually...I really need to get out of these clothes." I get up, heading for the door as all three stand. I stop them, my body beginning to tremble. "I'm just going upstairs. Please just let me get changed and give me a minute. I'm not...mad. Just really fucking need a minute. Some space. I just need...time alone."

I walk out, almost stumbling through the door as my chest hurts and a headache forms. The fog around my head worsens, exhaustion weighing on me. Slowly, I head up the stairs that don't feel familiar anymore. Once I get to my door, I find that it's open and walk in.

It's clean.

Movies that are still here are stacked in a neat little rack against the wall. Blankets are folded and placed neatly over the sofa. The kitchen has been cleaned; dishes put away. There're new baskets with my stuff in it, organized as I always kept telling myself I'd do. Staring at the space, I go to my bedroom and find new hangers holding up all my clothes. Bed is made and there's a new hamper. The place feels practically new, completely ready for someone to come back home to.

A sob catches in my throat as I tear off the sweats I've been in. I don't know what happened to the clothes I wore into the station, and don't really care. I tug on some cotton pants, short sleeved shirt, and one of the cardigans I left here from Leo's. Going back out into the apartment, there's a new dishrack in the kitchen and the fucking fridge is new, *including* the microwave. He updated my apartment. For when I came...back.

Emotions tear through me. This was him trying not to smother me, right? He wasn't leaving me? No, he'd not go through all that just to leave me. Or maybe he didn't want me near him so much? What if that was a lie, too? What if Roger was—?

No.

"Fuck," I mutter as I sit on the living room floor.

Thankfully my old television set is still here. I sit on the rug, holding my knees in close and stare up at the ceiling as I try to decipher my thoughts. Except they're a maelstrom. I've barely been in the city for three days, and I've sat in a mafia meeting, betrayed by my therapist, arrested, kept in an interrogation room for two days, and found out that Finn was involved with the mob.

Crud muffins, when did my life turn into a soap opera?

I rub my face, setting my chin on my knees and stare at the blank television screen. Anger. Betrayal. Guilt. All of it swarms me at once. I feel sick to my stomach, trying not to dwell on any of the horrid moments. How had I done this in the past? I'd spent *weeks* going through shit like this. Except, now, I don't know how to endure it anymore.

My head feels fucked. And I swear I can still smell piss on me.

Stomach lurching, I hold myself tightly and feel the dark emotions rise. They lurk over my skin, pulling at me like a demented safety net. Filled with holes, but familiar. Breath shaky, I lay down onto the carpet and look under the couch. They hadn't found it.

I reach for the k-bar that I've had hidden for years. It easily comes out, the old, chipped blade glinting in the dim light. Sitting up, I stare at the metal and flick my gaze to my arms and then legs.

Everything hurts. It aches and drowns me.

Almost in a trance, I shrug the cardigan off to reveal my naked forearms. It shakes as I hold my wrist up and clutch the knife in the other hand. The blade wobbles as my vision becomes blurry with tears.

I want the pain to stop. Please. *Please.*

"You're not broken." The blade rests against my skin.

"I want you to never cut yourself again." I freeze, feeling the sharp edge.

Elm Jed

"You're relearning how to be in a world that hurt you." I move the blade away from my skin.

"I love you." Tears stream down my face. Hands falling to my side.

So much. Too much to process and intake.

"Come on," I mutter to myself, knocking my head against my knees. "You're better than this…you're…"

You're self-destructive. His fuck suites. He'll leave you. Sarah. Became his whore. Lack of self-esteem. Clearly…you weren't ready yet. Sarah. No one even remembered. Lies. Why are you protecting him? Sarah. Trying to protect you. Knowing your history. Ex-mob owned this— SARAH!

I thrust the knife down.

It pierces floor.

I try to force the voices out, my breathing becoming erratic as I start to rock in place. The onslaught doesn't stop. I yank the knife out. The muscles in my hand ache as I clench the handle hard. The tip resting against my forearm.

"Once upon…once upon…" I try to recite the poem, but I can't think. I can't concentrate.

Parts of me scream inside. I can't get the actual words out. I can't move, apart from the constant rocking on the floor. The knife won't drop from my hands.

Three years. All lies. "You knew!"

I can't let go.

Please. It hurts. I'm spiraling, unsure what's real or not.

"You knew!" I can feel myself slipping again.

Self-destructive. Roger got to me. *Lies.* He got to—

There's banging below and I hear voices beyond the opened crack of the door. There's talking, and then I hear Leo yell, "I told you not to leave her!"

Nan argues, "Leonardo, let her be—"

"No!" He bellows.

"She asked—"

"Damn it!"

Heavy steps come up the stairs, and I'm still frozen. Fear of him screaming at me. Yelling at me as I clutch the knife painfully. Yet it's not enough for me to move. The fear of being found. Being seen like this. None of it is enough for me to get up and pretend I'm fine.

I'm exhausted.

I'm done.

The door abruptly opens. The rocking stops as Leo stands at the doorway. He heaves uneven breaths, jacket gone and shirt disheveled. The hard lines I'd seen earlier are long gone, replaced by alarm. His eyes widen when he sees the blade resting on my skin.

"I didn't," I whisper.

Although he's breathing hard, practically vibrating, he slowly closes the door behind him, double-locks it, and steps toward me with hands out. Every step is calculated in an attempt not to scare me.

"You told me not to." He stops, face crumbling as I admit quietly to him. "You said to never cut yourself again, but I couldn't let go."

Leo swallows hard, taking another few steps before he kneels before me. "Give me the knife, sweetheart."

I don't move.

He moves his hand closer, swallowing hard. "My dear Watson, hand me the knife."

My arm feels heavy, but ever so agonizingly slow, I place the handle of the k-bar into his hand. All the while, his eyes never leave mine. His hands tremble as he takes the knife, puts it on the floor, and slides it away from us.

"Good girl," he whispers.

"I didn't talk," I say unexpectedly. The dam is about to break, vision blurring. "I didn't break. I didn't talk. I didn't break."

Leo swiftly pulls me against him, wrapping his arms around me as I cry and scream against his shoulder. The shaking of his body worsens as he clutches me harshly, burying his face against my neck. "I know, sweetheart. I never left the precinct. I was on the other side. Never left you. I know."

I grasp him, wrapping my legs around his waist. I can barely hear him continue to tell me I was never alone. He'd been there. My sobs are muffled by his chest, letting everything out. Leo cradles my head, not letting anything between us as I feel his own tears fall upon my shoulder.

"You're safe, sweetheart. You're safe. I love you. I love you. I love you." His voice is music in the abyss. "I'm sorry. I'm sorry." Leo continues to apologize and say he loves me. Upon every word, his voice breaks more and more, becoming less of the stern, confident Leo I know.

"Stop," I whisper, breath catching as I press my face against his neck. "Stop, baby."

He quiets, but sits us on the sofa, while I remain wrapped around him. Silence comes over the space as we hold onto each other. The weight on my shoulders melts away, but there's another heaviness that fills me. Exhaustion beginning to win.

"Those were my crimes, not yours." His soft voice is muffled against my hair. "I was angry. So, fucking angry with you at first for staying, then I realized what you were doing."

"I had to protect you," I whisper. "Keep him away."

Leo pulls back, making me do the same as he clutches my face. His reddened eyes are brimmed with tears, and I realize this is the first time I've seen him truly cry. Streaks of them are along his stubbled cheeks and jaw. Green irises lined with gold flecks and redness.

He goes to open his mouth, but words don't come out. I shakingly wipe away some of his tears, keeping my hand pressed against his cheek as my chin quivers. "So, you were in the other room?"

"After I learned that bastard made you piss yourself, I threatened to stay on the other side as much as I could. Keep an eye on you."

"Controlling," I murmur, trying to sound amused, but my chin still quivers. Leo cradles my face, rubbing his thumb under my bottom lip. I lean into his touch. "I'm sorry."

He shakes his head.

"You watched me lose my shit, and then walked in with me—"

"Autumn." Those tear-filled eyes start to become strict again. He swallows hard and shakes his head again. The trembling in his body has barely relented, and I realize it's not just from panic, but anger. Pure wrath contained like fire in his eyes.

Without another thought, I kiss him hard. His breath catches, cradling my head as I plunge into him. Relief washes over me, tasting him and falling back into the safety that is Leo. His hand moves to the nape of neck, carefully handling me as we kiss fervently.

Breaking away, I place my forehead against his and breathe deeply.

"Let's get you to bed," he whispers as he stands up with me still in his arms.

"Leo."

"Anything else can wait until tomorrow." He checks the door is locked and then carries me to my bedroom. Quickly he starts changing, and I realize he's put some of his own clothes in my closet and dresser. Dang it, why didn't I notice that earlier? Leo pauses and asks me, "Have you showered?" I shake my head. "Do you want to?"

I swallow hard, biting my bottom lip hard. My gaze flicks to the discarded sweats from the precinct and I cringe. Leo doesn't wait much longer for my answer, before grabbing my pajamas and gently guides me to the bathroom. Although it's barely big enough for us both, he makes it work, quickly washing me. Finally, the smell of the precinct is gone, and he soon has us in bed.

Leo's chest presses against my back, holding me close under the covers. He kisses my damp hair, inhaling deeply as he strokes back the wet strands. He's not shaking anymore. Neither am I.

I whisper into the dark, "Nan told me."

His arms tighten a moment. "Is that why you were up here?"

I don't answer.

"We were supposed to tell you together," his voice rasps. "And not less than an hour after you—"

"She happened to tell me. I'm not mad, just uh...confused and tired." Somehow, the man is able to hold me closer. If he tightens his grip more, I may not be able to breathe next. "They don't...don't know about the cutting...how bad...only you," I murmur in shaky breaths. "She doesn't know, Leo. No one..."

He hushes me in a gentle tone, kissing behind my ear. "Shh, it's okay. I'm right here." I clutch his arms, nodding my head as I settle more into the pillows. "You're safe."

"I love you…mister."

"I love you, my dear Watson."

As I shut my eyes, Leo kisses my cheek and sleep finds me quickly.

Chapter 24

How to Breathe Again

It was weird waking up in my own bed again.

Weirder that a nightmare didn't wake me.

But the weirdest thing is watching Leo cook in my kitchen. There's even a bowl of sugary cereal on the counter for me. Maybe I'm dreaming. I stare at the man with the towel over his shoulder. He looks over at me, nodding toward the cereal. Yeah, I gotta be dreaming.

I shake off the oddness and take the bowl to sit at my small table. After a few bites, Leo's phone starts to buzz. Swiftly, he checks it then ignores it. Not even five seconds after, it starts to buzz again. He picks it up with a scowl and ignores whoever is trying to call him. He pours some coffee and brings over a mug for me alongside my sugar bowl. A kiss is laid on my cheek and, of course, his phone buzzes again.

Leo narrows his eyes, glowering at where his phone sits on the counter. The man vibrates with irritation, and I swear I see murderous intent on his face. My body locks up on instinct as he stalks toward his phone, picks up and growls, "I said *two hours*. Interrupt me one more time and you'll see how impatient *I* can be."

Someone tries to speak, muffled on the other end.

"Take care of it. Do your damn job. It's *three* now." He shuts off his phone, prowling toward my bedroom and something thuds. Poor phone.

Leo comes out, stopping in his tracks. He takes a few breaths, calming himself as he flicks off the towel to the counter before kneeling before me. My breath hitches, becoming frozen as he grabs my hand and cups my face.

"I'm not angry with you."

"I know," I murmur.

He kisses my knuckles, inhaling deeply and the hardness in his expression leaves. He relaxes, hazel eyes that I've missed look up at me. Leo always seems so vulnerable when he's on his knees. I'm not sure why he does it for me, maybe so he doesn't seem so looming with his height.

"Want some cereal?" I hold up a spoonful. Both of us slowly smile.

He shakes his head and I shrug, eating it instead. He finishes making breakfast and sits down. I'm half certain that chair may break under him. Did find it in a dumpster.

As I finish the cereal, Leo hands over a pancake and eggs for me to have next. I smirk at him, moving my gaze to the oven clock. It's past 8:30. No Nan. Leo eats quietly as I glance at my apartment door that has a new deadlock on it.

"Leo, did you forbid Nan from coming into my apartment this morning?" He pauses, jaw tensing. Busted. "She'd be up here by now with muffins."

"I told her I'd handle breakfast."

"Mister."

The harshness comes back, sliding toward me without remorse. "I wanted privacy with you. Figured you deserved some, too."

"I appreciate that," I say, putting my hand on his. He continues staring at me, brow becoming a bit more furrowed. Smiling faintly, I reach over and press my finger against the line above his brow. It vanishes as he relaxes. "Guessing it's because you're angry with her, too."

"She was supposed to wait for me. She didn't," he says darkly. "You spent over 40 hours locked up, and then she dropped that bomb on you, it almost pushed you over the edge."

I shake my head, knowing this 'hungover' feeling and exhaustion isn't helping *this* conversation.

"Not talking was eating at Nan. She probably felt *more* guilty with me being arrested, held for so long, and being coerced." Leo stares down at his plate. His hand on the table fists, knuckles cracking. I sigh, "You can be mad at whoever you want, Leo. Not gonna tell you can't be, but it wasn't their fault."

"They left you alone. You were right upstairs with a k-bar in your hand." His voice is tight. My chin quivers a moment, glancing over at the counter where the knife now sits. "You could've…"

His hand grips mine, rubbing his thumb over my wrist. Leo's gaze doesn't budge from our joined hands.

"That's my fault, not theirs," I say in a very quiet voice.

"No."

"Leo—"

"No." I can't take my eyes off his, and I want to cry. He brings my wrist up to his lips, kissing it tenderly. "I will blame every fucker who hurt you. I will blame that detective for screwing with your head. I will blame every person who's told you that you aren't enough or didn't deserve affection. And I will blame my own damn Crew and Nancy for not taking a fucking minute to think of giving you space after what you endured." He kisses my wrist again, inhaling sharply. "I am sorry that I didn't tell you sooner, but I promised I'd wait until she was ready to tell you in person."

"Was there anyone with you?" I ask suddenly. He brings our hands down, confusion pinching his face. "Just you saw, listened to my…ramblings?"

"You really want a purple room."

I snort under my breath. "Seemed like a good idea at the time."

"Yes, just me. The others were busy pulling judges and commissioners out of their beds."

Stiffly, I nod as understanding sinks in. I wasn't the only one in hell. We both decided to stay for the other, practically tormenting ourselves. Me wondering if he was still out there. Him having to watch me through glass like a caged animal.

"Do you need these two hours, I mean, three…" I smirk, and he almost does, too, "…for you or me?"

"Will I seem less controlling if I say both?"

"Maybe."

Leo hums. I squeeze his hand.

"Don't blame Nan and them, okay? They didn't know and tried to do what felt right." Leo sighs, giving me a singular nod. Well, it's something. "But I'd like having a few hours together. Just us."

A small smile comes over his face. He gets up, placing a brief kiss on my lips and then refreshes the coffee.

I don't think it's hit me thoroughly what I endured. I remember when I finally got out of the hospital years ago, and it all felt like a fever dream. It hadn't felt real. Every minute going back into this 'normal' routine with Leo, makes it all feel like a bad nightmare. All that's left are the uneasy feelings and small pit in my stomach. I brush it off, taking a bite of Leo's pancakes as I try to pretend that the last two days hadn't happened. Just a nightmare. Passed and gone.

"What would you like to do?" He asks as he sits down.

"First, I think I should ask how you updated the apartment."

Leo clears his throat before drinking his coffee, then asks, "Too far?"

"Too you." He quirks a brow. "Organizational stuff that I've talked about getting? New fridge? Cleaning up a little?"

"Wasn't certain how often you'd want to stay at the hotel." I quirk a brow back at him. "Within reason of our protocols."

"What about at your penthouse, apartment or whatever?"

"I'm barely there, why should I expect you to be?"

Should I be upset about that answer? Ask for a drawer or something? Who am I kidding he's already given me half a closet at the hotel. "And you like the bookstore."

I nod and take another bite of pancake. I look around, feeling out of place in my own home. I'm not sure if it's due to the small changes or being gone for so long. "Could we stay at the hotel tonight?"

"Of course, dear Watson. Wherever you want."

We finish breakfast, and Leo only lets me help clean up when I threaten to put marshmallows in his drawer. While he's changing clothes, I grab the k-bar and put it back under the couch in its designated spot. When he comes out, his eyes dart to where it had been but says nothing as I change into everyday clothes.

He suggests we watch a movie, picking out one of the few cartoon movies I still have here. *Swan Princess* plays on the small screen as I snuggle up next to him. I watch the classic as Odette and Eric sing about finding each other again, waiting for longer than forever and my heart clenches. I press closer to Leo, reminding myself this is real.

I decide to leave with Leo back to the hotel rather than later this afternoon. I may not be as angry as Leo is at Nan, but I needed more space. And I knew deep down the moment he left, I may not get. Worry gnaws at me that Nan may want to talk more, and I'll just slip all over again. And if I'm too far from Leo, I honestly may lose it.

I don't trust myself. I'm not sure if I'll grab the knife again. He's the only one who seems to help me keep my sanity. Dr. Wilson may have a few words about that on 'codependency', but she can go get buried neck deep in concrete.

Almost exactly three hours on the dot, someone knocks on the door. I pause packing some of my movies and open the door while Leo is busy in the bedroom. Owen stands there, straight-faced, but softens it when he sees me.

"Hey, Iron Buffalo," I greet.

"Thank fuck you're alright." He gives me a hug and I give him one back. "Scared the shit out of us."

For a moment, I think he's talking about last night. I force a smile. "Join the club, but I'm fine."

"Whatever happened in that room, don't let it get to your head."

He points at said head. "Meant to screw with you and that's it. Don't worry, soon that detective won't be able to be within ten blocks of you. You made sure of that."

"Thanks."

"Owen." Leo walks out, adjusting his cuffs. "Take her bag."

"I got it," I answer, keeping hold of it and moving past to the stairs. Both men make a sound behind me. "I can carry my own stuff, Leo. And Owen isn't a bellhop."

"Could always get you one for here," Owen muses.

"Cause Nan obviously needs someone else to boss around." I smile back at him, and he responds in kind. Leo follows us with a serious expression. I hold back a sigh. His sense of humor was already running low this morning and I'm sure it's gonna get worse as the day goes on. I walk into the bookstore, finding quite a few people in the store itself. Suddenly, my heart pounds as someone passes by and I flinch when a book drops. Quickly shaking it off, I head to the counter to say goodbye to Nan, who hugs me.

"How'd you sleep, dear?"

"Better than the night before," I try to joke, and she gives me a weary expression. I add a grin, which seems to help.

"Here, I've got some muffins for you, since *someone* wouldn't let anyone in this morning." She dips down as I glance at Leo. His expression is stone cold. Not a lick of apology. She puts a small container in my hands. "Now am I going to see you tomorrow then? Perhaps dinner? Talk some more?"

"I'll let you know. I need about three days of bad movies, I think." Nan purses her lips, flicking her gaze to Leo. She doesn't have a lick of apology on her face either. I'm starting to think I preferred it when they were conniving. In fact, maybe I should just not have known about her involvement at all. Let it go with her into the afterlife, really.

"Well, don't let him keep you all to himself. You've got—"

"We need to go," Leo interrupts, putting a possessive hand on my shoulder. Nan begins to glare at him, frowning when someone comes up to the register. "Let you get back to attending the store, Nancy."

"Yes, and *you* back to your work, Leonardo. Since it's so important to you."

"I understand my place, do you?"

"More than you perhaps, although convincing you of that may be impossible."

Yup, I'd like them to be conniving, chattering old biddies again.

I look at the woman who's at the register. "She'll be right with you. If you understand anything about in-laws, that's basically what's happening. I don't even have a ring yet and already I'm getting a glimpse into my future."

Leo stiffens beside me.

The woman starts to chuckle. "Married five years. And his mother-in-law is three states away. Still not far enough."

"Try the other side of the city," I mutter, placing a quick kiss on Nan's cheek. "Behave, Nan. Please. I'll be back soon, and we can talk, and maybe I'll get Isaac to show you how to make British tea."

"I'm Irish, dear."

"Another civil war for me, yay," I say sarcastically and head out of the store with Owen. I look back through the window, finding Leo scowling at Nan and half-expecting her to glare in return. Instead, she steps back with nervousness etched on her face. And then forces one of her sweet smiles, helping the woman at the counter.

"He won't hurt her," Owen murmurs. "He's just been pissed for the past three days."

"Yeah."

"He's fine. Always is." He walks me toward the car where Rudy stands.

"Morning, Rudy."

"Guten morgen, *bärchen.*"

I smile as he opens the door for me, and I climb in with Leo getting in from the other side. The other two sit in the front, and before we even make it halfway down the block, I press the button for the divider to go up.

"Check in," I say.

"I should be asking you that."

"No evading there, mister. I'm green. Check-in." He frowns harder. "Processing shit in my head, but still green."

He exhales sharply. "Yellow."

I take his hand, stroking my thumb over his skin like he does with me. "Wanna talk about it?"

"Already did this morning." Leo looks away from me, sitting back more fully. "I'm a possessive, controlling asshole boyfriend, according to Nancy. Not to mention having tendencies of overstepping boundaries in attempts of controlling you and your needs. You've asked for communication and honesty from me, and it appears that I fall short of that in every turn."

"Leo."

"I've had a lifetime learning how to prioritize situations in order to maintain control. Plans set in place to regain it whenever it is lost and taking back more ground than what was originally lost most times. And sometimes, when I do lose what I want, I've learned to move on. Find another hill to conquer and remain in the top seat, but..." he looks over at me, deep lines over his brow and a small curl to his lip, "...it's been some time since it's felt like those I trusted stood in my way of what I wanted. I am certain because of that, people are expecting me to lose that control."

I search his face for more meaning, but all I get is a cold, strict expression. The kind he wears when discussing business or speaking with someone he doesn't approve of.

"Do you feel like you are? Losing control?"

"No, but I cannot let others know if I'm not fine. Instead, it's masked behind what you call 'grumpy boyfriend' or simply not sharing anything private. Or being a territorial asshole. I can't allow myself to lose control, Autumn."

I don't want to lose control because of the consequences of being hurt. That loss being used against me. It's what would've happened within that interrogation room. It almost was.

For Leo it's not much different. Instead, it seems he's constantly in that room with a viewing glass for everyone to watch his every move. Perhaps, that's what dug at him, seeing me in a position he feels like he's in. Having your dirty laundry thrown at others to see, accused of crimes, and constantly pushed to the brink. You can only take so much before you snap.

"So, the stoic, impassive expression you always wear really *is* a mask? Is that why you're extremely private, and why the Crew was surprised you let me in? You don't let others in completely to…maintain that control?"

He kisses my hand in his, holding it there against his lips. "I gave up the liberty of relinquishing control years ago. I've made my deal with the devil."

"But you lose control with *me*."

Leo's face scrunches, staring at me with confusion as he drops our hands.

I shrug. "You do, not like yelling, throwing stuff, or whatever. You take the mask off with me, though. You feel and care deeply with me, even if others don't see it. And maybe you remain in small bits of control while cooking, dancing, or taking care of me, but you release it a bit. I mean, you don't get angry with me interrupting you, if I laugh at the worst moments, do weird things, or put you in fuzzy socks and it could be because you get to *feel*. Not have to…sit quietly behind a glass and hope no one finds something wrong."

Leo's eyes widen. "Autumn—"

"You're possessive and controlling *for* me, cause you don't want to lose that."

"No, that's not…I, I love you—"

I put my hand against his cheek, stroking down his freshly shaved face. "Not saying cause I don't think you don't. You just really protect what you love fiercely, others don't understand that. Not trying to give myself a big head here, but I also know I'm the only one you don't have to play boss, president, or some other role that takes a toll on you. Cause that's how I feel about you."

The harsh lines disappear. Softening as his face falls at my words.

"I stayed to protect you and I wasn't going to budge until I knew Roger couldn't touch you. I know, you would've handled it some way, but I couldn't just… not *do* anything. Not find a way to protect both of us. You're the only sense of freedom I've gotten in my entire life, even with the chaos that follows, I'd never change it. Maybe parts of me wishes I could go back to last summer before you. Before all this mess, except I don't ever want to go back to being that shell. Cause I was. Didn't know it at the time, but I was a shell. Whatever was left of Sarah Marie. What I'm trying to get at…don't tell me you're fine if you're not. You don't have to hide with me, please. I'll keep trying to tell you when I'm not, too."

Leo crushes his lips against mine. My breath hitches and I clutch his shoulders for support, falling against him as he kisses me fervently. Sparks fly down my spine, easing me as we kiss. He breaks away, placing brief ones on my cheeks and along my jaw. The car stops and there's a knock on the divider. Leo quickly knocks back, locking the doors. I smirk.

"How do you see through every wall I've built?" He asks.

"Cause we're too damn similar, mister Americano."

He snorts, brushing my hair back. "You've been through enough. I don't want to burden you."

"Hey." I kiss his cheek and nudge his shoulder. "Been through worse than stuck in an interrogation room and borrowed clothes. And it'll make me feel better knowing I could help you."

"Always worried about others more than yourself."

It's easier to focus on him, than me. I'd rather listen to him than my own thoughts.

"I'm fine, for now," he says quietly. "But I wasn't when you were out of reach. I'm not usually fine when you're not near me. I'm plagued by worry, and then I keep thinking back to when I left you in that bookstore. Fearful that it's the last time I'd see you and don't know it."

Guilt punches me, squeezing at my chest. His neck muscles tense, taking a deep breath and strokes his hand over my leg. I go to open my mouth, but he shakes his head once, kissing me tenderly.

"I trust you to come back to me," he whispers against my lips. "I do not with others." He kisses me again. "I will do anything to keep you safe. No matter the cost. Whatever you want of me; I will give you it. And if you ever are given doubt or made to believe differently, know that I will *always* come for you and love you, and strike down anyone who comes in my way."

"There you go again with declarations," I murmur against his lips. "Smooth talker."

"You'd call it that?"

"Yup, just like your *cute* tattoos." A smile forms on his lips.

Leo runs his hand through my hair, cupping the back of my neck and kisses me deeply. A sigh releases from me, leaning against him as he hums against my lips. My skin tingles, pleasure rushing over me as I begin to move onto his lap. Halfway there, someone knocks against the window again, snapping us back into reality.

He growls, glaring at the window and knocks back. I climb off him as he grumbles about work and annoying associates. I can't help but giggle as he adjusts his pants, biting my bottom lip. Amusement flutters over his face.

We get out of the car, coming out into the garage for the hotel. Chiari stands near the entrance, clipboard in hand and smiling. Another car is running near us, where Jameson waits looking disgruntled with Julio, who seems just as stern. Great signs.

"Isaac will be with you today," Leo states, taking my bag from me and handing it over to him, who walks off before I can say anything. "Chiari will get you anything else you need. I'll be back for dinner." He lifts my hand, kissing it briefly.

"You're leaving the hotel?" I flick my gaze nervously to the other car.

"For a short awhile, I've got business to attend to that I don't want near here." Oh…yay. "If you need *anything*, have Isaac contact me."

I nod, swallowing hard. I'm not sure why I feel so nervous with him leaving. Perhaps it's because we just dealt with police, and I'm certain he's not off to do *legal* things. Or not feeling sure with myself being alone. Not having him right by me, which seems pathetic. I should be used to being alone…right?

"Boss," Julio calls. "Need to go."

Leo kisses me once more. "I'll be back before dinner."

Elm Jed

He turns away, prowling toward the others. Julio flashes his gaze
to me, then hands a phone to Leo as Jameson gets in the car with him.
I wait until they drive off before I turn toward Chiari, who steps aside
with grin as I head into the hotel. Not even a few feet down the hall,
my best friend waits for me. Leanne and I collide, crying in each
other's arms.

Chapter 25

Ballrooms & Chandeliers

Vanilla and roses. That's what the ballroom smells like. Even the carpet.

Leanne and I are in the *Pantheon Ballroom*, lying on the floor amongst stripped tables and chairs. There's a dance floor off to the side. Everything is midway of being put away from whatever event was held here the night before. After spending over an hour with Leanne in the coffee shop on the hotel's first floor, I began to show her around the small bits of the hotel I knew, which included the ballrooms. At some point we just laid down and talked. It's been hours with me telling her the rest, spilling my guts out while Isaac stays in the hall.

My own little shadow.

Leanne is quiet next to me. I stare at the glittering chandeliers, amber warm light reflecting off the crystal. I'm sure they're real and not glass, especially if the floor smells of vanilla.

"So," I say, squeezing her hand in mine a little. "That's me, how have you been?"

"Cause that's the seg-way into a different conversation," she laughs faintly. We look at each other, and I smile at her half-heartedly. Well, how else do you change subjects of explaining being arrested under false pretenses, interrogated, and having a mafia boss boyfriend?

"Are you sure you don't want Trix to find you another therapist?" Leanne asks.

"I'm fine."

"Hun."

"I'm fine." I force another smile, trying to give her enough to let it be.

I'm not sure I can walk into a therapist's office ever again. Let alone so soon after Celine. I'd been such an advocate for therapy, but now I was rethinking my entire stance on it. What was real? What wasn't? Had there been progress or had it been in my head cause Celine *wanted* there to be progress for her own benefit?

I wasn't sure.

"You said Trix was okay, though, right?" I ask.

"Yeah, wishes she could call you and all, but I told her you were out of police custody. And that you're home, but guess I'll tell her you're staying...here." Her voice is weary, and I watch her dark brown eyes flit over the extravagant ceiling.

"I'd give you a number for her to call, but no phone...again." I clear my throat. "Seem to lose those a lot lately."

She nods her head, pursing her lips a little.

Son of a biscuit.

I sit up, looking down at my best friend of over a decade. Her gaze meets mine and I can see the unease in them. Don't blame her, I've told her a lot, not everything like Nan being involved with the mob before (still needed to process that myself) or that I self-harmed. And I didn't go into detail about the interrogation. All that can stay in that dark grey room.

"What is it?" I ask her.

"Just worried about you." She waves it off, sitting up alongside me. "That's a lot for anyone to go through. Not to mention, not many people can say they've been interrogated for *hours* and not lose their sanity."

Her voice begins to get sharp and agitated. Yup, best friend is not happy.

"Leanne." She huffs and meets my gaze again. Her mouth tightens, thinking. "Just tell me."

"It's not gonna help."

"Not asking you to. Just want you to be honest." I pull my knees up, gesturing for her to speak her mind. Last thing I wanted was to learn she was part of the mob or she was an international spy or something. "So, tell me."

"You're not gonna like it."

"Look, whatever you say, honestly can't be any worse than watching Nan and Leo argue."

"That bad?"

"She tried to scold him with muffins and in front of customers, too."

"Oof."

"Yeah, and she wasn't too happy that I wasn't staying at my apartment tonight."

"Why aren't you?"

I break the eye contact, looking at the folded sheets and stacked chairs. The walls are a deep beige with white and golden trim. Bright. Elegant. "Figured it was safer just to stay here."

Leanne sighs, folding her legs under her. She's wearing dark jeans, a flowy shirt and sweater. Pretty similar to what I'm wearing. When I first saw her downstairs, I thought she had skipped work to see me, until I realized it was Sunday. I'd been in the precinct all of Saturday and Friday, which now connected more dots why Roger tried to get away with some of his interrogation 'tactics'. Weekend shift bullshit.

Leanne frowns as she leans back on her hands. "Fine, but I'm just being honest. And remember I'm just the bystander, telling you how I feel about all this."

"That's fine."

"I don't trust him. Or any of the men or whoever is in his employ. But I don't trust Leo." My eyes stay fixated on her as she lets out a long breath, and then ruffles her twists as she scratches her head. "I know *you* do, obviously with all this and you should, but don't know if I ever can, hun. Any of them."

Her gaze moves to the closed doors, where Isaac most likely stands. "They're not gonna hurt me, Leanne."

"Deep down I want to believe you, really I do, but over the past month, that's getting harder to believe. I mean, you disappeared after he just *showed up* at the club to take you somewhere."

"I called you the next day."

"But then you still vanished, and then again *with* him. And don't get me wrong, as much as I don't trust Leo or his guys, I hate Caltz more, but...not knowing where you really were scared me. And I hated that you couldn't tell me."

I'm silent as she sighs, touching my hand.

"I just want you to understand where I'm coming from. And it's just that every time you get hurt or close to it, he's part of the why. Maybe they're not going to hurt you themselves, but you have to admit, hun, they're part of something that can." She sits up straighter, averting her gaze. "Part of something that *has* hurt you."

"Leanne, they're gonna do everything to protect me. It's okay if you don't trust them yet, don't expect you to if ever. Just trust in *my* judgement with them. Maybe give them time to earn yours."

She shakes her head, and I see a single tear run down her cheek. A whisper comes out of her, "I don't want to bury you again."

My heart cracks.

I grab her hand tightly. We're quiet. Me unsure what else to say or even tell her. Even with Leo's and the Crew's help, the danger that comes with them is all too real. I knew what world they were a part of. Top of the pyramid or not, there's no escaping the darkness that it comes with.

"I want to trust in your judgement, hun, and I know you love him, but...I'm not sure if I ever can. If it...it may *ever* feel right to me that you're with him, and I'm sorry. I'm sorry I can't."

"Don't be sorry," I murmur. "How things have gone the past month, I can't blame you. What you've heard."

"And not saying you'll want to, but if you wanted to leave…could you?"

Her brown eyes meet mine, tears gone as she searches my face. I nod and answer in a very quiet voice, "Yeah, I could."

"Would you?"

"Are you asking me to?"

She takes a moment, looking solemn. "No. We both know you'll do what you want. You're stubborn like that." I smirk weakly. "By why stay? Why chance it all over again?"

"Because I love him, Leanne. Really, truly do." She frowns, staring at me for more answers to give. To understand. She opens her mouth, but then closes it, face falling a little with guilt. Uncertainty.

"He's not going to change, Sarah. You need to walk away."

"I can't. I love him, I can't—"

I look away, swallowing hard. No, this time was different. If there's one thing I've learned to be true, it's not to assess present relationships from the past.

"He loves me," I add. "Very, very much. So, if that's the first thing you believe, let it be that."

"I'm not telling you what to do, like I said stubborn," she tries to lighten the mood. "Just saying how I feel. I've never met him beyond that night at the club, either. So, I get I'm only seeing an outside perspective. Maybe I'll feel better talking with him in person."

"Not being in an alley?"

"Exactly." She squeezes my hand. "I love you and I care about you so much, and I just don't know what to do to help. And be there for you."

"I love you, and I appreciate you being here at all, and as for help…" my voice trails off and I look over at the dance floor. I raise my brows at her, looking suggestively at the wood planks.

She chuckles. "Apart from laying on the floor like we did during mid-terms, want some nostalgia about that next?"

"Hey, did learn some new west coast moves while upstate."

She gets up, pulling me with her. "You didn't mention that earlier, let's see what you got."

I follow her to the area, while she pulls out her phone and I quickly tell her, "No *Man with the Hex!*"

She gives me a disgruntled look. "I'm not that mean," she says, scrolling through her phone and then starts playing a slower swing song. She takes my hand, beginning to lead me into a slower triple time swing. We start dancing around the floor like it was our college days again. And just like how I knew, the fast tempo song plays next and Leanne grins playfully as she pulls me into the fast dance. For a moment, dancing with Leanne, I can forget briefly how torn and strained I've felt with every conversation since I left the police station.

Yet, deep in my soul the sensation of drowning lurks in the back of my mind.

Leo

Captain Walton breathes heavily with Rudolph's hand on his shoulder. Mila stands to the other side of the seated police captain. The room within the warehouse is barely lit by a few lights hanging from the ceiling. A ghoulish glow is across the mostly bare room, apart from a table with some thin leather folded over and a few other metal chairs. Next to Walton, seated in a metal chair like him, is a deputy commissioner. They both swallow loudly as a door slams behind them.

Leo walks past the captain, Jameson and Drew remaining at the door. Carefully and silently, Leo pulls off his jacket and places it over one of the metal chairs. Unbuttoning the top of his shirt next.

"Gentlemen, I rarely dirty my hands for several reasons," Leo talks in a poised cold tone. "First is to keep my name out of people's mouths, remaining out of the limelight." He pulls his shirt off, placing it over his jacket. "Second is due to my own time. I don't *waste* it on those who can be handled by one of my subordinates."

He rolls his shoulders back, unbuckling his belt and slinging it off with a crack. Both men flinch as he places it over his shirt, wearing only his shoes, pants, and a black sleeveless shirt. "Although the third reason is why those who work directly for me *always* do their best to keep my hands off matters. It appears I'll need to remind you both what that reason is."

Walton goes to speak, "Luciano—"

Rudolph grabs the man's neck, holding it firmly as Walton chokes on his own words. Leo gives a menacing look at the captain, sliding his gaze to the other who remains silent.

Leo walks toward the table and tosses open the leather. Underneath are an assortment of knives, handful of handguns, and other metal utensils. He starts to arrange them, his body beginning to vibrate as the rage from the last few days begins to boil to the surface.

"Not even my own Crew like to be in the same room with me when I…*work* on certain individuals." He puts a serrated knife to the side and holds up one of the .45 revolvers. "It doesn't happen often, not of recent years, but lately I've come to be needed, bloodying my hands again."

He nods toward Drew, who opens the door and gestures for someone to come in.

"I've given warnings." The gun clicks as Leo spins the cylinder. "I've been welcoming in negotiating deals with you both, benefiting all of us. We'd come to an accord. After *everything* I helped you both with. Protected your families. Obtain the job titles you so desperately wanted. Security. Awards. Kept others on short leashes."

A man is brought in with a bag over his head, led by Waylon and another mobster. He's seated on a metal chair, handcuffed at his wrists and ankles. The other mobster leaves, while Waylon steps off to the side.

"I'm usually a very patient man," Leo continues, walking up to the man with the bag over his head. "Except when it comes to the woman I love."

Waylon yanks the bag off. Before them sits a man with dirty blonde hair and pale skin, a gag in his mouth. The deputy commissioner and Walton exchange a look, recognizing the police officer. Leo points the barrel of the weapon at the man's forehead. He whimpers, closing his eyes and quivers as Leo cocks the gun.

"Luciano, whatever he did—"

Mila squeezes the deputy's shoulder, making him shut his mouth as Leo keeps his attention on the gagged officer.

"This man knows a secret." Leo's expression becomes a hard mask. Threatening and thirsting for blood. "And after looking over report after report…his name was signed multiple times as one of the officers who released two men. Two men, who three months later, would rape and torture a young woman for over twelve hours. And *then*, he signed a deal to release said men *again* because those men were his suppliers."

The officer shakes, eyes widening as he grunts against the gag.

"Your little renegade detective talks a lot of smack, but a little digging and it seems he's covering for fellow officers with certain addictions. And *you* knew." Leo looks over his shoulder at Walton, who gulps harshly against Rudolph's grip. "These *officers* made a deal. One gets his supply, and Caltz gets bragging rights for arresting drug runners to continue his 'undercover' cases, while letting the bigger dealers run free."

Leo swiftly points the barrel lower without looking and pulls the trigger. The man screams against the gag as the bullet penetrates his thigh, shrieking louder as Leo puts another in his shin. Cracks come from the bone as the man struggles against the restraints. All of Leo's Crew, including Mila, remain unresponsive as Leo puts the gun back on the table and grabs a k-bar.

"Can't give Caltz a lesson…yet. His suspension and the charges against him will have to do for now, but an officer still on desk duty after multiple counts of hard drug use while a certain deputy commissioner keeps turning a blind eye…" Leo pauses, looking at the other man who frowns at him, "…it was bound to happen that this man's *demons* caught up to him."

The knife is flipped in his hand, and the mafia boss' body goes rigid for a moment. The entire room becomes cold, some holding their breath as Leo stares at the blade in his hand. His lip curls, handle creaking under his grip. Then, ever so slowly like a predator watching its prey, he cocks his head toward the gagged officer.

"After everything his contact went through, while infiltrating the mob, he *helped* let loose disgusting excuses of men for his *friend* to get high." The knife is clutched tightly in his hands, pressing against his skin as a reminder.

The fear in her eyes. The exhaustion. The hurt. Her screams at Caltz. The murmured *yellow* while she held the coffee he sent her. Her crushing the papers. Talking to herself. A coldness in her face that he did not recognize. Her tears.

"All of you are going to relearn today why you will do *anything* in your power to keep me 'hands free'…" he thrusts the knife down, partially cutting off the wrist of the officer who wails against his gag, "…so long as *I* draw breath."

Autumn

I hug Leanne close, and she makes happy noises. She pulls back and says, "Dinner this week, right?"

"I'll call you tomorrow *and* Trix, let her know, will you? So, she doesn't screen me?"

"Of course. Maybe get all three of us out on like Thursday or whatever."

"Well, I'm free." I mostly hold back a grimace.

It's late afternoon, yet it didn't feel long enough being with her. Leanne had a date and wouldn't give me much details on the guy, since she met him through work and their relationship is still fairly new. I give her a wink, then give her a kiss on the cheek as she does with me. I stand off to the side of the lobby, watching as she walks out of the bustling hotel. Dinner rush is beginning to come in for the Sunday crowd. Isaac comes up behind me.

"Who arranged for her to come?" I ask.

"I think you already know the answer to that, Miss Autumn."

Leo. Although Leanne's words echo in my head of her not trusting him, I know I just have to give her time. She doesn't know him like I do. Nan doesn't know him like I do. Knowing this, there's still a gap in my chest. Torn into different directions wanting others to understand. Crazy sounding or not. My head begins to throb, and I rub at my temple.

"Miss Autumn?"

"Guess I'm just getting hungry."

"We can head up to the apartment, and I can order dinner for you. Boss shouldn't be late, but you know how some of his meetings can be long."

I think of waiting for him up there. Grey walls.

A shiver runs over my skin, and I look over at the large seating area of the lobby. One part is up and out of the way with some plants and a small fountain. There aren't that many people around, most heading for elevators or checking in.

"Actually, I'm just gonna wait down here." I start walking for an empty couch.

"Here?" Isaac follows close behind. I sit, folding my legs underneath me as Isaac looks around. "It's perfectly fine for you to wait in the apartment."

"Never been down here long enough. And it's pretty," I say, pointing at the fountain. "All you're missing are the fish. Plus, good place to read."

"I can acquire one of your books, which would you like?"

"Kind of *Bernard and Doris* of you there," I smirk.

"Are you saying I remind you of Ralph Fiennes now?"

"Nah, you're still Bond." I shrug, and he grins. I answer, "Any book."

"I'll bring multiple. Please stay here."

I give him a mock salute as he walks away into the bustling crowds, disappearing down the hall. I lean back into the sofa, taking in the hotel completely. It always seemed like I was in and out, never seeing much of it. Staring at the porcelain, gold, and extravagant designs, my gaze comes back toward the front and down to the marble floor. Quickly, the first time I'd 'fallen' into the hotel comes back.

I hum and hug myself a little, remembering that night. Who'd have thought that moment would transpire to this? Then my mind serves up another memory, recent, as Roger pushes the papers towards me. They meld into more of Roger telling me to take the barista job, that it'll be far enough away from the mob. Out of their territory. And then Nan telling me I could stay with her, safe and sound.

Three years.

Three years I had not known where I truly was. Who was so close. Those I could've walked by. Been seen by. Lies and deceit, manipulated to believe I was safe. That I would be able to hide and never be found again. It was all a pipe dream.

Self-destructive.

"Miss Watson?" I jolt out of my stupor, realizing I'd been staring at the fountain water. I look up to find Oliver there with a tentative smile. "Sorry, did I interrupt some inner thoughts?"

"Just disassociating, entranced by the water." I wave it off and give him a smile. "How are you?"

"Good. I saw Mr. Morton leave, and wondered why you were still down here." My brows pinch together. "Mr. Luciano's head of security."

"Oh, right!" Isaac's last name was rarely used around me. "He went to go grab some of my books. Thought it'd be a nice place to sit and read. People watch."

"Well, if you need anything else, I'll be over at the front desk for another hour before my shift ends."

"Thanks, Oliver. And it's good to see you again."

He nods briefly, beginning to walk away, but stops. "Are the flowers to your liking?"

I stare at him, and it takes me a moment to realize he means the ones I'd gotten for the penthouse. That I've not seen for almost four days. "Yeah, they're lovely. Can see why ya'll have them as your florist."

"Mr. Luciano hires the best."

"Oh, I know."

Oliver grins, walking away and goes right to helping a hotel guest approaching the desk.

Right, there were flowers in the penthouse. I tap my fingers against the soft fabric. My leg starts to shake and there's a prick at the back of my neck. I rub at it, trying to make it go away as I go back to staring at the fountain.

"You're fine," I murmur. "Fucking fine. Police aren't gonna come and rush the building."

I take a deep breath in, trying to calm myself and see Isaac reappear with books in hand. A grin forms on my face as he places them next to me, taking a seat in the chair across. Focusing on the books, I decide on one of the romances he brought, needing a happily-ever-after. For the next thirty minutes, I do my best to stay within the world of the cupcake baker and cowboy. The puns are great, but even those don't seem to keep my attention.

I'm half-tempted to try the history book Isaac brought, when there's a commotion near the front. Isaac quickly stands, walking away and I notice a few people almost swarm the main entrance area. Craning my neck, my breath hitches as Leo and Jameson enter with a crowd of people. All of them are wearing expensive clothing, appearing like they're going to the opera instead of a dinner or to a hotel. Then again, far across the way are shops that the hotel owns and uses for such events.

Fancy Shmancy.

I stay where I am, watching as Leo listens with that furrowed expression of his. Jameson talks with some people that have approached them, shaking a few of their hands and even smiling. Leo touches no one. Owen stands directly behind Leo, whispering in his ear as Isaac approaches.

Almost like he can sense me, Leo turns his head and instantly finds me across the hotel. I bring my hand up, wiggling my fingers at him in a small wave. His brows ease, eyes glinting. Without saying a word to the others, he leaves them stammering as Jameson attempts to continue to keep their attention. I put the book down as Leo strides for me, catching attention from everyone who probably know he owns the place or just... I mean, the man *is* sexy. I'm staring for my own reasons.

He expertly unbuttons his suit jacket, a movement that makes me bite my lower lip and feel myself heat up inside. All the thoughts I'd been battling vanish as I watch him, entranced by the confident aura.

Leo walks behind the sofa I'm on, dipping his head next to mine as his hands land on my shoulders. He kisses my neck, inhaling deeply as he massages away the tenseness in my muscles.

"Dear Watson."

"Mister Americano."

He chuckles under his breath, kissing behind my ear. "What are you doing down here?"

"Thought it'd be nice to sit down here for a change." And not be in a grey-filled apartment by myself. "Because you *do* have a beautiful hotel here, Mr. Luciano."

"No hotel I create will ever compare to your beauty."

I lean away from him, giggling suddenly as surprise flits over his face. I attempt to bite back the giggles, noticing he was serious. Of course, he was. It's Leo.

His lips pull up slightly in a half-smile, hazel eyes shimmering. The small bout of laughter continues as he walks around, sitting down next to me as he places his arm over my shoulders. Leo does the only thing that makes the laughter stop. He kisses me. I hum against his mouth, inhaling deeply as comfort fills me.

Another kiss is placed at the corner of my mouth, then he crosses his leg over the other with leisure and grabs one of my books. He starts talking, but everything eddies out when I see the smudged crimson on his shoes. It's small. Barely noticeable, almost blending into the soles. But I can't forget what dried blood looks like. What it does when you try to hide it, attempting to clean it all off.

"They're part of something that can...has hurt you."

"Autumn?" Leo grabs my chin gently, lifting it and it brings me back to reality. His eyes search my face. "What is it?"

Swiftly, I give him a smile, pretending that the old fears deep inside aren't churning. "Nothing."

His face hardens a moment, adjusting in his seat and uncrossing his legs, taking the shoe out of my sight. "Check in."

I swallow hard. No way do I want to tell him that seeing his damn shoe may have rattled me. I told him I didn't care what he did behind closed doors, and I really did mean it. I knew what he did, what that would entail. Didn't I just tell Leanne that I trusted him? We have an understanding. Yet, thoughts of uncertainty swirl in my head.

I must've taken too long to answer, because Leo cradles my face and asks again in a kinder tone, "Check in, dear Watson."

"Yellow," I blurt. My head shakes, trying to wrangle the thoughts. "Probably just hungry, haven't eaten much today, the past few days for that matter. It was great seeing Leanne and talking, but maybe I'm more tired than I thought. There are people down here and just—"

Leo kisses me briefly, shutting up my rambling. "You're safe."

I stare into his gaze, then finally nod.

"Let's go have dinner." He looks over his shoulder. "Isaac." Leo puts my book off to the side, then promptly picks me up into a bridal style and I squeak. My arms wrap around his neck, blinking at him. "Don't try to fight me."

"Why would I? You're comfy."

He smirks, holding me tightly to his chest as he walks us to the elevators. People stare at us, most in awe and gaping. I ignore them all, focusing on Leo as I sink into his arms, all the roiling emotions fading with each step.

Chapter 26

Routine

I jolt awake.

I stare up at the ceiling, breathing heavily as the light sheen of sweat on my skin cools. It takes a couple of minutes for the pressure on my chest to subside. A hand skims down my arm, and I curl up against Leo's chest as he pulls me into his arms. I snuggle closer as he then rolls onto his back for me to lay across his bare chest and start tracing his tattoos. Swirls of dark lines blend into the fire and thorns. Latin words hidden amongst the imagery. As I trace the ink, my fingers come to his upper arm where there's a shield. Perhaps Roman or maybe a Spartan's knowing his lineage. Brain still waking up, I try reading the Latin surrounding it—*Mors ad umbras.*

"Death to our shadows," I murmur.

Leo turns his head to look at me. "You can read Latin?"

"Only other language I learned," I say softly, moving my hand down the marbled down to some roman numerals. "Just had to pick a language not often spoken. Took classes to…change up what I was studying."

My mind flits to the long hours in front of computers. Coding and lost in screens and gaming consoles.

"I know *Autumn* has a degree in English Arts, but what did you actually study?" Leo asks softly, brushing my hair back as I move my hands back to his chest.

"Computer forensics mostly."

"Really?"

I purse my lips. "Yeah, used to be a nerd, essentially. How you feel about that, having a nerdy girlfriend?"

He kisses my temple, stroking his hand down my back. "That there are more parts of you I get to learn more of everyday and love." I stifle a laugh. "Just like your fascinating sides which include reciting Poe, knowing some Latin, and delight in watching cult classics."

"I'm a well-rounded person. Although the one who can cook the best breakfasts, ride motorcycles, Waltz and Rumba, and *also* recite Poe should know he's just as fascinating."

He smiles lovingly. I lay my head on his chest, listening to his heartbeat while I trace my fingers over a tattooed skull.

"Did a nightmare wake you?"

"Yeah. Figured they'd return. May take a few days to wrap my head around things, hopefully they'll subside."

"Do you need to do anything today?"

I think, pinching my brows together. There's nothing planned. No job. No appointments. No friend dates, yet. Could go see Nan, but the sudden twist in my stomach may be a sign that I need more time. There's nothing to distract me.

"I don't have anything. Unless I go to the bookstore to work."

"Do you want to?"

"Shouldn't I?"

"That's not what I asked." He brushes back a few strands of my hair. "I'm certain Nancy can handle things without you, she's a...*competent* woman."

There's a tightness in his voice, and I'm pretty sure I'm not the only one not ready to be around Nan yet. I clear my throat. "Feel like I should do something, work or whatever."

"Not if you don't want to." I lean up on his chest, giving him a quizzical look. "You've had a rough couple of days since we got back to the city." I snort. That's putting it lightly. "It's fine if you don't do anything that requires much."

"Like yesterday?"

"No set number of days for you to rest. Take however many you need."

"Is this your way of trying to get me *not* to work?" I smirk, teasingly.

Abruptly, he pulls me down to him and kisses me. I squeal, humming as he flips us over and covers my body with his over mine. The heat of his skin reaches through the flimsy shirt I'm wearing, traveling down to between my thighs. I move my hands up his back, caressing the hard muscles rippling under my fingertips. Leo breaks the kiss, nipping at my chin. "Of course not, dear Watson. You can go work whenever you want, but you deserve *days* of relaxing, not just one."

"I did at the estate though."

"Take all the time you need of doing nothing."

"What about you, mister?" I cup his face. "Not the only who's been on an emotional roller coaster ride."

He kisses my neck, moving up and over my jaw. His voice reverberates against my skin. "All I need is you."

"You keep saying that."

"I keep meaning it." His hands move down my sides, caressing me as he continues to kiss my face and neck. "You were right yesterday. I can only relax, let go, with you…" his lips brush against my ear in a tantalizing manner, "…in you."

A nervous giggle comes out of me, and I can feel him smile against my skin. Hands flutter over my torso as he slowly begins to lift my shirt and massage my breasts. A moan replaces my light laughter. My hips press further against his, bending up closer to his touch. Arousal flourishes inside me, forgetting whatever nightmare woke me and focusing solely on him.

"My form of relaxation is hearing you laugh…" he nips at my ear lobe, squeezing my breast, "…seeing you smile or…" he does it again, placing a languid kiss against my lips which makes me moan,

"...that sound. Caring for you, loving you. I'm a complex man, but I am quite *utterly* simple with you, my dear Watson."

I grip into his hair as he continues to fondle my breasts, kissing me and pushing his hips against mine. His hand moves down my stomach, finger skimming over the seam of my pants unhurriedly. I sigh at the light touch. My breath hitches when he slips his hand under and starts to stroke further down.

"Check in," he whispers against my lips.

"Emerald."

He groans and kisses me deeper. His tongue tangles with mine, desire filling me to finally have him again in this way. To feel him inside. An intimacy I only get of him. Leo starts to spread my legs more, moving his hand closer and closer to—

There's a sudden loud knock at the front door, echoing into the bedroom.

Leo stops, turning his attention toward the noise. A scowl comes over his face as he moves his hand away from me as his phone starts to buzz on the bedside table. He growls, not moving from on top of me as he grabs his phone. I concentrate on not giggling at his 'unhappy camper' look, especially as his hard-on brushes against my thigh.

"What?" He answers with a strict tone. I can't make out the muffled sounds on the other end, but I'm betting it's either Jameson or Owen. Only two I know who have the guts to wake him up like this. *Maybe* Rudy.

I check the clock. Past eight.

The knocks come again. Leo grumbles. "Fucking give me thirty damn minutes. And tell whoever is banging on my damn door to fuck off. I'm awake."

He tosses the phone to the side. It's the look of utter annoyance on his face that I finally start giggling. I'm not sure why it makes me do so, but his grumpy face has become my favorite expression.

Leo looks down at me, and I quickly slap my hand over my mouth to muffle the sound. He narrows his eyes. "You think this is funny?"

"Given prior conversations, the timing is too perfect," I mumble against my hand.

"I could always tease you, leave you hanging would you be laughing then?"

I move my hand away, gasping in shock. "You're not that cruel!"

"I could be."

"Not with me, mister." I attempt to scramble from the bed…just in case.

Leo doesn't let me get far, encaging me against the mattress with his heavy body. I struggle for a half a second and give up as I see him smile down at me. "Going anywhere, dear Watson?"

"Tease me and I put marshmallows in your carbonarra."

His brows scrunch. "Your negotiation methods are questionable."

"But effective."

He thinks a moment. "Maybe I should have you work for me then."

"You'd hate me as an employee."

"Why is that?"

"I never sleep with my boss." Leo buries his face against my shoulder, laughing hard. I laugh with him, hugging his neck.

In the next forty minutes, Leo leaves with Jameson and Julio. Both men looking worried as they leave. Either it's from whatever reason they called him or due to Leo's fuming expression.

Betting on the latter.

I sit on the patio, bundled up in a blanket and sweater with my coffee. Leo quickly made breakfast, probably in attempts to keep himself from being fed cereal. It's cloudy out, chillier than it has been. Winter is just around the corner. The heater next to me helps keep me warm as I sip my morning beverage.

I stare out into the city, when the patio door opens and Chesty sits down in the chair next to mine. He smiles a little. "Hey, sister."

"Hey." I grin back. "Isaac usually gets the morning shift, well, I guess all day."

"He's needed for some other issues."

"Should I ask?"

He shakes his head, sipping from his own mug. "Nah. Business as usual for us. We'll take care of it."

I sigh. Right. I've not heard anything about how things have been taken care of. You'd think I'd be part of those conversations, but if Leo took care of the guy who attacked me months ago…who knows how he's gonna take care of the police. He'd tell me if I asked, but I really don't want to know.

My mind flashes back to seeing his shoe yesterday.

"You good?" Chesty asks. I blink, staring over at him. "Know Leo checked in with you, but you've been through the worst shit."

"I'm fine." He raises a disbelieving brow. "Just trying to make sense of it all but doubt that's going to happen. Lot to figure out."

"One day a time. Focus on what you can change. You'll drive yourself crazy trying to change what ya can't." I snort a little. "You got out, focus on that. Whatever he told you in that room, lies."

I want to tell Chesty more truths came out than lies. But I can't. How do I even explain what I've realized? Or the fact I've got no proof of it, only hunches and tiny connections. Instead, I just say, "Used to follow that advice, but lately it's been hard."

"When life hits you below the belt, it feels harder."

I stare out into the hazy sky above the city. Although I'm not sure how to talk about one thing, perhaps there was another side I could. Feel less alone. Maybe, Chesty would be one to understand. "Okay, if I speak frankly with you?'

"Sure."

Leaning my head back, I start talking. "What frustrates me the most are the people I can't change, well, how they feel or reacted to me or Leo. I can't force people to get along. To not be cruel. To understand or even listen. I can't seem to push all those voices away, ignore them. And not be worried, or have nightmares, or be anxious about how to juggle it all. Could try to not let all of that in, but it's almost impossible not to. Tried to numb it all out, but now I don't think I can."

"Want some advice on how to handle it?"

"Is it better than ice cream?"

He shrugs, and I nod for him to continue. "Think it's alright to be worried or anxious from time to time. During my time in the Marine Corps, and now, keeps you on your toes. Reminds you to fight. The hard part is when it paralyzes you. But, sister, you can't change people, not really. You'll have to learn to ignore their yapping, listen to your own gut."

"*That* I do know, but..." my voice trails off. The only sound becomes the light wind and cars honking below. My stomach sinks as different faces pass over my mind.

"Doesn't take away the hurt," he says, breaking the silence. "Betrayal can dig deep."

"Yeah...especially if maybe they were *trying* to do the right thing. Not sure if that makes it better."

"Least with bastards you know they're just that...bastards."

My fingers tap against the mug, thoughts beginning to whirl in my head. Although I know Chesty is right, there's this dark feeling in the pit of my stomach. It hasn't seemed to leave since I left the precinct. Questions combined with that smattering of anxiety.

They're just lies. But the truth could help...right?

"Does Leo have a fuck suite?"

Chesty sputters some of his coffee. He stares at me wide-eyed. "What?"

"Something Roger said, and I don't care or whatever... I just need to know that Roger was blowing smoke or something." I need *something* that he was absolutely wrong about.

He lets out a long breath and scratches at his beard. "He'd never use the hotel like that. Only place he's ever used is here, and pretty sure he's bleached the sheets after some of the people he's brought over." I snort. "Just observing."

I chuckle a little, finding a little peace in that answer. I knew about Leo's past with women, so it's not astonishing of how this place was used. Even Leo has admitted to that. See, Autumn? Just some bullcocky Roger was throwing at you.

"That detective really told you that?"

"That and a few other things, but it always seemed to be his go-to."

"Knew Ringer should've dragged his ass out," Chesty mutters. "No wonder he was so fucking pissed yesterday."

I watch Chesty carefully, eyes flicking down to his boots and finding them clean. He mutters more under his breath as I put my mug down, pulling my legs up. "Do you think Leo would go as far as…killing Roger?"

Chesty meets my gaze, holding it for a moment. Finally, he answers, "He's overprotective and controlling at times, but he's got a good head. Knows to think shit through. We wouldn't have followed him here if he didn't. He's in control, always has been."

"You didn't answer my question."

"You trust him?"

"Yeah."

"That's all ya need."

A sinking feeling hits me as the quiet comes back. My legs begin to itch, and involuntarily, I start rubbing at them. I stop, almost feeling the healed cuts pulsate up my legs. Swallowing hard, I try to focus on the outside and just anything that's around me.

"Got anything on the agenda today? Drag me to anything?" Chesty asks, giving me a half smirk.

"Nope. Stuck with nothing."

"Well," he says, standing and stretching a little as he scratches under his beard braids. "Could do *somethin'* to help get your mind off things and such. I could use it, too."

I point at the railing. "Suggest shopping and I'm pushing you over the edge."

"Don't have a death wish, but I do have some projects in the private parking garage if you're interested."

My entire body comes alive, perking up. "You have bikes here?"

"Always got some nearby to work on during downtime. Could also have you practice riding in tighter spaces." I scramble out of my chair as Chesty laughs. "Gonna turn you into a biker chick before Leo knows it."

"After the past shitty weeks we've had, I think he deserves a good surprise and I deserve to see him in shock...again. But also, *good* shock." I take my dishes inside.

"Unless you use his office chair again as your own private NASCAR," he says following me inside.

I stop, narrowing my eyes. "Animal?"

"He definitely wasn't gonna keep that shit to himself. Next time take pictures. Or invite us for a race. I'd give two desert eagles to see Ringer doing that shit. Knowing you, you'd get him to." We laugh, closing the patio door.

"Deal."

Chapter 27

Motors and Empty Chairs

I hop off the Harley Sportster, letting Chesty take over to back into the wide parking spot. An Indian Larry sits nearby with another chopper. Both were custom made by Chesty and Rudy, frames entirely rebuilt to have bronze coloring and dark brown seating. Works in progress.

I've spent the entire morning on the motorcycle, going slow, with Chesty teaching me to ride in smaller spaces, backing up, and navigating obstacles. The private garage is one I've rarely been in before, located below the main executive garage. It's easy to almost miss the secure entrance, not to mention the gates that enclose the front. There are SUVs and vans, while a few cabinets sit near a service elevator on the far side, the main private elevator on the other. The place is practically a bunker.

"Not too bad," Chesty says, putting down the kick stand. "Before we know it, we'll have you out on the road, zipping around traffic."

"One day," I sigh dramatically, following him over to the second chopper. We start working on gears, time passing silently as I hand over tools. "Thanks for the distraction today."

"Anytime, better than sitting in that penthouse." I think of staring at those grey walls and shiver. "Or shopping." He grimaces, and I chuckle.

"What about shopping for biker stuff?"

"That's different. Just like going record shopping or diving into barrels of new gadgets. Hand me the socket wrench." I pull one from the toolbox, handing it over. "Besides, if you ain't got nothing else to do, might as well learn some skills."

"Come in handy, right?"

"Right." He winks. "And can't let what we taught ya wear off."

"The horror," I tease. He gestures for another wrench.

I watch Chesty work, pulling my knees up as he explains each step and what the different parts do. He talks of engine lines and how the set up between the choppers are different. Most of the numbers he mentions blur together, but I get the gist of it. And listening to the slow tempo voice of the Marine Corps vet eases my brain fog. The anxiety that keeps returning disappears. Relief and sense of security comes over me, almost hypnotized by the piece of machinery. I grin as he goes over how he's going to reinforce the frame and seat, then what Rudy may do.

The elevator doors open, and Chesty is suddenly on his feet with his hand on the .45 at his back. He instantly unstiffens when he sees who it is.

Mila walks toward us as I get up. She's dressed in a suit of dark grey with a black v-neck shirt. Although he drops his hand, Chesty straightens his posture, stepping in front of me slightly.

"What's up, Mila?" He asks in a clipped tone.

She stops just a few feet from us, folding her arms over her chest. She looks at the motorcycles with a bored expression. "Her too with the bikes?"

"*She* thinks they're fun," I answer a little annoyed. You'd think I stepped on her Legos or something.

"Here for a *joy* ride then?"

"Mila," he warns.

"No, I'm here to be Leo's *Old Lady*." I glance at Chesty to see if I got it right, and his smirk tells me yes. "Or just biker bitch."

She scoffs. "You seem tougher than the other *girls*."

A prick hits my spine, running down with warning. Mila sure is starting to remind me a little of Bailey and I really don't want to dump coffee on her next. If I ever become a serial killer, that's gonna be my marker—coffee stains and latte foam.

"Nah, pretty sure they were just plain bitches. You should know, right?"

Her eyes widen slightly. Chesty coughs abruptly. Her jaw tenses, curling her lip a little. "Think you're *that* special?"

"Oh, I think I'm adorable. Ask Rudy."

She frowns more, taking a step toward us. Chesty pulls out his gun, keeping it pointed to the ground, but the safety clicks back. Mila glowers at Chesty. "You heard the boss, Mila. Don't try it."

I freeze, sweeping my eyes from his gun to her. Her face suddenly becomes bored like this was any other Monday. She says, "Just trying to understand what makes her so special."

"Socks," I say.

She scoffs, "Socks?"

"You wouldn't understand."

The woman rolls her eyes at me and then tells Chesty, "Boss needs you. Top office. Direct orders."

"Personal messenger, now?" He puts away the gun, and Mila snorts as she turns away. Chesty huffs next, glancing at our little mess. "Gonna have to leave you upstairs."

"Yeah." I rub the back of my neck, following him to the elevator. "Fun calls my name from the castle in the sky. Woo."

Chesty chuckles. "Shouldn't be that long."

"Isaac lies better than you." We laugh as we enter the elevator, Mila leaning against the wall. He presses the button for the penthouse and then the top floor. Crud muffins, something tells me I'm gonna have a 'wonderful' afternoon of nothing. And being alone. A chill runs down my spine, quickly going through my head what else I could do.

The doors open, and I walk out then turn to wave good-bye to

Chesty. Mila looks even more disgruntled, so I add, "Thanks for protecting my boyfriend, Mila. Don't let him scare you *too* much."

Chesty clears his throat as Mila's jaw drops as the doors close.

That'll make her think twice about throwing jabs at me.

I enter the quiet penthouse, already rubbing the back of my neck as I look around the spacious room and…grey. I look at the clock, hoping it's later than I think, but nope, only just past noon. The anxiety crawls up my back, traveling over my skin and making my heart rate quicken.

"Fuck, Autumn, you're in the safest damn place." I shake my head and walk over to the counter and see a note. Beside it sits a new phone. The note says,

FIGURED YOU'D NEED IT SOONER THAN LATER. ALL SAME AS BEFORE – ENIGMA.

Thank goodness for the *Forgotten Demons*.

Quickly, I text Leanne and then Trix, finding both their numbers already saved. Trix can't talk on the phone, but she does reply back that she's glad to hear from me. Leanne ends up creating a group text, allowing all three of us to talk. I occupy myself for the next thirty minutes texting them, thankful they're on their lunch breaks.

I end up asking about seeing them for dinner, maybe later this week. They both agree, in a couple days, given tomorrow seems full for them. Leanne's work is piling up and she's taking work home, while Trix is handling Dr. Wilson's "early retirement." Guess I should've known Leo would've had her fired.

Not sure what else to do with my time, I tell them I'll pick the place. I figured the timing and picking of the place would give the Crew enough to set up whatever they needed to do for security. I pause, realizing I don't really know anywhere off the top of my head for a reservation. There's the Mediterranean place we go to, and another Mexican place, but it's further uptown. Close to the women's center. And the precinct. My stomach drops as I try to think. Maybe somewhere closer to the hotel, but it's two nights from now…reservations are gonna suck trying to get in. Even for a Wednesday. Not to mention expensive. Dang it.

Unless…

As I start to call the front desk, I stop, glancing at the walls around me. My stomach twists again, and I decide to do a more hands on approach. I head into the bathroom, cleaning off the grease from working on the bikes and change out of my shirt and torn jeans. In exchange, I pull on a plain shirt, *not* torn jeans, and a sweater then head out of the penthouse. I'm okay to explore the hotel by myself, which includes the floor with the *Giglio Giardino*.

The buttons stare at me. Now to remember which floor.

I tap my thigh, running through the entire hotel layout in my head and press the third one. As I descend, I text my little main security team my whereabouts. Once done, I take a deep breath and my gaze sweeps over the fancy interior. Dark mahogany walls. Small loveseat and plush carpet of deep colors. It all matches with the shiny crystals in the ballrooms, the gold trimming of the lobby, and marble. My skin starts to itch, and I ignore it as the doors open.

I give myself silent victory for choosing the right floor as I walk out, heading toward the restaurant's entrance. The man from the first time I came is there, hair slicked back and wearing the same dark vest.

"Good afternoon, Miss Watson." I pause, blinking at him as he gives me a pleasant smile. "I remember you, of course."

"Oh, hi, um…I don't think I caught your name from before?"

His expression falters a moment. "Christopher."

"Right, sorry, I should've remembered."

"Not at all, miss."

"Is it always Christopher?"

"Yes."

"Okay. And you can just call me Autumn. The whole full name thing feels too formal."

His face scrutinizes me a moment, then swiftly goes back to his pleasant expression. "If that's what you'd prefer. How may I help you? Did you have a reservation for lunch?"

"No, but, was hoping you could help me with one." I smile a bit more, and we both relax, seemingly pushing away the formal bullshit.

"How may I help you, Autumn?"

"I need a table for three on Wednesday night this week. Is that possible? I know it's somewhat last minute for most smanzy restaurants."

"Smanzy?"

"Snazy and fancy together. Compliment, I swear."

"Wouldn't that make it…*snanzy*?"

"Doesn't have the same ring to it." He chuckles, opening his reservation ledger and writing something down.

"For Mr. Luciano, we always have a table ready for him, and I've been well-informed that you are granted such permissions as well. Any table. Any time."

Well, that makes some things easier. "Thanks."

"Will Mr. Luciano be joining you as well that evening?"

I pause, opening my mouth and closing it as I think. "I don't know."

"Was it not to be with him?"

"It's for a couple of friends and I, but now I'm wondering if…" I shake my head, he'll probably be busy anyways, "…I'm not sure."

"Why don't I put it down for four? Just in case. What time?"

"Seven."

"Reservations are set. If there's anything else you may need, such as allergies or preferences for the wine list, please be sure to let me know. The front desk can help you get in contact with me or the chef."

"Y'all are pretty good at your jobs." He smiles broadly, then a waiter comes up to whisper something in his ear. I give him a smile and wave, leaving him to do his job as I head back to the elevators.

Well, got that done. Unfortunately, it only took about 10-15 minutes to do. I'm slowly understanding why it's easy for Leo to get into places or have things done so swiftly. He hired good staff. Not to mention getting first dibs.

I step off to the side of the elevators, reluctant to go back up to the penthouse…apartment…whatever. Worry crawls up my back, causing me to shiver and look behind myself. Nothing. Just the occasional person entering the restaurant or using the stairs. Maybe the past weekend *is* getting to me.

The elevator doors open, revealing Chiari with a clipboard in her hands. A small bit of reliefs hits me. She gets off as I greet, "Hey Chiari."

"I was hoping to see you before you went to the top." I look at her quizzically. "I've been informed you were adventuring the hotel."

Of course, the Crew told her.

"Just making reservations, but that could be on the list. Anything to do, really. I've got movies, but I think I'm too antsy to sit still." I perk up a little. "Hey, does your coffee shop need a barista? I'll demonstrate and interview for you."

She laughs softly, and I take that as a no. She brings the elevator back, pressing a button to go down a floor. "Mr. Luciano has had standing reservations for you at the Day Spa and salon for weeks, how about finally appeasing his gesture?"

I blink at her. Why would he have—?

"When I fell into the hotel? The comped night and…that sneaky man."

"He was awfully serious about your little night off," she muses, getting on the elevator and I join her. We're not on long before the doors open to reveal a cream and gold colored hall. "Today seems like a good day, given your open schedule. And after the weekend you had, I think you deserve some pampering."

I clear my throat. How is it that it feels like a hundred days since then, but it wasn't even a week ago?

"How much did they tell you?" I whisper.

Chiari gives me a compassionate faint smile. "Enough. Whatever details help me to do my job, which includes looking after you. Have to stick together, right?"

"Right," I murmur as she pats my shoulder. I follow her down the luxurious hall, which is gold-plated with marble, reminding me of pictures of Rome from their height. Glass walls soon appear, flowers filling the spaces between and there's tiny waterfalls built into the wall. I'm beginning to think the *Italian Lily* is just Wonderland and the TARDIS put together. How the fuck is all this in here?

Chiari leads me to the main desk, and I peek past to see tall shelving filled with shiny bottles and towels. Candles are burning and it smells of citrus, and fresh linen. A receptionist with light skin, freckles across her face and down her arms greets us. Her light orange hair falls over her shoulders like liquid copper. She smiles at Chiari. "Good afternoon Chiari, who do we have here?"

"Hi, Wanda. This is Miss Watson, she's Mr. Luciano's special guest." Not sure how I feel about that. I must make a face because Chiari adds, "His girlfriend."

"Oh, so you're Miss Watson?" Wanda asks.

"Yeah, but just call me Autumn."

"Well, you see Mr. Luciano is very strict about—"

"Whatever she wants, Wanda. Per Mr. Luciano's request." Chiari interrupts with a smile, but there's something in her tone that makes even my body lock up.

Wanda quickly changes tactics. "Yes, of course, Autumn. Follow me and we'll take care of you." She gestures for me to follow.

I glance at Chiari, who says, "You'll be fine. The staff here is excellent. If you need anything, have them call for me or Isaac."

"Sure." She turns, leaving with long strides toward the private elevators, heels clicking. Glad I'm on *her* good side. Mila doesn't scare me that much, a strict Chiari though? I'll hold off on the coffee dumping.

For the next two hours, I sit in a robe that I'm practically guilted into wearing, slippers, and my hair is being blown out. I've not had control over my own hands for almost an hour, while my nail technician, George, paints them a light lavender. His blonde hair is pulled back into a bun, his light beard almost blending with his tanned skin. Lisa, my hair stylist, brushes out my newly, trimmed short hair. Her own is dark and curly, pinned to the top of her head. She asked multiple times about dying it or shaving the sides, but I wasn't feeling it. Didn't want to change more.

"How about that?" She asks, ruffling my hair a little with a soft smile. Her dark brown eyes shimmer through the mirror at me. "You have such the perfect face for short hair by the way."

"Thanks. Took a while to get used to it."

"That'll be me if I ever chop mine off," George mentions, scooting his rolling chair around. He shakes his head a little, acting like he's showing his off.

"If it's not me cutting and styling it, I'm divorcing him as a friend," Lisa mutters teasingly near my head.

"Like I could go to anyone else," he chuckles, checking over my hand. "This lavender is stunning on you."

I bring my other hand up, staring at the pastel color. I try to recollect the last time I've gotten my nails done, let alone painted. Must've been during college. Leanne would paint them. They were always too short and brittle the years after. She tried again when I moved in with Nan, but I always scratched the color off.

"Autumn?" George asks, and I blink, coming out of my thoughts. He rubs a lotion over my hands soothingly, watching me carefully. "Want anything else done today? Could have your toes match."

I shake my head. "No, this is fine. More than I've gotten in years."

"Well, come back soon, and we can change colors for the holidays." He smiles, showing off his long rainbow-colored ones. "Or if you ever want to try other shapes. I *never* get clients who will try anything other than *almond* shaped."

I smile and nod, getting up and head toward the locker area to change back into my clothes. The pit in my stomach doesn't go away, tightening as the creeping feeling over my skin doesn't relent. *The Raven's* first few stanzas are repeated in my head, trying to remember where I am. You'd think being in a spa would help with anxiety, instead it just seems to keep rising.

Get out.

I did everything to concentrate on George and Lisa's banter, who were comforting, but it barely worked. I force a smile as I leave, waving as I hope to be in a better mind space the next time I see them. The palm of my hand rubs into my forehead as I walk down the hall, almost bumping into a couple of women. They look down over me, one of them smirking as she clacks down the hall with her high heels. The other brushes her long hair over her shoulders, adjusting her fancy bag. Heavy pressure pushes down over me, engulfing my chest as I look down at myself and then to up to a mirror in the hallway.

My hair looks fluffier, lighter almost from what Lisa did. My complexion isn't as pallid as it was weeks ago, nor do I look gaunt. Gently, I run my hands through my hair and feel the soft strands smelling of fresh shampoo. The pit in my stomach worsens, squeezing at me as my hand begins to shake. Inhaling sharply, I head for the elevators and stop, staring at the distorted reflection of myself.

"Me and these damn doors," I mutter as they open, walking in and staring at the buttons next. I can't bring myself to input the code for the penthouse. Minutes feel like they tick by before I finally press for the floor with the ballrooms. I sit down on the velvety loveseat and rub my hands over the surface. I keep rubbing at it, my body starting to rock as I look up and see my reflection again.

"It looks fine. Blonde was never your color anyways."

"You always wanted to try short hair!"

"Try this color." I look at my nails. *"They'll grow back."* The lavender suddenly looks too sweet. Too spring. Too…innocent. I start to press my nails into my thighs, and quickly stop.

The doors open, and I rush out of the small space and move past each ballroom. It's in the middle of the day on a Monday. Not much going on up here. There are some people cleaning the other ballrooms. I come to the familiar doors of the *Narcissus Ballroom*, opening the doors. It's partly set up with tables and chairs, spread across the room with plain coverings. The dance floor is set up, and there's even a DJ station with tables along the walls, most likely for a buffet. No decorations yet.

I walk around, trying to distract myself, attempting to keep my breathing level. I've walked around the room twice, before I finally take my shoes off and test the wood flooring with my socks. Backing up, I take a running start and slide across the dancefloor.

No smile. Not a chuckle. Not even a glimpse of joy from it.

My stomach drops, worry clenching itself around my spine as the snippet of anger I've suppressed the past week starts to grow. I move back and do it again, but it doesn't help with the gnawing emotions of unease, fear, and resentment digging at me. They morph together and my entire body starts to shake.

Come on, come on. Think, you're fine. You're—

I look around only to find empty chairs and fucking tables. Silence. Alone.

Alone.

I begin to pace, leaving the dancefloor and start reciting *The Raven*. I speak the lines out loud. Again. The frustration doesn't leave. The darkness of fear at the pit of my soul swirls and overwhelms my thoughts and I can't think of each word. I mess it up, swearing to myself as I fist my hands. Dark thoughts claw at me, ones I've not had since New Jersey. No…not since two nights ago. Not since Leo walked in—

I want to scream. Hit something. Throw something. I want the pain inside to stop.

My entire body trembles as I stare down at my hands, anger filling me as I start to scratch at the fresh manicure. Deep crevices are created in the once perfect nail polish. Chips. Gashes. Too innocent. Too pure. Too pretty.

Screams drown out thoughts in my head. *Self-destructive. You failed. Broken. Notch on his bedpost. Like an alcoholic. His whore. Getting lazy.*

Lies. Deceit. Gaslit for years. Manipulated. Betrayal. Used.

My fingers dig into my thighs as I breathe heavily, ire pressing inward.

"You knew! You knew!"

They knew. They all *fucking* knew. How many lied to me? How many more will?

Something snaps inside me as I clutch my head, thinking of the knife in my hand the other night. The pain. The physical hurt to wash away the agony inside. I dig my nails into my hair and head, feeling the stinging pain.

"Broken," I rasp as pain shoots down my spine. "No…no…"

You failed. He'll use you. They broke you. Can't trust him. Bury you again. Broken and alone. You failed. You failed me first—

I grab the chair closest to me and slam it against the ground. "No! I am *not* a failure!" I grab another, tossing it and then grab the edge of a table, flipping it and something snaps as I throw it against the floor. "I am *not* replaceable! I am *not* a fuck toy! I didn't deserve it! *I didn't deserve it! I am not broken! No!*"

My vision blurs, all I see is red as I destroy the tables and chairs. I flip them, shattering several chairs as I crash them against the dancefloor with all my fury. Every dark feeling since I watched my therapist betray me collides. My insides writhe in agony. Not giving a damn anymore. The walls close in and all I see is grey. Humming of lights.

I tear at my hair, grabbing another table and flip it. "I am not fucking broken! I am not a whore! I am not a fucking pawn! I am human!" I scream, tossing another chair that crashes against others with a sickening break. "*I don't want to be alone! I don't want to be alone!*"

Wood splinters across the dancefloor as I grab another chair, slamming it down with a shriek. Something in the distance slams. "Autumn!"

"*Red!*" I yell, tearing at my wrists and let out another scream as I hit myself, tearing at my skin and nails.

Someone slams into my back. I start to thrash as they cross my arms over my chest, wrapping their own around my body as they do. I keep screaming, kicking forward as I'm held to keep from hurting myself or destroying anything else. Furious screams are released as tears begin to join them. My vision blurs as I try to break free from the rock-hard hold. I keep kicking, but they don't let go, trying to speak to me through the maelstrom in my head.

I can't hear them.

The voice doesn't pierce through the darkness. It's not who I need to hear. The one who stops the storms.

I feel myself breaking. As if I'm being snapped in half through my soul. Another cry comes out of me, *"I don't want to be alone!"*

Chapter 28

Not Fine

Through the fury and anguish in my head, Waylon's voice somehow reaches me. "You're not alone, sister."

I struggle to breathe, still writhing within the arms that keep me tightly in place. Other commotion comes from the doors. My body trembles, weakly struggling through gritted teeth. "I'm not broken! I'm not—"

"I know," he says against my ear. "I know. Get it all out. Let it out."

I loosen a furious scream, head throbbing. He tenses around me as I continue to scream, letting out the frustration, hurt, and agony stirring inside me. My voice begins to hurt, hoarse as I continue to scream and try to scratch and hit myself again when past images come back. Waylon doesn't release his hold, keeping me from causing more damage. Others are around. I can feel them close by, but I'm too focused on breathing through each shriek as the darkness surrounds me.

My throat burns enough for me to stop, eyes teary, but no sobs. I tremble in Waylon's arms, finally not trying to escape. My knees buckle, causing my legs to wobble as strength leaves me. My body about to completely give out, Waylon eases us down so that he kneels and I'm basically sitting on him. He doesn't let go. My head hangs, heart pounding in my chest and thudding into my head.

"I don't want to be alone," I rasp against my scratchy throat. "I don't want to be alone."

"You're not. Got your six, sister." He grips me hard against his chest.

"I don't want to be alone," I keep repeating, flickers of uncertainty of where I am. "Don't leave me in that room. He'll lock me in."

"Only shadows, sister." The voice lulls me a little. "Not there anymore, sister. Breathe. There you go."

"Don't let go," I plead. "Please don't let go."

"I won't." He adjusts, letting me sit on his legs more, bringing me flush against him. I'm completely incapacitated, held firmly by his vice grip. A different kind of warmth engulfs me with the compression around me and the hardness of his gut. The sensation of being held helps me gasp for air easier, allowing myself to fall back against him. "Yup, just breathe. There you go. Doing good, sister."

"Don't let go," I beg again.

"Not going to. We're just gonna sit right here like a couple people sledding on those trash tin lids." I want to laugh, but I can't seem to.

People walk over, and there's murmuring in the distance. It sounds jumbled as my brain tries to recollect where it is, concentrating on Waylon's arms around me. The press of his fingers. Someone speaks to him, and it takes me a few moments to register that it's Isaac and Jameson.

"We should fucking call him," Isaac says.

"We can't," Jameson counters. "You know who he's with, it'll cause—"

"He's going to be more pissed that we didn't—"

"That damn meeting is important," Jameson cuts Isaac off. "After pushing shit off and what he did yesterday, it'll jeopardize everything we've tried to stabilize the past week if he leaves. He *needs* to be there."

"Oh, for fucks sakes," Waylon mutters near my ear.

"It'll take him over forty minutes to get back anyways."

"Not if he takes the—"

"I am *ordering* you to—"

"*She* is his priority; he's made that clear—"

"Quit arguing before *someone* walks in and hears you," Waylon interrupts. "We know the costs, Sombra, and we know how important she is to him, Bond. How about giving me a damn minute with her and see what the fuck she needs. Ever think to ask *her* that? Like a couple dumb lieutenants." He mutters the last part.

I wait someone to address me, but I'm not sure what they're talking about. Is Leo gone? When did he leave the building? Out of the city? At that thought, I start shaking harder, anxiety pulsing through me. No, he wouldn't have left me behind. He wouldn't—

He'll betray you. No. Leo promised. He *promised.*

"Deep breaths, sister," Waylon's soft voice pierces through the thoughts. "I need you to concentrate for me. Can you talk?"

"Yes."

"Alright, not gonna tiptoe around the issues here, 'kay? Leo is across the city in a major meet-up. He's with other crime bosses, taking care of some situations that happened few weeks back." I clutch Waylon's arms. "He'll be fine. Ringer, Enigma, and Iron Buffalo are with him."

I nod stiffly. He continues, keeping his voice at a steady cadence. "Our protocol, sister, is to tell'em if something happens to you. We all know he'll leave in a heartbeat, but we can wait until he's done. None of us will leave you alone until he gets here, promise you that. I want you to understand the entire situation, so it doesn't just seem like Sombra here has his boxers in a twist again. 'Kay?"

Again, I nod, gulping hard.

"Want us to contact him? Or wait?"

I wanted Leo. Badly. I ache to see him and hear his voice, telling me I'm safe. That I'm not broken. Except the guilt aches worse. The consequences he'd have to face tears at me deeper. Fear already wrecks me. How much worse will I feel? The guilt could destroy me again.

"You'll stay?" I rasp.

"Yup. However long ya need. Got you."

"Wait. Wait until he's done."

Isaac starts to protest. "Miss Autumn, if you honestly need him—"

"No," I rasp, head pounding. "Don't tell him yet, I just, just..." my body trembles violently as I shake my head, causing Waylon to tighten again, "...don't leave me. I don't want to be alone."

There's murmuring, and the other two walk away. Doors open and thud shut, voices raising and then disappearing. I'm certain it's just Waylon and I in the ballroom. There's only silence, until from time to time he tells me to breathe like a mantra.

My legs start to fall asleep, and my arms begin to ache. I don't want to move though. I inhale deeply, letting out a long exhale.

"I'm scared," I whisper. "To be alone. Bad shit always happens when I am. I hate it...deep down I hate it."

"Your movies, that why you play'em? Don't feel alone?"

"Yeah, but I couldn't sit...I couldn't..."

"Shit, sorry, sister. Should've made sure someone replaced me earlier."

"No." I shake my head. "I didn't know it'd be this bad. I...I thought I could...this time..."

"What thoughts you get?"

I swallow hard. My chin quivers, struggling to say out loud what I couldn't even tell Leo. Say the words. What's going on in my head. But I can't.

"I'm gonna let go, and move us so we can talk, 'kay? But if you feel like you're gonna start hurting yourself, tell me." Waylon carefully releases me and helps me up on shaky legs. He grunts, standing and then grabs two chairs that I haven't wrecked. He sits across from me, practically knee to knee as he keeps his hands around mine.

"I want you to be honest with me," he starts as I stare at our knees. "If you can't say the words, squeeze my hand once for yes and twice for no." Wonder if Leo taught him that or vice versa. I squeeze his hand. "Now, I ain't a therapist, but dealt with enough Marines and soldiers with PTSD to notice some signs. Something tells me those thoughts are suicide and self-harm."

The moment he says the words, my eyes snap to his, finding calm eyes. He rubs my knee a little. "Nothing to be ashamed of. Wasn't sure at the estate, even after you had that flashback, but...coming back to the city and being interrogated, I'm guessing escalated those thoughts. Would I be correct?" I squeeze his hand once. "Did they happen at the estate?" I squeeze once. "Before that?" Again, I squeeze. "Did your ex-therapist know? That why she gave over your records?"

My throat tightens, feeling sick to my stomach as I squeeze his hand twice. He glances down at our joined hands, and then makes a soft hum.

"Were they just thoughts?" I flick my gaze to the doors, checking for anyone else who may be here. Waylon tightens his grip, which brings my attention back to him. "Just you and I."

A few minutes past, ticking by slowly until I finally say, "I used knives. Anything sharp. After she...I, Sarah died. By the time I thought of telling Celine, I stopped."

"Did you ever discuss having those thoughts?"

"No. I couldn't...didn't want to chance being taken back to the hospital. I...no one knew. Not Nan. Not Leanne."

"When was the last time you did?" My eyes lock with his. And I have to concentrate on breathing. "No judgement. No hospital. Promise. Shit happens, ain't gonna shame ya."

"Roger's house," I whisper. His lips tighten together, nodding a little. "Almost did the other night."

"Cause of the interrogation?" I shrug weakly. "It's okay if that shit messed with you. You're not weak."

"It didn't, it..." I shake my head, "...um, I don't think Roger got to me. But I...I did."

"What you mean?"

"I went inside myself, became me. The old me. And as shitty as it is to be locked in a room or pissing yourself it was nowhere...it wasn't that bad. Comparably to what I've...I've been through."

"Autumn, you can admit that it was that bad. Don't have to come out bleeding for it to hurt." I look away as a sob begins to work its way up from my chest. He squeezes my hand but gives me a minute before I look at him again. His jaw works a bit, beard moving as he thinks and flashes his gaze to the doors. "Gonna stay frank with ya, 'kay?"

"Okay."

"Why were you going to therapy for three years?"

"Cause I needed it."

"For?" I stare at him, unsure where he's going with this. "Not picking at what you talked about, that's confidential shit, but for what? In your head to you...for what?"

I continue to stare at him in silence. Why can't I answer him? I should be able to. My mind flicks over those early days, going through paperwork at the women's center. Trix being there. The police reports. The hospital.

"The uh, assault."

"Anything else?"

"Anxiety? Struggled with relationships in general, other things."

"Did you ever go over your trauma from undercover? What you did? What you saw and witnessed?" A tear falls down my cheek as I squeeze his hand twice. "In that time, did that therapist ever discuss how to handle your PTSD? Flashbacks?" I squeeze his hand twice. "But you did for the panic attacks?" I squeeze once. "Did you ever bring up what happened or why it all ended?"

"No," I whisper. "If I did, we just...didn't spend much time on it."

Waylon watches me for a moment. He sighs a little like he's trying to finagle his own thoughts. "For us military folk, when we get back from deployment we have this post-deployment shit we go through. Getting checked on with integrating back into society, go through what we did, and how shit changes in our world. What you did wasn't a deployment, but close enough where you were secluded in a dangerous place, and people dropped the ball the after."

"What do you mean?"

"I think that therapist may've been helpful with the assault, perhaps even your anxiety, but not what's at the root of it. You couldn't even tell her about yer thoughts of suicide or felt safe enough to. You're allowed to be angry, show that you are, no matter how big or small the thing is. Can't keep it bottled up until you combust. Over a year of keeping secrets ain't easy to stop, and I think your true emotions became the next secret cause…well, probably other things I don't know. No matter what you were focusing on, that therapist should've checked in on that shit if she knew what you endured."

"Telling me I wasted three years of therapy?"

"No." He pats my knee. "What I'm saying is you took care of certain areas that needed looked at, but I really do think the deeper wounds need proper care. If you're battling thoughts of self-harm and have recently done it, spurred on from recent events, we need to get you to a professional who knows what they're doing. Who can help navigate those feelings. Whether you think being locked up affected you or not, you should be able to talk someone who knows how to help."

My body feels numb.

I stare at our hands. Thoughts spiral, trying to decipher conversations between Dr. Wilson and I. They were always concentrated on the assault, changing my identity, and anxiety and how to conform into society as a woman, not a…operative. We discussed a few things, but it was always about Steve or the lead up to the end. She never pushed to know. I kept ignoring that it happened, pretending I was never Sarah Marie. Always Autumn. And she always pushed that I was Autumn, too.

She'd been one Roger had recommended. I never told her how betrayed I felt when Roger was promoted while I laid disfigured. I never told her how broken I felt when they performed surgeries I had no real say in. How used I felt by the police. Never wanted to admit I had been, sticking with "doing the right thing" and every lie Roger had told me. Until I went back to him and the rose-colored glasses I had made for myself, for Autumn, shattered.

That's why he hadn't gotten to me completely *in* that room, apart from my own vengeance and spite. What had was the thought of being used again. Losing my freedom. Or fear I'd repeat history with Leo. Stuck in a loop.

"Autumn," he says my name softly. "We'll get you to a therapist in the next 24 hours. Someone to talk to. I think you need it and it'll help, since it's something you're used to, and know it helps."

"Okay, and I'm sorry."

"Don't be. You said we all have bad moments, right? Just need help getting back up. Not alone in doing so. We understand it's a lot, not gonna expect you to be okay with everything overnight. Or being fine after someone fucks with your head. Just tell us."

"I decided to stay," I whisper. "I should've…"

"Nah, from what they told me, what he did was cruel and invasive. You didn't deserve that. Somethin' tells me you weren't the first he's tormented like that."

My chin quivers, a few more tears beginning to fall down my cheeks. The burning in my throat aches, tightening as I nod my head as I struggle to swallow. "I just wanted to be strong enough. Not be weak, not be a burden…when you all have…"

"Hey." Waylon wiggles my knee, making me look at him. He moves his hand up to the nape of my neck, bringing me in close. "You're not broken. Not weak. Far fucking from it. Don't compare yourself to us, we all handle shit differently. We ain't perfect either. Not to mention some of us had training to prepare for this shit. You didn't. Still haven't. But you ain't weak."

"Thanks."

"Got a family with you this time. Like I told you, brothers. Being left alone in hell will mess with your fucking head, and you've been left there multiple times. That's what those fuckwads did to you. You did nothing wrong. You survived, but you're allowed to be angry they failed you. You can be mad they failed you. Even us." I shake my head. "Caltz should've never gotten his hands on you in the first place. We fucked up."

"No. No, you all tried. You tried." Tears fall down my cheeks as I reach forward, hugging Waylon. He stands up, embracing me as I continue to silently cry. No screaming. The tears just fall.

"Let's get you upstairs. Good to walk?" I nod, and he eases back, keeping his arm draped around my shoulders as he leads us out of the room. There are people outside, but I keep my head down not wanting to see who's there. No one speaks to us as Waylon takes me to the private elevator, the doors closing as he rubs my arm. "One last thing, Leo should know—"

"He does. He stopped me the other night." He goes still next to me. I stare at the warped reflection of us, not able to focus on any immediate features. "But I told him I was fine."

"He know about in Jersey?" I nod. "Alright."

Once inside the penthouse, Waylon sets up in the television room. He goes to pick out a movie, but I choose one instead, playing *The Last Unicorn*. I stare at the screen, pulling a blanket over myself. The rest of me becomes numb. Exhaustion begins to take hold. Waylon stays within eyesight, talking low on the phone as I watch the unicorn warn the old woman. About more than halfway through the film, Waylon sits next to me, and I feel calmer. Safer.

From myself.

When the film finishes, he suggests another, and I go through the organized stacks of my movies and pull out another classic. *The Pebble and the Penguin*. I'm enamored by Hubie as I always have been, smiling at his nervousness. Waylon chuckles with me, until the front door opens, and he quickly gets up. I pause the movie, carefully standing and dropping my blanket as I peek around the doorway.

Waylon, Julio, and Isaac all speak with Leo in hushed tones. Leo's back is turned toward me. Isaac nods before leaving with Julio close behind. Waylon dips his head closer to Leo, whispering and pauses when he sees me. Leo turns, hazel eyes almost burning into me and my legs ache where the cuts were. My eyes stay on Leo as Waylon leaves, the front door shutting and locking as Leo approaches me slowly with concern etched on his face.

I clutch my arms, and whisper, "I told them not to contact you."

His brows furrow deeply, stopping only inches from me as he

caresses my cheek. His hand moves gently to the nape of my neck. Eyes search my face, flicking down to my arms. "Did you—?"

"No." I won't let him finish what I know he asks. I bite my lower lip and shake my head. "No."

He pulls me into his embrace, keeping his hand against my neck as I wrap my arms around his torso. Leo kisses my head and inhales deeply, but his exhale feels shaky. The pit in my stomach comes back, gnawing at me as I clutch to him and not finding relief yet. I bury my face against his chest, sick at the guilt and self-hate that stirs under my skin.

"If you needed me, I would've come," he says.

"You can't do everything yourself. Waylon handled it."

"Autumn."

"I lied," I murmur, chest beginning to shake. Leo moves back, eyes searching my face again.

"What?"

"I told you I was fine. That I was fine, but I don't...I don't think I'm fine. Those thoughts, the dark thoughts they came back and just...just..."

"Are you having those thoughts now?" I shake my head. "What caused them? Do you know?"

"They usually happen when I'm alone. Everything crashes in, and then I can't figure out what's in my head or, fuck." I step away, beginning to run my hands through my hair and my muscles tense as I feel where I'd torn at my scalp. I pace trying to regain control of my emotions. It all feels like it's tumbling again, not darkness falling this time, but more so feeling pressure around my chest.

"Autumn." I continue to pace through the large living room, eyes flashing to the bare walls and anxiety pricking at my neck. "Dear Watson." I stop, looking across the room to him. Apprehension covers his face as I see his hands flex at his side, twitching. I focus on him, controlling my breathing again as I try to get the images out of my head. The voices and betrayal raging deep.

"You said you were on the other side of the glass, right?" Leo nods his head once. "Did you see the newspapers Roger brought in?"

Leo's jaw flexes. "Yes."

"Do you remember that day? Where most of those articles were from?"

His brows furrow deeper, coming a step closer. "My publicist thought it'd be good to hold a charity event here for the anniversary of the hotel's opening." A flash of that moment comes back, cold and barely feeling my toes. "Was there a reason he showed it to you?"

"I don't know." I hold myself tighter, knowing how caring Leo is doesn't mean he'd remember. It was a blip in time. Even I barely remembered. "Why did you go into Blue Java the day we met?" I ask instead. Maybe there was a reason there, an odd twist of fate instead—

"I've always gone to Blue Java for small public meetings." My heart stops.

"This job will be perfect for you."

"I thought I told you that. It'd always been in the mornings though."

The line clicks as Roger hangs up. The job application in my hand.

"Why didn't you when I worked mornings?"

"You were gone. I didn't want to go back at all."

"Stay in that area."

Roger's words practically roar in my head. Warning pricks at my skin as more pieces click. The job. The date on the newspaper. Leo practically owning the women's center, which Roger sent me to. Too much not to be coincidence. Anxiety pulses up my spine, making my stomach clench as I wonder how much of the three years were really mine.

"You knew!"

Had I always been a puppet?

"Breathe." Leo is suddenly right in front of me. He touches my shoulder and I have to shake off the odd haunting feeling that threatens to drown me. "Autumn, it was pure coincidence that I was there that afternoon. I'd missed my usual meeting with Juanita, and we moved back the time. That's all." He pushes my hair back and I focus on his touch. He tilts my chin up. "You're safe, dear Watson."

He pulls me into his embrace again, holding me firmly as he caresses my back. I lean into him, not realizing how short of breath I was until he begins to help calm me down. Swallowing hard, I grasp onto him, putting all attention on his gentle caress. I do everything to shove the horrifying thoughts away. That it wasn't just me, but him who'd been played, too.

Minutes tick by, exhaustion beginning to pull at me. "Sorry, it's been a long day."

Leo hushes me softly, threading his fingers through my hair gently and kisses my forehead. He pauses briefly, feeling the strands. "Cut your hair."

"Yeah." I pull back, holding up my hands between us. "Nails were done, too, but kinda fucked'em up." The paint is destroyed. Leo takes my hands, moving his thumb softly over my knuckles.

"Come with me." He guides us into the bathroom, stopping me before the counter and gestures for me to sit. Unsure, but trusting him, I get up on the counter as he goes to one of the cabinets. He comes back over with a bottle with pale blue liquid and some cotton. He pours some of it onto the cotton, then begins to apply it to my thumbnail, soaking away the lavender.

"Why do you have nail polish remover?"

"My main housekeeper prefers to use it for stains, along with other items, so I keep bottles here." He dabs more remover, moving to my other fingernails with precise movement to soak then rub. "She has to use approved cleaning supplies for the hotel, but here I'll listen to her advice."

A small giggle comes out of me, and he flicks his gaze over to me. A small smirk comes over him as he continues. He's gentle and affectionate, wiping away the light color on my nails. Although what could be a calming color, I feel less and less anxiety as I watch it disappear. He moves to the other hand. "Lavender isn't your color."

"No?"

He shakes his head, humming a little. "Something more of a fall color."

"You mean autumn?" His smile is gentle. "I'll get another color."

"No rush." Leo finishes, tossing the cotton away and then turns on the sink, soaking a washcloth to clean my hands. I watch him in fascination as he does, and then he grabs some lotion to start massaging into my skin. My eyes close. The calluses of his hands are rougher than usual, but not to the point of scratching at my skin. His fingers press between each of mine, moving over the tendons with ease. A long sigh releases. The last of the rigidness dissipating along with any worrying thoughts.

I feel Leo move closer, until his lips brush over mine. "You are safe, dear Watson." A gentle kiss is placed upon my lips. "I love you. Trust me."

"I do," I murmur against his lips. "It's everyone else."

"Look at me." My eyes flutter open. His face barely inches from mine. All I see are hazel eyes. "Trust in me. No one else matters."

I want to tell him he's wrong. There are others that do matter. Whether I care for them or not. I think of telling him this, when my stomach rumbles loudly. I bite my bottom lip as Leo glances down.

"When did you last eat?"

"Breakfast?" I scrunch my face, realizing how long. Another day forgotten.

Leo mutters, "They should've made sure—"

"I never said anything about being hungry. In Waylon's and others defense."

"Except you never say when you're hungry. You'll starve before you do," Leo says, slightly chastising me as he goes to put the remover away. My shoulders involuntarily hunch, shrinking within myself as I get off the counter. Leo notices when he comes back, sighing as he rubs my shoulders. "I'm always worried about your health and eating habits." He kisses my cheek. "I'm not mad at you."

Hearing those words help alleviate uncertainty. "How do you feel about pizza rolls?"

He snorts. "I'll order dinner. Not pizza rolls. We've both had a long day. Get changed for bed, and then we can resume your movie. I'll have tea ready for you."

Leo leaves and I shake off the last of the lingering bad feelings. I head to the closet, stripping out of the clothes I almost ripped off myself earlier. In only my underwear, I debate whether taking a shower when Leo speaks behind me, "Autumn?"

I let out a small screech, spinning as he watches me from the doorway. Instinctively, I start to cover myself up, but stop as I rub my calves together, trying to act nonchalant. "Yeah?"

"Breathe," he says quietly, and I do just that and give him a smile. He holds the phone up. "Did you make a reservation at Giglio Giardino?"

"Yeah, for Leanne, Trix, and I. Only place I knew I could reserve short notice."

"You had me down as a maybe?"

"Wasn't sure. I was gonna ask, but…" I shrug, and wrap my arms around myself feeling chilly, "…do you want to join?"

Leo smiles, walking over to grab my cotton robe as he talks on the phone. "Reservation for four. I'll want the 45' Pinot or 37' Merlot, it will depend on the special that night. Be sure it's one of the more private tables."

I take the robe from him, smiling back as he goes to leave the bedroom, but he pauses. "He'd like to speak with you."

"What?" He holds the phone out. Pulling the robe on, I take it and answer, "Hello?"

"Good evening, Autumn," Christopher answers. "I hear you've had an eventful day."

Oh, goody. The hotel staff rumors have commenced.

"A bit."

"Well, Mr. Luciano ordered dinner for you both, but didn't mention dessert. I thought you'd need some, perhaps some of our 'smanzy' tiramisu? Or chocolate mousse lava cake?" I chuckle, and Leo raises a brow.

"That's a tough decision, Christopher."

"My preference is the tiramisu."

"That one then. Thank you."

"Of course, Autumn. Please inform Mr. Luciano that everything will arrive within the hour." He hangs up soon after and I hand the phone back.

"Should I be concerned?" Leo asks as I head into the closet.

"Not yet," I muse, now wondering how many know I've danced in the hotel. Or damaged it.

Leo tosses the phone aside, beginning to strip off his button-up and then his undershirt. His belt snaps as he takes it off. I find myself staring at him, blinking quickly when he looks my way and I duck further into the closet. I begin pulling out pajamas, jolting when Leo wraps his arms around me. He nuzzles his face against my neck, inhaling deeply.

"Will you still be doing that if I decide we watch a Nick Cage movie?"

He kisses my neck. "Always."

"Hmm, well it's your lucky day, mister. I'm already invested in the classic cartoon out there. So, you've been spared. For now."

Leo trails his hand up, placing it gently against my neck. I lean back against him, closing my eyes as his warmth engulfs me. I'm safe. Even from me.

Chapter 29

Rebuilding

I sit across from Dr. Rory Maxwell. He's a large man with dark skin, a short fade and trimmed goatee. His eyes a deep mahogany, which seem kind along with his expression. The polo shirt and tweed jacket give me professor vibes. Not to mention a thermos of tea. Gotta give him points for coming prepared.

I clear my throat, glancing around Leo's office, the one I first visited, which feels like eons ago. Chesty and Leo thought the familiar space would be helpful, not to mention I wouldn't have to leave the hotel. Outside, Drew and Isaac are keeping watch with only a door between us. I notice now how this office seems to have a gothic scholarly aesthetic. A complete opposite of Leo's actual office. Why couldn't he choose *this* instead of damn grey walls?

Dr. Maxwell flips through some papers. He was given some of my background information this morning, with my permission. Didn't really want to go through the whole spiel...again. He places the papers onto the coffee table between us, crossing one of his legs over the other in an easy manner.

"How would you prefer we start, Autumn?" I blink at the baritone voice, something I'm not familiar with in this kind of setting.

I've only ever had female therapists. He's the first man I've sat in front of. Chesty doesn't count. Officially.

"Not sure. Well,…" I point to the papers, "… do you need more information? Or something Waylon mentioned to you?"

"Let's not focus on paperwork…" he gestures toward the same folders, "…or what others have said. I'd rather hear from you. Your perspective, thoughts, and feelings."

"Gonna be here awhile then," I nervously scoff.

"This session can be an hour, two, or even four. I've been instructed to take all afternoon if we must. Whatever you need."

"Seriously?"

"Yes." He smiles. "It'd appear that Mr. Luciano and his closest people care deeply for you. They want to be sure you're safe. From others and yourself."

Anxiety ticks up my spine and I adjust on the couch.

"What's going through your head from that comment?" He asks, and I just stare at him. "Or rather, *which* of the comments made you uncomfortable?"

"Oddly, not the self-harm part," I murmur, trying to encourage myself to just freaking talk. I've done therapy before, but this felt harder. Anxiety keeps pricking at the back of my neck, twisting into my stomach. He waits for me to answer, keeping an inviting expression. I loosen a breath. "It's hard sometimes. Believing others care about me, which I know people do, but…it hasn't always been men."

Sure, let's start with a subject I know. My anxiety with men. Simple shit.

"You have trouble believing men?"

"More like trusting. In the past. Haven't had a good track record."

"What do you think that track record is?" I watch him a moment, but his warm look doesn't budge. "In your own words."

"Well, there's specific events that I could pinpoint to. Want that?"

"Not exactly." He picks up his thermos, sipping it. "How would you define your interactions with most men?"

"Simple conversations. Nothing beyond skin deep. When I was a barista, usually only for work, but nothing too personal. I've always been an open book, but there's a line before giving certain stuff out and not, ya know?"

"Being an open book of what you're already comfortable with does not always equate to being vulnerable." My eyes meet his. "Discussing subjects ranging from sexuality, mental health, general preferences, and such doesn't always mean we're trusting who we're speaking to. It means you trust yourself, know yourself confidently of who you are. What you believe in. While vulnerability is trusting to show parts of yourself without fully knowing how you feel about those subjects, know how to explain, or not knowing how that person will respond. You gave those open subjects to people because either you were confident in your own self or knew *how* that person would react. Thus, having more female relationships. With men, you've not had similar reactions. Or their reactions were harmful. Except with Leo and his Crew, who you became vulnerable with. Trusting."

"Paperwork give you that?" I blurt, and he smiles softly. "Sorry."

He shakes his head, waving it off. "We'll call it a third-party view with background in seeing similar patterns."

"Ah."

"Why did you open yourself up to them?"

"Because Leo trusted them. He considers them family."

"Why did you trust Leo?"

"He tries. Even at times when I keep expecting him to leave. Give up. Walk away." I stare past the doctor, shifting in my seat again. He's silent, but I can feel the question from him. The constant *why*. "It seems to be a pattern for me."

"From who?"

"Parents. Never really cared. Didn't even show up at... Sarah's...*my* funeral. Then there's the long list of things Steve did, but I think leaving me in the gutters to die was the least of the issues. The police, soon as I gave them what they wanted, they left me to my 'new life' to enjoy." I swallow hard, throat tightening as I breathe a shaky exhale. "Ex-therapist, who practically said I wasn't getting any better. Roger..." my stomach plummets, and I start to rub my thighs and shake my head, "...Leo isn't them, though. Sometimes he fucks up, but at least he tries."

"It's good to be self-aware. Understanding where our pain comes from." Dr. Maxwell pauses, causing me to look at him again. "Allow yourself to feel the emotions that come from these instances you share."

"Thought I was."

"Your voice is calculated," he says, leaning back. "It's careful, like a survivor who's gone through the events they've endured. Rationalizing each event, which is fine, but at times it makes us...gatekeep our own emotions. To not truly comprehend how we feel."

"If I did that every time I talked about it, wouldn't that set me back? Get angry all the time and hateful? Whole point is to be happy right?"

"Emotions are neutral. It's what we do with them that changes the outcome and what they become. Stopping ourselves completely from feeling fear, worry, or anger will only prolong suffering inside. We have times to be aware, not let emotions control us, and we use things to cope through those harder moments. It doesn't mean ignore those emotions. We recognize them, feel them, let go, and move on."

I blink at him, unsure how to respond. Dr. Wilson always talked about 'not lingering' on anger. Much like how I was about forgetting and move on.

"I have these...fuzzy sock moments," I say quietly. "Finding whatever brings me joy or forget the awful feelings. Maybe I was really just using my coping mechanisms to ignore other emotions."

"You said you do it to find joy?" I nod. "No matter what the thing is?" I nod again. "Without thinking, tell me why you like these fuzzy socks."

"To remind myself I can be happy. Allow myself to feel." Realization settles in and a slow smile comes over his face. "The blowup yesterday was from emotions I kept bottling up, not allowing myself to feel. Be vulnerable with...myself." Dr. Maxwell still just smiles, tilting his head a little. "Not sure how you did that, but you're good."

"Sometimes starting with one subject we can align it with what the root of the issue may be if we follow the breadcrumbs." I relax into the couch finally, smiling back at him. "Handling emotions should be with finesse, not yanking at strings in hopes something will open. So, why don't you tell me about these neglected emotions of late. Let's work on you becoming vulnerable with *yourself*."

The next couple of hours I talk and talk. Everything comes out of me with Dr. Maxwell, opening up about the worst of what's happened and my thoughts. He's deliberate with his advice and answers, allowing me time with the harder subjects. He soon knows everything, even the smaller details I could remember being under-cover and the week I spent with Roger. The more I let out without fear of repercussion, the more relief fills me. Until we reach a subject I've been actively avoiding.

"I'm certain we've gone over quite a bit, more than even you thought possible," he says, stirring honey into his new mug of tea. "What about the interrogation?"

"What about it?" He raises a brow, giving a look that I'm labeling as 'don't try it.' "It wasn't that bad."

"Knowing what you've endured of your past, perhaps, and that's how your brain is compartmentalizing it. But I'd like to hear why it wasn't that bad."

My spoon goes in circles in my own tea, chewing a little on my bottom lip as I shrug. "I was by myself, talked to myself, pissed myself, and screamed at Roger. Honestly, did all that while under-cover at some point."

He sips his tea, then sets it down to settle back into his chair as he folds his hands. "It is commendable that you endured such treatment, but I guarantee you that *no one* can come unscathed from spending over 40 hours locked up. Questioned about personal subjects. Locked in an empty room with harsh light. Pushed in directions you don't want to go in." I avert my eyes from Dr. Maxwell, leg beginning to shake a little. "Or because we learn things about ourselves that we didn't want to."

I bite at my bottom lip, taking a deep breath.

"You are not weak in saying that Roger got to you. That he got under the surface."

"He didn't, he…didn't."

Dr. Maxwell hums a little. "Earlier you mentioned about loss of control yesterday." I continue staring at the carpet. "How the change of your hair and nail color may have triggered you." I nod, staring down at my clean fingernails.

"Reminder I'd lost myself," I murmur. "That Sarah…died. Freedoms I lost. Choices. Maybe those choices didn't matter."

"Why would they not matter?"

"Not really your choice when you're manipulated into them."

"What choice was that?"

His deep gaze meets mine, keeping that eye contact as I clear my throat. How could I explain all of it? Make it make sense that it wasn't the interrogation room or Roger or pissing myself that made me lose it. It was the truth clanging through me like a bad omen.

Readjusting myself, I exhale sharply and lean forward. "For the last three years, I thought I was free. I thought I'd gotten out and there was finally hope in finding a normal life. Whatever that meant, and then I find out that's not the case. Almost every major decision I've made since then was manipulated or I'd been lied to."

"Was it something Roger said?"

"Yeah, but also Nan," I admit. "I don't want to hate or be angry with her, but I am. And Roger, I knew how much he'd become my… my jail keeper instead of handler, but more lies were revealed. More of my choices in the past meant nothing when I thought they had. How am I supposed to feel about that? What am I supposed to do?"

"As we do with any emotion. We feel them. And we let go. Those decisions are long past, you can't change them, but you can control what you do now."

"I don't think I can just let it go."

"Then remind yourself it wasn't your fault." My expression drops. "If you're not ready to let go, alright, but you have control now."

"Doesn't feel like it, honestly, felt like I had more while undercover. Trusted no one." I shrug, folding my arms over my chest. "Doesn't hurt as much when you expect *everyone* to betray you."

"Who are you waiting to betray you?"

"What?"

"It sounds as if you're waiting for someone else to do so because of what happened in that interrogation room." I can only stare at him, heart beginning to pound. "Just say how you feel. No matter who it is. Who did Roger shake for you?"

"Leo."

My body locks up, hating saying his name and admitting it. Dr. Maxwell barely moves, no surprise or judgment on his face. "What in particular about him?"

"Not what you may think."

"Tell me then."

I swallow harshly, slowly letting out a breath as I try to keep my breathing level. "I trust him. I feel safe with him. Leo is just that... safe person no matter what. I shouldn't listen to Roger, knowing he's just playing with my head, but I know I'm not an easy person to deal with. My anxieties, depression, self-harm tendencies...it can be a lot for anyone. I love him, but I'm scared I won't be enough. He already didn't tell me the truth for months, even though I understand why, it's the same reason I didn't tell him the truth but...what if there's another lie? What if I lose it and he can't do it anymore? What if there's a worse secret?"

Dr. Maxwell leans his elbows onto his knees. "How did you feel when you realized he lied to you?"

"I ran."

"Not that moment. The moment you fully understood what he'd been hiding. Deep down, what did you feel?"

"Angry."

"Did you tell him?"

"No."

"Because?"

"What if he wouldn't take me back?" A tear slips down my cheek.

"I'm already practically a burden on him, how would he feel if I was angry at him? After everything he's done?"

"Just as you can't neglect feeling emotions, you shouldn't need to neglect them with others. From what you've told me, he sounds like he very much cares for you. And it is never good to make assumptions or decisions for another without knowing how they'll truly react."

"So, be vulnerable?" I smile faintly as another tear falls. A smile pulls at his lips, and he leans forward to hand me a tissue. I take it and wipe away the tears.

"Relationships are always a give and take, even the most independent person needs another to lean on. Right now, you are depending on him and learning how to move forward. One day, I'm sure you can in return, in your own way, give him that. *You* know what you and Leo have, not some detective, best friends, or even me."

"Sure, about that, being independent? Cause I don't feel like it most days. I actually feel like a kid some days who needs their hand held."

"You survived the mob on your own." My hand grips the tissue. "I believe you're self-sufficient in more ways than one. Finally, after years, you're at a resting point. In a place that's safe. You're not trying to use Leo in any way. You'll have that control you want back soon enough. We'll work our way back up, give you new tools and new foundations to rebuild from. Everything you've done was not a waste, whether the decision was truly yours or not. You're here now. And now, it's time to build yourself a new building."

"And the old one?"

"Take the pieces which served you, and then put them into the new one. It's better to build with what we know was successful anyhow. Whether others have told you not, you've implemented many successful things."

A smile pulls at my lips, and I whisper, "Thanks."

"You're welcome." He sits back and grins. "I'm assuming you'd like to continue our sessions after today? Work on it together?"

"Yeah, I think so." I glance down at my mug. "We're gonna need more tea though."

Leo

Leo's knuckles go white.

The chairs in the ballroom weren't heavy duty, but Autumn still bends and snaps their legs like twigs. She demolished eight chairs, dented and cracked the dancefloor, too. Four of the tables are busted. Everything was being cleaned up after a wedding event. His brows furrow as she screams, ripping at her hair and scratching at her nails as the audio of the footage crackles from her high-pitched screaming.

His chest constricts, struggling to remain calm.

"Should've known she had that in her," Julio whispers a few feet over. "Had to survive the mob somehow."

"She's relentless like a pro-boxer," Rudolph murmurs.

"Just needs a boxing bag, instead of hotel furniture," Owen comments.

"Quiet," Jameson warns, glimpsing at Leo.

The security room becomes deathly still, all the men watching the footage Leo insisted on watching multiple times. He leans over the table, directly in front of the main monitor. Jameson stays near his right, while Owen is on his left with Waylon. Julio and Rudolph stay near the doorway. The place is small, especially with the large bikers all standing with arms crossed.

"How long she been with Maxwell?" Rudolph asks.

"Two hours now," Waylon answers. "Drew just got them tea."

"She's talking."

"Yeah, thankfully."

She'd been quiet this morning, sitting in Leo's upstairs office until Dr. Maxwell arrived. Leo's jaw clenches, hoping it's enough as he watches Waylon put her into a stronghold. She screams and cries, yanking at him. Jameson, silently, presses a button to quiet the audio. Leo stops the tape as Waylon and Autumn sit alone on the dancefloor.

His head hangs, breathing heavily as one of his hand clenches the table harder, making the material creak loudly. Jameson places a hand on his shoulder, causing Leo to tense.

"Not your fault," Jameson whispers.

"I should've been here."

"You have other duties—"

"I should've fucking known, if anyone would've known how far she'd—"

"Quit blaming yourself," Waylon warns, and all the men freeze. Leo snaps his head toward Waylon. "You heard her at the estate. Not yours to take. Been around jumpers for over a decade, you don't always know." Leo's jaw muscle tightens, frowning deeply. "She learned how to hide in the open, probably not realizing what that was doing to her."

"Survival," Owen comments. Leo stares at Autumn again, hair in disarray and turned away from the security cameras. "She had no other choice. Us vets..." he motions to himself and Waylon, "...we know what that's like. What you have to do, but it can fester inside you."

It becomes quiet again as Leo stares at the monitor.

Jameson murmurs, "She's not Matteo." Leo stiffens. "Or Gabriel."

Leo glares at him, eyes darkening at the mention of his brother's name. He brushes off Jameson's hand, standing up straight as he presses the button for the footage to continue silently. "Update."

Each of them exchange a look. Owen takes the lead. "The homicide case of the three men is closed. They have their murderer, trial should be cut and dry."

"Who?"

"Dealer for Enzo."

"Good. The detective?"

"Suspended, charged, and under investigation."

"I want him fucking fired."

"Commissioner should come through, but Juanita should have it handled," Julio adds. "But he's still a hero amongst his precinct and others for what, well, *she* did. We'll have to be careful. Sarah Marie doesn't even exist in the reports for the takedown, which may be good on our end for keeping her out of the limelight."

"There any actual worry of it being found out it was all her?" Rudolph asks.

Julio sighs, making eye contact with Owen who tightens his jaw muscle. Both glance at Leo who doesn't tear his eyes from the screen. "Unless someone overtly wanted to find her, like us...no. Long as those involved stay quiet, like the detective, no will ever know."

Leo growls fisting his hands "Put a damn restraining order on Caltz. Don't want him within five blocks of her."

"Already done. Same with the hotel itself."

"Good. How close are we to getting the other two?" Leo asks.

"Rossi doesn't care if we nab him, apparently dude sucks at his job," Owen says.

"I want him before the end of the month."

"Done," Waylon says.

"I'll get the other out of jail by that time," Julio adds.

"Her bastard of an ex?"

"Nah, he's the tricky one," Julio huffs. "Given his deal with the feds, max security and all, gotta use different channels. Get too close, someone may sniff out what we're doing. Like I said, unless someone openly wants to find her, but releasing Steve could tip off those like Gabriel."

"Gotta treat this with finesse, boss," Owen adds.

"Not to mention, Caltz being suspended and possibility of being fired...he may get bored and start poking his nose in other places. Prison may be one of those, best to wait and hold our cards," Jameson suggests carefully. "We're playing chess, not checkers here."

"When are we not playing chess?" Rudolph asks in a low tone.

Leo inhales deeply, making all the men quiet.

They wait for his response as the minutes tick by. Slowly, Leo turns toward Jameson with a dark, sinister look. Jameson meets his gaze straight on, not at all phased by the mafia boss. He nods once and walks out of the room. The others follow suit in silence, leaving Leo and Waylon within the security room. Once the door shuts, his expression softens a touch as he whispers to Waylon, "Thank you for helping her."

"Don't need thanks, Pres. She's one of us."

Leo looks back at the screen as Autumn and Waylon sit, talking to each other. His voice becomes hoarse as he watches with an ache around his heart. "What did she tell you?"

Waylon sighs, rubbing the back of his neck. "Chesty." Leo looks over at him, who gives a grim expression. "Tell me."

"Not my place."

"Waylon."

"You knew about her cutting at the detective's?" He asks abruptly, folding his arms. Leo's expression is stone cold, but he nods once. "Didn't say shit?"

"Not my place."

"Oh, fuck you, boss," Waylon snorts, shaking his head. Leo pauses the tape as Autumn and Waylon get up to leave the ballroom. "I won't say what she said, but I'll tell you my opinion. And that's I don't know how helpful that fucking therapist was. Maybe with the assault, but not the almost two years of undercover work and being used like a..." he swallows hard, "...soldier left in war."

More of Leo's face softens. "Waylon."

The veteran shrugs, staring at the monitor next. "Kind of reminds me of myself and other vets when we left the service. Don't know where you fit. People pretend to help, but don't. No one warns ya you'll never be the same, society ain't gonna be the same. Never know who to trust next. She was put through hell without backup, without training, or help of any kind. Before and after. And all she wants to do is be good enough."

"She is."

Waylon snorts. "You've been through a lot Leo, but you've not been used by government schemes. That shit fucks with ya. From what she told me, I'm tellin' ya, she's waiting to be left behind again."

"Like you eight years ago." Both men smile faintly as Leo huffs a sigh, straightening himself more. "What do I do?"

"What ya did for all of us, but with more lovey-dovey stuff." Leo's soft look quickly turns into a glare. Waylon snorts at him. "She'd go through hell for you, even though she's been there plenty times. Can't stop her from going back, like any of us, but remind her she's not alone. And that she's a fucking fighter."

Autumn

I shake Dr. Maxwell's hand, feeling better than I have over the past few days. Weight that's been pressing on my shoulders has eased and it's like I can breathe again. We talked for four hours, deciding on another session soon.

"Thank you," I say again.

"It's been wonderful talking with you. I look forward to more, but we'll keep it shorter next time. Not to worry others, eh?" He grins, patting my shoulder as he opens the door.

"They'll just send in paratroopers or whatever." We laugh, walking out to find Isaac and Drew sitting in chairs across the way.

"I'll speak with Owen on putting together a schedule for future sessions," Dr. Maxwell informs, looking over at Isaac and Drew as they stand. "Good start today."

"I'll talk with Owen," Isaac says, shaking his hand. Both nodding.

"She's a bright, smart, courageous woman," the doctor smiles at me. "Just need to find some new tools."

"Yeah," I murmur. Drew gestures for Dr. Maxwell to follow him, while Isaac escorts me toward the elevator.

"Feeling better?"

"You've no idea," I say as we round the corner. "Thanks for yesterday, I know you were just trying to help."

"Always my pleasure, Miss Autumn." He grins, blue eyes shining as we approach the private elevator. "Boss is still working, big surprise, all the way up or penthouse?"

"All the way up. I'd like to see him."

He nods as we step inside, and I sit down on the love seat and rub my head. It's quiet as the elevator ascends and Isaac remains standing, flicking his gaze to me.

"I really am okay, Isaac. I'm sorry if I scared you."

He shakes his head briefly. "I've just taken a liking to you since you kicked me in the dick."

"Start of a beautiful friendship," I smirk.

"Very much so, Miss Autumn."

The elevator doors open. Isaac pauses outside of Leo's office doors, gesturing for me to wait. I wink at him, and he does it back as he peeks inside. He opens the doors, and we walk in quietly. Leo is on the phone, pacing before the large windows while Owen works on his digital pad to the right. Jameson leans over Leo's desk, stacking papers and signing some. Jameson gives me a passive look as he leaves the office, gesturing for Isaac to follow. Leo continues talking, speaking gruffly in a language that's not English. Italian?

I approach Owen silently. "Should I come back?"

"Nah, he'll want to see you after this," Owen mutters under his breath. "Overseas issues."

"Matteo?"

Owen flicks his gaze to Leo and back to me. "Renato. Don't press."

I go over to one of the chairs in front of the desk, sitting with my legs underneath me as I wait. As I listen to Leo talk, I realize he is speaking Italian. It's fluid coming out of his mouth, and he has a deeper accent that flows with the words. Course he'd speak it flawlessly and sexily.

He stares out the window, waving toward Owen, who walks up to show him something. Leo nods, waving him away after Owen whispers something in his ear. I smile at Owen as he leaves, who gives a small grin back and I'm left alone with Leo. Time passes and I concentrate on breathing slowly to keep my anxiety down, remembering what Dr. Maxwell said. Leo and I have talked and been honest, I can do this. Finally, he hangs up and lets out a harsh sigh.

I ask tentatively, "Check in."

Leo turns swiftly with surprise, but relief replaces it. "Green." He tosses his phone onto his desk, sitting down and moves a few folders and papers to the side. "How was your session with Dr. Maxwell?"

"Really good," I answer. "Covered about all of it and then some. Gonna try to have regular weekly sessions. Isaac and Owen will probably figure out a schedule."

Leo leans back, giving a faint smile. "Good. I'm glad it'll work out."

I bite my bottom lip gently, pulling at my hands a little as the air suddenly feels thick. We watch the other in silence. Leo quirks a brow, like he knows that I have something on my mind. I clear my throat, reminding myself it'll be fine.

I exhale and say, "I'm angry at you."

His eyes widen slightly, but move back to normal as he leans forward on his desk. He folds his hands on it, and genuinely asks, "Alright, what can I do?"

I slump a bit. Wasn't mad at him *right* now, which makes this harder. Kind of difficult staying angry at someone who cares enough to remedy the situation at every turn. I flashback to him apologizing at my apartment door, the one and only time I'd been truly angry with him outright.

He hadn't left then either.

"Okay, I *was* angry with you, but been told I should try feeling some emotions instead of bottling them up and you seem like the best start."

"Being angry with me?"

"Yeah, which I didn't say anything before cause I worried you'd leave me or won't love me anymore. Maybe you'll hate me."

He instantly straightens. "Never."

"Hold on, let me explain a bit." I hold my hand up, and he nods. "I know those fears are just that...fears. Ones I need to own up to and not let keep controlling me. I can't pretend they're not there though like, like…my back against hard surfaces during sex." I point to his desk. His gaze follows my hand, face completely neutral. "We're both aware, so we work around it, but we don't *ignore* it. Some days I can do it cause it's a good day or just good sex." He smirks. "Careful, mister. What I'm trying to say is I know you won't leave me if I get angry with you, but I can't just ignore that fear any more than the emotion. I need to face it, until one day…"

"…you lay down on the desk."

"Yeah."

"What *were* you angry at me for?"

"Lying to me about being a mafia boss." Leo's entire face falls, hands dropping completely onto the desk. "I understand why, just as you understood why I didn't tell you about my past. I was still angry. And you even warned me that you couldn't tell me everything, but when Jameson confirmed it, deep down I was angry. Angry you lied to me. That I felt betrayed. I felt used again. And…" I take a shaky breath, stomach clenching as he watches me silently, "…Roger got into my head. Probably did because I never told you I was angry, and I wasn't sure *again* how real this was."

Leo is frozen. His eyes digging into my soul.

"I am sorry for lying to you," he says finally in a rough voice. "It was never my intention to deceive you."

"I know and holding onto what trust I knew was real between us kept me going in that interrogation room. And my only fear was me walking out, and they'd take you instead. All of it, all of us, was for nothing."

"Never, my dear Watson. Never." A small smile grows on me, but then he asks, "Do you hate me then?"

I get off the chair and walk over to him, pushing his chair back to sit across his lap. Leo watches me with some surprise, but he unstiffens as I loop my arm around his neck and put my forehead against his. "Never, mister Americano. Never."

Leo strokes his fingers over my cheek and down to my neck. He lays a tender kiss on my lips, and I sigh as I kiss him back, pulling him closer as he hums. Leaning back into the chair, Leo breaks the kiss with brows less furrowed. "Anything else?"

"No, but I may need a neck brace for the emotional whiplash of the past week. I feel like I've been through multiple seasons of *ER* or *Grey's Anatomy*, and I don't even watch those shows."

"Sounds like an early night to me. How about some carbonara?" He keeps me in his arms, standing up to walk us out of the office.

"Are you cooking?" I ask, and he raises a brow. "Another reason I can't stay mad at you."

"My cooking?"

"And cute tattoos." Leo stops, smiling at me. "Obviously not the only reasons."

"Obviously," he smirks.

Chapter 30

Dinner Dates

"Miss Autumn." A knock sounds from the bedroom door as I pull on my cardigan. I open it to reveal a solemn faced Isaac. Well, that's not good.

"Uh-oh, what did Leo do now?" He raises a brow. "Come on, only time you give me that…" I gesture at his face, "…is when you have to deliver news from him."

He snorts, a grin almost pulling at his lips. "He's going to be late for dinner."

"Okay." I shrug, turning away and heading into the closet to look for shoes.

"Are you alright?"

"Yeah, why wouldn't I be?" I sit on the ground to put on the short heels. They have black lace that'll match the dark slacks I'm wearing and burnt orange blouse. Concern flickers over his face. "Did he say he won't make it at all?"

"No."

"Then he'll show up later. And honestly, I'd be more surprised if he showed up on time." I start to strap the heels on.

I'd overheard earlier today in Leo's office that there was trouble with one of his importing companies down the coast. Not to mention

403

I could hear murmuring about Matteo and other matters I try to ignore and let be. I'll hold onto the hope he'll be there like he said he would be. Especially, since I slept without nightmares the night before and feel good enough to keep my dinner date with Trix and Leanne. I won't even let a late Leo damper my mood in seeing them.

It'll go fine. They'll get along. And everything will work out.

Hopefully.

I stand, pressing the heels down into the carpet. Comfy enough. Sighing, I button the black cardigan and start heading out of the bedroom with Isaac close behind. Briefly, I check the clock and notice I'll be close to fifteen minutes early at this rate. Well, not terrible to head on down.

"Ready, Bond?" I ask, grabbing my phone.

"You've got time, Miss Autumn."

"I'm an early bird...for nighttime," I smirk as I open the front door. Isaac quickly gathers his things and follows me. "You should remember from when I worked."

"You do have quite the punctuality." He strides past as I pause to smell the flowers on the hallway table. They're lilacs with other flowers of deep blues. A small smile rises on my face, touching the petals delicately before I join Isaac at the elevator. "I'll leave you at the restaurant when your friends arrive or earlier if you don't want me making contact with them."

"Why would I not want you to make contact?" He raises a brow. "You're a bodyguard, Isaac, not invisible."

The elevator dings, opening its doors for us. He pushes the button for the restaurant and asks, "Did you talk to Nancy today?"

"No," I mutter. He sighs. "I will! Just need a bit more time. She's knows I'm okay."

"I won't tell you what to do." I raise a brow at him next. "But perhaps give her some slack. You've always said open communication is key in stable relationships."

I narrow my eyes at him. "How dare you use my words against me."

"One must use the knowledge one has."

My hand bops his shoulder, and he grins. "I'm telling the Crew to call you Dr. No."

"You can threaten better than that." The doors open as I roll my eyes at him, walking out.

There are people bustling in the hall. They're all dressed in finery, much like how many were on my first date with Leo. Thankfully, my confidence doesn't feel as low. Off to the far-left side there's some chairs and I head over to wait. Which, I don't have to for long before Leanne walks out of the elevator. She's wearing a light blue dress with ruffles down the skirt, her hair pinned up with glittery barrettes.

"Fancy place you got here!" She exclaims as I head over to her. She hums as she hugs me, and I breathe deeply. Smiling, she pulls back and looks me over. "Looking fancy too."

I shrug, waving her off.

"Given one of your party is here, I'll give you your space. There's a matter I can attend to downstairs," Isaac says, nodding at me and then at Leanne. "Good to see you again, Leanne. And I'll see you tomorrow, Miss Autumn."

I give him a fake salute and he smirks, disappearing through the stairwell. Leanne gives me an inquisitive brow. "Don't start. Felt like it took forever for him just to call me *that.*"

"Fancy," she repeats.

I clear my throat, glancing at the clock. "Still a bit early, but we can check about our table until Trix gets here."

"What about Leo?"

"He's running a bit late." She hums again, and I roll my eyes at her. "Guys are perpetually late, especially when I have a habit of being early."

"I'm just teasing," she says with a grin, rubbing my shoulder. "Besides my boyfriend has a habit of being late, too. Can't say anything."

"Is this the one with the blonde hair you met at a conference?"

"*Jim,*" she emphasizes. "And yes, that one."

"Been like three weeks now, right?"

"Yeah, both of us been busy. He's copy editing and helping with marketing for schools, while I'm overviewing curriculums. Still fresh and new. The best part of the relationship now, where anything can happen."

"Yeah. Come on, let's go be early birds and get first pick of appetizers."

"*Now* we're talking." She hooks her arm in mine as we approach the maître d station where Christopher stands. "Evening, Christopher."

"Hello, Autumn. Wonderful to see you, did you enjoy the dessert the other night?"

"Yes, it was great. Thank you again."

"Of course, I can be sure that some will be on the menu tonight for you." He winks, then turns to Leanne. "And good evening to you."

"Evening," Leanne replies.

"Is your other guest and Mr. Luciano coming later?"

"Leo's gonna be late, but the other—"

"Is right here. Trix!" Leanne lets go of my arm, walking over to Trix, who's eyes are large as they look at the furnishings of the hotel. Christopher continues to grin as Leanne and Trix hug.

"Did I look like that the first night?" I whisper.

"A bit," he muses. "But it is always a delight to see people who appreciate the place. We work hard to keep it pristine and presentable."

"If the décor doesn't cause awe, the food certainly does. Could have food from here almost every night, though pretty sure that's not exactly possible."

"If you wanted, you could, Autumn. Almost all the hotel staff are happy to oblige you." I blink at him as he gives me a kind expression. I wonder if he knew what happened the other day, and honestly, if the staff would hate me for causing such a ruckus. Didn't even have the gumption to ask Leo what the damage was. "Your table is ready whenever you are."

"Thanks, Christopher." I turn to tell the other two, but then Trix's arms are thrown around me. I laugh, hugging her back tightly as my arms shake a little. "You're okay."

"I'm not the one..." her voice trails off, glancing at Christopher and then just smiles faintly at me, "...you know."

"I'm fine." I smile at her, squeezing her arms a little. "Kicking and screaming still."

She smiles softly. Trix wears a patterned pink blouse with white slacks, black heels, and her head is wrapped in light violet scarf. "I'm glad you're safe."

I squeeze her hand and she does so back. "Table is ready, we can go sit and wait for Leo. Get you two some drinks."

"Mr. Luciano has already ordered wine for the table, which you can begin with," Christopher says, gesturing for us to follow him.

"Impeccable service," Leanne says, glancing at Christopher and then me.

He leads us through the bustling restaurant toward the back, just a few tables away from where I had my first date with Leo. We're seated at a round table near a window, plants and vines climbing up the walls. I sit facing away from the entrance, while Leanne and Trix sit at the window, Leo's seat is against the wall next to me. There are two bottles on the table next to a decanter, both a type of red wine and Christopher pours Leanne and Trix a glass of their choosing. He leaves, while one of the waiters brings over breadsticks and me a glass of water before I even ask.

"Attentive, huh?" Trix asks as they leave.

"It's Leo's hotel and they know me, so..." my voice trails off as I sip my water. My gut wrenches a little in worry about how tonight will go, but I push it aside to focus on a good evening.

"A toast," Trix starts off, holding up her glass of Pinot. "To Autumn being home, safe and sound again. And all *three* of us together again."

We clink our glasses, sipping and both their eyes widen. Leanne comments, "Wow, that's good."

"What label is this anyways?" Trix grabs the bottle and her mouth drops, staring at me. "Do you know how expensive this is? It's an exquisite Italian wine."

"Trust me when I say that the bottle doesn't compare to other things he's gotten," I say, knowing how often I just don't look. His money, his decisions. Long as I get my cereal, don't care.

"Comes with the territory of dating a billionaire," Leanne says.

"He's not…oh, never mind."

"Not complaining, given it was probably his money that got you out of that police station," Trix says quietly.

I want to argue it wasn't, but my stomach begins to twist. I put my water down and grab a breadstick. "I've been gone and need full updates from you Trix. And your help to get more info from Leanne about this guy she's dating."

My diversion tactic works. Both leap into talking about work and Leanne going on about Jim. I feel better seeing her happy discussing him and then Trix going on about this girl she met. We talk for the next thirty minutes as I feel relief having conversations I've grown to love.

We're laughing when our waiter, Tyler, comes to place a dish of seared scallops and lobster on the table. Trix almost coughs on her wine as Leanne looks at me with shock.

"Tyler, we didn't order this," I say.

"It was requested for you, Miss Watson," he responds, making swift eye contact.

My heartbeat quickens. "Is he here?"

"Just arrived and is speaking with the maître d."

I nod and he leaves as I bring my attention back to my friends. Except, they're not looking at me, but share a similar sly smile. Leanne tries to hide hers with her hand as I turn around in my seat.

It feels like our first date.

Leo strides assuredly toward our table, wearing a black dress shirt, which is open slightly, and black suit trousers. He passes tables with a poised expression that says he's fucking in charge. People stare, some watching in a way that tells me they understand who he is. I remain seated this time, smiling a little as his eyes stay wholly on me. He's practically smoldering with sensuality and confidence.

Leanne clears her throat. "Maybe it was just a bad night, but I don't remember him being that hot."

"I bat for the other team, but…knows he owns the place, huh?" Trix comments.

"Shh," I hush them and they both chuckle as he approaches.

A shiver runs down my spine as his hand lands on my shoulder, bending slightly to place a chaste kiss on my mouth, then whispers against my ear, "Apologies for being late."

"Thank you for letting me know before." His eyes shimmer. "And thank you for the appetizers."

He takes his seat beside me, placing a hand on my thigh as he addresses my friends with a stoic look. "Trix. Leanne. Good evening. Apologizes for being late, but it's good to see you two. And in better circumstances than of late."

That business air is around him, shrouding him in confidence and a suave manner. He takes the Merlot, pouring himself a glass and I have to keep myself from giggling at him. It's been a while since I've seen this side of him in public. He squeezes my thigh playfully.

"We get being busy," Trix finally says. "Work happens, you know?"

"That it does, have you ordered dinner yet?"

"We weren't even looking at the food yet, until *this* came," Leanne answers, gesturing at the platter. "Quite the spread. Do you always order the most expensive things?" She holds her glass up with emphasis.

"Leanne, I'm sure he's just trying to give a good impression," Trix says. "Since our first time meeting him, Autumn disappeared for a month and then was arrested when she came back."

Oh, the best friends were getting ready to swing, huh? Why couldn't I have friends that weren't protective?

Leo appears unphased, as he barely blinks and picks up his wine glass.

"Unfortunate circumstances, yes, thankfully we've been able to move forward. But none of this is due to that," Leo speaks in a collected tone. "I do my best to give the best to Autumn, which can include her friends and family if she wishes. If either of you think it's to *woo* you, then you'd be wrong. She chose the restaurant, not me, because she adores the staff and food. She's always taken my advice wholeheartedly when it comes to the menu here, since it *is* my restaurant and I know the selections well."

Both look at me completely speechless. Leo sips his wine, then waves over Tyler who arrives promptly. Tyler smiles pleasantly. "Good evening, Mr. Luciano. It's a pleasure to have you."

"Evening, Tyler. How's your father?"

"Much better, he's in hospice now."

"Good, if you need anything don't hesitate to ask," Leo says in a stern, but gentle tone.

"Of course, sir."

"What are Raoul's specials tonight?"

"The chicken parmesan, the lobster risotto, and the Fiorentina steak at your request."

Leo looks at me. "Chicken?" I nod. "Leanne, Autumn has told me you prefer seafood, so I'd recommend the risotto. And Trix, I've heard you prefer steak."

Both exchange a look. Trix asks, "A *real* Fiorentina steak?"

"Yes, unless you'd prefer wagyu, I can order that from the other restaurant."

"No, that's fine." She stares at me with shock.

"Leanne?"

"Sounds good."

"Very well. Tyler, one of each and a Fiorentina for myself." Tyler nods, walking away with a brisk pace. Leo settles into his seat, stroking my thigh gently. Leanne and Trix exchange another look, adjusting in their seats. Leo still has a stoic expression on his face.

Suddenly, I start to laugh. It bursts out of me, and I slap my hand over my mouth to stop, until Leo catches it and pulls it down. My friends gasp as I laugh more, Leo beginning to smile as he stares at me. Giggle fit not showing signs of slowing down, nerves take hold to just laugh it out. In a few minutes I finally stop, and say between short breaths, "Ya'll should know he also helped create the menu."

Casual dinner banter did start back up at some point. Except, it wasn't long until the "question maelstrom" began. Every question I think they've thought of since I mentioned his full name came bubbling to the surface. A few he had to evade, due to Trix being the only one to not know who he actually was. Otherwise, he handled every question with care. My gaze would flick to Leanne as she asked some questions, reminding myself this was just the regular 'grilling the boyfriend' thing others have talked about. Except, I knew Leanne didn't trust him. From how Trix questioned him, I doubt she did either.

This dinner may not be the help I thought it would be.

Leo hadn't seem phased, taking everything in stride with his usual passive, composed tone. He gave them his half-smile, that's it. I knew why. All three were being careful and it was driving me to want a drink of that damn wine.

We're near the end of dinner when Christopher stops by. "I hope everything is up to standard."

"It was delicious," I say, grinning.

Christopher gives Leo a look, who's jaw ticks. "Now?"

"I was told it was urgent, Mr. Luciano."

Leo nods as Christopher gives us a smile and leaves. A kiss is placed on my cheek, before he says, "I'll be back."

He gives a curt nod, walking away with only *slight* menace. Least he didn't seem to make any of the waiters want to piss themselves.

"Well," Trix breathes out. "Quite the boyfriend."

"Can we even use that term for him? He seems a bit too *mature* for it," Leanne comments.

"Knew he was, but he's another level of…" Trix shrugs, grabbing her wine glass, "…I don't know. Just another level."

"He's confident. Has to be," I argue. "His position kind of

requires that. And *he* wanted to be called boyfriend. His words, not mine."

"Still kind of imposing," Leanne murmurs, flicking her gaze toward the front. I sigh, and she gives me a look.

"So, since he can't *woo* us, instead he's trying to intimidate?" Trix asks.

"Not what he was doing. He's just like that."

"All the time?"

I sigh again, grabbing my water in hopes it'll turn into wine. Trix puts her glass down. "Not saying he's bad, Autumn," Trix says. Leanne raises a brow, and I frown at her. Not now, Leanne. "He's just...not who we were thinking? I mean, you have to admit the man is cold."

"He's not cold."

"He was when taking care of Caltz and Dr. Wilson." My throat tightens. "And honestly, maybe it's just confusing because that kind of person never seemed to be your type."

"Kind of person?"

They exchange a look, and Trix reaches for my hand. "We're not trying to be mean, just...trying to understand."

"Okay, what are you not understanding?" Again, they look at each other. "Quit that, and just say it. I already know Leanne doesn't trust him, and obviously that hasn't changed."

She shrugs, folding her arms. "And I told you why."

"What else?"

Trix sighs, and I wait for something of an answer as my stomach clenches. Suddenly, the chicken I had wants to come back up.

"How serious is he?" Trix asks suddenly. My brows pinch together, looking between them. "Come on, Autumn, he's this cold, strict, business guy. Yes, he's helped you and all, but...everything seems to have gone awry lately. Lot of it seems to come from, well—"

"Him." Leanne finishes, keeping her gaze with mine.

"He loves me," I state.

"At what cost?" Leanne's whisper is faint, and I see fear flick over her eyes. Trix leans back in her seat, noticing the small stand-off between us. "I don't want you getting hurt again."

I pull my hands off the table, yanking at them as I remember Dr. Maxwell saying no one will understand Leo and I other than ourselves. Except, how much longer can I keep defending him? Getting my friends to understand that I need him and vice versa? As I stare into Leanne's worried eyes, I have a sinking feeling she's only ever going to know him as the "mafia boss and brother to the man I sent to jail." As for Trix, he's the hotel mogul, playboy in the newspaper articles.

And I hate that I can't blame them for thinking that. Because of everything shown on the outside, that's *exactly* how it looks. Just as he said about Nan viewing him.

"I'm a possessive, controlling asshole boyfriend." Suddenly his words hurt more, making my heart ache. He's fine being the villain...but I'm not.

"I need a minute." I stand on wobbly legs, needing air.

Trix tries to stop me. "Wait, Autumn—"

"Please, just give me a few minutes. Order whatever dessert you want." I walk away shakily, anxiety tickling up my spine as my hands begin to tremble. I can hear them murmur behind me as I head for the front, keeping eye contact away from everyone.

My hand moves to rub at my chest, but I clench it at my side as I walk past the maître d station and toward the elevator. I can't breathe. I can't—

"Autumn?" I stop, looking over my shoulder at Christopher. His gaze searches my face and then approaches me quietly. "What can I help you with?"

I shake my head, beginning to rub at my arms. "I...I just need... one thing to go right...just one *fucking* thing to go right. Life doesn't work that way, huh?"

"That's the fickle thing about life, isn't it?" He gestures toward the chairs in the small alcove. I don't move. "Autumn, why don't you take a moment over here?"

I press my hand against my head, trying to focus on my breathing. Anxiety pulses through me, and the voices come back like a wave. *Get out.* A part of me wants to run again. Dash down through the halls I still have memorized. There's nowhere to run to.

No ex-handler.

No friends.

No Nan.

All of a sudden, I feel isolated. More isolated than that damn interrogation room. Roger's questions feel like bruised, crumpled flower petals. Easy to toss aside. Trying to defend staying with a mafia boss and brother of someone who wants me dead? Funnily enough not easy to explain. The deep abyss I'd been in only two days ago begins to swallow me whole once again as the screams in my head begin to wail.

Chapter 31

Emerald Eyes

My hands begin to move toward my hair, threatening to yank at the strands again. Roger's voice echoes in my head. The smell of piss. Fending off questions. Newspapers. No. He didn't get inside my head. *No.*

"Autumn." I shake my head. *That's not my name.* Christopher continues to say my name, but I remain silent as I try to reign in the dark thoughts. How'd I think I'd be fine after only a day and *one* session with a new therapist? I should've known, I should've—

"Autumn." The voice this time isn't Christopher's. It's familiar, filled with worry as heavy steps approach.

"I believe she's gone non-verbal, sir. I've tried to get her to move without touching her."

"Thank you, Christopher. Keep others away," Leo speaks, stepping before me. "Check in."

"Red, no yellow, I—" My voice catches in my throat, mind continuing to spiral. A whimper leaves me, knees shaking as the walls begin to look grey.

"Good girl. You still answered."

"There's nowhere to go," I murmur. "If they take you, there's nowhere to go."

"Not going anywhere. Breathe." I do as he says, taking a deep breath, but it hurts. "I'm going to touch you." I nod and his hands take mine, removing them from my head. "Look at me, dear Watson."

Slowly, I do. Affectionate hazel eyes meet mine as his fingers stroke under my chin. He starts to walk back, keeping hold of my hands and I follow. Leo stops just before one of the chairs, maneuvering me to stand before one. "Sit down." Again, I do as he says, listening to the slow cadence of his voice and breathing.

Leo kneels before me, one of his hands stroking over my leg. Abruptly, I remember where we are, and panic starts to rise. "We're in public. Someone is—"

"Christopher will keep them away. Focus on me, dear Watson." Muscles trembling, I nod stiffly. "You're safe. I'm right here."

"I want to be normal," I blurt in a quiet voice.

"I know."

"I don't want these panic attacks."

"I know."

"I hate this."

"I know, sweetheart. Breathe with me." He takes a deep breath in, and I mimic him. He does it again, making me take long inhales of air, and exhaling through my nose. "Good girl."

My hands shake and my gaze begins to flicker toward the walls.

"*Once upon...*" Leo starts off, nodding for me to say with him, "*...a midnight dreary—*"

He speaks the poem with me. And I notice the slow tempo he speaks is similar to how I say it. We continue through the poem, and the parts where he usually forgets are clear this time. Leo speaks *The Raven* word for word with me until the end. By then, the wrench around my chest has eased and my stomach doesn't want to hurl up its contents.

"Thank you," I murmur.

"Always." He leans forward, kissing my forehead with tender care. He pulls back, and asks, "What happened?"

"It's nothing."

"You just had a panic attack, so it is *not* nothing."

I shake my head, starting to pull at his hands to get him to stand. "Please get up."

Leo stands, pulling one of the fancy chairs over to be closer to me. He sits similarly to how Waylon did the other day, keeping his knee against mine. One hand strokes my leg, while the other holds my hand. "Dear Watson, look at me," he insists gently, and I do. "Was it because I left?" I shake my head. "After?" My nod is barely one. Quickly, anger moves over his expression, flickering his gaze past me.

"They don't trust you," I say, huffing with some exasperation. Might as well tell him, he'll find out at some point. "They think you're strict. Cold." I run my hand through my hair, rubbing at the back of my head. "The questions, I think, just reminded me of the interrogation. Neither meant it, they're just protective…like Nan."

I close my eyes, sighing as I lean back in the chair. Leo doesn't make a sound, continuing to stroke his thumb over my wrist. The touch is what I focus on, making my breathing match the pace.

"I'm learning how to accept people caring for me," I murmur. "But if y'all could get on the same page and not fight with each other, that'd be great."

Leo squeezes my hand, and I open my eyes. A somber expression on his face.

"It's never gonna get easier, is it?" I ask. "Whether it's Roger, Dr. Wilson, Nan, Leanne, Trix…jealous coworkers…" I snort a little, placing my hand over his on my leg, "…you're gonna be their bad guy."

"Do you believe I am?"

"No, you're Batman, remember? Only person who orders an Americano past 8pm." A small smirk rises on both our faces. "I should've known they weren't gonna accept you with open arms after one dinner, but I was hoping. Gotta be pretty childish to believe in the whole everyone will get along spiel, huh?"

"No." He raises my hand, kissing the knuckles softly. "It makes you hopeful." I snort at him, and he leans forward to kiss me. I accept the warm gesture, sighing against his lips as he kisses me tenderly.

He fixes my hair when he pulls away and I chuckle under my breath at his attentiveness.

This. Why couldn't they see *this*? The Leo who helps me back to reality. The one who listens and tries to make me feel less alone. The patient, gentle side of Leo.

"You are moonlight and starlight combined," he says suddenly with a definite, assured tone that makes me straighten. "You reflect everything that is good in this world, providing light in the darkest of nights. Some may think you'd have no light, after everything you've endured, but you do. It does not matter the pain, struggle, or faults you feel you have, because you are undeniably human and good. Even in the darkest of moments, you're always trying to show off the beauty that is to be human. To love, to forgive, to be compassionate, to endure. Everything about you is magnificent. Your constant search to find joy in life and curiosity is magnificent from your nervous giggling..." I blush, and he smirks, "...making coffee, fighting for sugary cereal, watching movies, reciting poems, or dancing like no one is watching. I love you passionately for all these facets of you, but because you deserve to be loved in a manner that mirrors how you approach life. Even in the moments when you think you don't."

Tears arrive in my eyes, a couple falling. Leo quickly wipes them away, kissing where they'd fallen.

"It is your hopefulness that makes the nights seem less dire. You are not broken." My breath hitches. "It may never be easier, but I will be right here." He kisses my hands again.

"I love you," I whisper.

Leo smiles a moment. His expression quickly falls, becoming serious when he looks past me. I follow his gaze, finding Trix and Leanne standing completely still. Trix clutches Leanne's arm, tears brimming her eyes. Leanne's face is neutral, but I visibly see her swallow.

"Autumn's and my relationship is none of your business," Leo speaks in that composed tone again, but it's a touch softer. A quiet warning. "No matter how much either you two, Nancy, or others want to pry, to me your opinions do not matter. I'll be quite frank. I do not give a fuck what your thoughts are about me. Hate me. Fine."

Leo pauses, looking directly at Leanne who begins to frown at him. "I'm used to being hated," he continues. "Autumn is not accustomed hearing such things. The only advice I'll implore for you to follow is to respect *her* decisions in staying in a relationship with me."

"We just want her to be safe," Leanne says.

"So do I." Leo stands, adjusting his shirt, but keeps a hand around mine. "I have quite a handful of power, and I will use it at any turn to protect her. Out of respect for Autumn and her love for you both, I will give you this warning once."

My entire body wants to stiffen, but Leo gets me to stand and places a hand at the small of my back. He strokes down my spine, and finally I look up at him. No anger, hate, or malice is in his eyes. Just resolve.

"Question me all you want. Give me the third degree. Don't trust me. But *do not* question her decisions that she has clearly made herself and respect them. Just as she would with either of you when it comes to your relationships, jobs, or personal hobbies."

They look at each other, Trix lets go of Leanne's arm and folds her arms over her chest. Leanne looks to me, the frown slowly disappearing.

"We can agree that all three of us have love for Autumn," Leo states. "She is *everything* to me, and you mean a great deal to her. I'm willing to get along as much as we can. Are we at an understanding?"

Trix clears her throat, letting out a long sigh. She smiles faintly, and nods. "You're right. It's not just your decision, but yours, too Autumn. We should respect it even if we don't understand, and you have been helpful."

Leo moves his hand up my spine, back down again, keeping my breathing level.

"We should act like adults," Trix continues, then looks me in the eye. "Sorry, hun. Didn't mean to push you. Past week just had me worried, well, past month or so."

I nod faintly.

Leanne walks up to us, stopping before Leo with her head held high. His serious expression doesn't budge, watching her with furrowed brows. Leanne doesn't flinch away, not like how Nan did, she holds her hand out to him. He takes it, shaking it briefly. He goes to pull away, but she keeps a hold on his and she warns, "My only warning…don't hurt her. I'll find a way to get you."

My breath hitches, staring up at Leo who keeps his gaze on Leanne. Slowly, a faint grin pulls at his lips, and he shakes her hand once more. "Never would, but duly noted."

"Good." She drops his hand and puts her hands on her hips. "Christopher said you loved the tiramisu, thought to order it for dessert. Shall we? Try this again?"

I smile at her. "Yeah."

She offers her arm for me.

"I'll walk her in," Leo states. Leanne narrows her eyes at him, and Trix starts to chuckle.

"Met your match, Leanne," Trix says, leading the group back to the restaurant.

"Apparently." She raises a brow, following Trix as we do. Leo offers me his arm, and I take it with a laugh under my breath. He smiles, holding me close as we follow my protective and very brave friends into the restaurant.

Chapter 32

A Chair is Still a Chair

I grab the coffee pot, glancing at Leo as he furrows his brows heavily. Data sheets are strewn across the counter, brought in this morning by Owen. It's not even nine yet. Leo is in his usual business attire, flipping pages, signing some, and putting them into folders. We've had breakfast, which I made for once. Was it oatmeal, fruit, and toast? Yes. It wasn't cereal, I'm calling it a win.

It's been almost a week since the dinner. It was quiet during dessert, but some neutral conversations occurred. Leanne apologized the day after, jostled by how he came in and was more upset she'd triggered a panic attack. She said nothing of trusting him, and I won't push. I'll have to follow Leo's lead and not care. If I can.

Trix and I have talked on the phone every other day. She's been shaken ever since the incident with Dr. Wilson, and I think she's debating leaving the women's center. Knowing they had a therapist that willingly gave up my medical records without my consent, she's understandably upset. She lost her trust in them. For now, she's staying, still working on her projects for different colleges. I finally chewed out Nan. Okay, not really, but after another session with Dr. Maxwell, it was easier to explain to her why I was upset. Mostly about the lies. She apologized profusely, but I still have to keep my fingers crossed that Leo doesn't threaten her again. Although given her track record of pushing his boundaries, I'm not gonna hold my breath.

The rustling of papers brings me out of my thoughts, and I bring over the coffee pot to refill his mug. Leo looks up from his seat. A warm smile growing on his face. "Come here."

I put the pot back and straddle his lap with his arms around me. He murmurs against my ear, "Good girl."

A giggle escapes me, shivers running down my spine. His warm smile turns molten. Leo kisses me, crushing his lips against mine. I hum at the sweet contact as he holds me close, hand traveling up my leg and then squeezing my hip. A tiny gasp releases when he nips at my bottom lip.

"Leo," I gasp again. "We both know you've got a long day."

"All the more reason to start it off—"

I clutch his face, making him stop as his gaze heats with want. "And betting you ten bucks that in like five minutes, Jameson is gonna start knocking. Then you'll just be grumpy rest of the day."

"They can wait."

"You're wily this morning."

"You cooking is a turn on." He grabs the back of my neck, massaging his fingers into my nape.

"Doubt toast and oatmeal compare to what you do. I'll take the compliment though."

"It's the thought that counts, dear Watson," he murmurs, kissing my cheek. He places another down my jaw and neck. Warmth travels through my body as I hum, skin beginning to heat at his touch. His hand on my hip tightens and my muscles down below pulsate, hips starting to grind against his growing erection. My breath hitches as his lips devour mine. I grip at his shoulders as he moves his hand down my spine, kissing me deeply.

"Leo," I moan against his lips.

"Check in."

"Fuck...green."

"Do you want me to stop?" His hand starts to travel over my

thigh. I shake my head, clenching my legs around him. Heat strikes me as he runs his fingers over the crotch of my leggings. My hands now gripping into his hair, Leo traces his fingers along the seam, alighting my senses as I push against him, wanting more.

"Son of a nutcracker," I rasp, kissing him fiercely as I become enflamed by his touch. Leo starts to move his hand under my clothes when the front door opens.

He rips his hand away, breaking our kiss and yanking me against him to hide his erection and my own flushed reactions. I immediately start giggling as I hear Jameson and Julio swear from the hall. Leo scowls as I try to stop the quiet laugh, burying my face into his shoulder.

"Called it," I giggle.

"When the fuck did I lose my privacy?" Leo growls. "Or is knocking too much to fucking ask?"

"We needed to leave by nine," Jameson answers as the door closes. "Boston and Chicago are already on the conference call with Owen. These negotiations need to end *today*. Among other things."

Leo tightens his arms, and my laughter dies down. I mumble against his skin, "You owe me ten bucks."

Leo looks at me with the grumpiest expression and a smile breaks out over mine. He sighs, kissing me quick before helping me off his lap. I bite my bottom lip, trying not to chuckle as he adjusts his pants and tosses the sheets he was looking at into another folder. It's handed off to Julio, who takes it as I pass him toward the coffee pot to refill my mug.

"Sorry, boss," Julio says, beginning to leave. He winks at me, "Sorry, *hermana*." I wave it off and he leaves.

"Leo—"

"Five damn minutes, Jameson," Leo practically snarls. "I know what these negotiations are worth. They're not going to fall apart in the next ten minutes."

"Coming from the one adjusting his pants."

"Maybe I need to get *you* laid instead."

Jameson growls, "Oh, fuck off. That's not—"

"You've been a pain in my—"

"Okay, quit it!" I quickly stand between them, hands up to keep them from going at each other's throats. Both scowl at the other, furrowed brows at the ready. "Go to your corners, grab a towel, cool off." They turn their attention to me. "I've seen *Rocky* enough times. Corners."

My heart rate picks up, the tenseness in their voices causing my skin to prick. I ignore it. All week it's been like this, hearing about small arguments and fights within the Crew. Leo has snapped at them multiple times, including Jameson and Drew. Not sure what's entirely wrong, but whatever it is, it's getting under all their skin.

Jameson straightens, adjusting his navy suit. "This doesn't concern you."

"Does if you're arguing before coffee kicks in," I argue.

"You don't—"

"Careful," Leo warns.

"Fucks sake, she's a grown woman!" Jameson points at me. "Not like she can't—"

Leo takes a menacing step toward him, expression hardening in a manner that makes Jameson step back. I step more in Leo's way. Something *definitely* isn't right.

I look at Leo, who sneers with a sinister gaze. "Hey, mister." He snaps his head to me, and instantly his demeanor eases like he's realizing I'm there. The menacing look disappears as I turn to Jameson. "I don't know what's going on, don't wanna know. Business is business, I guess, but if you're gonna start acting like frat guys, I'm putting you in timeout to discuss your feelings."

Jameson crosses his arms over his chest, scoffing. "You're not the boss—"

"No, I'm not. *I'm* the tired girlfriend who doesn't want to start the day with a panic attack." Jameson moves a worried look to Leo behind me. Yeah, that'll shut him up. If I have one, Leo will lock everyone out of the penthouse to stay with me. "I'm banning pissing matches in here, *including* for Leo. So, go to the elevators, smell the flowers, take a breath and I'll send him out shortly. Cool?"

The man stares at me, brown eyes boring into mine. I keep my ground. He looks like he's about to argue, but I feel Leo shift behind me. Instead, he sighs and answers, "Fine."

He starts to walk out, but I stop him and quickly run over to the kitchen cabinets. I pull out a thermos, pouring coffee and sugar in, and then hand it over to him. He looks incredulously at it. "It's not a Cubano but take the damn caffeine."

Jameson purses his lips, taking the thermos and leaves the penthouse in silence. Leo runs his hand over his face, rubbing at his temple harshly. I walk over, grabbing his waist to get him to look at me. "Check in."

"Yellow," he exhales harshly.

"Do you want to talk about it?"

"Apparently, I don't have time." He glares at the front door.

"Spark notes?"

Hazel eyes search mine, taking a moment. "These negotiations… deals just consist of transferring some power to people, moving a shit ton of money. Multiple people's livelihoods depend on this outcome. I've pushed it off due to *other* situations of late but waiting this long may have made things worse. Could take all day to convince three boards to agree to my terms."

I caress his cheek, stroking my thumb over his skin. "You're a smart man, Leo. You'll figure it out. If it takes all day, then it does. I know you'll get done what needs to be done, and all those people will be taken care of. You're good like that."

The hardness along his face vanishes, replaced by the tenderness he always seems to have for me. I take his coffee and pour it into his own thermos, then set it down and help straighten his suit. He smiles gently. "You're human, Leo. It's fine to be frustrated or feel like there's too much pressure, no matter how good you are. Just try not to take it out on your Crew, they're just trying to help, I think. You're all a little cranky."

"We have our rough patches."

"Don't I know it," I smirk. Leo kisses me, more of the tension in his body seeming to go loose. "Since I'm gonna be at the bookstore today, I'll probably stay there tonight."

"Inform Isaac—"

"Already have, and Rudy and Drew will probably take shifts tonight. But if you need me..."

Leo shakes his head, placing another kiss on my cheek and grabs his thermos. He begins to leave the penthouse, the mask of 'strict businessman' starting to surround him. He looks back at me. "Thank you, my dear Watson."

"Anytime, mister Americano." He smirks, disappearing through the door. And for some reason, there's an uneasy prick against my neck.

"It's been a couple years since it's been, well, this bad," Drew comments, handing me some books.

"Just from the pressure? Or things getting fucked up? I'd imagine getting a new hotel up would've been worse," I say.

"Nah. Him and Jameson are too good at that. Cause of the reputation at this point, that shits easy."

I've been working in the bookstore all day, staying busy reorganizing books for Nan's new shelves. A little 'present' from Leo for her to keep her nose out of his business. There's been people streaming in and out, typical for this time of year before the holidays. And there's been reports of a "hot hotel mogul" being seen here. Not just diehard small bookstore readers.

Drew helps me carry some books toward the back, while Isaac remains stationed near the register with Nan. "Shit just bubbles up, ya know? We're all still covering our asses cause of Caltz and the shitstorm he started. Heads are on a swivel, hyperawareness spikes."

"Yeah." I move down the aisle, putting books away as he follows.

He's quiet, and then asks, "How was your session the other day?"

"Only two hours this time," I smirk, crouching to move some books over. "It was good. And I feel better. Bit more stable." I pause, putting the books away and look up at him. "How often do you all see a therapist? Although you don't really have to tell me that."

He scratches his facial hair, and shrugs. "Nah, it's okay. We try to stay consistent, whatever our schedules are."

"Does anyone else see Dr. Maxwell?" I stand up quickly and shake my head. "Wait, that's rude to pry, sorry."

"You're fine." He pokes my shoulder, handing over another book. "We see guys flown in from Cali. Safer that way. Only Chesty and Iron Buffalo talk to Maxwell occasionally. Heard good things about him. All our therapists have been…vetted, multiple times."

"Kind of have to."

"Yeah, can't have whatever our inner thoughts are get out into the open cause they decide to…" his voice trails off, and then he clears his throat.

"Throw you under the bus?" I finish.

"Shouldn't have brought it up."

I sigh, walking past. "What happened to me probably are all your worries and fears come true. If Leo said he never wanted to see or talk to someone again wouldn't blame him. Can't imagine what his inner thoughts could…"

I stop, pinching my brows as I *can* imagine. If he talked to a therapist about his anger, who he hated, or feared…it could all be used against him. Suddenly, all I see is that empty penthouse I first entered, calling him out on being alone. *Safer that way.*

Drew puts a hand on my shoulder, and I jolt. He rubs my shoulder a little and gives me a half-grin with those warm brown eyes. "Appreciate you caring about him. He knows how to take care of himself. And he seems to be in better control of shit since you've been around."

"Sure, about that? From how Jameson sounds, it seems like I've made it worse."

"Nah, Leo's just not burying himself in work anymore and I don't think Sombra knows how to handle it. Change ain't easy, even for us unruly bikers."

I snort at him, pushing him teasingly. He grins bigger as I put more books in his hands. "Speaking of unruly bikers, I need new reading material and Chesty has a new engine coming in for his chopper project."

Drew helps me finish the reshelving, and then goes through the mechanic and motorcycle books that Nan has. He hands over ones he thinks are best, including a few about MC history. I buy a few, against Nan's wishes, but I'll always pay for my own books. At closing, Isaac leaves, switching with Rudy. I have a short slightly tense dinner with Nan, then head up to my apartment and get ready for bed, while Rudy insists on staying on my couch. How it's going to hold the giant man, I have no idea.

It's late as I stay up reading about Harley engines. The night wears on and midnight passes by the time I shut off the light. Try as I might, I can't sleep. No nightmare or anxiety rising, just…nothing. I toss and turn in my old bed, feeling out of place as every few minutes I reach across for Leo.

It's just me.

I lay on my back and stare at the ceiling. A tightening band comes around my chest, pushing me down. I sit up, rubbing my head and glance at the clock. Almost 2am. "Shit."

Could try watching a movie. Not sure if that'll help.

I get out of bed and walk out to the living room. Rudy sits on the couch, watching one of my 80s films. He must hear me, cause he gets up and pauses the movie. "What is it, *bärchen*?"

"Uh, this may sound silly, but ever stay at a friend's house or relative's and something feels off? Like you can't sleep or sit still?"

He rubs the back of his neck, face scrunching in thought. "When I left home, I stayed with friends before coming to the U.S. Felt something was missing. Now it doesn't matter where I sleep." Rudy purses his lips. "Second friend's apartment always smelled like fruity flowers." He shudders a little.

"Well, this place smells like fruity flowers."

He chuckles. "Can't sleep?" I shake my head. "Wanna watch a movie?"

"No, I think I'd like to go back to the hotel. Leo may not be up, but I could sneak in."

"I'll wake up Drew, and let security know we're moving." He turns off the television, grabbing his jacket and begins to leave. "Meet you downstairs, unless you want me to wait."

"Nah, I'll be down soon. Meet you at the car, Ringer." He winks, walking out as I head back into my bedroom. I start to pack a bag, when I realize, I don't need to. Instead, I change into some sweats and pull on a sweater. I write a quick note for Nan, saying I'll be at the hotel then put away the movie Rudy was watching. I pause, looking over the neatly stacked movies and pull-out *Taxi Driver*. I glance inside the case before putting it and a few others in my small bag as options to watch this week. I head out, sticking the note on the door for Nan to see.

I tiptoe down the steps and through the bookstore, finding Drew out front on his phone. I lock up the store, climbing into the car with Drew beside me and Rudy driving. As the car door shuts, Drew hangs up.

"Sorry for waking you," I say.

"Don't worry about it. Part of the job." Rudy drives off, heading toward the hotel. It's late, but there's still some traffic. It's sparse enough that we get to the hotel in record time, pulling into the private garage. I get out with Rudy walking me to the door and then the elevator, where he waves me in as they open.

"He came back an hour ago." I stare up at my gentle giant, and he shrugs. "Long day."

"Tell me about it."

He smirks. "Night, *bärchen*."

"Night, Rudy." I step into the elevator but stop the doors from closing. "Hey, how do you say good night in German?"

"Gute nacht."

"Gute nacht," I repeat. He smiles, causing those little wrinkles at the edges of his grey eyes. The doors close and I fall onto the seat, leaning my head back. The tightening around my chest leaves, beginning to finally relax. Guess the hotel is becoming a safe space of some kind.

Buttons blink as I pass each floor, finally stopping at mine. I step quietly, coming to the front door and carefully unlock and open it. The door shuts silently as I ease it back, tiptoeing as I go, but stop in the hall just before the kitchen. There's light coming from the main living space. The fireplace crackles, casting shadows over the walls and providing an eerie glow. It's quiet aside from wood snapping as the fire consumes it.

Leo sits on the couch watching the flames. A crystal of scotch is on the coffee table and there's a half-filled glass in his hand. He's still wearing what he had on this morning, jacket thrown over the couch's back. His elbows are planted on his knees, unmoving. He shows no signs of noticing I've entered. Silent and alone.

Suddenly, I wonder what he did all those nights when we were apart. I'd go home to watch movies, read books, or Nan would make me come down to dinner. I never thought what he did. Always figured he'd go straight to bed, take a long shower or something. He just sits there watching the fire with a blank expression that appears…broken.

My throat tightens, tears threatening to come at how lonely he appears. Alone.

The small bag I have, I place on the counter with some noise. Leo's head snaps to me, sitting up alert as he puts his drink down.

"Just me," I say, moving out of the shadows. Leo stares at me with confusion, slowly leaning back against the couch like I'm a dream. Like I shouldn't be here. "You're up late."

He takes a moment, finally responding, "So are you, did you have a nightmare? Or—"

I shake my head, sitting down next to him. "Couldn't sleep, guess I'm not the only one."

Leo sweeps back a few strands of my hair. His hands are trembling. Without a word, I crawl onto his lap. His arms wrap around me as I hug him to me. He inhales deeply, kissing my neck as he strokes my hair. I hold Leo close, placing my head against his chest to listen to the beat of his heart. Faint.

"My apartment doesn't feel like home anymore," I whisper.

"Do you not feel safe?"

I shake my head, moving my head to look directly into his gaze. Exhaustion covers them. I caress his face, kissing him lovingly and slowly. "It's not home anymore. You are."

His breath hitches, arms tightening. "Are you staying?"

I nod faintly and Leo buries his face into the crook of my neck. His hands still tremble, but now his arms do, too. "I'm right here, Leo. You're not alone…I'm right here."

He shudders, saying nothing else as the fireplace crackles. The quiet builds around us, ticking on as I feel his silent, hot tears soaking into my sweater.

Chapter 33

Interruptions

My breath catches.

I blink quickly, turning in bed and calming when I see Leo asleep on his stomach. With a sigh, I sit up, rub my head, and check the time. I pause, surprised it's almost 8:30 in the morning. No alarm, no phone ringing, or knocking has occurred.

Maybe because of how late he got back, it means a later start.

I leave the bed, and strip off my sweater as I head to the kitchen. I yawn as I start coffee for the morning. Once the coffee pot begins brewing, I notice the crystal of scotch is still on the coffee table, along with Leo's unfinished drink. He carried me to bed not long after I arrived, both of us falling asleep quickly. As coffee bubbles behind me, I walk over to put away the liquor, and then pour his drink down the sink.

For a moment, I stare down at where the amber liquid disappeared, remembering how lonesome he was. The stillness that chilled my bones. Not wanting to think about the melancholy I'd felt seeing him just staring into the fire, I walk over to the patio windows and sit on the sofa's arm. I close my eyes, embracing the morning light. Its warmth helps me inhale deep as I peer out over the cityscape.

I release a sigh as I hold my arms around myself.

I told Leo I'd move in. Though, I'm not sure if that means entirely *here* or to his actual penthouse. Okay fine, this place is an apartment, but it's still huge.

There's rustling from the bedroom, and I'm about to call out that I'm here, but Leo appears with his lounge pants hanging low. They're barely holding onto his hips as he seems to instinctively know where I am. His hair is mussed and there's stubble along his jaw. Colorful tattoos across his torso become vibrant as he enters the sun's glow. He doesn't say a word as he approaches, coming before me as he reaches to cup my face and kiss me tenderly. My heart flutters, the softness of his approach and kiss makes my body become very aware and awake. I reach out, placing my hands against his chest to feel the heat of his skin.

"Good morning, my dear Watson," he murmurs against my lips.

"Morning," I say breathlessly. "Sleep well?"

"With you next to me? Always." He kisses me again, his tongue skimming over my lips as I close my eyes and succumb to him easily. "And then I woke up, remembering you telling me you're moving in. That I'm your home."

I pull back enough to catch his gaze. Hazel eyes flecked with gold burn with yearning. The radiance of the morning creates a halo around his head, but shrouds most of his face in shadow. There's a gentleness about him that makes my heart ache.

"Yeah, I did."

His eyes seem to shine more, a faint smile on his face.

My hands trail up his chest, and then moving down toward his hips where his pants hang low. His own hands slide to my shoulders. My eyes travel down, following the inked creations on his body. I stroke a finger above the seam, and he shudders at the touch, loosening a sharp exhale.

We've not had sex since before I was arrested. It's been almost two weeks. We just haven't had time or been abruptly interrupted. Even now, I'm half expecting someone to come knocking. Yet, I ask in a rough voice, "Check in."

Leo places his hand under my chin, tilting my head back. He

moves the other to rest his palm against my bared neck. A calmness settles over me.

"Emerald," he answers.

"Why emerald?"

"You are the first woman I've ever hoped to live with."

His answer makes my heart ache, but I focus on him as he leans down and kisses me again. I run my hands over his hips, smiling against his lips. My fingers trail under his pants, beginning to pull them down.

"You're getting bold, dear Watson."

I pause, unsure if he means it in a good way or not. Leo kisses the side of my mouth, bringing a hand down to grasp one of mine to help tug his pants off.

"Good girl, show me what you want," he murmurs, kissing my neck next.

A shiver runs down my spine.

Swallowing hard, I start sliding back over the edge of the sofa and tug him towards me. My back lands against the cushions as Leo places his hands on either side of my head, leaning over me. My legs hook around his bent waist, trying to pull him closer. Leo licks up my neck, kissing my jaw and then places another searing kiss against my lips. In the background, I can hear the coffee finish brewing, bubbling in the distance.

I rasp, "I want you—"

A heavy knocking comes from the front door.

We freeze, and it feels like my heart just sank through the cushions.

Leo stops, snapping his head up and practically snarls, "You've got to be *fucking* with me."

"Well, not yet," I attempt to joke. Leo looks down at me, and I try to smile, wanting to hide my disappointment. I add quietly, "It's okay."

Leo's eyes search my face, and I swear he may actually murder whoever is at the door. The knocks come again, and he stands up fully as I sit up on the couch. I begin to stand but pause when I notice Leo stalking toward the door, very much naked and with an erection.

"Uh, Leo?"

He stops at the edge of the kitchen, folding his arms over his chest. The door unlocks, opening and in walks Jameson and Drew. Thank goodness I wasn't naked yet. Although, the two get enough of an eyeful from Leo. I bite my lip, trying not to laugh as they both exclaim profanities.

Drew grumbles under his breath, immediately walking out and says, "You're on your own, Sombra."

Jameson starts arguing in Spanish, and Leo argues back in the same language. I blink rapidly as they exchange words gruffly. Leo takes a sudden step towards him, and Jameson throws his hands up, taking the hint.

"You've got an hour," Jameson mumbles, and then immediately leaves, slamming the door behind him, but not before I hear him exclaim, "Culo!"

I immediately burst out laughing, holding onto my sides. The absurdity keeps me laughing even as I look up and watch Leo turn towards me, raising a brow.

"You heard him, we've got an hour," he says.

Immediately, I clam up and straighten. My heart races from laughing, but now it thumps for another reason as his wrathful expression changes into a smoldering one. My eyes flick to his hard-on.

"Same position?" I point at the couch. The way he's looking at me, I may melt right here on the spot instead.

Leo smirks, and it helps the sudden tension at the base of my spine vanish as I smile back. He gently orders, "Take your clothes off and sit at the counter."

My brows go up as he starts moving but disappears into the bedroom. I scrunch my face together, confused, wondering why we don't just go back to the sofa. Maybe he wants naked coffee first?

"Autumn."

Oh, shit, right!

I squeak and start to undress. I pull my shirt off, and then yank at my pants, but trip over my own feet and stumble forward. My body slams into Leo, and he easily catches me, wrapping his arm around my waist. Instantly, my hands go to his chest, and I stare up at him. The burning within his gaze is still there, whilst there's also amusement.

"Hi," I whisper.

"Hi," he responds, kissing my forehead.

Leo swiftly picks me up, wrapping my legs around his waist as he walks us to the long counter and sits me on one of the barstools. He sets a container on the counter, and then says against my neck, "I wanted you to tell me what to do, but I'm going to make this hour count."

"Oh?"

"Help remind you sex can be fun."

"Oh?" I giggle.

"And then I'm going to make you breakfast naked."

"Oh." My voice goes up a notch.

"Turn around and face the counter." Leo kisses my cheek, stepping away.

I do as he says, following where he goes. I flick my gaze to the counter, noticing it was lube he set down. He grabs a small bowl, and then opens the freezer. Clinking sounds follow as I put my elbows on the marble and watch him as he comes back and places the bowl next to the bottle. My brows pinch together. Did he just fill a bowl with ice cubes?

I jolt when Leo grabs my hips lightly, pulling them back a little to the point I feel like I may fall off as I straddle the stool.

"Arch your back, sweetheart," he says, wrapping an arm around my waist. His other hand caresses my side, causing shivers down my spine.

His chest becomes flush with my back, the heat of his skin engulfing me. I arch my back, feeling his erect cock brushing against my ass. I inhale sharply as Leo kisses my neck, stroking his hand over my thigh and toward the apex of my thighs. I swallow hard as he traces his fingers over my skin, unable to move as he keeps me in place against his chest.

"Check in," he murmurs.

"Green, but unsure what you're doing?"

"You trust me?"

I turn my head a little, finding his gaze. "Yes."

Those smoldering eyes have me in a chokehold, practically darkening.

"Lean forward, place your chest on the surface. If it triggers anything..."

"Say red or yellow," I finish quietly.

"Good girl." He kisses me briefly before his arm loosens around me.

I lean forward, pressing the top of my chest against the counter and my breath hitches at the chilled surface. It's cold against my skin, causing it to prickle . My nipples even harden at the coolness, but no signs of panic.

Thank fuck, already had enough interruptions.

Leo strokes his hand down my spine, causing another shiver over my body as he teases me below. He then reaches over, opening the lube. Swiftly, he tosses the bottle back onto the counter, sliding some of the slippery stuff on his cock. His non-slicked hand runs up my back, touching me softly. I'm not sure how this position will work until he adjusts my hips a little and I feel his cock at my entrance. I blink, reaching up and placing my hands on the counter as he enters me slowly. He barely thrusts, causing my body to vibrate as pleasure travels up from my core. I moan, yearning for him to fill me, and completely bury himself inside as he rocks his hips forward. My nipples harden more as I press into the cold marble, sliding my hands over the surface as Leo pushes forward. Laying my cheek on the counter, I breathe heavy as he continues the slow, sensuous pace. A hand remains gripped around my hip, while the other caresses my back. Finally, he thrusts all the way and I moan against the marble.

"Check in." His heated skin comes over my back, his torso

covering mine from above as he slides his hand around to clutch my neck gently.

"Green," I rasp.

We remain locked in this position with him flexing his hand against my neck as I arch my back to drive his cock deeper. It rubs against my clit, and my legs start to tremble already. Leo kisses the nape of my neck, making a guttural moan that flutters hot breath over my skin.

"Leo," I gasp.

"We're gonna go slow, sweetheart; an easy morning fuck."

I let out a breathy laugh, but my breath hitches as he pulls back and thrusts into me easily. He gently holds me in this position as he languidly fucks me from behind. There's a safety that washes over me, having his hand against my neck, whilst his other grips my thigh. Pleasure courses through my veins as I quiver beneath the tattooed mafia don who fucks me slowly.

Suddenly, he lets go, standing fully as he reaches over to the bowl. I suck in a breath as I glance at the ice cube in his hand. He pops it into his mouth briefly. Still confused, one of my hands starts to tremble, unsure what he's about to do until he reaches forward and traces the ice along my forearm. I gasp at the cold. As he continues to drag the ice up my arm and to my shoulder, he pushes back into me, making me moan.

Leo begins to glide the ice slowly along my spine. I partially yelp, trying to sit up as his cock thrusts into me. A shiver rushes over my skin as he does it again and I suddenly start to giggle. The cold sensations mix with the heat of Leo's touch and slow thrusts. I giggle again, almost ticklish, as he travels it over my shoulder and down my clavicle. My breathless laughter is combined with moans as Leo rocks his hips. He drops the ice on the counter, leaning over me and kisses my neck.

"Check in," he murmurs. I can hear the amusement in his voice.

"Green," I continue giggling as my body slides over the cold surface. The chilly sensation creates more giggles to erupt out of me, even as Leo's cock enters me deeply.

"Good girl," he whispers. "See? Sex doesn't have to be *fucking* serious."

I laugh again, but am cut short as Leo plunges forward again. Tingling runs up my spine, legs shaking as the oncoming orgasm starts to grow, the seat rubbing against my sensitive areas as I straddle the barstool. Leo grabs another ice cube, but kisses the nape of my neck with it in his mouth. He drags the ice with his mouth across my skin, and I can't help the loud gasps at the wet mixture of temperatures from his mouth. One of his hands squeezes my hips and my body becomes alight. He drops the ice cube, allowing it to slide down my back and clatter to the floor. He grabs another, sliding the ice again over my skin. Every sensation pulses through my body.

The dripping, cold ice. The heat of his skin on mine. The gentle, yet rough rocking of his hips. The grip of his hands. His mouth. The slippery marble against my chest. And the coiling of pleasure and ecstasy, clutching at his hard cock inside me. I come hard abruptly, the orgasm rolling over me like a wave as I try to grip the marble counter, but slip as I lose control. I swear I see fucking stars as I moan against the hard surface. I'm catching my breath when Leo drops the ice, suddenly pulls out, turns me around, and lifts me into his arms. My brain feels fuzzy from the orgasm and flurry of sensations, trying to determine if he's already come or not as he carries me to the bedroom. He lays us down on the bed, his body covering mine.

"Leo?" I barely get his name out before he drives his cock back into me. I gasp, clutching at his shoulders as he thrusts his hips. His arm goes under my leg, folding it up and creating a different angle that makes my entire body shudder.

"I want to see your face when I come," he groans, moving faster. "And when you come again."

"Again?" I gulp.

I'm not sure if he sees the uncertainty on my face, because he comes in close and presses his lips against mine. He murmurs gently, a complete contrast to the pounding of his hips, and says, "Come for me again, sweetheart."

I kiss him hard, grabbing at him as his cock plunges inside me.

Shivers run down my back, new sensations overwhelming me. The softness of the bed and the heat of his body against mine. Sweat covers his skin, my fingers slipping over him. Leo kisses me fervently, groaning into my mouth. He pulls away, putting his forehead against mine as he grunts loudly. His movement slows, pushing forward into me as far as he can go, while his body shudders. Leo lets go of my leg finally as he kisses my chest. We both lay there, breathing hard and it's a few moments later I realize I didn't come with him.

Sudden disappointment washes over me that I didn't orgasm again. That first one almost knocked me out, but he wanted another, and I didn't, and well…usually I have.

"Check in," he murmurs against my skin.

"Um, green."

He pulls back, looking down at me with pinched brows. "What is it? Was the ice too much?"

"No uh, I just…didn't come again," I whisper. I half-expect to see disappointment on his face and start rambling before it appears. "It's okay, I came in the kitchen, and honestly that was pretty fucking good. The ice was fun, and different, so you don't need to feel bad, and I'm sure—"

Leo suddenly kisses me, stopping my panicked rambling. I hadn't realized I was gripping his shoulders so hard and loosen my hold. Hazel eyes meet mine and not at all filled with displeasure, but affection.

"Are you satisfied?" He asks.

"Uh, yeah." He raises a brow, silently asking if I'm telling the truth. "Yes, Leo."

"That's what matters," he says softly. "I'll always try my best to give you the most pleasure, dear Watson. Sometimes multiple orgasms aren't going to happen. And it's okay if you don't have that every time."

I blink quickly up at him. Oh.

"You didn't disappointment me, dear Watson," he says, before kissing my jaw. Those words help me melt underneath him. I'm not sure why I needed to hear that, even though I was worried about *him* when it was *me* who didn't orgasm again. Except, that first one could hold me over the next week honestly. Fingers crossed I dream about ice cubes tonight.

He then murmurs against my ear, "Good girl."

I tighten my arms around him, hugging him gratefully. "Thank you."

Leo rolls over slightly so he doesn't crush me as he lays down completely.

"You're right, that was pretty fun," I say. "Except the interrupting part."

"I'm changing the locks and adding a fucking barricade."

I immediately start laughing, knowing he's completely serious.

L eo kept his promise. He's cooking naked. Apart from the apron he wears to not get bacon grease accidentally flung on him.

My head is propped in my hands as I lean on the now dry counter. Leo cleaned up our mess quickly before I had a chance to help. We're coming up on his 'deadline' before the others return. I'm just in my robe, deciding to get dressed after he leaves. Right now, I'm far too busy watching his tattooed ass cook breakfast. I'm slowly learning to not hide from staring at him.

Leo comes over to replenish my coffee, smirking at me as I bite my lower lip. He leans in close over the island and kisses my nose, making me wrinkle it.

"What are your plans today?" He asks, going back to the stove.

I shrug. "Could start packing."

His smile grows, still concentrating on the food, but I grin at his expression.

"I should tell Nan I'm moving out so she can rent out that—"

I'm interrupted by ringing. I glance over my shoulder at my phone on the coffee table. I head over to grab it as Leo says gruffly, "Our hour isn't up yet."

I glance at the caller ID, and sigh. "Speak of the woman."

"Hour counts for her, too."

I give Leo an exasperated look, and he gives me a very serious one. "You know she's not your enemy, right?"

The look I receive tells me I might be wrong. Then again, everyone this morning is practically his enemy. Rolling my eyes, I sigh, "She doesn't know, and I did leave in the middle of the night."

Leo grumbles as I answer the phone on the last ring.

"Are you alright?" She asks instantly.

"Good morning to you, too, Nan." I sit at the counter.

"Yes, good morning, now are you alright?"

"I'm fine, just couldn't sleep."

"You could've woken me up," she retorts, and I lean my head back with a sigh.

"Well, I was just restless and decided to come to the hotel."

She makes a snort of disinterest. Oh, goodie, love that sound in the morning.

"Spending quite a bit of time there," she says. "I understand that you and Leo are pretty serious, but you've barely been home."

Leo comes over, setting down a plate. "Won't be home for long," he says dryly.

I cover the phone with my hand and shush him. Nan already seems to be in a tissy mood and I don't need fuel added to the fire yet.

"Was that Leo? Isn't he usually *working* by now and what does he mean for long?"

The phone isn't on speaker is it or am I just that unlucky? I glance at the phone. Nope, apparently the two have been gifted sonic hearing.

"She's moving in with me," Leo says loudly, stepping away to the oven as I flick him off.

"Moving in? When was this decided? You just got back," Nan gasps on the other side. I inwardly groan. Just when I think they're done fighting, they pull me back in. I feel your pain Corleone, on multiple levels.

I put the phone on speaker, giving in as I lightly tap my forehead against the counter as they somewhat argue.

"Last night," Leo answers.

"So, it's not official."

"It is. She's moving in."

"To the hotel? That's hardly a home, Leonardo, even *you* have to admit that. She needs—"

"I know exactly what she needs, Nancy," Leo interrupts, turning off the stove. "We decided she's moving in."

"We or do you mean *you*?" Leo glares at the phone.

"Okay, enough of that," I say, grabbing the device from the line of fire. "Nan, yes I'm moving in with him. We'll figure out details later."

"Well, dear, I just thought you and I would discuss something like this before you agreed."

"Yeah, well, no one discussed with me about buying the building I lived in. Or how about the apartment I was living in was owned by the mob, but at least this time I *know* which mobster it is."

Nan becomes quiet and Leo stares at me, swallowing hard as his jaw tenses. I sigh deeply, rubbing my forehead. Oh, goodie.

"I said I was sorry," Nan says quietly.

I start to pace, turning off speaker mode and hold the phone closer. "Yes, I know Nan, it's fine. Just been a long night, okay?"

"And ever since you came back, it just...well, feels like he keeps taking you away."

"He's not."

I continue pacing, noticing Leo disappearing into the bedroom. Son of a nutcracker.

"Nan, I forgive you for the whole mob thing and such, okay? Really. I just want to move on, but I need *you* to move on, too. Leo's gonna remain in my life, and I need you to accept that, which includes all pieces of him."

"What makes you think I don't?"

"You want the long list or the short?"

"Don't chastise me, dear, I'm not the one who locked you away in your apartment."

"We just wanted some privacy."

"You or him?"

"Nan," I warn.

"Alright, fine," she sighs heavily, and there's some clinging as I hear her opening the store. "Perhaps, I'm being too harsh." There can be miracles. "I do accept he'll be in your life, I very much mean that, but that doesn't mean I won't worry."

"I'd be concerned if you weren't."

"And he just seems, well, selfish at times. I understand a man in love, but he should learn to share you. There's other people in your life, dear." Leo leaves the bedroom, dressed in slacks and a black undershirt. "Not to mention his obsession with work."

If she knew what he did this morning, she may say differently.

"He seems to only care about being right or in charge, rather than other people." Was this the same woman who let him up to my apartment behind my back? Pot calling the kettle black, Nan.

"Well, I doubt you'd still say that when I tell you what he's offered," I abruptly say, and begin scrambling for whatever idea is forming in my head.

Leo pauses, glancing back at me with confusion.

"Oh?" Nan asks.

"Yeah, he's offered a full spa day for you at the Italian Lily, it's a beautiful salon. Hair, nails, the works."

His frown deepens and I gesture for him to keep quiet. She can take my free appointments. I can go without painted nails.

"Oh, well, that's…nice of him."

Leo starts to walk over, and I give him a pleading look.

"Are you sure this isn't *your* idea, dear?" Nan questions.

"No, it's…" Leo gestures for the phone, and I bemoan inside, "…hold on."

I hand it over and he says, "You are free to use the salon services however often you want, Nancy. Free of charge to you as it is to Autumn, I'll foot the bill. I'm sure Autumn would enjoy sharing that time with you."

I was *not* gifted with sonic hearing, and only hear muffled words on the phone.

"Later this week you can have your first appointment with Autumn, and after I'll treat you both to one of the hotel's restaurants." More mumbling. "Very well. Now, if you don't mind, I have exactly fifteen minutes left with her this morning, she'll call you after."

He hangs up, holding the phone out to me. I quietly grab it, his face a mask of stoic calm. He gestures toward the counter, and I follow the silent signal to go sit. Leo places my plate

before me, then sits beside me as we usually do. My hands start to shake a little, somewhat perturbed by the conversation and my short outburst with Nan.

It's okay to be angry, I tell myself.

Gently, he places a hand on my thigh, and I stiffen.

"Breathe," he instructs gently. Oh, shit, I've been holding my breath. I let out a long exhale. He rubs his hand over my thigh.

"I was mad at her, not you," I whisper.

"Look at me, dear Watson." I slowly bring my gaze to his, and I'm met with caring, calm eyes. "I walked out of the room so I wouldn't grab the phone and tell her to fuck off. You were frustrated."

"Story of my life," I mutter.

"I didn't help by bluntly telling her you were moving in with me, I'm sorry." I shrug. "And I was irritated that no one seems to think you can make your own decisions."

"My track record isn't really the greatest." Briefly my mind flits to many conversations and my own shame for the situations I've landed in.

I go to look away, but he catches my chin and keeps my gaze with his. There's a hardness to them, but I know not towards me. I place my hand over his upon my thigh, helping the shaking subside. Quietly, I reach for him, hugging his torso from the side as he drapes his arm over my shoulders. He kisses my head as I press my face against his shirt, wishing we had more time.

"You're my home, too, Autumn," he murmurs. He strokes my hair back. "You need to eat before it gets cold."

I smirk softly, pulling away and notice his small smirk, too. We start to eat breakfast quietly, until I break the silence. "Think we'd get another hour if they opened the door, and *I* was naked?"

He pauses drinking his coffee, sliding his narrow gaze to me. "Don't even try it."

I start giggling as my overprotective boyfriend scowls at the idea of the Crew seeing me butt naked like him.

Chapter 34

Ghosts of Her Pasts

Nan chats with Wanda, possibly booking enough appointments to put a dent in Leo's income for the rest of the year. Of course, he's not gonna tell her no if it keeps her docile or from arguing with me at every turn about him.

She and I spent most of the day getting our nails done, massages, and her with her hair. I just wanted to try repainting my nails again. They're a burnt orange done by George. I apologized for already destroying the last set and he just shrugged it off. Said he chips his nails all the time. Maybe it was because I could hear Nan chattering away with other ladies or just the color change, but I dealt with it far better than before.

Leo sighs beside me, who came down to join us for an early dinner.

"I offered *a* day, you agreed to the rest of this," I say, crossing my arms. He snorts, and then his phone rings. He answers, stepping away to answer.

It's been a few days since I came back to the hotel. I'll start moving in about a week, get settled before the holidays start. Then maybe tell my friends I moved in with him. Surprise them with their own spa days. Leo won't woo them, but I might.

Nan hasn't relented in her conversation. I sigh, sitting down on one of the plush benches as I wait for her and Leo now. I lean back, swinging my legs a little and smile as I skim my converse shoes over the tiled floor.

"Having fun?" Isaac approaches.

I grin up at him. "Perks of kinda being short. Leg room."

"Somewhat jealous, Miss Autumn." He points his foot, showing off his long legs. How did I ever outrun him? Pure luck apparently. "Everything is set for dinner. I think you're about to become the *Giglio's* favorite customer."

"Either sneak me pizza rolls or have the chef stop making delicious dessert."

"You mean the tiramisu."

"It's good!" I exclaim, throwing my hands up and a few customers look over, puzzled by my outburst. Some scowl at me and I shrink a little. "Oops, I've upset the fancy birds."

Isaac chuckles, nodding at my attire.

I grin proudly as I flick the lapels of my jean jacket. Found it in the bottom of my closet.

Leo approaches, speaking in Italian with a strict tone and covers the receiver to speak with Isaac. "Check with Owen about the footage. Julio and Mila are handling the other matter."

I freeze at the mention of Mila's name. I've not seen her since Chesty practically pointed his gun at her. No doubt he told Leo and she's been banned from my presence. That's what I assume.

"Contacts came through?" Isaac quirks a brow.

Leo nods once, going back to his phone call and switching languages. Isaac gives his goodbye, leaving as Leo sits on the bench, crossing his leg over the other as he continues his conversation. He hums, face completely neutral as we wait. Slowly, I put my left hand over his right. Without missing a beat, he takes my hand, bringing it up to silently kiss my knuckles. A certain peace fills me as I watch him.

"Ciao." He hangs up, putting his phone away with a heavy exhale. He kisses my hand again, having it linger near his mouth.

"Check in," I ask quietly.

"Green." Our hands settle on his lap. He gazes down at them, thumb stroking over my fingers. "This color matches you."

"Yeah?"

"Just like your favorite season." I smile, leaning my head on his shoulder. We sit in silence as the entire floor of the Day Spa bustles with people. It smells of lilies, lilacs, and warm vanilla. The ambiance is relaxing with the soft lighting and piano playing over the speakers.

Calm. Peace. This small mundane moment, just sitting here with him. For a little bit, we're a regular couple. It's odd waiting here like anyone would. Just existing. It's a relief as I take a deep breath. I look up at Leo, smiling as I see his thinking expression with furrowed brows. He turns his attention to me, furrowing his brows more. A small giggle leaves me.

"What is it, dear Watson?"

"Just enjoying the moment." He hums, kissing my head.

"Well, aren't you two just a sight," Nan comments as she approaches. She smiles mischievously, tilting her head before digging into her purse. "Don't move. I mean it." She pulls her phone out, getting ready to take our picture. "Now. Smile. Leonardo, you, too."

I grin wide, knowing he's not going to. Nan huffs and relents, taking the picture and Leo places another kiss on my head before standing up. I follow suit as he heads for the elevators.

"You two do make a lovely couple," she comments. She shows me the photos. I stare at the couple in the picture, almost stumbling over my own feet as I realize this is our first picture together. We look…cute.

"Thanks, Nan," I whisper. "Can you send me that?"

"Oh, of course, looked like me and Finn waiting on the bus," she muses as we catch up. "Leonardo, I've heard your recommendations for dinner are the best. You best be ready to impress me."

"Impress you?"

"Yes, although you've not cooked for me yet, I guess this will have to do," Nan subtly chastises. The woman is getting bold.

Leo gives me a glance as we get into the elevators. I give him a "don't look at me" look and take his hand. "Well, Nancy, perhaps *you* should choose from the menu. Given your knowledge of recipes, it should be easy for you to see which is best to try."

She makes a noise, waving him off and I have to hide my face against his side to keep from laughing. Please let this frenemies relationship that's brewing stay amusing. I'll take it over the blatant arguing.

Apart from Nan comparing notes with Leo during dinner, it's uneventful. Some higher power had mercy for me. I just sip my cappuccino as they discuss recipes, until Christopher comes over to whisper in Leo's ear. Leo pulls his phone out, and I glance at the entrance to see Owen on the phone, grim and solemn.

"I need to handle something," Leo says, leaving with Christopher close behind. I grab my cup, concentrating on the warm drink.

"Does that often, hm?" Nan asks, grabbing her after dinner coffee to sip, too.

"Enough that if he doesn't leave during dinner, I get worried." I shrug. "Usually only takes a few minutes."

"He's consistent..."

"Nan, I've had almost two sold weeks in therapy, I don't need discussion topics. No stirring the pot more."

"I'm not."

"You got a new a perm, you're wily."

She waves me off, settling in her seat. "Not trying to fight him, dear. Honest. He's just a worthy adversary to keep my wits about me."

"Uh-huh."

"How have things been? Between you two?" I raise a brow at her. "The man would blow a gasket if he heard me, but I'm asking as a concerned guardian."

I snort, shaking my head as I put my cup down. "Quiet lately. From everyone on the outside, and already told you about me moving in with him. I can help you find someone to rent my old apartment."

"We'll see if I do. With no worry of losing the store, I could keep it open for family to stay." Something about that sentence makes my heart ache. People converse around us, utensils tinkling as I look toward the entrance. I can barely see Leo, Owen, and now Julio. "Have you two talked about the future?"

I pinch my brows together. "Really? Aiming for *that* talk instead?"

"It took Leanne *and* I to convince you to move in with me," she says, and I inhale sharply as I think about that time. That was different. "You seemed to have agreed with him—"

"I brought it up. Not him. Why does everyone think *he's* the only one making decisions?"

"It's just not like you, and for so long you avoided such conversations." She pats my hand. "Not a bad thing, dear, but you've always been independent. Given Leonardo's strict regimen would've thought he suggested it. Safety wise, this hotel may be the best for you in his eyes. I'm no ninny, and my bookstore isn't Fort Knox."

"Believe or not, I make most of the decisions about our relationship it seems, but it's always mutual when it counts," I retort, going back to my cappuccino. Suddenly hankering for an Americano.

"Have you two talked about your future then?"

"You sound like Leanne and Trix."

"It's a valid question."

"We're taking it day by day, figuring it out. Pretty sure neither of us know what our future holds, I mean it's been a month, since you know what, Nan."

"Well, *he* may think differently," she whispers.

One day is all I ask. No questions. No musings. Nothing. I'm *this* close to locking myself in the penthouse and watching Nick Cage movies all day as a reboot. Actually, that sounds like a great idea. Eleanor, wait for me.

"What do you mean?" I ask exasperated.

"No man fights that hard to keep a woman without a plan. And you have said he's been agitated and under pressure of late."

"Nan, I was arrested and interrogated for over 40 hours. He's had two large business deals outside the U.S., new hotel going up, along with other things I can't talk about in public," I whisper.

"That's not what I meant." I gesture for her to continue, and she sits back plucking a chocolate into her mouth. "I mean he's acting like a man with a ring burning in his pocket."

The coffee cup almost drops from my hands. Quickly, I put it down and stare at her. "What?"

"Dear, did you really think that wasn't in the cards?"

"I…well, I-I, no…Nan—"

She waves me off, smiling tenderly. "He's acting like Finn before he proposed. A bit tense and walking around like he's carrying the biggest secret in the world. Nothing scares a man more than being on the brink of popping the question, no matter *what* others may say they always worry about the answer."

I slump in my chair, staring at her. Sure, Leo and I have had some heavy conversations, but nothing of marriage. One time we discussed family, but that was for other reasons, it was never about our…future together.

"Not telling you to make you worry, dear." Nan pats my hand again, rubbing it a little. "Just saying what I see, and you two have moved quickly the past few weeks. And he's a man in love, even though he's a bit demanding at times."

I snort. She only started thinking that *after* he told her what to do.

My gaze flicks to the empty seat next to me. Funnily enough, apart from the surprise of Nan asking, there's no churning emotions inside me. No anxiety pricks at my skin or yanks at my spine.

"If he *did* ask, do you know your answer?"

"Yes." My response is without hesitation. I look at Nan who now is the one blinking in shock. "Without thought, yes."

The shock begins to evaporate on her face. "Oh."

"What?"

"I…I wasn't expecting that."

I open my mouth to explain when Christopher approaches and gives us both a tight smile. "Apologies, but Mr. Luciano said he won't be able to return. There's some urgent business for him to attend to."

"Is everything okay?" I ask.

"He wouldn't say, but everything has been taken care of, as

always. He also asked to speak with you, Autumn." He gestures for me to follow, and I get up as Nan watches with wide eyes. "Tyler will be with you shortly, Ms. O'Malley."

Nan comes out of her stupor, whether from the abrupt interruption or my answer to her question. "No, no. We're done anyhow. Why don't I go wait in the main lobby downstairs for you, dear? If Leonardo is going to be busy, you can come back to the bookstore with me. I need that back-alley camera checked again."

"Again? It was working fine last time I looked at it." She shrugs. "Alright, but I may have to check with Isaac or Julio cause of the new ones they put up."

She pats my shoulder, somehow leading the charge out of the restaurant and Christopher raises a brow at me. I shrug as we leave. Leo and the others are gone, prompting me to look at Christopher weirdly as he nods toward the private elevator. He escorts Nan to one of the public ones as I get on, almost running into Isaac who's apparently waiting for me within. My heart rate picks up, glancing at the floor chosen. Apartment.

"What's going on?"

"He wants to tell you himself," Isaac says as the doors shut completely. I swallow hard, not liking the closed off demeanor of my shadow. Worry travels over my skin, prickling. He touches my shoulder lightly. "No need to worry, I assure you. Promise."

I nod as the elevator climbs, and then the doors open. Leo stands in the hall with Jameson and Owen, all three with serious expressions. Once I step out, the two swiftly step past me to join Isaac on the elevator. The doors shut, leaving Leo and I alone in the foyer.

"Not at all ominous," I mumble.

"I wanted this to be private." He walks toward me, placing his hands on my shoulders.

"Check in, first."

I swallow hard. "Green, but you're worrying me."

Leo touches my cheek in an affectionate manner, far too gentle as he speaks with an all too controlled tone. "I promised you that you would decide the fate of the men who tortured and assaulted you."

My hands shake as my stomach plummets. "We have the last two, apart from Steve. They're being held somewhere where they can't escape. I am guaranteeing you *now* that they will *never* harm you again."

My mind goes blank. No memories come forward. Nothing. All of it becomes a fog like a lost memory as I stare at his chest. Frozen.

"I know what I want done with them, but I'll keep my promise with you of doing what you want." Leo places a hand at the nape of my neck, stroking his thumb over my skin.

Time passes slowly as I try to comprehend what he's saying. I actually get to decide. I get to make the decision of what happens to *them*. Justice. Justice for me, the other women they hurt, and for the woman I'd never get to be again.

"Look at me, dear Watson." I do as he says. "Take your time."

"This doesn't feel real."

"I'd show you that I have them, but I will not bring them into your presence. Or risk harming you by you seeing them again." A sharp breath comes out of me, gripping onto his arms. "You don't need to answer now, if you can't decide."

I relax at his words, taking a few deep breaths and concentrating on the steady gaze before me. I trust him. Enough that I know he'll make them suffer more than anything I could think of.

"Whatever you want," I finally answer. His face darkens. The hold against my neck becoming firmer. "Whatever you decide. I just don't want to see them or, or…"

"Alright." He kisses my forehead. "Alright."

"I trust you, Leo. I trust you to take care of it."

He pulls me into his firm embrace, cradling my head against his chest. "Is Nancy still here?"

"Lobby. Suggested going to the bookstore."

"Do that. Chesty and Animal will go with you. Isaac will come get you later." As he cups my face, I nod in response before he places a tender kiss against my lips. It's languid and soft as if he's trying to purge the last of my worries. "I love you, my dear wonderful Watson. I vow they'll never touch you again."

"I love you," I whisper against his lips, kissing him again more fervently. He clutches me, pressing deeper in a brief desperate want. Leo abruptly pulls away, leading me back to the elevators, getting on with me to head downstairs. We're quiet until the doors open on the first floor, where Waylon and Drew are already waiting.

Leo nods once at them, then places another kiss on my lips before I walk out. I'm a few steps away, fear striking me. I turn back as the doors begin to close. "Check in."

With murderous wrath written on his face, he responds, "Red."

My fist is met with shiny, golden doors. Body trembling at how dangerous the man I love became in seconds. I stare at my reflection against the elevator doors. Should I stop him? Not for those fuckers sake, but his.

A hand lands on my shoulder, and I flinch away. Waylon's standing there, holding his hands up in a surrender kind of fashion. "Breathe, sister. You're good." I swallow hard. "Let's get you out of here."

Drew and Waylon lead me through the hall, down toward the garage. Chiari brings Nan around, and I force a smile with her as we head toward the car. Drew suggests Nan riding in the front with him, while Waylon and I ride in the back. As we start to leave the garage, Waylon puts the divider up and looks over at me wearily.

"He'll be fine," he reassures me.

I stare at the headrest in front of me, running my hand through my hair. "Chesty, that look on his face."

"He's fucking furious, yeah, but he'll have the others with him." He grips my knee, making me look over at him. "We've been tracking these guys since you came back. He's been itching to get them in his grasp, he'll take his anger out on them."

"Still worried."

"I know. Sombra will look after him, always has. Along with the rest of the *Forgotten Demons*. We've got his back, make sure he doesn't leave the deep end."

I loosen a shaky breath. "I know."

We're quiet the rest of the ride, and it feels too soon as we park outside the bookstore.

We get out of the car, Nan meeting us on the sidewalk. "Are you alright, dear?"

"Yeah, fine, uh, didn't you have a new shipment of children books?" She nods. "I'll go organize them with Waylon and scan them in."

Staying quiet, I head into the bookstore and get to work. Waylon helps me bring the boxes from the back organizing and getting the books ready to be on shelves. After a couple hours, even though he assures me that someone else can look at it, I check the security camera Nan mentioned before it gets too dark. Anything to distract myself from what Leo may be doing.

I'm up on the ladder, investigating the camera and notice a couple pieces have been replaced. I follow the wiring, seeing the connection it has to the others Julio and Isaac had installed. Well, that's why it's on the fritz. It's an older model than the others, can't run on the same hardware. Someone thought otherwise. I glance over my shoulder at Waylon below me.

"When Enigma had the new cameras installed, did he have Nan's old cameras added to the security network? I think whatever he used may have caused the one's I installed to go dark or aren't able to manage sending information to Nan's monitors and his."

His brows go up, then he scratches the underside of his beard. "Gonna be honest, sister, I've no fucking clue yer talking about."

I snort. Right, Waylon nor Drew did the computer stuff.

"I wanna go check the other camera down the alley," I say, getting down as Waylon grabs the ladder.

"Something wrong?"

"Wondering if whoever put up the new ones tried to *upgrade* the older ones but used the wrong equipment. When I installed them, I used older models and completely gutted the insides, but they're still not gonna work with most newer models." The burly biker just stares at me, and I finally chuckle after a quiet afternoon. "Imagine someone putting a 4 cylinder on a motorcycle that can only run on one. Could work, but gonna caput on you more likely."

"Look who's learning," he smiles. "That what wrong up there?"

"Basically." He carries the ladder down the alley with me, pausing underneath to set it up as I stare down where the camera I put in almost two years ago. A tickling goes up my spine.

"Keep fucking forgetting your actual background," he chuckles, securing the ladder.

"Well, you teach me about engines, and I'll teach you about electronics."

"Thought you did the coding stuff, not this." He waves his fingers in the air as I climb the ladder.

"Wanted to learn what I was creating programs for," I answer, getting to the top and start investigating the camera. Definitely newer, which means I know less about.

"You ever tell Enigma how you bypassed his firewalls?"

"Weren't firewalls, but close enough." May need to if I wanna know how these cameras work. I'm out of practice. Instead of spending a day rebuilding engines, maybe I should do one with Owen and Julio on their computers. It's been over three years since I touched one. Even the thought of using one makes me shiver. Excitement and unease.

After a few minutes, I finally see what parts they put in that were meant for these newer cameras. This is why I don't like people touching my stuff. That and maybe I have some of Leo's territorial traits when it comes to *my* technology. "These were put up while we were at the estate, right?"

"Yeah, got people we hire for it."

"Tell them not to touch the older models, cause they don't know jackshit about them." I get down from the ladder, brushing myself off. "What Enigma and Isaac installed is fine, but that..." I point at the camera closer to the back entrance, "...and others I installed are not to be touched, unless by Enigma or me."

"They special or something?"

"Somewhat, I'm gonna head up to my apartment. I should have

the right stuff to make them work again. If not, I'm dragging Enigma or Iron Buffalo out here to collaborate."

"And listen?" He smirks and I give one back. "I'll update them after we see if you can fix it."

"Can you move the ladder back under that one? I'll be back down."

"I'll head up with you."

"I'm fine, Chesty," I try to assure him as I pause at the backdoor.

"Orders not to leave you alone, sister."

"I can go up and grab what I need, promise." He stares at me for a moment, and I give him a small smile. Perhaps a couple hours ago it wouldn't have been a good idea, but the distraction of work has helped. Something to keep my mind occupied.

He hums, scratching his gut and nods. "Don't take too long."

"Aye, aye sir," I give a small salute, and he chuckles as I head inside. I know Dr. Maxwell said to not bottle things up, but I'm not ready to fall into the chasm of worry just yet. Distraction it is. And it's been working anyways.

I head up the stairs, opening the door to my soon-to-be ex-apartment and head for my bedroom. I put my phone down on the bedside table and go toward one of my drawers to look for the correct wiring but stop.

Why was my front door open? I've not been up here all day and neither have the others, not to mention I've not been back since I left with Rudy. Pretty sure I locked it. I couldn't have been that—

My spine goes stiff, caution racing over my limbs. Nerves prick at my skin more harshly than it ever has, not since the day I ran in the park. I look around the bedroom, noticing nothing is out of place. Books on the bedside table. Bedsheets strewn about from my tossing and turning. Clothes on the floor.

It's fine. I just forgot to lock the door. Hearing about those men and seeing Leo like that has just spiked my anxiety. The faulty wires on the camera. Simple mistakes. That's all. Don't overthink.

Yet, I still freeze and listen. My apartment door clicks shut. Breath hitching, panic yanks at me, causing my hands to shake. Warning screams at me, and I silently go to the bedside table, pulling out the .22 hidden underneath. Keeping it firmly between my hands, I prowl out of the bedroom and into the living room.

Footsteps creak behind me.

I go to swing the gun around, but an arm wraps around my neck, placing me into a chokehold. The gun is knocked out of my hands as I'm rammed into the wall, choking on a cry. It clatters against the rug as a larger barrel of a gun presses against my head. The pressure around my neck tightens, and I shove at the body behind me.

The gun's handle hits my temple and I go down, falling hard to the floor as my head spins. Blinking against the pain, I turn to face my attacker. My blood goes cold as I stare up into harsh, empty eyes. The tan he once had is gone, paler than I've ever seen him even when he was high on coke. His head is shaved, only scraggly bits of facial hair grow on his jaw. The sneer on his face is volatile, filled with malice. He speaks in a low, taunting voice as he points the gun at my head.

"Miss me…

Sarah?"

Autumn and Leo's Story

Continues in

<u>My Emerald Fire</u>

The past rarely comes back roaring from the distance.
It will sneak through the holes of your defenses…

…and gnaw at you from
the inside out.

Books Also By Elm Jed

Paranormal Mafia

Mafia, Murder, and Mayhem Series

Vinny the Vampire & Me

Sweet Cheeks & Her Mob Boss

The Wolf Boss & His Darling

Prequel: Memories of the Underground - Volume One

Suspense Romance

My Dear Watson

My Forgotten Demons

My Emerald Fire

About the Author

Elm Jed is a Marine Corps veteran, who's been writing since they were ten years old with a degree in Theatre. They live with their husband, who is their biggest supporter from making sure they're caffeinated to listening to them ramble for hours about chaotic ideas. They spend most of their time jotting down ideas, reading novellas that make them laugh, or attending Renaissance Festivals with their greatest friends.